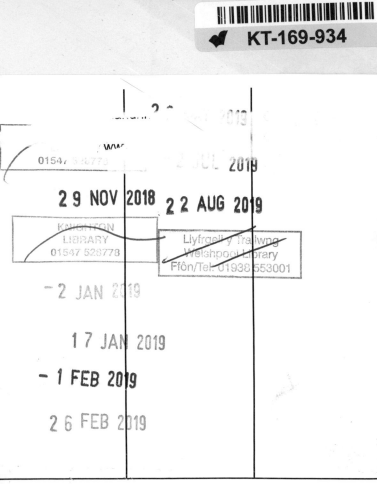

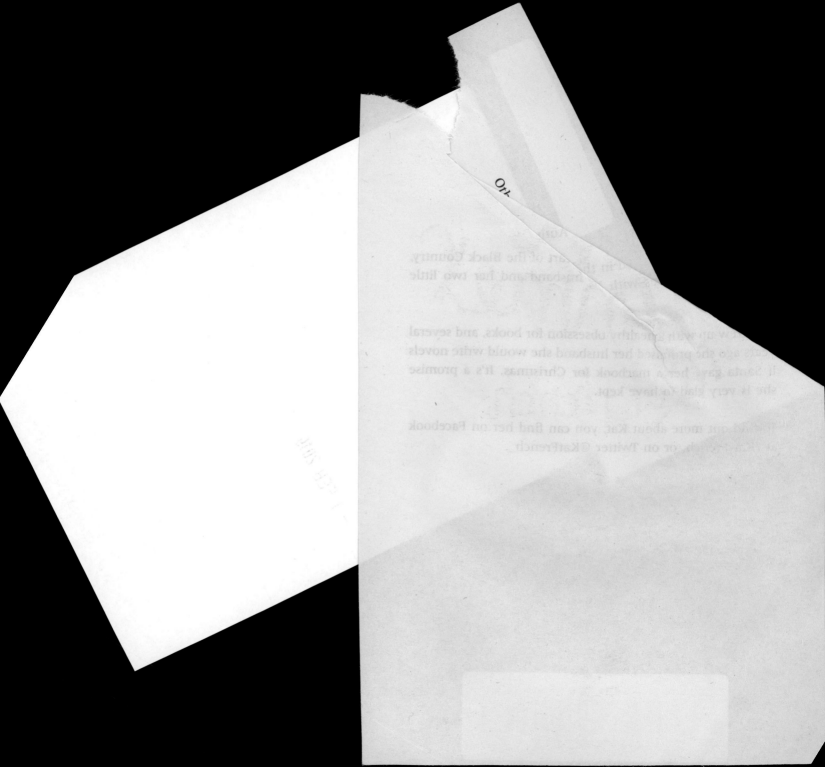

One Hot Summer

Kat French

avon

AVON

A division of HarperCollins*Publishers*
1 London Bridge Street,
London SE1 9GF

www.harpercollins.co.uk

A Paperback Original 2016

1

A catalogue record for this book is
available from the British Library

ISBN-13: 978-0-00-757762-0

Typeset in Meridien by
Palimpsest Book Production Ltd, Falkirk, Stirlingshire

Printed and bound in Great Britain by Clays Ltd, St Ives plc

MIX
Paper from
responsible sources
FSC C007454

Acknowledgements

Thanks first of all to my lovely editor Caroline Kirkpatrick, it's been an absolute joy to work with you on this book. I love that you fell for Robinson as much as I did! Thanks for your positivity and support, I'm going to miss you a great deal.

Thanks to everyone else on the Avon team at HarperCollins too, you're all so supportive and generous with your time and enthusiasm.

Much appreciation to Sabah Kahn at LightBrigade PR for being all round brilliant.

Love as always to my superstar writing bezzies, collectively known as the Minxes of Romance. Thanks for sharing in and feeding my enduring love for all things country – one day we should all hit Nashville together. Imagine that! Music City would never be the same again.

On that, a huge and general thank you to all of the fantastic stars of modern country music for inspiring mc daily as I wrote this book – I'm so buying some proper cowboy boots and a Stetson one day. A piece of my heart is now forever country.

Love and gratitude as ever to my own special, gorgeous

people, my family and friends. Your endless enthusiasm and interest doesn't go unnoticed or unappreciated, love you all!

Last but never least, thank you to the readers, the bloggers, and all of the wonderful, sometimes crazy people who keep me company on social media. You make me laugh, you inform me, and you support me. Thank you times one million.

For my beautiful minxes –
Sally, Rose, Jojo, Romy, Suzanne, Lorraine, Sri and Lacey.
May the words be ever in our favour.

xx

CHAPTER ONE

The *Daily Mirror* headline that morning:

MCBRIDE OR MCMISTRESS?

Spotted! It looks like the sexy on-screen romance between married TV star Brad McBride and his sexy co-star Felicity Shaw has spilled over into reality, if our sensational pictures are anything to go by. Shots of the couple smooching in a booth at The Roof Gardens emerged this morning, along with further images of a distinctly sheepish McBride leaving Shaw's London flat in the early hours of New Year's Day.

'They couldn't keep their hands off each other in the club, they didn't seem to care who saw them,' one reveller, who didn't wish to be named, told the *Mirror*. 'I saw them leave in a cab just after midnight; from the way they were going at it in the club, I bet that cabbie had an eye full!'

Representatives for both McBride and Shaw have so far declined comment.

'Alice, it's not what it looks like. I can explain.'

Alice slowly lifted her eyes from the salacious images splashed across the morning papers to the man standing in front of her with his hands spread wide, his eyes saying the opposite of his mouth. Brad McBride. He'd been a burn-your-fingers hot struggling actor when she'd met and married him more than half a decade ago. All that had changed when he landed a role in a new cop drama that had caused a sensation on both sides of the pond, catapulting him straight from struggling-actor status to celebrity darling, and from Alice's darling into the arms of his leading lady, if the papers were to be believed.

It was pretty tricky not to believe them, truth told. There weren't many conclusions to draw from the photos of Brad and Felicity Shaw besides the glaringly obvious ones. Brad could always have been inspecting Felicity's tonsils with his tongue in a purely platonic way, or maybe she was sitting in his lap with her dress around her thighs because her legs had suddenly stopped working, and there was always the outside chance that he'd been caught leaving her bijou townhouse looking rumpled at dawn because his car had mysteriously broken down right outside on the night of the infamous New Year cab strike that never was. That would be the same night three days ago, the very same one that Brad had called her on to say that he couldn't make it back for the weekend as early as planned because filming had run over schedule. It had surprised her that they'd filmed during New Year week, but Alice hadn't made a fuss. She'd had to get used to her husband being public property since he'd been catapulted into stardom, and as his wife she'd quickly had to get used to being photographed for publicity and showbiz events. She didn't enjoy it but knew Brad needed her to smile for the cameras, and she'd be forever thankful that it had allowed them to buy Borne Manor, the Shropshire country pad of their dreams. Or Alice's dreams, in any case. Brad had liked the place well enough, but London was calling for him in a way it just wasn't for Alice. It seemed simple enough – they'd keep their London flat as a base and buy the Shropshire house as their long-term family home. Except there was no family as yet, and it seemed from the photographs that Brad had decided that life with Alice wasn't quite bright lights, big city enough for him any longer. Folding her arms wearily, she looked her husband in the eyes.

'Go on then.'

His eyes narrowed. 'Go on then what?'

Pack your case and leave. 'Explain,' she said. 'You said you could explain the pictures.' Alice glanced down at the newspaper on the table. 'I'm listening.'

She wrapped her dressing gown closer around her as she slid into one of the dining chairs, weary already even though it was barely eight a.m. The expensive dove grey cashmere robe had been a Christmas surprise from Brad just a week or two ago. Alice found herself wondering if Felicity Shaw was at that very moment wearing the same thing. Her husband was big on efficiency; she could well imagine him doubling up on identical presents.

Brad paused, tongue tied and uncertain.

'Erm, well . . .' He shoved his hands through his dark hair and then scrubbed his palms over his cheeks, unable to meet her eyes head on. If she'd have been looking for classic signs of lying, the red flags were all there. Touching his face and covering his mouth, rapid eye movement, shallow breathing beneath his expensive shirt. It was a poor show for an actor, really, Alice thought, detaching herself mentally from the situation for self-preservation purposes. She watched him wriggle on the hook, slippery, trying any which way to get himself off it. She wasn't going to help him. She couldn't. All of her efforts were concentrated on holding herself still in the chair rather than flying across the room and tearing his face off.

'Alice, I'm so sorry,' he said, suddenly urgent, crossing the room and pulling out the chair beside hers. He sat facing her, his kneecaps against hers, close enough for Alice to smell the familiar scent of his favourite shower gel. 'It was nothing. She doesn't mean anything to me.'

Alice looked down at his strong, tanned hands as they closed over her clasped ones in her lap. Hands that wore the wedding ring she'd placed there, hands that she'd trusted to hold her heart safely, hands that had held another woman when they should have been holding her. She didn't say anything. It's difficult to speak when your heart suddenly fragments into a million pieces. She could feel it splintering, and it physically hurt all the way from her scalp to her toes.

'It was one night, baby, a stupid, stupid mistake.'

His words washed over her skin, scalding, not in the least bit soothing. Did he imagine that it would be less of a betrayal if he said it had only happened once? Which it hadn't, of course. Lots of little things had happened over the last few months that hadn't quite added up, a dinner receipt here, an inconsistency in Brad's recollections there, and each time Alice had allowed herself to sweep it under the carpet, or had at least looked for innocent explanations instead of jumping to the worst-case scenario. This though . . . these pictures . . . there wasn't a best-case scenario to find here, only the ugly truth of deception and infidelity. Those warning signs did nothing to deaden the blow of evidence; hard facts turned out to be a lot harder to swallow than suspicion. Dread prickled cold and clammy beneath her skin and her morning coffee rose bitter in her throat. She knew that what she said next mattered. Go, or don't go.

'Tell me what I can do, Alice. I need to make this right again.' Brad squeezed her hands. 'You name it and I'll do it.'

Was it really her responsibility to tell him how to right his wrongs? And why did he assume there was something he could do to balance the scorecard again? Even so, finding the strength required to say the things she needed to say next was the most difficult thing she'd ever done.

'There's only one thing you can do now, Brad. Pack a case. Leave.'

'No! I won't.' Urgent desperation thickened his voice. 'Alice, please, we can work through this. I love you, and I know you love me.' He gripped her hands tighter still. 'Our marriage is worth that, surely?'

Oh, he had no idea how badly he'd just screwed up. She nodded, digesting his words slowly, fury heating her blood.

'You didn't think it valuable enough to stop you screwing Felicity Shaw, yet I'm supposed to think it's worth fighting for. Is that what you're saying?'

She lifted her eyes to his and watched him scrabble for the right words when there weren't any.

'That isn't what I meant,' he said quietly. His phone buzzed in the pocket of his jeans. They both glanced down, knowing in her eyes, guilt in his.

'You better get that,' Alice said, keeping her voice even as she stood, scraping her chair back on the flagstones. 'I'll go and find you a suitcase.'

Three months later . . .

Throwing Brad out had hurt like hell. Gwyneth Paltrow had been way off the mark when she'd used the term conscious uncoupling for separation. Alice felt more like she'd had her heart amputated without anaesthetic, or all the life sucked from her body by an industrial-strength Dyson. It came as a surprise most mornings when she looked in the mirror and found herself still standing up.

'I cancelled your newspaper delivery yesterday,' Niamh said, handing Alice a mug of coffee before taking a seat alongside her on the garden bench out the back of Borne Manor. The sun hadn't long risen, and there was that chilly hint of new-day promise in the pale blue sky.

'Did I ask you to?' Alice said, frowning. She couldn't recall doing it, but that didn't mean much lately. She talked to Niamh most mornings and could barcly remember what they'd said within half an hour of her leaving. And it wasn't just Niamh. It was everyone and everything since Brad had left. Her brain was soup. And not a silky smooth consommé, either. It was more like yesterday's leftover dinner liquidised into a thick unappetising gloop, trying hard to work and failing.

Niamh shook her head. 'Nope, but I did it anyway. You need more pictures of Brad the Cad and Felicity-no-knickers like you need a hole in the head.'

'But . . .' Although Alice knew that Niamh was right, anxiously scouring the papers and magazines for images of him had become part of her post-Brad daily routine. He'd taken out a costly subscription to all of the nationals when they'd moved to Borne; Brad had taken pleasure and pain from searching for mentions and reviews of his performances.

This was just another form of that, really. Alice didn't enjoy it. In fact she had to brace herself for it and her shoulders didn't drop from around her ears until she'd closed the last page of the last newspaper, but in another way she kind of relied on it, in the same strange way you can come to rely on visiting a sick relative in hospital because the alternative of losing them altogether is even worse. By cancelling the papers, Niamh had kicked the power cable out of the life support machine of her marriage. She'd argue, but Alice knew that any doctor in the land would have pronounced it dead anyway.

'But what?' Niamh said, leaning down to find a stick to throw for Pluto, her rescue dog turned loyal companion. 'You'd rather torture yourself slowly than go cold turkey? If I had a bullshit buzzer I'd press it right now, Alice.'

They both watched an ecstatic Pluto hurtle down the frosty lawn and career off towards the woods in search of the stick. He'd be gone a while. He was the dearest of dogs, but he was blind in one eye and his good one wasn't brilliant.

'I bet Davina had a field day, didn't she?' Alice muttered, picturing the owner of the local shop-come-post-office. Dark haired and sly eyed, Davina was the village ear to the ground and man-eater. There was always talk of scalps on her bedpost amongst wronged wives after a few gins in the local. She wasn't exactly what you might call a girls' girl; she'd happily gossip with mums at the school gate in the morning and try to bed their husbands in the afternoon. She'd had plenty of cracks at Brad since they'd moved into Borne Manor a little over eighteen months ago, a fact which he'd always reported back with glee to Alice. She hadn't been concerned, back then. The fact that he told her all about it meant he wasn't interested, right? Looking back, Alice wasn't so sure. Maybe if Davina had caught Brad at a weaker moment he might have accepted more than a book of stamps and a punnet of strawberries.

Niamh laughed beside her. 'Oh, she tried to fish. All doe eyed, twisting her hair around her fingers as she asked after you and Brad. Proper concerned she was.'

Alice sipped her coffee and watched Pluto mooch about at the edge of the woods. The gardens and land that came with Borne Manor had been one of its big attractions; Alice had imagined kids building forts and camping in the woods, and Brad had pictured rolling garden parties and summer balls attended by the rich and famous. He was a man who'd let his fledgling fame go straight to his head – in his mind's eye he was already one good dinner jacket away from David Frost. Pushing all thoughts of her errant husband to the back of her mind, Alice dwelled instead on the worrying red letter that had arrived a few days ago in the mail.

'I might lose this place, Niamh,' she said, facing facts as she cupped her hands around her mug for warmth against the March morning. 'The bank letters are coming thick and fast, and Brad isn't happy to keep paying the mortgage indefinitely. I can't possibly pay it. I don't even have a sodding job.'

'So divorce him and use the settlement. Ask the bank to wait.'

'You know that won't happen soon enough. Even if I saw a solicitor today it'd drag on for months.' She didn't mention that she wasn't ready to start divorce proceedings. Divorces needed strength, and she couldn't see herself feeling very Fatima Whitbread for a while yet.

'Is there any chance that Brad might try to take the house?'

'Over my dead body,' Alice shot back, even though she had no clue how she'd stop him if he actually tried. This was her house. It might have both their names on the deeds, but she knew every brick and slate, she loved every nook and cranny. She knew its history and its stories, because she loved the place enough to find out. From the moment she'd set eyes on Borne Manor, she'd wrapped her heart around its mellow stone walls and vowed to love it for ever. Much like her wedding vows, really. The difference was that Brad had let her down. Borne Manor hadn't, and she wanted to repay it in kind.

Quite how she was going to do that though was anyone's guess.

'How long do you have?'

Alice shrugged unhappily. 'Two months, maybe?'

Niamh sucked in a sharp breath of cold air. 'We better think of something fast then.'

We. Not you, we. Not for the first time in the last few months, Alice found herself grateful for Niamh's friendship. They'd been neighbours ever since Alice and Brad moved to Borne, but it was only since Brad's departure that their friendship had blossomed beyond the occasional coffee in the village or chat at the gate. She'd knocked on the door of Borne Manor and asked if Pluto could possibly go for a run in the gardens as it was safer for him than being on the common, and she'd been around most mornings since at sun up for an early morning coffee on the back bench and an hour setting the world to rights. Alice suspected that word had reached Niamh's ears of her troubles and she'd reached out to help; she was that special kind of person. In actual fact they weren't neighbours, exactly; as owner of the row of four tied cottages next to the manor, Alice was officially Niamh's landlady. Not that she went along the row and collected rent; specified arrangements with most of the cottage owners had been included as part of the sale particulars.

Number one housed Stewie Heaven, ex seventies porn star, a perma-tanned man who seemed to have a wig to suit every occasion. Alice had only seen him on hops and catches as he wintered in Benidorm, but from what Niamh said he'd arrived home a week or so ago and was as verbose as ever about his exploits. He paid rent to Borne Manor at the princely sum of one pound a month, a nefarious peppercorn arrangement with the previous owner for services rendered. No one knew the precise nature of the services, and no one had the stomach to ask.

Hazel lived at number two, a woman as round as she was tall and who told everyone who cared to listen that she was a practising witch. She lived with her sofa-surfing son Ewan, a perpetual student, and Rambo, her talking mynah bird, who could often be found perched on her open windowsill shouting obscenities at passersby. Hazel paid double Stewie's rent at two pounds a month, secured on the basis that she'd cleared the manor of an unwanted poltergeist some twenty years previously.

Which left just Niamh, who'd returned to Borne to nurse her ailing mother after a stroke last summer and stayed on after she died a couple of months later. It was written into the sale of Borne Manor that Niamh's mother and any of her surviving children should be allowed to live rent free in number three until such a time as they no longer wanted or needed to. There was no explanation offered, and Alice saw no reason to question it. Brad had wanted to when news reached him of Niamh's mother's death, but Alice had uncharacteristically put her foot down and refused to allow it. She was glad every day now that she'd made a stand; Niamh had turned out to be the perfect friend in her time of need.

The end cottage, number four, presently stood empty after the passing of Borne's most senior resident, Albert Rollinson, who Hazel assured them now haunted the row of cottages in spirit form, stealing their morning papers to check the runners and riders at Aintree. Fond of a bet and a pint, if Albert was there at all he was the most benign of ghosts. He'd make Casper look angry. Freed of its peppercorn rent arrangement with the death of Albert, the estate agent had secured a buyer for the tiny two up two down and agreed a sale a couple of months back, but as of yet no one had moved in.

'Pluto!' Niamh called, putting her cup down on the cobbles and standing up. 'Here, boy! I better shoot. I've got a sitting this morning, some farmer from three villages over who wants a painting of himself naked for his wife's birthday. Where would a man get the idea that any woman wants that?'

Alice laughed despite her gloom. 'Maybe you could offer him a strategic bunch of bananas or grapes to drape himself with. Tell him it's arty.'

Niamh huffed as she leaned down to clip Pluto's lead on.

'I don't have bananas. Or grapes. Do you think he'd be offended if I suggested an out-of-date fig?'

'His wife probably wouldn't notice the difference,' Alice said, making them both laugh softly as she opened the side gate for Niamh. 'Call me if he gets frisky. I'll come over with the contents of my fruit bowl.'

'No worries on that score. I've got my bodyguard to protect me.' Niamh fussed Pluto's wiry head and he rolled his good eye towards Alice in farewell.

'See you tomorrow. Same time same place.'

'It's a date,' Niamh called over her shoulder, raising her hand as she disappeared down the road towards the cottages. Alice closed the gate slowly and returned to the bench, sitting down to watch the rose pink and gold clouds that streaked the early morning sky. One of her favourite parts of the day was already behind her and it was barely break-fast time.

Would it always feel like this? Would every day always be a new mountain to climb? Mount KilamancalledBrad-forbreakingmyheart might not roll easily off the tongue, but it was there on the map of Alice's life and its recent eruption threatened to leave her homeless.

Bending to pick up the empty mugs, Alice looked out over the rolling gardens towards the woods. Through the trees she could see silvery glints of the vintage Airstream caravan she'd impulse bought on eBay last autumn with the intention of giving it a kitsch make-over for weekends away with Brad. His celebrity life made it difficult to go to hotels and cities without him being noticed, so she'd harboured hazy images of them camping out in the Airstream, maybe even taking it over to France for long weekends of wine and cheese and sex. The sight of it made her heart heavy these days. Maybe she could live in it if the bank repossessed the house, claim squatters rights in her beloved garden. Sighing, she turned and headed back into the warmth of the kitchen.

Sliding ready-made lasagne for one onto the kitchen table, Alice placed the most alcoholic bottle of wine she could find and a glass beside it and sat down, the tick of the kitchen clock the only sound in the too quiet, too big kitchen. It hadn't seemed that way when she lived here with Brad; the kitchen had been the central hub of their lives and one of the rooms she loved best of all.

But then it had also been the room where the ugly end scenes of her marriage had played out too; the traded insults, the wall that had needed repainting after Alice hurled a cup of coffee at Brad and only just missed. She liked to tell herself that she'd intended to miss, but he sure had gone from bringing out the best in her to the worst in her in a very short space of time.

If this were a movie, Alice could see herself sitting alone at this table, a solitary figure as the end credits rolled and cinema goers were left bereft of their happy ending. Maybe it was melodramatic to cast herself as the crazy cat lady already given that she was still shy of her thirtieth birthday, but some days she really did just want to give it all up and go and sit in the attic in her wedding dress until the cobwebs choked her.

Picking listlessly at the pasta, Alice's gaze slid to the unopened pile of bills. Ignoring them wasn't helping, she knew that. She'd eat this cardboard dinner, and then she'd be brave and open them, because just the sight of them was making her feel ill and that was no way to go on. Flicking the TV on for dinner company proved little solace. *EastEnders* blared from BBC1, all garish lipstick and shouty arguments in the Queen Vic, and Alice had a self-imposed ban on *Central* in case Brad and Felicity unexpectedly appeared and scorched her eyeballs out with their passionate on-screen clinches. That left her with a straight choice between a nature documentary about hedgehogs or yet another re-run of *The Good Life*. She went for the latter, and ended up thinking how lovely Tom was to Barbara even though they didn't have two pennies to rub together, and remembering how much happier she and Brad had been before he got famous and switched his wellington boots for Armani ones.

Pushing her dinner away and pulling her wine towards her, Alice laid her head on the table and allowed herself to indulge in a few tears. And then she poured a second glass of wine and cried some more; bigger, snottier, shoulder-shaking sobs that made her knock her drink back too quickly and refill her glass for a third, ill-advised time. Within the hour she was at her own pity party for one, which frankly beat the pants off her lonely, sober dinner for one, or at least it did for the glorious half an hour when she turned the radio up loud and wailed along to any sad song she could find on the dial.

When the bottle was finally as empty as her stomach, Alice flopped back into the chair again, her cheek on the dining table, her eyes closed because all she could see when they were open was that humungous, frightening pile of bills again. If I close my eyes, it might disappear, she thought. She'd heard all about positive thinking from Hazel down at the cottages. Maybe if she wished really, really hard, they'd be gone when she opened her eyes. Alice tried. She really did give it her very best shot, which only served to make it an all crushing blow when she opened her eyes and found the pile of bills still there, even bigger than when she'd closed her eyes, if that was even possible.

Any traces of wine-fuelled high spirits abandoned her there on her kitchen table, as did her resolution that she could find a way to hold onto her beloved manor.

As she fell into a heavy, troubled sleep she thought for the second time that day of the Airstream in the garden. Only this time, she saw herself living in it on a muddy campsite like a scene from *My Big Fat Gypsy Wedding*, and all of her new gypsy friends coming out with sticks and big growly dogs to defend her whenever Brad the terrible turned up in his Range Rover and poncey Armani boots.

'I'm going to live in the caravan.'

Niamh looked at Alice as if she'd just said she was planning to fly to the moon and should be back in time for lunch. Alice just nodded, her eyes trained on the edge of the woodland and the caravan that lay beyond.

'It came to me yesterday after you left.'

Niamh frowned. 'I only cancelled your newspapers, Alice, not your whole life. Have you had a knock on the head?'

'I'm serious, Niamh. I thought about it all day yesterday and it might just work.'

It was more of an economy with the truth than an actual lie. She hadn't thought of it yesterday, she'd thought of it at about four o' clock that morning as she'd peeled her cheek from the dining table and made her way blearily up to bed. Her dreams had been full of the Airstream, muddled and messed up, but they'd sown the seed of a more plausible idea that had gripped her from the moment she'd properly woken up.

Pluto dropped his ball at Niamh's feet and she picked it

up and hurled it across the grass. 'You're going to have to spell this out. I'm not seeing how you moving into the caravan will help.'

'Because if I live in the caravan, I can rent the house out to someone else to pay the mortgage.'

Niamh paused. 'Are you allowed to do that?'

A frown creased Alice's brow. 'Why wouldn't I be?'

'I don't know . . . I just thought there were rules around that sort of stuff.'

Alice chewed her lip. 'Then I'll get it sorted so I can. I mean it, Niamh. This is the only way I can think of not to let Borne Manor go completely, or at least until I'm ready to leave on my own terms, rather than because of Felicity bloody Shaw.'

Niamh fell silent for a moment and then reached down and felt around on the ground behind the bench. When she straightened she held a half-empty bottle of rum in her hand, the emergency supply they kept there for extra cold winter mornings or moments of dire need. Moving from the grandeur and luxury of Borne Manor into a caravan that probably wasn't even watertight definitely fell into the latter category. Tipping a good snifter into each of their coffee mugs, she clanked her cup against Alice's.

'Let's drink these then and go and view your new home.'

'It's . . . it's . . .' Niamh paused, stepping into the caravan behind Alice ten minutes later. It had taken almost five minutes to prise the door open, and the first thing that hit them was the pungent smell of damp when a hard tug had finally wrenched it from its seal.

'It's kind of cute?' Alice finished for her, seeing the same battered wooden interior as Niamh, though through more rose-tinted glasses. 'Let's open the windows, get rid of the damp smell. It'll be fine once it's aired.'

'You think?' Niamh's gaze swept from the lumpy double bed at one end of the caravan to the threadbare seating at the other, taking in the tatty kitchenette and holey lino on the way. 'Is there a bathroom?'

Alice stepped along the central aisle and they both reached for a wall to steady themselves as the caravan lurched downwards at one end.

'Oops! Legs must need putting down.' Alice smiled nervously. 'The bathroom's in there,' she added, waving an expansive hand towards a slim door beside the bed. 'There's a loo and everything.'

She looked back over her shoulder at her friend's doubtful expression. 'Don't pull that face. Work with me here, I need your vision. You're an artist; can't you see it as a blank canvas ready to be made gorgeous?' She ran her hand over the faded wooden kitchen cupboard. 'A rub down here, a lick of varnish there . . . some pretty curtains maybe?'

Alice watched Niamh study the interior, silently willing her to see beyond the shabbiness. Slowly, her friend began to nod.

'Yes? You see it?' Alice took Niamh's fledgling encouragement and ran with it. 'I looked on the net today, you should see some of the vintage Airstream makeovers I've found. It might be a bit of an ugly duckling now, but it's got potential, and that's the main thing, isn't it?' Alice needed Niamh to share her vision; not least because she couldn't sew so much as a button on while Niamh could operate her state of the art sewing machine with her eyes closed.

'It's an old girl, but she's got good bone structure, so just maybe,' Niamh said, ever cautious.

Alice nodded. 'She's Greta bloody Garbo!'

'Steady on. Let's start at Dot Cotton and work our way up.'

Suitably sobered, Alice ran through the basics she could remember from the eBay seller she'd bought it from. 'Everything works. The water, gas, electrics, everything should be fine once it's had a spruce up.'

'Heating?' Niamh pulled the sleeves of her jumper over her fingers as she spoke.

Alice nodded again, even though she couldn't precisely remember the heating being mentioned. 'I'll be snug as a bug.'

'A bed bug, probably,' Niamh said, casting a glance over the tired-looking mattress. Alice followed suit and then breathed in deeply.

'I'll just bring my mattress topper down from the house. It'll be fine.'

They both turned as Pluto appeared in the doorway, a heavy breathing thud of paws as he dropped his damp ball on the grubby floor and rolled his good eye at them hopefully.

'Not on Alice's new carpet, Plute!' Niamh scolded, earning herself a nudge in the ribs for her sarcasm as they headed out of the caravan and back to normality. It didn't escape Alice's notice that it was a degree or two warmer outside than it was inside the caravan, despite the early morning frost. She made a mental note to order the highest possible tog-rated quilt later. Was arctic-tog even a thing? Dithering as they crunched back over the lawns towards the house, she really hoped so.

CHAPTER TWO

'Are you sure this is the place?' Robinson Duff frowned out of the passenger window of the taxi as it slowed to a halt outside Borne Manor. Set well back from the road along a sweeping drive, the house was nothing like Robinson's sister had led him to believe. She'd used words like modern and cutting edge, he distinctly remembered their telephone conversation when she'd raved about having found him the perfect place on the internet.

This place wasn't modern. As soon as he was settled they'd be having another conversation, one that began with something distinctly like 'why the hell have you posted me out to Middle Earth for six months? What do you think I am, a fucking hobbit?'

Lounging splendidly in the watery afternoon sunshine, it was cute on a grand scale, the kind of house you might see on the English Tourism website alongside rolling green countryside and adverts for Shakespeare.

Robinson didn't do cute. Jesus, the mellow stone walls were practically pink, and was that wisteria winding its way around the huge, old, wooden front door? It made him think of fairy stories and afternoon tea, not usual or welcome thoughts for a man more accustomed to packed stadiums and the technicalities of a recording studio. Who the hell lived in a place like this? Goldilocks, maybe?

'This is definitely you,' the driver confirmed, glancing at the satnav app on his iPhone clipped to the dashboard. 'I'll get your bags out of the boot, shall I?'

Robinson unhooked his seatbelt with a resigned sigh. 'Looks that way.'

Inside Borne Manor, Alice paced barefoot across the cool flagstones of the square entrance hall. She'd fallen for the house as soon as she'd first set foot on those flagstones, picturing the grand stone fireplace alive with flames in winter and a cheery jug of flowers on the central table in spring-time. The sound of car doors slamming had her heart bumping around behind her ribs. The new tenant must have arrived. Her heart didn't know whether to soar or sink.

One of the benefits of being with Brad had been access to decent legal advice, and this had served her well over the last couple of weeks when she'd decided to rent the house out. Brad hadn't been bothered; as long as he didn't have to cover the mortgage payments, he was fine with whatever Alice wanted to do where the manor was concerned – or so the message came back from the solicitor who'd also been responsible for making the switch from mortgage payer to landlady a relatively easy one. Alice herself hadn't needed to be involved in the legal ins and outs, so she'd spent her days clearing out her personal effects in order to prepare the house for its new inhabitants.

It had all happened with quite indecent speed once the

ball was rolling; from 'on the market' to 'six-month rental secured' within a few days of being on the agent's books.

It was mildly surprising that the new people hadn't even bothered to come and view the house before signing on the dotted line, but Alice was just relieved to know that she was still the legal owner of Borne Manor, even if she didn't get the joy of living in it, for the next few months at least.

Three raps on the doorknocker. It was time to meet the lucky new people who'd get to call the manor home, and then it would be time for Alice to move into her own new home too. She took a deep, calming breath, arranged her smile, and then reached out for the door handle.

Robinson watched the taxi disappear off down the drive and then knocked the huge blacked doorknocker three times and waited. It struck him as weird that the homeowners had insisted on meeting him here themselves rather than arranging for a key to be waiting.

In truth he'd have preferred to skip the tea, biscuits and guided tour, but then he was in England now, the homeland of, well, tea, biscuits and guided tours, so he steeled himself to suck it up and get rid of them as soon as he possibly could.

Setting his Goldilocks fantasy aside, he laid himself a private bet that the door would be opened by an elderly guy in tweed or his equally elderly wife in a woollen twinset and pearls. Or a butler, maybe? He'd seen enough movies about big English houses, there was an outside possibility of staff in a place like this.

Maybe living here for a while wouldn't be so bad if there was someone around to help keep the fridge stocked with beer. Maybe he'd get *really* lucky and land up with a guy who liked to shoot pool, too . . . Robinson's daydream came to a halt as he heard the catch on the inside of the door move, and a second or so later it swung wide.

Well, hell. Maybe there *was* something to those fairy stories after all, because it seemed that he'd been right first time around. This house was straight out of the pages of a beautifully illustrated children's book, and even odder still, it appeared very much as if Goldilocks actually did live here.

Okay, so maybe she'd switched the pinafore dress for ripped jeans and a sweater that slid off one shoulder, but her hair was bang on the money. Golden ripples that fell past her elbows, and nervous, startlingly blue eyes that looked into his as her lips curved into a slow, uncertain smile.

'Mr Duff? I'm Alice McBride.'

She stuck her hand out and Robinson dropped his bags onto the wide stone step so he could take it. Glancing over her shoulder to make sure the three bears weren't anywhere in sight behind her, he slid his hand into hers.

She glanced over his too, and then managed to frown and keep that fixed little smile in place all at the same time.

She had a surprisingly strong handshake for a girl who appeared so delicate on first glance.

'Come in, come in,' she said, letting go of his fingers at last and stepping aside to allow him entry into the hall. More fairytale stuff. The hallway was big enough to count as a room in its own right, and the fire crackling in the hearth took the chill from the air. His hostess glanced around outside in the empty driveway for a moment and then banged the front door shut and turned to him.

'Will the rest of your family be joining you later?'

'My family?' he frowned, nonplussed.

Alice faltered.

'I'm sorry, I just assumed, given the size of the house and all . . .' she trailed off, and a rose-petal warmth tinted her cheeks that had nothing to do with the warmth from the fireplace.

'Maybe later. It's just me for now.'

Robinson didn't elaborate, and found himself irritated by her automatic assumption. The last thing he planned on doing was sharing his domestic arrangements with strangers. He'd come here to get away from prying eyes and nosy neighbours, not hurl himself headlong into the middle of village gossip.

Alice recovered herself well, switching that polite smile of hers straight back on.

'Shall I show you around, or would you like a cup of tea? You must be exhausted after all the travelling.'

How very English. Welcoming as she was clearly trying to be, what Robinson really needed her to do was to leave him alone to get his head together.

'Actually, you're right. I am exhausted. Maybe we could take a rain check on the grand tour until tomorrow? I'm sure I can find somewhere to lay my head.'

He noticed how Alice blinked two or three times as she deciphered the request to leave hidden behind his polite words.

'Right. Right, yes, of course.'

She spoke haltingly, that smile still there but no longer touching her eyes. She seemed momentarily stuck, wiping her palms on her jeans as if she wasn't sure which way to go. He looked down at her bare feet and hoped she wasn't planning to tackle the gravel driveway without shoes.

'Okay, so I'll leave you to it then,' she said eventually,

and then, oddly, she added, 'it's just this way,' and turned and disappeared through one of the wide doorways that led off the hall.

Curious, he followed her and found himself heading into the kitchen.

'This is the kitchen,' she said, redundantly. He watched as she trailed her fingers over the central island as she passed it, almost an affectionate stroke. 'The oven can be a bit temperamental, I can show you how to coax it, if you like.'

'I'm not much of a chef,' he murmured. An understatement. He'd barely cooked more than bacon and eggs in his life.

'Right.'

She reached the backdoor, and then turned with her hand on the latch.

'I'll be off then,' she said, her eyes moving from him to sweep slowly around the room.

Was it an English thing to leave by the back door? If it was he'd never heard of it. He watched as she stepped outside and pulled on a pair of bright red rain boots from beside a bench by the door, her curtain of hair swishing around her shoulders as she straightened. That resolved the shoe issue, at least.

'Let me know if there's anything you need.'

He nodded, and then realised he had no idea where she lived.

'How do I find you?'

She glanced away from him across the gardens. 'Easy. I'm over there.'

Turning away, she started to tramp across the damp grass.

He watched her go for a few seconds, confused.

'You live in my garden?' he called after her. She paused, then turned back around.

'Well, no, not exactly,' she said, holding up her finger. 'If you check the lease you'll see that you get the house and the top lawn. I've got the rest of the land.'

He frowned, lost.

'My place is just the other side of the trees,' she said. 'I can have a fence put in to divide the garden more clearly, if you like?' She looked at him testily. 'I didn't because it seemed a bit unnecessary, but maybe I was wrong.'

Robinson realised that he hadn't just been being polite when he'd said he was tired. He was exhausted all the way down to his bones, and try as he might he couldn't work out what the hell was going on here. He needed a bath, a beer, and his bed, wherever that was.

'I'll give it some thought,' he said, and she gave him the smallest of perfunctory waves and set off again across the grass.

In the caravan a couple of hours later, Alice went into battle with the archaic heater and lost. She wasn't altogether surprised; disappointed, but not especially surprised given that it was a game of luck to get the gas rings on the cooker to work and the water pump was distinctly dodgy. The eBay seller who'd sold her the caravan had certainly added a gloss of efficiency to the advert that wasn't strictly true, but Alice wasn't to be deterred. This was home now. She was just relieved to have a roof over her head, even if it was made of tin and not one hundred per cent draught proof.

Making herself a sandwich as she warmed the kettle to fill two hot water bottles, Alice considered her new neighbour. The last thing she'd expected when she opened the door to Borne Manor that afternoon was a six-foot-two cowboy, much less a cowboy with broad shoulders, clear green eyes and something about his guarded manner that rendered her mildly speechless. He was . . . interesting.

Climbing into the huge bed, Alice set herself up for the evening. The memory foam mattress from the house had been a pain in the ass to lug down to the caravan, but boy was she glad of it now. She was equally glad of the myriad pillows and the cloud of quilts, and especially thankful for the luxury fur throw she'd given to Brad for Christmas that he hadn't bothered to take. The rest of the caravan might be lacking in amenities, but the bed was hotel luxurious with her five-hundred-thread-count bed linen thrown into the mix.

Warm and fed, Alice lay back and pulled the quilt up to her nose. Through the trees she could just about make out the honey glow of lights in the kitchen up at the house, and she could imagine standing by the Aga to warm her bum as the underfloor heating warmed her toes.

Bah. Who needed all that jazz anyway? She wiggled her toes on the hot water bottle and switched her Kindle on, the only light inside the dark caravan. Clicking through to the internet to browse for something new to read, Alice scrawled through the recommendations and huffed softly as a scorching cowboy romance appeared on the screen. The blurb promised a hot Texan bad boy who could do a lot more than play the guitar with his wicked hands. Her index finger hovered over the buy button for a second, and then she thought better of it and scrolled forward to the next recommendation. Cowboys might make good romance novel fodder, but she'd had her fill of romance for at least the next twenty years. All that romance had got her lately was a broken heart, a dodgy heater and a no-fixed-abode address. Resolute, she clicked buy on the latest gory thriller to hit the top of the charts and settled down to read.

Up at the manor, Robinson picked up the coffee he'd just made and turned out the kitchen lights. Beyond the windows he could see only evening darkness, no sign of any lights or life beyond the tree line. This really was turning into the strangest of days. Bizarre as it was, it would seem that he'd flown straight out of Nashville and become the lord of his very own English manor, complete with fairies at the bottom of the garden.

CHAPTER THREE

'There's a cowboy living in my house.' Alice shrugged her damp coat off and left it on the hooks just inside Niamh's front door. She'd huddled inside the hood of her parka and made an early morning dash from the caravan to the cottages, eager to talk about the new tenant of Borne Manor.

Dropping into the armchair by the fire, she gratefully accepted the mug of tea Niamh had already made for her in anticipation of her arrival.

'A cowboy?' Niamh perched on the seat of the other armchair. 'As in Elvis and horses and all that stuff?'

'Are you sure Elvis was a cowboy?'

Niamh shrugged. 'I've definitely seen him in a Stetson, and he sure sounded like one, ma'am.'

Alice raised an eyebrow at Niamh's dodgy attempt at an accent. 'Not as much as this guy does. He has a guitar, and he wears his jeans like a cowboy, and he speaks with this deep drawl.'

Niamh considered Alice's words for a moment then held

up her palm. 'Whoa. Back up there a second. He wears his jeans like a cowboy? What does that even mean?'

Alice floundered for the right words and pulled a face. 'You know . . . all low slung and snug. As if he's just got off his horse or something.'

'Please, God, tell me he's good-looking?'

Alice paused, trying to decide how to answer.

'He's sort of striking, yeah. He's got that laid-back, tanned cowboy thing going on.'

She looked at Niamh, who raised her eyebrows and waited for more. Alice shrugged, not wanting to over commit about the handsome but somewhat grumpy man living in her house.

'I don't know, really. He's just got this capable way about him. Charismatic, I suppose.'

Niamh laughed into her coffee mug.

'I think I need to see this man for myself. Think he'd fancy sitting for me?'

Alice shook her head. 'Doubt it. He seemed a bit grouchy, to be honest. Although . . .'

'What?'

Alice glanced across at Niamh's canvas on the easel behind the armchairs, at the all too evident beginnings of yesterday's octogenarian nude.

'Nothing,' she said, her eyes dancing as she looked back at Niamh. 'It's just that from the way those jeans fit him, I think you might need more than an old fig in your fruit bowl.'

A little later that morning, Robinson pulled back his bedroom curtains just in time to catch his resident woodland nymph running across the grass towards her mystery residence beyond the trees. Although she was more Eskimo than nymph this morning; he wouldn't have recognised her except for her telltale red boots and the long blonde trails of hair escaping the hood she'd turned up as protection against the lashing rain. 'Welcome to England,' he muttered, scrubbing his hands through his hair to wake himself up. Jetlag was one hell of a bitch to shake.

His thoughts turned back to his new landlady as he brushed his teeth. Where had she been so early, anyway? Or had she just been coming home after a night elsewhere? He pushed the disturbing thought away and headed downstairs. He didn't really object to her coming and going, but it was going to be kind of hard to keep a low profile if his garden became a thoroughfare for a steady stream of Alice's friends and lovers.

Maybe that fence she'd mentioned was going to be necessary after all.

'Alice?'

Even though she'd barely had one conversation with him, Alice recognised Robinson's voice straight away. No one else in Shropshire, or in England for that matter, had that odd mix of gravel-rough and silky smooth when they said her name. She swung the caravan door open, frowning at the grey, drizzly day beyond the canopy awning.

'Morning,' she said, keeping her guard well and truly up. 'Have you decided you need that guided tour after all?'

'You live in an Airstream.'

Alice looked at him steadily, taken aback by his bluntness. 'Yes. I do.'

His face had confusion written all over it. 'You moved out of that huge house into a van in your own garden?'

It nettled her that he didn't keep his confusion to himself, mostly because she wasn't any more ready to elaborate on her situation than he'd been when he'd arrived yesterday.

'Is that a problem to you?' she said, not quite challenging, but not quite polite, either.

He looked mildly taken aback, shaking his head with a tiny shrug.

'I guess not, so long as you don't plan on throwing all-night parties down here.'

Alice considered her options for a moment. If she argued her right to do whatever the heck she pleased down here, then she'd also need to prepare herself for a reply that involved six-foot fences and privacy rights. On balance, she decided not to go in hard straight off the bat, mostly because it was still early and her brain needed more coffee.

'Lucky for you I'm not the party sort, then.' She nodded slowly. 'You better come in out of the rain.'

Stepping back into the caravan, she flicked the gas on beneath the kettle, glad that the cooker co-operated easily for once.

'Coffee?'

Robinson stepped inside the caravan, and Alice watched him silently size the place up. She knew perfectly well what he must be thinking.

Why would anyone move out of the manor into this? He looked at the eclectic collection of rugs she'd used to cover the old lino for warmth as well as appearance, and the faded cherry-red leather banquette seating covered in a mish mash of pretty cushions Niamh had made along with the new curtains. It wasn't a palace, but the interior of the Airstream had a feminine, kitsch charm now that hadn't been there before Alice and Niamh had set to work on it. Alice was particularly fond of how the polished chrome roof over her bed had come up; its curves and bolts all looked fabulous by candlelight at night. It was unexpectedly intimate, having him look at her bed. In the close confines of the caravan he was in her kitchen, her lounge and her bedroom all at once, and the breadth of his shoulders seemed more pronounced in the small space.

'I love these old things,' he said, surprising her as he ran an appreciative hand over the coach built cupboards. Okay, so maybe she hadn't read his thoughts well at all. 'My folks had one when we were kids. All of our holidays were spent pulled up beside one lake or another, climbing trees and running riot.'

Alice patted the worktop, basking a little in his approval of her new home despite herself.

'I'm not sure she's up to dragging around the country just yet, but I'm happy enough in here. Sit down,' she said, motioning towards the banquette that ran around the opposite end of the caravan to the bed. He passed behind her where she stood at the cooker, close by necessity. He didn't touch her, but all the same her body was unexpectedly aware of his in a way that made the hairs on the back of Alice's neck stand up.

'Sugar?' she asked, flustered. What the hell was her body playing at? She was in the completely wrong place in her head for her body to be making such rash overtures, and it scared the hell out of her.

He shook his head, taking the mug she held out and placing it on the table in front of him. Alice picked up the drink she'd been part way through and joined him, perching a safe distance away on the end of the banquette opposite.

'So, Mr Duff. How was your first night in the manor?'

She successfully fought the urge to say 'in my manor', or even worse, 'in my bed'.

'It's Robinson, please.'

Alice frowned slightly, unsure she was happy to be on first name terms when her body had just acted in such an irresponsible fashion to his. *Robinson Duff*. Did something about his name ring a familiar bell? He must have sensed it in her, because he sighed a little and looked less comfortable than a moment ago.

'I'm sorry,' Alice said. 'It's just your name. I feel as if I've heard it before somewhere.'

He picked up his mug and drank slowly then lowered his eyelids, staring into his coffee.

'I doubt that.'

He dismissed her words with a careless shrug.

Alice frowned, unconvinced, her head on one side as she looked at him.

'No... I'm pretty sure I have,' she said, sensing his annoyance and not understanding where it came from.

He sighed audibly.

'Maybe you have, maybe you haven't. It's a pretty common name. Does it really matter?' His carefully controlled look aimed for bland, but his eyes told a different story. They told her to back off. Alice received the message loud and clear and held her tongue, even though she wanted to point out that, actually, Robinson Duff wasn't a very common name at all.

'I used to be a singer, back home,' he said, his tone flat, his eyes back on his coffee. 'Next subject.'

Alice wished he'd look up. It was hard to read his expression without the luxury of seeing his eyes, but the quiet melancholy in his voice spoke of a heavy heart.

'Must be it,' she said, privately planning to look him up later. She'd heard of him, she was certain.

'Where *is* home, Robinson?'

He didn't reply for a few long beats.

'Here, now,' he said, finally glancing back up.

He said it in a way that closed that line of enquiry down too, told her very clearly that he'd rather talk about something else. Alice didn't push it; recent events in her own life had taught her that some things are difficult to say. If Robinson needed to keep his secrets, she was okay with that. She just hoped he wasn't planning to keep them for ever in her house, because some time soon she was going to want it back again. It was clear from his testy attitude that although they were going to be neighbours, they weren't going to be friends. Alice found she was fine with that, because something about Robinson Duff made her profoundly uncomfortable. He was too much of a man; all broad shoulders and vitality and charisma. Her body approved, but her head and her heart didn't, which put him right at the top of her 'best avoided' list. Wiping her palms down her jeans, she donned her professional landlady hat. She could be that, at least. She could be his landlady.

'Want me to give you a guided tour of the house? There's a few eccentricities to the place you should know about.'

His expression cleared back to neutral, as if he too found their professional relationship easier to navigate.

'That might be a good idea, darlin'. I managed to find a bath and a bed without getting myself into too much trouble, but it sure is quite the house.'

Robinson's accent was pure cowboy, as Dallas as Bobby Ewing and the way he said *darlin'* sent a second unexpected and unwelcome prickle of awareness down Alice's spine.

She wanted to ask him not to say it again but knew that to do so would make her sound gauche and mildly militant.

'It's yours, I take it?'

She looked at him hard. What had they been talking about?

'The house,' he prompted. 'You own it?'

Back in the room. 'Yes. Yes, the manor's mine.'

Robinson looked at her for a few silent seconds before he spoke again.

'And will your family be joining you in the Airstream soon?'

He loaded the question with just the right balance of sarcasm and innocence, but he didn't fool Alice.

Right. So that was how they were going to play it. She knew she'd read his fleeting expression of annoyance properly yesterday when she'd asked if his family would be coming to stay, and he was firing an answering shot across her bows.

It was her turn to play her cards close to her chest. Robinson's eyes were full of questions, and she chose not to answer any of them.

'You'll like the village,' she said, deliberately changing the subject. 'There's everything you might need, and The Siren's a decent local.'

'Local?' he said, frowning.

'Pub,' she explained. 'If you fancy a drink, it's usually fun in there . . . a good crowd . . .' Alice trailed off, aware that it sounded quite a lot like she was asking him out, which she absolutely wasn't.

'I'm pretty private.'

And that sounded quite a lot like a knock back.

'I didn't mean . . .' he said, after a second, and then just shrugged and let his sentence hang in the air.

'It doesn't matter,' she said, over bright and too quick, then pushed her cup away from her on the table and stood up decisively.

'Come on. Let me show you around the manor.'

Robinson followed Alice hurriedly across the lawns and in through the back door of the manor, pausing with her to shed his coat and wet boots.

'Is it like this much?' he asked, already disenchanted with the English weather.

'April showers, I'm afraid. There's talk of a hot summer though, if that's any help.' Alice smiled as she stepped out of her boots, hanging her wet parka up. 'Come and warm up by the Aga.'

She moved across the kitchen tiles, her feet once more bare.

'I'm sorry,' she said, when he joined her by the stove. 'I said that as if it's my kitchen, didn't I? Old habits.'

'Change takes a while to get used to,' he offered, wondering how the hell she'd wound up living in an Airstream in her own garden. Maybe in time she'd know him well enough to tell him. She was a very different kind of woman to those who'd filled Robinson's life back home; there was a quietness about her, a self contained way that intrigued him despite his quest for privacy and peace. He hadn't got the measure of her yet, but one thing was abundantly clear: she loved this house.

After a quick and complicated lesson on the Aga, Robinson resolved not to buy anything that couldn't be microwaved and followed Alice back into the lofty entrance hall.

'Dining room,' she said, pushing open a wide door to reveal a high-ceilinged room with double aspect views over the lawns. The furniture was scaled to match the room, the long table grand and suitably aged beneath the central chandelier, but somehow the pretty interior decor choices allowed the room to avoid standing on ceremony. It was impeccably done, like the rest of the house, as far as he could see, a perfect blend of relaxed luxury and welcoming informality.

'This is the living room,' Alice opened another door to show him another equally large, airy room with French doors onto a terrace, this time with oversized ivory sofas that beckoned you to sleep on them and a fabulous original stone fireplace. Logs filled a basket beside the hearth, and Robinson made a mental note to light a fire in there later that evening.

'There's satellite TV in here, and the music system is decent,' Alice said. She probably assumed that was important to him. In a previous life, it would have been pretty darn crucial.

He nodded, non-committal, and she led him back into the entrance hall towards the sweeping staircase. Pausing by a door under the stairs, she backtracked on herself and opened it.

'Down there's the cellar,' she said, feeling around on the wall for the light. 'I'll show you, because you'll need to know where the electric box is. The lights can trip sometimes if you overload the system.'

She stepped down and then turned back to him. 'Mind your step, it's pretty steep.'

Robinson followed Alice down the steps into the coolness below the house.

'Is this the part where you kill me and store me in the deep freeze down here along with all your previous tenants?'

'Keep paying the rent and I'll let you live a while longer

yet,' she murmured, flicking the lid down on the fuse box and pointing out what he needed to know.

Robinson really didn't need the explanation. He knew his way around electrics. Before hitting pay-dirt in Nashville he'd made a living on building sites as a carpenter, and he'd worked around enough electricians to have more than a rudimentary grasp on the basics should he ever need it. All the same, he let Alice demonstrate and nodded in the right places, because it was clear that sharing her knowledge of the house gave her pleasure. When she turned to close the box up he inspected the room behind him.

'You play the drums?' he couldn't keep the surprise out of his voice.

Even from behind he didn't miss the way her shoulders tensed. She turned slowly, her expression carefully bland. 'Not me. They're my husband's, not that he used them much.'

'Your husband?' She'd ducked out of answering his earlier question about family, and Robinson instinctively looked down at her hands and found her fingers bare of rings. She didn't miss it and met his eyes steadily when he quickly looked back up again.

'He's away just now,' she said, her voice way too breezy for the troubled expression on her face. 'Feel free to make use of the drums if you'd like.'

He wouldn't. He wouldn't make use of the drums, nor would he play the gorgeous baby grand piano he'd spotted in the living room earlier. He wasn't even sure he'd play his beloved guitar again; he'd brought it only because travelling without it felt like leaving one of his limbs behind. He hadn't been anywhere without it since he was fifteen years old; not even his honeymoon. Right now it was propped against the wall in the corner of the bedroom, almost out of sight, even if never entirely out of his mind. Just because he wasn't playing it didn't mean that his fingers didn't ache to hold it and strum its familiar strings. Would this bitterness ever leave him? Lena really had done a number on him; she hadn't just hacked his heart up, she'd as good as hacked his hands off too. He didn't know which hurt more any longer; losing Lena, or losing the will to play, to sing. Forcing the thoughts away, he followed Alice back up the cellar steps and onwards up the staircase towards the bedrooms.

'The house has seven bedrooms in all,' Alice said. 'Five on this floor, and then a further two en-suite rooms upstairs in the attics. You might want to take one down here though, the ceilings up there aren't really designed for people over five foot.' Alice nodded towards the second-floor staircase as she spoke, towards the rooms she'd once hoped would house her children. Squaring her shoulders, she continued on down to the far end of the wide hallway.

'This is my favourite of the bathrooms up here,' she said, leading Robinson through a door off to the left. 'A loo with a view.'

One of the many things that had enchanted her when they'd first viewed Borne Manor had been the magical corner bathroom with huge picture windows looking out over the gardens. She'd since spent countless candlelit hours in the huge roll-top bath that stood central in the panelled room, a fire in the hearth in winter, a book in her hand whatever the season.

Drawing the door closed, she moved back down the hall, opening each of the original oak doors to reveal the pretty bedrooms that lay beyond.

'And this one's the master,' she said, opening the door that up to a day or two back had been her own bedroom, and just a few months ago had been the room she'd shared with Brad.

'Yeah, I've . . .' Robinson's words dried up as he and Alice stood in the doorway and surveyed the unmade bed, the guitar propped in the corner and the suitcase he'd thrown open on the floor last night in search of his razor.

There was no reason for it to come as shock to see her bedroom being used by someone else; part and parcel of renting your house out furnished, after all, was that the tenants used your things. They cooked in your kitchen, they watched your TV on your sofa, and they slept in your bed. Nonetheless, Alice needed a minute to find the right words, or to find any words at all. It was a shock to imagine him sprawled out in her bed. Had he slept on her side, or on Brad's? It was hard to tell from the way the quilt was tangled on the sheets, it looked as if he'd spent the night tossing and turning.

Robinson seemed to realise her discomfort, because he reached past her and pulled the door shut again.

'I think I've got this one covered already,' he murmured.

'Quite,' Alice said, trying to pull herself together. 'Quite.'

Walking ahead of him, she took the stairs at a skip and walked briskly back to the kitchen, her bare feet silent on the familiar flagstones.

'Thanks, Alice. I'm sure I'll have a hundred questions while I get used to the place,' he said, resting his ass on the kitchen table as he watched her. That's my table you've got your backside on, she thought. That's my table and you're sleeping in my bloody bed.

'Maybe you could make a list,' she said flatly.

Touring Robinson around the manor had reminded her all too vividly of the life she'd planned to live there, and left Alice ungraciously resenting his presence rather than being glad of his rent.

He nodded easily. 'I know where to find you.'

'I'm out quite a lot,' she said quickly, a complete lie to deter him from dropping by. 'Leave a note under the Airstream door if it's urgent.'

She saw her dismissal register on his face and couldn't get out of there fast enough. Pushing her feet back into her wellies at the same time as grabbing her coat, she had the door open in seconds.

'Right. I'll leave you to it. Have a good day!' she called brightly into her hood, and then ducked out into the rain and made a dash for the safety of the Airstream. She was glad of the rain. It hid the tears that streaked her cheeks, and the wind took the sound of the sobs that choked from her body as she ran.

Robinson leaned against the doorframe and sighed heavily. It didn't take a rocket scientist to work out that Alice McBride was a girl with a damaged heart. Watchful eyes. Defensive words. Bare fingers. Walls around walls around fragile hearts to keep people out.

He recognised the symptoms, because he'd been an in-patient on the same ward for a while now. From the way she'd reacted just now he'd say she'd probably been there for less time than he had; her pain seemed fresher, less under control. He wasn't in a position to offer her any hopeful words of wisdom; just keep breathing and hoping it hurts less tomorrow didn't really offer any kind of solace.

CHAPTER FOUR

Alice swung the door of the Airstream open to inspect the post-storm evening. The blustery weather had finally blown through, leaving behind it a still calm and the hopeful smell of damp spring grass and cherry blossom trees laden with sodden, velvety flower heads.

It was a little after ten, and through the trees she could see the kitchen lights of the manor, indicating that Robinson was home. Not that it came as a surprise; from what he'd said earlier he wasn't planning on throwing wild parties any more than she was. Picking her way down the caravan steps in her bare feet, Alice tip-toed across the wet grass to flick on the fairy lights she'd threaded around the edge of the awning in a moment of kitsch overload the previous week. They winked into life, candy pink, apple green and lavender blue interspersed with creamy yellow, all reflecting prettily off the shiny silver sides of the Airstream. She hopped and skipped her way back inside the caravan and pulled on her red wellingtons, then slung a woollen shawl around her shoulders as she reached for her rescued garden bottle of rum and a tumbler.

Sitting on the caravan step, her hands wrapped around her glass, Alice did something she rarely allowed herself to do. She let herself remember. She remembered the first time she and Brad had viewed the manor, the way her throat had unexpectedly tightened with tears as she'd looked out of the windows at the lush, rolling gardens. She let herself feel all of the things she'd felt back then. The swooping joy. The nervous excitement. The anticipation of forever. It was as if the place had wrapped its arms around her and welcomed her in, welcomed her home almost. It had kept her safe over the turmoil of the last weeks and months, and even now, living as she was only in the gardens, she felt under its protection. Borne Manor was her home, her beloved place, and her sanctuary. Drinking deeply, Alice's eyelids closed as she let the heat of the alcohol slide down her throat, warming her from the inside out. *Sanctuary.* If she had to sum up Borne Manor in one word, she'd choose sanctuary. And that was precisely the moment when the big idea floated into her mind like the blown seeds of a dandelion clock.

'Any left in that bottle?'

Startled from her thoughts, Alice opened her eyes and found Robinson standing just outside the cover of the awning. He looked like a man who could use a drink; tired eyed and crumpled around the edges, from his faded jeans to his creased, straight out of the suitcase checked shirt that followed closely against the cut of his body. Made from the kind of worn, brushed cotton that Alice knew would be peach soft underneath her fingers, it hugged the breadth of his shoulders and defined the curves of his biceps as he shoved his hands in his jean pockets and tipped his head to one side, waiting for her to answer. God, yes, she needed to answer. Clearing her throat, she shot him a small smile.

'You're in luck.' Pulling herself up, she stepped inside the Airstream and took down a second glass, sloshing a decent measure of rum into it. 'There's a deckchair leaning against the caravan, if you want it,' she called out, watching him casually through the window over the sink. He was quite alien; exotic and out of place, not at all English. She saw him frown at the chair for a second and then pass it over in favour of perching on her cool box as a makeshift stool, his elbows on his spread knees as he rubbed both hands over his face and then scrubbed them through his hair.

'Jetlag?' she said, stepping down out of the caravan to hand him his glass.

'I'm just about caught up, I reckon,' he said, looking up and accepting the rum, taking a drink before cradling the glass in his big, tanned hands.

Alice settled back onto the step and pulled the shawl around her shoulders, aware that she looked mildly eccentric in her frilled white cotton slip and red wellies, her pale knees poking out under the hem. His eyes moved along the tree line towards the house beyond.

'It's quite the place.'

'It is,' she said after a moment's pause. 'You'll find it's a great place to relax.'

He looked at her steadily. 'Is that what you think I'm doing here?'

The directness of his question took her by surprise, although the mild tone of his voice took any sting from his words.

She studied him for a second. 'Sorry. That sounded like I was prying and I really wasn't.'

'You weren't all that far from the truth,' he conceded, rolling his glass between his palms, his eyes fixed on the swirling liquid. 'Not to my mind, anyway. My sister on the other hand called it escaping, my record label called it reckless, and my ex-wife called it running away. Take your pick.'

Wow. So *that* was an unexpected information dump. An opinionated sister and an annoyed ex-wife, not to mention a record company chasing his tail. No wonder he looked ragged around the edges. She should have given him a bigger measure of rum.

'That's quite a list,' she said, keeping it simple.

'You don't know the half of it.'

Uh oh. That sounded ominous.

'I'm not going to have to beat them all off with a big stick, am I?' Alice remembered back to the days of being hounded by paparazzi around Brad's affair, of how much more difficult they'd made her life just when it was falling to pieces anyway. She looked back now and wished she'd been strong enough at the time to get rid of them, trampling her gardens and invading her privacy. She wouldn't let that sort of thing ever happen here again, even if it wasn't strictly her own privacy that she'd be protecting this time around.

He shook his head, a complicated look in his eyes as he huffed softly. 'I don't suppose this place has a drawbridge hidden around somewhere to pull up in case of emergency?'

''Fraid not, cowboy. No moat, either.' Alice silently questioned her own words. Cowboy? Just because she called him that in her head, it didn't mean she should have ever let it out of her mouth. If it surprised him, he didn't say.

'Figures. We could always dig one?'

Something in the way he said we rather than I unsettled her, bringing with it an image of being holed up against the world with Robinson in Borne Manor.

'There's a trowel around somewhere if you get desperate.'

46

God knew she'd reached the point of desperation herself a few times recently. 'There's one or two people I'd like to throw in it,' she muttered, unguarded.

He raised his eyebrows. 'I'll buy another spade, in that case.'

Alice traced the frilled edge of her slip with her finger against her skin. 'Deal,' she said, softly.

They sat in companionable silence for a couple of minutes, an owl hooting somewhere in the trees ahead.

'Cowboy?' he said eventually, favouring her with a speculative sideways look that said her nickname hadn't passed him by.

'Am I wrong?'

He raised one shoulder, a half shrug, an acknowledgement. 'I own a ranch and I sang country, so I guess you could call that cowboy.'

She noticed the way he'd used past tense to refer to singing.

'You don't sing any more?'

The pretty glow of the fairy lights picked out his profile, pastel hues illuminating the unmistakable twist of his mouth. He looked as if he'd swallowed something bitter. Was it pain, or distaste? It was hard to tell.

'I kind of lost my love for it.'

For the second time that evening Alice felt as if she'd spoken out of turn. It was clearly not a subject he wanted to get into.

'I'm prying again. Ignore me.'

He drained his glass. 'I'll make you a deal, Goldilocks. You don't mention my singing and I won't mention your absent husband. How does that sound?'

Ah. So she hadn't got away with her borderline nutcase behaviour up at the manor that afternoon, then.

'Goldilocks?' she said, picking him up for his nickname as he had with her earlier.

He smiled then, his eyes glittering in the darkness of the evening. It was the first time since he'd arrived that Alice had seen him look genuinely amused, and his slightly crooked grin warmed her unexpectedly.

'This place,' he gestured around with his empty glass. 'It's all just a little bit fairytale, isn't it? Or it seems that way to my eyes, anyhow.'

Alice couldn't argue with that.

'And then there's you, all blonde hair and rosy cheeks, living in my garden like a pixie.'

'My garden,' she countered, half laughing at his fanciful description.

He rolled his eyes and then corrected himself. 'Fine. Your garden. Either way it's all a bit fuckin' *Alice in Wonderland*.'

Alice looked at him. 'You know you're mixing up your fairy stories, right?'

His eyes met hers straight on, and for a second they connected, amusement sliding into seriousness, each recognising a kindred broken spirit in the other. And then he shook his head a little, breaking the moment, and Alice looked down then back up again and held out her hand to take his empty glass for something to do. She stepped back up into the doorway of the Airstream as he stood to leave, touching his hand against his forehead in the smallest of goodbye salutes.

'Thanks for the rum.'

She watched him push his hands deep into the pockets of his jeans, a gesture that was fast becoming familiarly his, his broad shoulders bunched beneath the cotton of his shirt as he sauntered away.

'Watch out for the three bears in the woods, cowboy,' she called out, crossing her arms over her chest.

He spun slowly, still walking away. 'I'm a crack shot,' he said, flashing her that smile again as he turned away and disappeared into the darkness of the tree line.

Alice considered him for a moment as she pulled the Airstream door closed and knocked back the last of her rum. All of those mixed up fairy tales and unexpected revelations had left her confused by Robinson Duff and his wolfish smile. Worryingly, if she were to liken herself to any story-book heroine right at that very moment, it would most probably have been Red Riding Hood.

'Morning, mine *chatelaine*!' Stewie boomed, doffing his shaggy blond wig at Alice as they passed each other the following morning by Niamh's garden gate. Alice grinned in reply as he marched on by, the tails of his silk smoking jacket swishing beneath the hem of his rain jacket. Newly returned from his beloved Benidorm, his tan rivalled the orange juice nestled alongside his newspaper in the crook of his arm and his Turkish slippers provided scant protection against the damp pavement. It didn't matter. Stewie's penchant for all things colourful and over the top was part of his larger than life charm; he wasn't a man who you'd ever catch buying a sensible cardigan in Marks and Spencer.

Niamh's front door opened and Pluto scampered down the path, his claws clattering on the old cobbles.

'Salutations, Pluto!' Stewie shouted, not breaking his stride until he reached his own gate further down the lane.

'Morning, Stewie,' Niamh called, sticking her head out of the front door, still in her PJs. 'Loving the blond!'

'In homage to the divine Marilyn, darling.' He stroked

his spare hand over his wig, his voice carrying easily over the cottage gardens as he opened his own door. He disappeared inside, and then just his hand poked back out holding the blond wig to give it a good shake.

'Plus it's long enough to keep the rain out of my eyes,' he called, and then whipped it back inside and closed the door with a flourish.

Alice followed Niamh back into the cottage trailed by Pluto, who despondently nosed his wet ball balefully back into the house and glared at her with his good eye as he curled up on his rug by the fire.

'Sorry, bud. Next time.' Alice fussed him behind the ears and he closed his eyes and deliberately ignored her, having heard her lines before. She straightened again, fidgeting around on the edge of the chair.

'Out with it then.'

Alice looked up at Niamh's words.

'You've got news. I can tell by the way you're bouncing around like an over-excited kid.'

For a moment she considered denying Niamh's assumption, and then cracked under her friend's expectant gaze.

'I know how I can keep the manor. It came to me last night.'

Niamh nodded for her to go on.

'I was sitting looking at the gardens of the manor, at the tree house, and then beyond that there's the old boathouse down by the lake, right?'

A frown of concentration creased Niamh's brow. 'Well, yes, but I don't see . . .'

'I'm going to turn the gardens of the manor into a glampsite.'

Niamh studied her intently. 'In the tree house, and the

boathouse? Alice, that place is rotten through. I know, I paint there sometimes.'

Alice waved her hand, undeterred. 'Picture it, Niamh. The tree house, expanded to be big enough for a love nest for two. The boathouse, shored up, a perfectly secluded honeymoon spot to watch the sun go down over the lake. A tee-pee somewhere, or a yurt, even. There's so many quirky places you can stay in now, I could have all sorts.' She watched her friend's perplexed expression closely, waiting for it to clear. It didn't. 'I know it seems impossible, but nothing ever is really, is it? You just have to want it hard enough.' Reaching into her bag she pulled out her laptop. The Airstream was too distant from the manor to get reliable net reception. 'Let me steal your Wi-Fi and I'll show you what I mean.'

An hour later and Niamh's printer had worked overtime to provide the images that now filled a red file Niamh had dug out of the cupboard beside the fireplace.

'I love this,' Alice said, tapping her fingers against a shot of a converted vintage grain lorry. 'Where could I get a lorry from?'

'Let's not run before you can walk,' Niamh cautioned, but her eyes shone with excitement that mirrored Alice's as she closed the file. 'Let's start with the tree house and see how it goes.'

Alice knew it was sage advice and went to close the laptop lid, and then had second thoughts and flipped it open again.

'Alice . . .'

'Shh. I'm not going to search for wooden igloo's again, promise.' Her fingers flew over the keys and pressed enter.

'What are you looking for then?'

Alice clicked on the first link that came up. 'Robinson Duff.'

'The country music star?'

It was hard to decide between looking at the screen and looking back up at Niamh. She chose the latter.

'You've heard of him?'

Niamh blew her dark fringe out of her eyes. 'Heard of him? Jesus, yes. Hasn't everyone?'

Alice scanned the screen, her eyes slowly widening. 'Everyone but me, it seems.' Image after image of Robinson filled her screen; publicity shots, paparazzi shots, and fan pictures of him on stage playing to packed stadiums. Wow. Her mouth formed the word, even though no sound came out. 'He's pretty famous, isn't he?'

'I have his latest stuff on Spotify.' Niamh reached for the TV remote and clicked through the on screen apps. 'Just a sec . . .'

Music filled the room, followed by a voice that Alice recognised easily as that of the man she'd drunk rum with last night. It was a song she was vaguely familiar with from the radio, just as she'd been vaguely familiar with his name when he'd first said it. He must think her totally clueless to have not known precisely who he was from the get go. She certainly felt it now.

'He's the cowboy.'

Niamh nodded, humming along to the track. 'Cowboy through and through.'

'No, Niamh. He's THE cowboy. The one who's living in my house.'

To say Niamh looked shocked would be an understatement. She stopped humming abruptly, her brown eyes rounding to at least twice the size they usually were. 'Robinson Duff is living in Borne Manor?'

Alice nodded. 'Right this very minute, and for the fore-seeable future.'

'Have you heard him sing yet?' Niamh's fingers curled around Alice's forearm. It was difficult to tell if she was actually breathing.

'Not a dickie bird.' It felt somehow disloyal to tell anyone, even Niamh, what Robinson had said about his career. She hadn't realised last night quite how big a deal it was for him to give up on singing.

'What the hell is Robinson Duff doing here in Borne?' Niamh whispered, shaking her head in childlike wonder.

'Beats me, but I'm pretty sure he wants to fly under the radar, so don't tell anyone else, okay?'

Niamh drew a dainty cross on her red polka dot PJ top with her fingertip. 'Cross my heart.'

CHAPTER FIVE

By lunchtime, it was apparent that Niamh's crossed heart wasn't to be entirely trusted. Alice returned from the supermarket to find most of the residents of Borne cottages clustered on deckchairs and upturned buckets outside her caravan, and Pluto darting excitedly in and out of the trees.

'Darling girl, you're back!' Stewie boomed from his fully reclined deckchair as she got out of the car and opened the boot. 'Let me help you with those bags.' He nudged the skinny goth teenager to his left in the ribs with his blue suede cowboy boot hard enough to shake him off his bucket onto the grass. 'Hop to it, Ewan, there's a lad.'

Ewan shot Stewie daggers as he clambered to his feet, wiping wet grass from his behind as he slouched over towards Alice.

'Err, I'm okay, actually, thank you, Ewan, there's not much,' Alice murmured, looking at Niamh through narrowed eyes. 'What are you all doing here?'

'It's your caravan warming!' Niamh jumped to her feet and threw her arms wide, an equally wide and unconvincing da-da! smile on her face. 'Surprise!'

Stewie followed her lead and offered up jazz hands, and Hazel, Ewan's mother, nodded vigorously. Ewan, for his part, slumped back down onto his bucket and nodded once, lifting one shoulder in a half-assed way. For him, that counted as a show of enthusiasm.

'Right,' Alice said slowly, looking from one to the other. 'So you're all here to see me, yes?'

Three pairs of eyes flickered guiltily towards Borne Manor and its newly resident superstar, and then resolutely back to Alice. Hazel stood up from the caravan step, a jingle of bangles and beads as she shook out her floor-length skirt, the tiny mirrors around the hem clicking like a belly dancer's hip scarf.

'I thought you might like me to perform a blessing ritual,' she said, rolling her shoulders gamely and closing her eyes.

Alice cleared her throat. 'Err, I'm good, thanks, Hazel.'

Hazel opened one eye. 'You're sure?'

Alice unlocked the Airstream and opened the door. 'Well, it's not much, but you're all welcome to come in,' she said, knowing full well that none of her guests were remotely interested in seeing inside her new home. Niamh knew it well enough already, and the other three could barely drag their eyes away from Borne Manor in the distance.

'Tea?' Alice called out of the window when none of them moved to come inside.

'Whisky?' Stewie suggested instead, straightening his jet-black Elvis-style wig.

'Out of luck, I'm afraid,' Alice said, noticing the stonkingly huge John Wayne-style gold belt buckle he'd added to his outfit. Cowboy boots. Elvis wig. Country buckle. It was perfectly clear that Stewie's attire had been chosen to make an impression on someone, and it sure wasn't Alice. *Hmm.*

'I hope no one takes sugar, I'm all out,' she said, opening the overhead mug cupboard.

'Shall I pop over to the manor and grab some?' Hazel said, leaping up, only to find herself rugby tackled back down onto the step by Niamh.

'I'll go, I know where it is.' Niamh smiled through gritted teeth, locked in battle trying to hold Hazel down.

Alice stepped into the doorway and watched her neighbours as they had what a fair number of people might term an actual fight on the Airstream step. After a minute or two she cleared her throat pointedly.

'Err, ladies?'

Niamh and Hazel both looked up, panting and out of breath. Alice raised her eyebrows at Niamh and then drew a telltale X over her heart with her fingertip.

'Cross your heart, eh?'

Niamh looked sheepish. 'It wasn't my fault, Alice. After you left I was so excited that I blasted out a few of Robinson's best tracks and Rambo hopped along the sill into my living room.'

Hazel nodded, instantly back in cahoots with Niamh. 'He did, Alice. I had to go round and get him, you know how Niamh isn't a fan of birds. Not that my Rambo would hurt a fly, mind.'

'He bloody swore at me,' Niamh said, indignant.

'I beg your pardon.' Hazel puffed up like a peacock, back to being offended again. 'That bird's got better manners than bonny Prince Charlie himself. If he swore he was only repeating whatever you'd said to him.'

Alice caught Ewan's eye behind his mother's back and shared a disbelieving look. Everyone in Borne knew Rambo, Hazel's beloved mynah bird. He spent most of his days perched on Hazel's open windowsill shouting obscenities at passersby, cackling with wild laughter if he managed to make someone jump. Hazel always alluded to a shady gypsy past if she was quizzed on how Rambo had come to be her glossy black familiar, dropping her voice an octave and drawing a veil over the exact details. She knew perfectly well that he swore like a sailor yet chose to defend his honour whenever anyone dared mention it.

'Anyway,' Niamh said, rolling her eyes. 'Hazel came round to fetch Rambo back and happened to mention that Robinson Duff was her absolute favourite, and the words sort of, well, fell out of my mouth before I could stop them . . . you know how it is . . .' Niamh trailed off. 'I didn't tell Stewie, though. Hazel did,' she added, as if that made it any better.

'I didn't,' Hazel shot back. 'I'm the soul of discretion, me. I only told my Ewan, and that doesn't count. He's family.'

All three women looked at the teenager, who twiddled nervously with his nose rings. 'Rambo?' he muttered, trying to make it sound a convincing suggestion. He might have blushed. It was difficult to tell under the mop of dyed black hair and dark make-up.

'Err, where *is* Stewie?' Hazel said, suddenly noticing the empty deckchair.

Ewan inclined his head towards the manor with a disinterested expression. 'He went that way while you two were fighting.'

Alice sighed and sagged against the doorframe, sending a silent apology across the gardens. Quite what Robinson would make of Borne's answer to Elvis was anyone's guess.

'Oh. My. Bloody. God.'

Alice followed Niamh's shocked gaze and spotted Pluto leading Stewie back across the gardens, and she could only agree with her friend. Even though she'd already had the benefit of meeting Robinson, she saw him with fresh eyes now she knew exactly how famous he actually was. There was a distinct swagger to Stewie's walk as they drew nearer, like a kid on bring your pet to school day who's brought a real live tiger in.

'Robster,' he said, hooking his thumbs through his belt loops and inclining his head towards Niamh. 'This little lady is Niamh, our resident artist.' Niamh stood up and bobbed an awkward curtsey, then swooned slightly as Robinson smiled easily and leaned in to kiss her on the cheek.

'An artist, huh?' he said, making conversation.

Niamh nodded, struck stupid. 'I draw naked men.'

Alice noticed how Robinson looked slightly taken aback by Niamh's response.

'Wow. That must be rewarding, right?' he said, eventually.

Alice could only admire his ability to find anything at all to say. Stewie shot Niamh a dark look, as if she'd tried to stroke his tiger, and ushered Robinson along.

'And this here honey is Hazel,' he said, although he didn't really need to perform introductions as Hazel was already out of her seat and practically pressing all five foot of her entire body against Robinson. Stewie coughed and muttered 'bit forward there, old girl,' under his breath, and Alice found herself wondering if it had been some time since Hazel had been near an attractive man.

'It's your aura,' she breathed, holding Robinson's face between her heavily ringed hands. 'I'm drawn to you like a magnet.'

'She's a bit bonkers,' Niamh supplied, drawing a spiral in the air beside her temple.

Hazel tossed Niamh daggers over her shoulder and then

swung back to Robinson again. 'Mother nature is here, can you feel her energy flowing between us, Robinson? You're a male pole, and I'm a female connector. We should . . .'

'Uncool, Mother. So uncool,' Ewan interrupted hastily, standing up. 'You're practically mounting him. Give him some space, man.' He stepped between his mother and a relieved-looking Robinson and stuck out his hand in the unsure way only a teenager can. He might not be a country music fan, but he was as awed as everyone else to be in the company of someone usually seen only on TV or magazine covers.

'Mr Duff,' he said formally, more like a forty-year-old businessman than a seventeen-year-old student. Robinson took his hand and shook it warmly.

'Call me Robinson,' he said, turning Ewan's cheeks pink for the second time that afternoon.

'And you've met Alice,' Stewie said, still trying to hold on to his role as circus master.

'I have indeed had the pleasure of Alice's company already,' Robinson said, finally looking her way. His rich, honeyed drawl gave nothing of his mood away and his expression was difficult to read. She didn't know him well enough yet to be able to tell if he was okay with this minor invasion, bemused by it, or even annoyed.

'Don't just stare at him, girl,' Stewie laughed loudly, edging towards hysterically bombastic. 'Get the man a drink. Whisky, Robbie?'

Robinson glanced at his watch. 'Might be a little on the early side for me.'

'Coffee?' Alice suggested instead, reaching another cup down.

Stewie led Robinson over to the recliner he'd recently vacated himself, dusting it off for dramatic effect and then bowing low to indicate the new king of Borne should take his rightful throne. It would have been quite theatrical had it not been for the fact that he bowed so low that his Elvis wig fell off and plopped into the deckchair in front of him like an errant guinea pig. Stewie styled it out, retrieving it whippet quick and slapping it on his head back to front as he straightened up.

Alice stepped across the camp and handed Robinson his coffee, bending her knees in the smallest of maid-like gestures. 'Coffee, m'lord,' she said, handing him the mug. 'I think I might have a plastic crown somewhere . . .' she added, earning herself a narrow-eyed look from her tenant. He looked as if he was about to say something but was distracted by the arrival of Niamh on his left and Hazel on his right, each perched on an upturned bucket, his unlikely pair of handmaidens.

'Can I say I love your music?' Niamh said, thoroughly starry eyed. 'I saw you live a couple of years ago, in Manchester? You might remember me; I was the one at the front with the banner that said "I'll be your Mrs Robinson".'

'Here's to you,' Stewie said, raising his glass.

'I think you'll find Mrs Robinson was a more mature woman, actually,' Hazel said, lowering her voice until she was almost at an Eartha Kitt growl, then licked her lips and pulled the clip from her long dark hair and shook it out wildly. 'I recently celebrated my fiftieth earth year, and I have to say I've never felt more intimately in touch with my body.'

Ewan dropped his face into his hands and groaned. Stewie, however, perked right up.

'In my professional opinion, older women have a lot to offer a younger man.'

Given that Stewie had been one of the most prolific porn

stars of the seventies, Alice really didn't want Stewie to take that line of conversation any further. She was saved from having to throw herself into the breach by Robinson, who cleared his throat to get everyone's attention. Even Pluto stopped hopefully nosing his ball around the floor and laid his chin on Robinson's knee.

'Guys, listen. I know we've all only just met and all, but I need to ask y'all to help me out.'

Niamh and Hazel looked ready to throw themselves off the nearest cliff if Robinson asked it of them, and Stewie didn't look far behind. He barely even noticed when Alice reached out and turned his Elvis wig the right way around for him.

'I'd appreciate it if I could count on your discretion about me being here. I'm hoping to keep it on the down low if I can, you know?'

They all nodded gravely.

'Your secret's safe with us,' Stewie drawled, possibly not even aware that he'd slipped into an American accent.

Niamh nodded and drew an imaginary zip across her lips, and Hazel crossed her hands over her heart and dropped her head.

'You guys are the best, thank you.' Robinson stood to leave, and Alice grimaced as Hazel reached out and almost stroked his jean-clad backside.

'See y'all soon,' he said, tipping an imaginary Stetson and strolling away towards the manor. Alice found herself wondering how he'd look if the Stetson had been real.

'Did anyone even *bother* to ask him for sugar?' Ewan muttered, pulling a face as he took a mouth full of his lukewarm coffee then tipped it out on the grass.

CHAPTER SIX

Alice tapped the back door of the manor later that afternoon, slightly nervous that Robinson might not be talking to her after the inaugural meeting of the Robinson 'Robster' Duff fan club.

'It's open,' his voice carried through the open window, and Alice pushed the door, taking a moment to appreciate the way the familiar old handle felt in her hand. Every little last thing about Borne Manor was beloved, from the smoothness of the worn oak banister to the creak of the floorboards on the third step of the attic stairs. As she'd closed her eyes to sleep in the caravan last night she'd walked slowly through the rooms in her head, savouring, remembering, and making herself believe that one day she'd live there again. She just needed some time, and for her glamping plan to work.

'It's only me,' she called out, kicking off her boots by the door and walking through the kitchen into the hallway in time to find Robinson jogging down the staircase barefoot in just his jeans. Unsure whether to be flustered or cool, Alice opened her mouth to say something and then closed it again, because the only words in her head were oh my god I've never seen a six-pack in real life before. His tousled hair was darkened by dampness, and the towel in his hand confirmed his just out of the shower status.

'I know. I saw you coming from upstairs,' he said, absolutely unfazed by the fact that he was half dressed. Alice was finding it difficult to be so laissez faire, given the fact that his skin was the kind of deep burnished gold that only a lifetime spent in the sunshine can give a man and the light covering of hair that trailed down his torso disappeared into his low-slung jeans like a fishing line that made you want to see what was at the end of it. God, she needed to pull herself together. What was happening to her? Her emotions were all over the place since the move into the Airstream, all of the upheaval seemed to have given her libido a scandalised kick up the backside as far as Borne's newest resident was concerned. It felt strange and confusing to be heartbroken over one man and lustful over another at the same time, all topsy-turvy and wrong.

'I wanted to apologise about earlier,' she said, following him back into the kitchen, biting her lip at the sight of his naked shoulders. She couldn't help it. She was a broad-shoulders girl, and Robinson's were world class. They did things, odd things to her insides. Maybe it was her inner cavewoman, but seeing a good pair of shoulders made her want to be thrown over them and carried up the stairs.

'Don't sweat it,' he said, opening the fridge and pulling out a couple of beers. 'Beer?'

Did she want to drink beer with the half naked and totally gorgeous superstar hiding out in her manor? Oh, go on then.

If only Brad could see her now, he'd rue the day he

decided to screw her over with Felicity bloody Shaw. Robinson knocked the lids from the bottles and handed her one, then reached casually for the T-shirt he'd draped over the radiator and slid it over his head. Bye then, shoulders. Bye then, abs. Alice bid them a silent farewell as they disappeared beneath the dark cotton. Did he have his clothes made for him, she wondered, noticing the way the material seemed to cling to every slope and angle of him.

'I didn't run around the village announcing your arrival,' she said, leaning against the Aga as she always had. 'I only told Niamh, and that was sort of by accident really because I looked you up on her laptop.' Too late, she realised that she'd made herself sound like a stalker. 'It was just that your name rang a bell and I wasn't sure why,' she added in an attempt to make it better, only of course she'd probably insulted him by saying she'd never heard of him. God, this was difficult! One of the benefits of being separated from Brad was that she no longer had to deal with the fragile egos of the famous, and here she was again. Closing her eyes, she tipped her head back and drank deeply from the bottle, and when she opened them he'd pulled out a stool at the breakfast bar and perched on it.

'Niamh who paints naked men, right?'

Alice grinned. 'Amongst other things. She's brilliant, actually, my best friend in the village.'

Robinson drank from his bottle, tipping his head back, drawing Alice's eyes to the way his throat moved as he swallowed. Slapping down the Mills and Boon heroine in her head, she looked away until he spoke again. She was in a spot of trouble here. Maybe one of the classic symptoms of heartbreak was inappropriate lust for the first good-looking stranger to come your way.

'What's Stewie's story?'

Alice started to laugh. 'I haven't seen his Elvis wig before, it must be new.'

'He has more than one wig?'

'God, yes. He's got loads,' Alice said. 'He used to be quite a prolific actor.'

'No way,' Robinson said, looking interested. 'Anything I'd know him from?'

'Maybe, maybe not,' Alice said, wondering how best to sum up Stewie's colourful career. 'If I tell you that he was professionally known as Stewie "The Snake" Heaven, you might get an idea of the kind of movies he starred in.'

Robinson started to laugh, that sexy, crooked smile lighting up his whole face as it had the previous night. 'Holy fuck. Naked painters and porn star neighbours. And there I was thinking this place was going to be dull.'

'You missed out the fact that Hazel's a practising witch,' Alice said, spreading her hands. 'Welcome to Borne, cowboy.'

He laughed under his breath and drank deeply from his beer. To Alice he looked every inch a guy in a bar kicking back, utterly relaxed. He tipped the neck of his bottle towards her.

'And then there's you, Goldilocks.'

Her new nickname had never sounded so sexy. 'What about me?'

He shrugged. 'If I was to guess, I'd say you and I have something in common.'

'You would? What would that be?' Alice wasn't entirely sure it was good for her to know.

'Feel free to tell me to shut up anytime you like, because I know I said I wouldn't mention this again, but your wedding band is only just as faded as mine.'

He looked at her left hand, and she looked at the telltale band of paler skin on his ring finger. She had no clue what to say next, so kept her eyes on his hands rather than look him in the eyes. He had good hands. The kind of hands your body might feel sexy in, and your heart might feel safe in. But then Brad had nice hands too, and he'd used them to twist her heart so badly that she wasn't sure it would ever go back to its original shape again.

'Almost six months,' she said softly. The time had gone by in a strange mix of lightning fast and torturously slow, and it was only in the last month that she'd finally removed her wedding ring and buried it at the bottom of her jewellery box.

'Ten for me,' he said, and she finally looked up and saw her own broken heart reflected there in his eyes.

'Are you going to tell me it gets easier?' she said. Just about everyone else did.

'Only if you want me to lie to you.'

She shook her head and sighed hard. 'I've had enough of lies to last me a lifetime.'

He clinked his bottleneck against hers and huffed in understanding, the way that only someone else who's been pissed on from a great height by the person they love best can. She wasn't sure how the conversation had turned so intimate, but she knew that she needed to steer it back towards less shark-infested waters because talking about Brad always left her feeling bitten raw. Robinson seemed to sense it too, because he suddenly slid from the stool.

'Before I forget,' he said, disappearing into the lounge and returning with his hands full of the expensive camera Brad had given her a year or two back for her birthday, even though she'd never expressed even the briefest of interest in photography to him. 'This was on the side. I figured you'd put it out and then forgotten to take it with you.'

Alice looked at the camera, debating whether to be honest and say she'd never even used it and had put it out to give away or to just take it from him and hide beneath his cover story. Seeing it there in Robinson's hands, Alice had the most peculiar feeling of a plaster being ripped from a wound only to find the wound hadn't healed at all and it would have been better left out in the open.

'Do you mind if I grab something from the cellar?'

Robinson laid the camera down on the breakfast bar. 'Go for your life, as long as you're not planning to start playing the drums in the garden.'

Alice threw her empty beer bottle in the bin and headed for the cellar door. 'No. Nothing like that. Just something I should have done a long time ago.'

Robinson listened to the sounds of Alice dragging things around noisily in the cellar beneath him, cursing every now and then and huffing out of breath. He'd checked a second time if he could help and received a polite but firm refusal, and he sensed that whatever it was that she was looking for down there, she wanted to find it on her own. She was a difficult woman to read. On the surface she was fragile, coltish and bambi-like, in a way that brought out his protective instinct. But she was also funny, and in turn feisty, and he'd glimpsed steel in her eyes too when she was pushed. If she was his sister, he'd be ready to punch the man who'd broken her heart. But she wasn't his sister, and she had a physical effect on him that was anything but brotherly. He'd screwed a couple of women since Lena had left him, both brunettes with hard bodies and hot tempers, both pseudo replacements of the woman he really wanted, the one who now slept in the bed of his best friend. Alice was the polar opposite of Lena. Was that what he found attractive about her, that she held none of his wife's Latino appeal and therefore posed no threat to his heart? He knew he was doing the woman in the cellar a disservice by thinking such thoughts, but they were the only ones that made any sense of the way his body reacted to hers.

Back in the sanctuary of the Airstream, Alice warmed soup and toasted bread, consciously avoiding looking at the size-able dark purple leather case on the table. It had taken some effort to lug it back across the garden; she'd shrugged off Robinson's repeated attempts to help.

She ate standing at the work surface looking out of the window, the case behind her out of sight.

Washing up stretched things out for another ten minutes, and she swept each rug on the floor individually until the whole place was spick and span. A quick glance at her watch told her it had just turned nine in the evening; she could always just go to bed. She could fill up her water bottles and have a luxuriously early night, read until her eyelids drooped and she nodded off, leave the case unopened until morning. Everything was easier in the morning, right? She got as far as filling the kettle for her bottles before she sighed and placed it down without lighting the gas beneath it. Even if she warmed the bed, there was no way she'd be able to sleep without at least opening the case. It might as well have had a huge red flashing light on the lid or a high-pitched alarm strapped to it for all the rest she'd get with it sitting there like an unexploded bomb.

Finally, when she could stall no longer, she took out a

soft cloth from beneath the sink, slid into the padded banquette and drew the box slowly towards her. Over eight years had passed since she'd last snapped open its silver clasps. She rubbed the cloth over the cracked leather lid, taking the time to run her index finger over the metallic embossed initials inlaid there. B.A.C. Benjamin Alan Collins. Her father. The box had been his long before it had been Alice's. He'd given it to her on her twenty-first birthday, as it had been given to him by his own father on his twenty-first. *A tradition*, he'd smiled, knowing just how much the gesture would mean to Alice. She'd been nervous at first about telling her dad she'd decided to follow in his footsteps as a professional photographer. As a multi-award-winning photojournalist known for his specialist work in war zones, Ben Collins was internationally renowned as one of the best in the business until he'd lost his life during an especially dangerous assignment out in Afghanistan. His posthumous award for bravery had been a fitting tribute for a man who knew the dangers of his work but still threw himself in whole-heartedly because he also knew a powerful image could speak a thousand words. He believed he could make a difference, and he had, both to the world and to Alice, his only child, the little girl he'd raised single handedly when her mother left them before Alice could even walk. Because of his unerring love and attention, Alice had never missed the mum she had no memory of. When Ben was away working he made sure she was safe, sharing her care with his parents who adored having such a hands-on role in their granddaughter's life. It had worked well, right up to the moment Ben Collins took a bullet through his heart, breaking Alice's at the same time. She'd closed the lid on the leather case two months after her father's funeral and from that day to this it had remained sealed. Today was as good a day as any to open it again.

Alice slid her thumbs over the catches, closing her eyes as she lifted them. They were stiffer than they used to be from lack of use, and the lid didn't release easily from its resting place. She gripped the top corners and gave it a shake to free it, and finally it unglued itself and came free. Alice paused, pulled in a deep breath, and then opened the lid.

As she'd known it would, a rush of sensation hit her. The smell of her childhood, the reverence of handling her dad's most prized cameras, photographs, of course, alongside the thick wedge of sympathy cards and the medal in its case. There was a unique scent to the box that time hadn't diminished, something woody and intangible, a mix of the box itself, the possessions it held, and the man who'd owned and loved it. Alice vividly remembered countless occasions sitting alongside her dad, the box open on the floor in front of them. He'd allowed her to handle his cameras even when her hands were too small and clumsy to take the necessary care, and he'd made her the proudest kid in junior school when he'd given a talk to her class and allowed her to show her friends inside the box too. He'd taught her how to handle a camera, the intricacies of lens selection, how to best work with the light. He'd gifted her his practical knowledge, but far more than that, he'd given her his passion for capturing a moment forever on film, a fleeting expression, an undeniable emotion.

This wasn't just a box. It was the next best thing to sitting alongside her dad again. Alice reached in and touched her fingers against the leather tan slipcase of her father's Nikon, and automatically ran her nail around the serrated edge of the lens casing as she had as a little girl.

She'd shut all of her memories inside the purple leather box, and along with it she'd sealed any of her own aspirations to wield a camera for a living. Over the six months after her father's death she'd spent less and less time at class, until it reached a point where her tutors could only despair at the fact that such a naturally talented student had turned her back on her vocation. She couldn't separate her love for photography from the loss of her father, one tainted the other, and the only way she found to handle her grief was to reinvent herself. Being someone else had helped, in a way; at least it had allowed Alice to move on. Meeting Brad had inadvertently cemented Alice in her new role, because they needed her wage to support his acting classes and low-paid between-jobs. Somewhere along the way she'd allowed herself to believe her own spin, to forget how much she loved everything about the world she and her father had shared. She'd stopped constantly viewing the world through a thumb and finger viewfinder to find the best angle, so much so that she'd never felt able to tell Brad about her long-cherished dreams of a life in her father's footsteps. Life was duller, but kind of easier. Well, no more. Having her world tipped upside down and shaken like a snow globe had left her sitting all alone on her backside in the snow without any footsteps beside her. Not her father, nor Brad. For the first time in her memory she was on her own, and the only set of footprints in the snow were her own. It was time to stand on her own two feet.

CHAPTER SEVEN

'You're going to break your neck up there.'

Robinson stood at the base of the tree and craned his neck to look up at the tree house above. He hadn't seen much of Alice since she'd lugged her mysterious cargo out of the cellar a week or so ago, and it had seemed to rain incessantly in between. He'd spent his days watching god-awful daytime TV, and his nights trying out the various bedrooms in the manor in the hope of a decent night's sleep. So far, he'd yet to find any real peace here. Maybe it was the drab, grey weather, maybe it was the otherworldliness of the manor, and maybe it was the fact that he was so far away from his real life that he felt completely alien. He'd almost reached the point of knocking on Stewie's door for a beer and a tour of his wig cupboard. Almost, but not quite. The damn rain had finally knocked off this morning, and when he'd opened the kitchen door and heard banging he'd followed the noise and found Alice playing girl scout in the garden. He'd spotted her red wellingtons first and had to look twice to check she really was dangling from the branches of a large old oak at the far end of the garden. Close up, she was clad in denim jeans that looked sprayed on from this angle and a black sweater that hugged her curves.

'Probably,' she responded cheerfully, peering over the edge of the tree house. Her blonde hair had been tamed into pigtails that swung in the breeze and her pretty face was free of make-up.

'You look about thirteen years old. Are you playing house up there?'

'Something like that,' she grinned and then disappeared. 'Come up.'

Robinson tested the bottom of the rickety planks that had been fashioned into steps that circled the broad tree trunk and, finding it sturdy enough to stand his weight, he made his way far enough up the tree for his torso to poke through into the house above. The floor was strewn with tools and nails and a hand saw leaned against the wall.

'Should I even ask what you're doing?'

Alice laid down the lethal-looking hammer in her hand and puffed a stray strand of hair out of her eyes.

'Probably not.'

He nodded, glancing around the interior of the tree house. 'Teddy bears' picnic?'

Alice shook her head. 'Better than that.'

'Grown-up picnic?' As Robinson's mouth formed the words, his brain conjured up images of very adult picnics indeed. The kind where you might eat strawberries from the navel of your naked lover.

'Not exactly,' Alice hedged, rubbing the booted toe of one wellington behind the ankle of her other. Was he imagining things or did both her face and her body language say shifty?

He hauled himself fully into the tree house and took in his surroundings.

As befitted the manor, the tree house was larger than your average kids' hideout. He'd had a variation on the theme growing up back home in Tennessee, and once he was holed up in there with Fitz and Derren it was pretty much full. Not this place. You could have fit all of the kids from his elementary class up here with room to spare.

'You've had enough of Airstream living and are moving house again?'

He wouldn't put it past her. Alice reached for the latches on the inside of the shuttered window and flung them wide, letting in a stream of warmth and sunlight that from behind gave her an instant halo. She *was* kind of angelic to look at, all peaches and cream, and it only made him wonder what lay beneath. Lena, and pretty much most of the women in his life back home, were fiery and direct; you knew what they were thinking way before they decided to open their mouths and let you in on it. He didn't find that with Alice. She held herself in a reserved way that made him itch to scratch the surface and see what lay beneath.

'Pass me that saw?' she said, gesturing behind him and not answering his question. He did as she'd asked and then watched as she held a length of wood against a gap in the side of the tree house and marked it with a pencil she pulled from behind her ear.

'Tools of the trade,' he murmured. He'd spent ten years fixing up houses with a pencil behind her ear before he'd accidentally hit the big time when the guy whose house he'd been working on turned out to be a manager from Music City. Robinson had sung to pass the time while he built Donald Marshall's porch, and it turned out to be the last job he ever worked as a carpenter. Marsh, as he was known in the business, had gone on to become one of his closest friends and his biggest supporter. Right about now he was probably regretting ever hiring Robinson Duff, either to fix his porch or to pack out stadiums.

Alice took the piece of wood out onto the deck of the tree house and knelt down, lining up her pencil mark with the edge of the deck before setting about sawing it down to size. There were several things Robinson wanted to say. Your saw's too blunt. You need a vice to cut wood properly. You're going to cut your goddamn hand off doing it like that. Yet he said none of them, holding his tongue until she managed to get through the plank and the spare end fell down towards the ground. Belatedly Alice peered over the edge to make sure she didn't have any concussed visitors and then straightened up and headed back inside with her freshly sawn wood.

'Don't tell me. You're planning to get a really tall dog?' He guessed again at Alice's intentions for the future of the tree house.

'Pluto wouldn't like another dog in his garden,' Alice said with difficulty as she held a nail between her teeth. God, she was a walking health and safety hazard.

'My garden,' Robinson said mildly, picking up the hammer and handing it to her. Alice raised her eyebrows as she positioned the wood over the gap in the wall.

'My garden,' she corrected, as he'd known she would.

'But you can't get to it without coming through mine,' he countered, not at all bothered by the fact. In fact he'd made sure to move the hire car that had been delivered that morning over so she could easily get in and out.

Alice narrowed her eyes as she banged the first nail in to place and let the wood swing down while she dug another nail from her pocket. Christ. She couldn't keep nails in the pockets of her jeans. She was giving him a heart attack.

'If you wanted to be really bloody minded I could get to the Airstream from the farm behind the manor,' she said. 'I'd have to swim across the stream, but I could do it.'

'Or you could just build yourself a bridge,' he suggested. 'You seem to have the determination, even if your skills could use work and your tools look like they belong in a museum.'

Her eyes opened a fraction wider. 'Probably. They were here when we moved in. Brad wasn't exactly what you'd call a DIY fan so we never bought new stuff.'

Robinson filed away that nugget of information about Alice's husband along with the thing she'd said a while back about him owning a drum kit but never bothering to play it. He wasn't finding much to admire about the man, besides his estranged wife.

'And err, hello? My skills could use work?' she said, seeming to suddenly hear what he'd said and fixing him with an appraising look. 'And you're qualified to judge me because . . .?'

'I know enough to know you should be wearing eye defenders when you're using the saw, even if it's blunt, and the way you're storing nails in your pockets is highly likely to result in your femoral artery being pierced.'

She looked unsure for a second, as if she recognised that he was right but didn't want to give him the satisfaction of seeing her pull those nails from her pocket.

Straightening her shoulders back a little, she said, 'I should get on.'

'Because you're going to use the tree house for . . .' he waited for her to supply the rest.

'Yes,' she said, without elaboration. 'I am.'

If she was trying to be secretive to wind him up, it was working. He remembered the sophisticated camera he'd handed over to her last week and a horrible suspicion surfaced in his mind.

'You're not building a hide for the press to spy on me, are you?'

He knew he'd said the wrong thing instantly. Her face told him so, but she didn't go off the deep end. She looked at him in silence for a few long moments and her eyes told him that he'd hit a nerve before she segued into cool, professional landlady mode.

'Your privacy, or indeed your fame, is not my concern, Mr Duff, but you can rest assured that I have no affection for the press and I won't permit them on my land.'

Mr Duff, huh? So they were back there again. She'd perplexed him with her secrecy and he'd offended her with his accusation in return, and no doubt he'd also left her with the idea that he was a cock with an over-inflated ego.

'I'll leave you to your work, Mrs McBride,' he said, like for like, inclining his head in goodbye as he descended the ladder. At the bottom of the tree he paused, considered an apology, and then thought better of it and shoved his hands deep in his pockets as he made his way back to the manor without glancing back.

Alice stood on the deck of the tree house and watched him saunter away across the grass, her heart still banging too fast in her chest. She'd had her fill of the paps and reporters during her break-up, and her father had had scant regard for the invasive methods they used. Over her dead body would she have them back here again. In some ways

Robinson Duff was nothing like Brad, but in other unsettling ways he was obviously cut from the same fame-hungry cloth. If she didn't need the six months rent he'd paid in advance so badly she'd ask him to pack his precious celebrity bags and leave her in peace.

Alice flopped down on the banquette later and laid her forehead on the table in front of her. She ached in places she didn't know it was possible to ache, and she wasn't convinced she'd ever get the grime out from under her fingernails. Day one of renovating the tree house could be considered a success on most levels; she just needed her body to get the memo.

'Alice.'

Crap. Robinson was outside. She hoped he hadn't come for round two, because she was officially all out of fight.

'Unless the manor's on fire, come back tomorrow,' she grumbled loud enough for him to hear, knowing she sounded horribly inhospitable but she was too tired to play nice.

'Well, technically no, it's not on fire, but I do have a bit of an emergency over there.'

Fear prickled her spine and had her on her feet and shuffling to throw the door open. He didn't look in too much of a panic, but then he was a laidback cowboy so she wasn't going to take any chances.

'What's wrong?'

'Plumbing problem in the bathroom. There's water everywhere.' He grimaced and looked apologetic. 'Would you mind coming and taking a look? I'm guessing the house has its own secret tricks and tips that I haven't sussed yet.'

Alice's heart thumped in alarm.

'Crap! I'm coming, hang on a minute.'

The plumbing wasn't prone to problems but one thing was for sure, getting anyone out to fix pipes in an old and complicated place like the manor was going to cost a fortune she didn't have. Sighing heavily, she shoved her feet quickly into her boots and gestured for Robinson to lead the way over to the house. Once there, she left her boots by the door and dashed ahead of him through the house and sprinted up the staircase, crossing the fingers of both of her hands tightly that when she reached the bathroom it was going to be something obvious.

It wasn't. She braced herself for disaster as she flung open the door of the corner bathroom, but as far as she could see there was no disaster. In fact, it looked fabulous. A jug of wild flowers had been set on the washstand, and the creamy fat candle had been lit on the deep wooden windowsill. Nicer still, the bathtub was filled with fragrant bubbly water, and the whole room had been warmed by the fire he'd lit in the hearth.

She turned slowly to look at Robinson lounging behind her in the doorway, almost bashful.

'What's this?' she said, her heart still racing, not understanding.

'An apology for me being an ass today,' he said softly. 'I figured the Airstream shower might not cut it tonight.'

Alice didn't know what to say. He'd completely blindsided her. A small churlish voice in her head told her to say thanks but no thanks, you nearly gave me a sodding heart attack, but the much louder 'oh my god the bath looks so lush and inviting' voice shouted it down.

'I don't know what to say,' she said, because she honestly didn't. It was such a simple gesture really, but it spoke of thoughtfulness, and a kindness that she hadn't expected.

Over the years with Brad he'd always been the one who needed bolstering behind the scenes; she'd fallen into the groove of being his support system, his cook, his cleaner, his secretary and sometimes his surprise bath runner. He hadn't been a terrible tyrant of a husband and it had happened so gradually that she hadn't felt the sting, but as Brad's self worth and confidence had risen, he'd eroded hers in equal measures. Put short, Alice couldn't remember a time when anyone had taken care of her like this.

'The robe was hanging on the back of one of the bedroom doors,' he said, nodding towards her cashmere robe placed over the Victorian wooden airer along with two fluffy white towels. The grey robe would cover her from neck to ankles, yet still there was an inferred intimacy to wearing it around him. She faltered, and then decided to just see how she felt after her bath. If worst came to worst she could always put her work clothes back on again.

'Take as long as you like,' he said, and before she'd turned around he'd closed the door and left her alone. On instinct she opened the door and leaned around the frame.

'Robinson?' she said, halting his passage along the corridor. 'Thank you for this.'

He studied her for a long second.

'Go get in before it gets cold,' he said, and his tone said that he also appreciated her gratitude. 'I'll throw some food together and see you downstairs when you're done.'

CHAPTER EIGHT

Downstairs, Robinson battled to get to grips with the Aga. He wasn't the keenest of cooks, but back home he *could* at least turn the damn oven on. Where were the controls? This thing was straight out of *Downton Abbey*. Hunkered down on his haunches in front of it, he tried to decide which of the doors to open first. It would probably have been easier to concentrate if he hadn't been distracted by the fact that there was a mermaid in his bathtub. The house was big enough for him not to be able to hear her up there, but it didn't stop his mind from wondering how much better that bubble bath looked now that she was in it. The weather here had been such that he'd seen barely more than Alice's bare feet and the graceful sweep of her neck, but he had a rich imagination and had no problem filling in the blanks. Her skin would be silk smooth and pale as double cream, probably flushed pink from the heat of the fire and the bathwater. Her hair would be piled up on top of her head, and she'd be resting her neck back on the roll top of the bath, her eyes closed. Or would her eyes be open as she watched the flames dancing in the hearth? He hoped she was relaxed. In his head she was. Blissfully, bonelessly relaxed. Were the bubbles deep enough to submerge her completely, or would they afford him a glimpse of her body here and there? He decided that they probably would. He could see the gleam of her shoulders in the candle light, and lower, the hint of her breasts just beneath the foam. If he blew softly, the bubbles would reveal them. Instinct told him her nipples would be pink, like the roses beneath the front windows of the manor. The chill of being exposed would stiffen them, and the smallest of smiles would cross Alice's mouth. Did she just arch, the tiniest of movements to give him a better view? He followed the line of her body down, the soft curve of stomach, the flare of her hip . . . in Robinson's head he was already pulling his t-shirt over his head and shucking off his jeans to slide into those bubbles and pull her against him, skin to skin. Jeez, she'd feel warm. Hot. A darn sight hotter than the casserole Hazel had dropped round earlier would be if he didn't decide which of these oven doors to open and put it in. Robinson scrubbed his hands through his hair and stood up, way too far down the road towards bathing with Alice to think straight about kitchen appliances. Maybe there was a microwave around here instead.

Upstairs, Alice sank back in the cradle of foamy bubbles and could have cried with pleasure, both physically because her body ached and emotionally because she loved this room so much. She let her lashes close, and for a few moments she let her head and heart pretend that she lived here again. It was a toss-up which she missed more these days; the manor itself or the man she'd hoped to live in it for ever with. It was so hard living in such close proximity without being able to come and go as she pleased. Her life was busy and her head full of plans and schemes, but it was distinctly lacking in luxury. This was what she missed. This room, this bathtub, this bliss. But there was more to it than that. Since Brad had left, she'd lived here alone. Borne Manor was too big for one; it was too big for two really, but being alone in the manor had been decidedly lonely, and being here right now with Robinson reminded her of how she'd hoped married life would feel when they'd first moved in. The reality had never quite lived up to her expectations, in all honesty, and it wasn't the house's fault, it was Brad's. It was a hard truth to acknowledge, but this simple experience of having a bath drawn for her and dinner cooked downstairs had never happened before. Her eyes moved around the room. The jug of flowers that were all recognisable from the gardens of the manor, the glow of the fire, the creamy candle reflected against the dark windows. She'd bathed in this room count- less times, but she couldn't have created this atmosphere for herself because the necessary element that made it special was the intent behind it, the thoughtful gesture, the planned surprise. Robinson had gone further tonight to please her than her husband had in as long as she could remember.

Alice padded into the kitchen to find Robinson had laid two plates on the scrubbed table, a couple of wine glasses and an open bottle of red beside them. She was glad he'd opted for the simplicity of the kitchen table rather that the formality of the dining room, it had been her own choice when she'd lived here most of the time too.

'Better?' he said, looking up from the other side of the room where he was fiddling with the dial on the microwave.

'About a million times,' Alice said, feeling self-conscious

in her robe even though it was as demure as her usual clothes were in terms of coverage. The crucial difference was that one good tug on the robe's belt and she'd be naked. The thought had her double-checking to make sure she'd tied it securely. 'Need some help?' She crossed to stand beside him and tried to peer through the smoked-glass microwave door. 'What's in there?'

'Hazel dropped a casserole in earlier,' he said, pinging the door open to show her the bowl of hot stew bubbling inside. 'I think it's probably ready.'

'Really? She never brought me so much as a welcome to the village card when I moved in,' Alice said, smiling as Robinson slid the hot dish onto the table. 'You obviously made a bigger first impression on her than I did.'

Privately, Alice had to acknowledge that this didn't come as any great shock. She reached for a serving spoon from the drawer on autopilot, then remembered it wasn't her kitchen any longer.

'Sorry,' she said, hovering the spoon halfway between the table and going back into the drawer.

'It's fine, Alice, relax,' he said, pulling out a chair for her. 'I wasn't sure where to look. You helped.'

He had an easy way about him that encouraged those around him to feel easy too, and Alice found herself sitting down and letting him ladle food onto their plates. Sniffing the steam, she tried to decide what it was and failed.

Robinson picked up his cutlery. 'Hazel mentioned wild boar and sweet potato, I think?'

Right. So that would be why Alice couldn't identify the intense looking meal in front of her. Knowing Hazel she'd probably thrown in a few extra ingredients in the hope of impressing their famous new neighbour.

'That's, an, err, interesting combination,' Alice tried, waiting for Robinson to try his before she braved hers. He flicked his eyes up to meet hers for a brief second and then dipped his fork in and put it in his mouth. A few seconds later, he nodded, his eyebrows raised.

'It's . . . it's not bad, actually.'

Alice tried a little and had to agree, although Hazel had gone in heavy-handed with the chilli.

'I think she said she'd put chocolate in it too?' Robinson poured wine into their glasses. Alice nodded, wondering what other ingredients Hazel might have thrown into the pot. As the unusual concoction slid into her body, she couldn't help but ask herself if there were a few aphrodisiacs in there along with the wild boar and chocolate. Sipping her wine to wash the food down, she watched Robinson eat for a few moments. He really was a ridiculously good-looking man, all cheekbones and dark lashes as he looked down at his plate. His faded red t-shirt did nothing at all to hide the strength of his shoulders and deeply tanned biceps, and the fine downy hair on his arms had been turned burnished gold by sunlight. He wasn't model hot. He was healthy, real-man hot, and at that moment Alice found herself inexplicably attracted to him on the most basic of man–woman levels. He looked up at that moment and seemed to see right inside her head, sending a flush running up from her neck to her hairline.

'Okay?' he said softly.

She nodded. 'Think so.'

'Did I do the wrong thing?' He drank a little wine, watching her. 'I didn't stop to think about how this might make you feel, Alice.'

'How can being kind be wrong?'

He shrugged. 'I see how much you love this house. I didn't mean to remind you of what you're missing.' He paused. 'Happy memories and all that.'

He really was a perceptive man. 'I do love this house, Robinson, you're right. But my memories . . . they're not all happy ones.'

The expression on his face told her that he knew exactly where she was coming from. He ate in silence for a couple of minutes, and then laid his cutlery down again.

'I guess we're both doing the same thing in our own way, Alice. I'm here because I couldn't stand to be back home any more. Are you in the Airstream for the same reason, because you didn't want to live in the house without your husband?'

Alice shook her head.

'It's not that, to be honest.'

She swirled her wine around in her glass, trying to find the right words.

'This house was never Brad's dream. It was always mine. We didn't get to make that many good memories here in the end.'

'That surprises me,' he said. 'It seems like a decent kind of place to lay down foundations.'

Alice nodded. 'I thought so. Brad just . . . I don't know. His life was in London, being here turned out to be too much of a compromise for him.'

'You weren't tempted to sell up and go back to the city with him?'

Alice huffed softly. 'We never had sensible conversations about it. He made his choices without talking to me, including the choice to go to bed with his co-star off screen as well as on.'

Robinson's green eyes glittered. 'Tough on you, darlin'.'

She couldn't deny it. 'It was. It is.'

Robinson refilled her wine glass.

'At least you've only run as far as the end of the garden. I'm half way round the world and can officially say love still sucks.'

Alice touched her glass against his.

'Here's to the official launch of Borne's broken hearts society.'

'Let's throw our very own pity party, Goldilocks,' he said, pushing his half-eaten food away. 'I think I'm done with that.'

Alice did the same, surprised that she'd eaten so much in the circumstances, and wondering again if Hazel had hidden any secret potions in the casserole because the way he called her Goldilocks warmed her insides when it should probably have pissed off her inner feminist.

'What will you do when your six months in Borne is up?'

Robinson pushed his chair back and picked up the plates. 'Honestly? I don't have a goddamn clue. I kind of work on a day to day basis. Week to week, if I'm lucky.'

'But don't you need to get back to work at some point?' she asked. Surely someone with such an all-encompassing life as his would have to go back at some point. She thought of the snippets of his concerts she'd seen, all of those fans, all of that fame. His residence in Borne could only ever be temporary.

Robinson's expression turned melancholy, and he splayed his hands out palm down on the table in front of him. 'My fingers always ache for my guitar when I don't play it,' he said, his eyes hidden from her by his lowered lashes.

She remembered seeing his guitar upstairs in the master bedroom. 'Can't you?'

He shook his head slowly. 'Right now, Alice, I can't see myself ever making music again.'

Alice couldn't even imagine how hard it must be for him to have lost his creativity. He was such a big, vital man, but looking at him now she could see that there was a huge part of him missing. His music.

'Tough on you,' she said, giving his own phrase back to him because it was so entirely appropriate for the moment. She also reached out and laid her hand over one of his, because it seemed entirely appropriate in the moment to comfort him.

His gaze stayed locked on his hands, on her hand over his, and she lowered her gaze too when his fingers curled around hers, warm and strong. It started out as a thank you for understanding gesture and slid slowly into something else as his thumb stroked back and forth over the sensitive skin at the base of her wrist, over her racing pulse. Alice watched the motion, feeling her breath catch in her throat. He was heartbroken, she was heartbroken, and it was every kind of wrong, but Robinson's touch against her skin made her desperate for him to keep going. All the same, she gasped in surprise when he reached out and dragged her chair close enough to his for their shoulders to almost touch and then stroked the back of his fingers along her jaw.

'Alice, I'm gonna go out on a limb here and be real honest. When Lena left me she took my heart with her in her suitcase, but sitting here right now, all I can think about is whether or not you're naked beneath that bath robe.'

CHAPTER NINE

Much as Alice wanted to undo her robe and show him, she didn't. Reaching up she covered his hand with hers and regretfully moved it from her jaw to her lap.

'Robinson, don't. It's not going to make either of us feel better.'

'Are you sure about that, Alice?' he whispered, massaging her fingers, his face so close she could feel his breath on her cheek. 'Because right now I'm feeling a whole lot better.'

God, it was tempting. He was gorgeous, and his body was hard and sexy and warm, and her lips wanted to kiss his slightly open ones more than anything.

'No, you're not,' she said, laying her hand on his cheek. 'Not really. You're lonely and you're hurting, just like I am.'

A small, sad smile tipped one corner of his mouth. 'You're not her, and I'm not him. It's just you and me here tonight. Alice and Robinson. Is that so very bad?'

Alice shook her head, not answering him because she was finding it almost impossible to deny him or herself.

'I'm not looking for love, and I don't think you are either,' he went on. 'We've both been there, got the t-shirt, and had it ripped from our backs. Our cards are already on the table.'

'That's exactly why it's a bad idea,' she whispered.

'As bad ideas go, this one feels pretty good in here.' He tapped his chest with two fingers. 'And your eyes tell me it feels pretty good in there too.'

He reached out and touched the same fingertips against the silken lapel of her robe, coming to rest against the pulse at the base of her throat.

'If I kiss you, maybe we'll know for sure if it's good or bad,' he murmured, his fingers drifting around her neck into her hair. There was something in the barely there touch of his hand against her skin that made her arch into him, the space between their mouths so small that one tiny movement was all it would take. Alice hadn't kissed anyone else but Brad in years and years, and she was nine parts wildly turned on to one part absolutely terrified.

'I'm scared,' she breathed, her lips barely moving.

'Don't be,' he whispered, and then he moved forward and covered her lips with his, and Alice found that she wasn't. She wasn't, because his kiss was so slow and gentle, his lips hardly moving on hers, his fingers cradling her head. Alice closed her eyes and breathed him in, and her hand curved over the warm strength of his shoulder. His body was heaven under her hands, solid and hard where his mouth was soft and sure. He reacted to her touch, gathering her closer, opening her lips with his to let his tongue slide over hers. It was the best of first kisses, the kind that melted every bone in your body and made your blood sing a chorus of hallelujahs in your veins. It happened in her mouth, her body and her heart, like a box of fireworks all exploding at once. She barely registered when he pulled her across onto his lap and wrapped his arms around her, because all she wanted was to be closer and for him not to stop. His hands skimmed down the length of her spine, making her arch and press into him, her hands in his hair pulling his mouth harder onto hers. The change in him was instantaneous; he seemed to let go of his restraint and kissed her properly, deep, open mouthed and crazy hot. Alice didn't need to question whether or not he was turned on, she could feel the heat and the hardness of him under her ass and it made her gasp. He moaned in his throat and sank his teeth into her bottom lip as his hand cupped her breast through the thin layer of her robe. She may as well have been naked, because when his fingers closed around her nipple it felt that way.

'I guess that answers my question of whether or not you're naked under this,' he said, sliding his mouth from her lips to her ear and mouthing the sensitive skin there. He wound her hair around his other hand, using it like a tether to tip her head back and expose her neck to his lips.

When he slipped his hand inside her robe and held her breast, Alice gulped down air at the intimacy of his skin touching hers. He moaned her name, kissing her slowly again now as his thumb drew equally slow circles around her nipple. It was agonisingly sexual, magic and delicious and new, so very different to the way Brad had touched her that her eyes opened and locked with his as he flattened her breast with his palm. Neither of them breathed as he massaged her skin, watching each other's eyes as he pulled his hand back and rolled the tips of his fingers around her nipple.

It was erotic, and it moved her deeply, so much so that tears filled her eyes and crept down her cheeks. Robinson eased his hand from her robe and wiped away her tears with his thumbs, drawing her back into his chest and pressing his mouth against her forehead.

'It's okay to feel like this with someone else,' he said, stroking his hand over her hair, understanding her without the need for explanation. They stayed that way for a while. He smelled so good; clean and woody and male. Alice breathed him in, wrapping her arms around him and burying her face in his neck, not wanting to leave but knowing she needed to.

'I should go.'

He held her a little tighter and sighed against her hair. 'Yeah.'

'Thank you for kissing me,' she smiled shakily. 'I think I probably needed someone to do that. Someone other than him, I mean.'

'Glad to be of service, ma'am,' he said. 'Consider me available if you ever need your boundaries testing some more.'

'You're top of my list, cowboy.'

'You have a list?'

She liked his easy, lighthearted way. 'I've just started one. You're the only man on it so far.'

'I kind of like being the only one on it, Alice.'

She wasn't sure how to respond. She didn't really want a list.

'Come on,' he said. 'I'll see you home.'

A pang of sadness surfaced when she remembered that this wasn't her home any more.

'You don't need to do that.'

He stood up with her in his arms and set her down gently on her feet.

'I know I don't need to. I want to.'

'I can practically see the Airstream from here,' she said, pulling on her boots as he opened the back door.

'Yeah, but I hear there's bears in the woods,' he said, grabbing a leather jacket she didn't recognise from the coat hooks and wrapping it around her shoulders. Butter soft and battered, it had the same comforting woody, unique smell as his neck.

'I don't need protecting,' Alice laughed as they walked across the moonlit grass, but she really did mean it. Her life was going through the mother of all changes, and if there was one thing she was learning it was that she didn't need anyone else to take care of her.

'I'll keep that in mind,' he said, looking up. 'Stars are out tonight.'

Alice tipped her chin up and gazed at the dark studded sky. 'I heard on the radio this morning that the weather's about to change. They said we're in for a long, hot summer.'

Robinson led the way through the trees, their footsteps the only sounds in the late darkness. At the Airstream he swung the unlocked door open, peering around inside it before stepping aside.

'All clear. No bears waiting to eat you for a midnight snack.'

'That's good,' she said, unaccountably nervous that he was going to kiss her again. She looked over her shoulder into the caravan. 'I won't ask you in for a nightcap.'

He shoved his hands down into his jean pockets and nodded, a small smile on his lips as he looked at the ground. 'Wise.'

'Take your jacket back,' she said, starting to shuck her shoulders out of it.

'Keep it for tonight,' he said. 'It suits you.'

She nodded, drawing it close. 'Night then.'

'G'night, Alice. Sleep tight.'

He might have winked, a barely perceptible gesture as he turned and walked away. She watched him until he was out of sight, and then closed the door and crawled into bed, his jacket still wrapped around her beneath the covers as she fell asleep.

Robinson heard the front door knock loudly the next morning and debated whether or not to answer it. It wouldn't be Alice, she would have used the back door, so it had to be either one of the residents he'd met the other week or a stranger. The latter would be preferable, because after the email he'd just received from his manager he wasn't in the mood to entertain guests. It was barely ten in the morning and five minutes ago he'd been seriously considering searching the cupboards in the manor for a bottle of tequila.

'Hang on,' he called out, his southern-boy good manners winning out in the end. Glancing out of the window before he opened the door he saw a flashy sports car he didn't recognise in the driveway and frowned, opening the locks and pulling the heavy door back. A guy he'd never seen before stood on the step, slightly shorter than he was and a lot more groomed, from his sharp hair cut right down to the mirror shine on his no doubt highly fashionable shoes. Robinson's hackles rose, automatically assuming either press or a sales man.

'Hi there,' the guy said, and Robinson nodded in silent reply, waiting for more.

'Is Alice here?'

Robinson narrowed his eyes, reassessing the situation. 'She doesn't live here any more, dude.'

The guy glanced away down the drive and then back again, sliding his shades off and into the open collar of his shirt. 'Do you happen to know where she went?'

If there was one thing Robinson knew it was how to protect privacy, both his own and other people's.

'Who wants to know?'

The stranger on the step seemed irritated by the question, as if he should already know who he was.

'I'm Brad McBride. Her husband.'

Robinson nodded, suspecting as much and wondering if it'd be bad manners to land one on McBride's chiselled jaw. Blood sure would make a mess of his carefully put together outfit. But then this was the guy who'd made a mess of Alice's heart, and that stain was way more difficult to wash out.

'My solicitor mentioned the idea of renting the manor out, you must be our new tenant,' Brad said smoothly, holding out his hand to shake. 'I'm sorry, I didn't realise things had moved so quickly.'

Our new tenant? His arrangement was with Alice, not this guy.

'Sorry, man. I don't know where she is. If she should call by I'll mention you were looking for her. Any message?'

Brad opened his mouth to speak and then closed it again as Alice's voice rang out from deep inside the house, calling Robinson's name. Robinson cursed himself for unlocking the back door earlier; she must have let herself in to the kitchen.

'I brought your jacket back,' she called loudly, and then she wandered into the hallway, barefoot as ever, his leather over her arm. She stopped halfway across the hall when she saw who stood on the step.

Brad was quick to make a judgment call on what he saw.

'You don't know where she is, huh?' he said, dropping his nice guy demeanour.

'It's not my fault if you don't know where your own wife

is, city slicker,' Robinson said, needling him deliberately because it felt good.

'Where she is or who she's shagging, by the looks of it,' Brad said, twin spots of colour sparking up on his cheekbones.

Alice stepped forward and stood beside Robinson. 'What do you want, Brad?'

'To talk with my wife in private, if that's not too much to ask around here these days.'

'It is,' Robinson said. 'This is my house for the next six months. Make an appointment through my lawyer if you want to come in.'

Alice laid a hand on Robinson's arm. 'It's okay, I'll talk to him.'

Robinson looked down at her, knowing he was interfering where he had no place. And then, even though again he knew he had no place, he dipped his head and kissed Alice brief and hard on the mouth. He caught her unaware, so much so that her mouth opened a little in surprise. His tongue brushed over hers momentarily, sending a shiver down his spine, and her eyes widened a little when he broke off and stepped back.

'I'll be in the kitchen if you need me,' he said, touching her cheek, and then stalked out and left them to it.

Alice took Brad through to the lounge, where he pushed the door closed and spun around to face her.

'What the fuck do you think you're doing?'

'I'm sorry?'

Brad jerked his head towards the door. 'Him. Who even is he?'

Alice sighed. 'He's the new tenant. I told you about him,

or at least I let your solicitor know that the lease had been agreed.'

'New tenant and a whole lot more besides, by the looks of it,' Brad levelled at her. 'You didn't waste any time letting someone else stick their tongue down your throat.'

She stared at him for a few long moments. 'I'll remind you, as it seems that you've forgotten, that you left me for another woman. What did you expect me to do, Brad, sit around and pine for you? Is that the problem here? You don't want me but you don't want me to have anyone else either?'

'You're still my wife,' he said.

'Yes, and I was your wife when you decided to sleep with Felicity Shaw. It didn't seem to stop you then.'

He ran his hands through his hair. 'I don't fucking believe this,' he muttered, and Alice could see that he genuinely didn't. Self-belief had always been one of Brad's strongest traits; it must be a difficult pill for him to swallow that anyone could move on from him. Was that what she'd done? If he'd turned up even so much as yesterday then the answer would have been no, but that was then and this was now, the day after she'd made out with Robinson Duff at the kitchen table. So yeah, maybe she had moved on just a little bit and she was selfishly glad that it seemed to hurt Brad on some level, even if it was his pride rather than his heart.

'Why are you here?' she asked him quietly.

'You know, I even felt bad about coming here today to say this, but not any fucking more,' he said, posturing by the fireplace. 'This is my house and I want it back. I want Borne Manor.'

CHAPTER TEN

'Why did you do that?'

Alice stormed into the kitchen and rounded on Robinson ten minutes later. Brad had pushed every last one of her buttons and she was just about ready to explode.

He leaned on the Aga in her favourite spot and folded his arms over his chest, unrepentant.

'He deserved it.'

'And that was your decision to make, was it? Did you stop for even one minute to think about what I wanted? Don't bother answering that, I'll do it for you. No, Robinson. No, you damn well didn't.'

Robinson shrugged. 'If you want me to apologise, I'm not going to, Alice, he needed a dose of his own medicine. He's only lucky I didn't hit him.'

They faced each other across the kitchen.

'You know what this is, don't you? This is you taking your marriage problems out on mine. There's a man out there somewhere in the world that you wish you'd punched, and your crazy, screwed-up logic somehow thinks that taking it out on Brad is going to even up the score. Well it might make you feel manly in your own eyes, but it makes you look a twat in mine.'

A pulse flickered along his jaw and his eyes flared with anger. She didn't care. He wasn't half as pissed off as she was right now. She yanked the back door open so hard it banged back on its hinges and then turned back to him, furious.

'Don't you ever kiss me again, Robinson Duff, not for revenge nor anything else. Is that perfectly bloody clear?'

Where was that goddamn tequila when he needed it? Robinson slid down and leaned his back against the Aga, knees bent, head in his hands. Alice was right and he knew it. There were things he wished he'd said and done differently with Lena, and maybe he had acted out of turn just now. He'd already been wound up tight by Marsh's email that morning. It didn't matter how many tickets had been sold or how much money had been sunk into the plan, there was no way on earth that he was going back to do the damn concert or any others behind it.

He'd come halfway around the world to get away from all of the crap back home, and all he'd wound up with was a raft of new fucking problems to go with the old ones that had followed him across the globe.

'Two glasses of red, please,' Niamh said, leaning on the bar at The Siren that evening.

'You may as well give us the bottle, Dessy,' Alice said beside her. 'We're going to need it.'

Dessy raised his eyebrows in shock. 'Sounds juicy, darling. Shall I bring a third glass for me?'

Alice shook her head. 'Girl stuff.'

'I always wanted to be a Girl Guide,' Dessy said sadly, rolling his shoulders in his floral shirt. 'Broke my heart when my mother made me be a Beaver.'

Alice and Niamh found an empty table by the fireplace and slumped down.

'I'll be so glad when I'm done with this commission,' Niamh grumbled. 'If I have to look at Brice Robertson's wrinkled todger for much longer it'll put me off sex for life.'

Alice smiled despite her own turmoil and filled their glasses. 'Are you almost done?'

Niamh nodded. 'It's his last sitting tomorrow, thank God. I'm going to get blind drunk tonight so I can get away with wearing dark glasses all day.'

The idea of drinking until she couldn't remember her troubles appealed greatly to Alice. 'Brad came round this morning,' she said, picking up her wine glass.

'What? Why? You should have come and got me, I'd have given him what for.'

Alice huffed. 'Robinson made a good job of that in your absence.' She was still hopping mad with their resident cowboy.

Niamh perked up. 'Ooh, do tell. I was going to ask you how he was getting on.'

'He went all macho, then kissed me and strutted off in a temper.'

Niamh's hand covered her heart and her eyes went round as pennies. 'Robinson Duff kissed you? Fark! Was he good?'

'Did you miss the part where he went all weird and macho and stuck his oar into my business without asking?'

Niamh flapped her hand, agog. 'No, I heard you and we'll come back to that in a minute, but come on. You kissed

Robinson Duff. I want the gossip before we do the serious stuff.'

Alice twisted her gold bracelet around her wrist. 'He was angry. It wasn't a romantic kind of kiss.'

'I don't get you,' Niamh said, looking pained. 'He just kissed you suddenly out of the blue to piss Brad off?'

'Sort of,' Alice hedged.

'But he's a good kisser, right? Please say yes. You'll crush my dreams if you say no.'

Alice rolled her eyes. 'When he wants to be.'

Niamh studied her friend over the rim of her wine glass. 'It wasn't the first time he'd kissed you, was it?'

Much as Alice didn't want to feel as if she was betraying Robinson's confidence, she really could use her friend's ear and advice. 'No. He kissed me in the kitchen last night too.'

'And?'

'And what?'

Niamh slid forwards on her seat. 'And tell me you kissed him back and realised that your absent husband is not actually the be all and end all when it comes to men. That his kiss was so hot that your lips blistered and you dragged him upstairs and had your wicked way with him three times with his Stetson still on?'

'Niamh . . .!' Alice said, glancing around to make sure no one had heard. 'No, of course I didn't drag him upstairs. He ran me a bath to surprise me, and we had dinner together. We were talking and the kiss just sort of happened, you know?'

'I so wish I had your life,' Niamh sighed dramatically. 'It's not fair that you get to see a sexy cowboy todger when I have to look at Brice Robertson's. It's like a shrivelled toad.'

Alice ejected that particular image out of her head speedily.

'I only kissed him, Niamh, and I won't be doing it again in a hurry after the way he acted this morning.'

'What, you mean the time he gave your cheating big bad ex what for and showed him what he's missing?'

Alice sighed. 'Robinson did it for himself, Niamh, not for me. He's got a million issues with his own screwed-up marriage and decided that meddling in mine would make him feel better.'

Niamh's mouth thinned out. 'If it means that Brad got a taste of his own medicine then I don't see why you're so mad.'

Alice drank a huge mouthful of wine. 'Everything's messed up, Niamh. Brad came to tell me that he wants the house.'

'The manor?' Naimh said, all romantic thoughts cast instantly aside. 'He wants Borne Manor?'

Alice nodded miserably. 'That's what he said.'

'What for? He never even really liked the place!'

'Reading between the lines I think Felicity is behind it,' Alice said. 'He used phrases like "perfect country bolt hole" and "why should you have all the peace and quiet?"'

She shook her head, remembering back over the heated conversation she'd had with Brad after he'd declared his intention to take the manor. It had been so obvious that the words and phrases he was spouting were being fed to him by his jealous girlfriend. She could only thank her lucky stars that she'd made the decision to lease the place out when she did, and even more lucky stars that it had all gone through so quickly. One superstar in particular had saved her bacon, and she'd thank him if she didn't feel so much like killing him. Even if Brad did want the manor, Robinson had a watertight six-month lease and was entitled to stay there until the end of October, giving Alice much needed thinking time and space.

'But you're gonna fight him, right?'

Alice nodded slowly. She'd never been more determined or sure about anything in her life. 'That glamping plan just got a whole lot more urgent.'

The much promised sunshine made an early appearance the following morning, flooding the Airstream with shafts of light that bounced off the polished domed ceiling above Alice's bed. Her eyes still half closed, she basked in the gentle warmth adding to her sleepy comfort as it filtered through the polka dot voile screens that shielded the windows. Stretching, cat like, she contemplated bringing an early coffee back to bed. Opening one eye, she looked at the kettle and wondered if she could will it to boil itself. If the coffee could just see its own way into a mug and over here to her in bed, that'd be just about the perfect start to the day. That was the thing with caravan living. Everything was so close you could almost touch it. Truth told she didn't hate it. Much as she adored the manor, being in there on her own had quite often been a lonely experience. The Airstream was cosy and compact, a protective tin bubble around her from Brad, Felicity, and even from Robinson.

'Alice!'

She groaned and cocked her ear to listen as someone banged on the door.

'Alice, open up. I've got coffee.'

Hmm. It sounded like Hazel. Alice looked at the kettle again, impressed with her own ability to summon coffee. Or maybe there was more to Hazel's magical skills than anyone gave her credit for. Either way, she pulled herself up and scrubbed her fingers through her hair.

'Coming,' she called, climbing out of bed and pulling her robe on over her PJs. Tying the belt reminded her of the last time she'd worn it with Robinson in the kitchen at the manor. Snatching her hair back with a band she found in the pocket, she shook the memory into the recesses of her head. It was way too early for that sort of thing.

'Morning, Hazel,' she said, opening the door to find her neighbour had made herself at home on the chairs out there. 'This is a surprise, come in.'

'I better not, love,' Hazel said, her eyes on the caravan roof. 'Rambo followed me. He'll want to come in too.'

Alice leaned out and peered up at the mynah bird perched above her doorway. He peered back down at her with his shiny, black bead eyes.

'Filthy bugger! Change your sheets!' he screeched, a perfect mimicry of Hazel's tone.

Alice jumped and shot him a filthy look as she stepped out of the caravan to join Hazel on the deckchairs.

'Sorry about him. It's all he's said since he heard me telling Ewan off about the state of his room yesterday.'

Alice smiled and sipped from the hot-pink mug of coffee Hazel handed her.

'Well, this is nice,' she said, wondering why on earth Hazel had come calling.

'Don't start without Stewie!' A voice carried over the lawn, and seconds later Stewie himself bounced into view, resplendent in black silk pyjamas and a lime bandana knotted around his head in lieu of his usual wig. He carried a china cup of tea in one hand and, oddly, a paintbrush in the other. Before Alice could stop to ask what was going on, Niamh jogged into view too, catching up with Stewie as they reached the Airstream and took any seat they could find.

'Is this another thinly veiled attempt to get an audience with Robinson Duff?' Alice said, fussing Pluto's furry head and looking expectantly from one to the other. 'Only I don't think he's as much a morning person as you lot obviously are.' She looked discreetly at her watch. It wasn't even seven-thirty.

'He's a filthy bugger!' Rambo yelled like an abusive cockerel, and Alice closed her eyes for a second.

'Nothing to do with our Robster this time,' Stewie said. 'Although how is the old dog? Might call over there when we're done and see if he fancies a flutter on the gee-gees. Needs to get out a bit, that boy.'

Alice wasn't sure that Robinson would appreciate the offer but kept her own counsel. Who was she to know what would or wouldn't please him?

'We want to help,' Hazel said, mysteriously.

'I can paint,' Stewie chimed in, holding up his paintbrush. He held it in a way that suggested he'd never painted anything in his life.

Alice looked towards Niamh urgently, asking her to help her understand what was going on.

'I told them,' Niamh said, her pretty face pensive. 'It affects us all, Alice. You own the cottages and we want it to stay that way. What you're looking at here is your work force.'

Alice couldn't help but wonder if Niamh had lost her mind as she looked around the little gathering.

'And there's Ewan too, if he ever gets out of his bed, that is,' Hazel added darkly.

They all looked up expectantly at Rambo, who took supercilious pleasure in remaining silent.

'I'd never even heard of this glamping until Niamh

explained it this morning,' Stewie said. 'Marvellous idea. Don't come knocking when the caravan's rocking, eh?'

Alice flinched and swallowed a mouthful of coffee. 'When did you even get time to talk about this?' She was looking at Niamh again.

'Six a.m. crisis meeting, darling,' Stewie said, tapping the side of his nose.

'I'd just popped into the garden to channel the transitional energy between night and day when Niamh called over the fence,' Hazel explained, nodding sagely.

'And there I was, doing the walk of shame after a reunion night with some old colleagues.' Stewie really was an old rogue. Alice didn't even want to think about what might have happened at a reunion night for ex porn stars.

'Filthy buggers!' cackled Rambo, on cue.

'Quite right too, Rambo old son,' Stewie agreed with a twinkle in his eye, not at all insulted. 'My knees are shot this morning.'

Niamh cleared her throat to disguise her laughter. 'Right then. Where shall we start?'

Alice glanced around them all in their various states of undress. 'Do you think it might be a good idea if we all get dressed first?'

Stewie pulled himself up out of the chair. 'Good idea, troops. On your feet and quick march back to the cottages.'

Niamh hung back until the others were out of earshot. 'I know you probably think this is crazy, Alice, and it sort of is, but the point is that we want to show you how much we care about you and won't let you go down without the mother of all fights, okay? This manor is yours, and it's staying that way. You're not on your own in this.' Niamh squeezed Alice's shoulders. 'I'm going home now to have breakfast and put some work clothes on, and you should go inside and do the same. You just became general of the oddest freakin' army ever.'

By lunchtime the 'army' had all been hard at work in their designated roles for a couple of hours; Hazel had decided to spend the day walking the site to decide where to position any future accommodation in order to maximise on chi. So far Alice had found her with all four limbs wrapped around the old oak at the far end of the woods and sitting cross-legged on the deck of the boathouse with her eyes closed communing with the spirits of the lake. Even Ewan had rolled up mid-morning and taken up the task of gathering and chopping wood with Stewie, to use for both the tree house renovation and other projects as they got going.

Alice and Niamh worked in the tree house, laying flat on their bellies on the deck with a large paper plan of the land in front of them and the file containing all of the information and paperwork Alice had collected so far.

'Will you need a licence to operate something like this?' Niamh said, writing it down on her to-do list.

'It's already being sorted by my solicitor,' Alice said. She didn't pretend to understand the ins and outs of the law and was only glad to be able to hand it to someone who did.

'Loos?' Niamh pulled a face as she said it.

'Compost ones.' Alice said, having looked into the matter a day or two back. 'You can have them delivered and installed in little huts.'

'And what about Robinson? Have you told him what's happening?'

Alice's pained expression told Niamh more than she could have in words.

'Alice, you have to! If you're seriously hoping to have the first two units ready to rent within eight weeks it's going to affect him more than anyone else.'

'I know, I know,' Alice sighed. 'And I will. I just know that he's not going to love the idea, that's all.' Robinson had come to Borne for privacy, to get away from the world. He wasn't going to like the idea of the world coming to camp on his doorstep one bit.

'Well you better do something spectacular to get him on side then, because if he makes it clear that he's not happy to the council then the whole scheme could fall in. I don't think you'll get any complaint from the village in general, but he's your closest neighbour. We need him smiling. Talk to him sooner rather than later, yes?'

Alice looked over towards the manor, her stomach flipping a slow, nervous somersault. They weren't exactly on good terms. 'I will. Promise.'

CHAPTER ELEVEN

Alice made her workforce a cuppa around five o' clock and then sent them all home, waving them off back to their respective baths and beds from the deck of the tree house. She'd been doubtful when they'd all turned up like a ragtag team that morning, but just having them around and willing had served to make the whole thing seem a bit less daunting. Even Hazel's site-scoping mission had thrown up some interesting ideas, admittedly more about which trees were rare or protected than about potential chi, but useful none the less. Good old Stewic had loved having Ewan as his junior. Alice feared that he might be regaling his apprentice with stories that weren't fit for a seventeen year old's ears in order to keep his attention, but even she had to admit that the resulting log pile was pretty impressive.

Throughout the day she'd been making notes in the file as people shouted random ideas up to her, and she intended to spend her evening pleasurably going over them. There was something she needed to do first though. She squinted up at the setting sun, knowing instinctively that the perfect time was coming. Climbing down the tree ladder, she headed back towards the Airstream at a dash.

It fitted in her hands perfectly. She hadn't handled it in over eight years, but Alice's fingers automatically loaded the film she'd ordered into her dad's Nikon and adjusted the shutter speeds, her mind and fingers working on instinct as she considered the lighting conditions. She jogged through the trees, aware that every minute counted if she was going to catch the shot. Sunset had been her dad's most favourite time of day to capture images, and he'd passed his love and quest for the perfect shot on to his daughter. She didn't let sentiment cloud her judgment as she settled on the edge of the dock at the boathouse a few minutes later, the camera beside her on the boards, her arms stretched out in front of her as she made a viewfinder with her fingers.

She could almost hear him coaching her, almost feel him sitting beside her talking her through it when she reached for the camera and lifted its comforting weight to her face. It was a pure pleasure and nostalgia to use and she lost herself completely in the moment. All those years she'd avoided doing this, and in the end it was comforting rather than painful to let herself enjoy the creative process her father had taught her to love. At the time of his death she'd let herself blame his career, his obsession, his relentless professionalism . . . photography had taken her dad away from her. Now, though, time had allowed her to feel what she couldn't back then; his hands on the camera she now held in her hands, his practised eye pressed against the same viewfinder. It was a gift to be able to use it, and a gift to have had him as her teacher for all those years.

She took her time, drawing solace and pleasure from

going through the motions and waiting for the optimum moment. As the light dwindled she lowered it from her face and turned it over in her hands, the leather strap warm and reassuring around her neck. Smiling, she remembered the ever-present pale band around her father's neck from where the same strap had protected his skin from the punishing heat on location shoots.

'Should I strike a pose?'

Alice looked up and found Robinson standing by the boathouse.

'Sun's gone now. You missed your chance.'

She was still sore with him for his behaviour with Brad. It wasn't so much that she was concerned about whether or not Brad had the wrong idea about them. Maybe Robinson didn't even realise it himself, but in acting the way he had he'd rode rough shod over her feelings and choices for his own agenda.

'Old school,' he said, coming closer and nodding towards her camera.

'It was my dad's.'

'He's not around any more?'

Alice shook her head, her eyes on the water. 'He died some years ago.'

Robinson sat down beside her on and deck and didn't speak for a few moments. 'Looks like he knew his kit,' he said eventually, reaching out and touching the Nikon briefly.

'One of the best photojournalists of his day,' Alice said. 'He died on location in Afghanistan.'

The words came out succinct and unexpected. She didn't have a clue why she'd told him something that she hadn't managed to tell her husband in all the years they'd been together.

'You must be very proud of him.'

Alice didn't reply, because it wasn't the kind of statement that needed a response. He picked up a stone and skimmed it across the darkening lake.

'I'm sorry for kissing you, Alice.'

She nodded.

'The second time I mean. Not the first.' He glanced sideways at her. 'I'm not sorry for that one.'

'Thanks for apologising.'

Robinson sighed. 'I was wound up and pissed off about something else and ended up taking it out on you. I wish I hadn't.'

'I wish you hadn't too,' she said, but without heat because he obviously meant what he said.

'You mean the second kiss too, right?'

She rolled her eyes. 'You know perfectly well what I mean.'

'Because the first one was kind of hot, wasn't it?' He bumped shoulders with her and she shrugged, smiling.

'I can't remember,' she lied. 'I'd had a glass or two of wine.'

'You remember just fine, Goldilocks.' His smile creased his cheeks and his eyes glittered in the dwindling light. 'I can always remind you, if you need me to?'

His little finger toyed with hers where their hands lay flat between them on the deck, and the tiny movement was enough to distract her completely. He leaned a little closer and met her gaze, half joking and half serious.

'You know, I think I do remember after all,' she breathed, afraid he was going to kiss her again. Kissing Robinson again right now would be a bad idea. She was already emotional, she was entirely likely to drag him back to the Airstream and do things she'd regret in the morning.

Standing up, she dusted her jeans down with her hands, the camera safely slung around her neck.

'I'm glad we're friends again,' he said, getting up too and walking with her towards the Airstream. Were they friends? He was alone here in England and she was really the only person he'd allowed into his life on any real level, so she was probably as close as it got to friends for him right now.

'Want to talk about whatever had wound you up yesterday?' she said, keeping it casual.

He kicked the dust with the toe of his boot as they crunched over the gravel path. 'Not much to say really. I'm supposed to be someplace else and I don't want to be there, not now or, the way I feel right now, ever again.'

'Work, you mean? Or with your wife?'

'Ex-wife,' he corrected. 'And no it wasn't her turn to wind me up today. I mean she did, because just the thought of her winds me up pretty much every day, but this was work stuff.'

His description of his glittering career as a famous country music artist as 'work stuff' was just about the understatement of the year.

'Do you have commitments you need to go home for?'

'That's just the thing, Alice. Home doesn't feel like home any more.' He shoved his hands down into his pockets as he walked, his arms stiff, his shoulders bunched. Everything about his stance said stressed. 'Let's just say I wasn't doing so well there.'

'And here? Are you doing better here?' she ventured.

His mouth twisted. 'Yes and no.'

As answers went, it was frustratingly vague. Alice opted for silence in the hope that he'd elaborate. She was in luck.

'Being here, I have space. I can breathe, I can relax, I can forget about the shitty stuff. But in the back of my head I know it's all still there waiting for me. Trouble's kind of patient like that, you know? It can play the long game.'

Alice did know. She was becoming adept herself at burying her emotional problems underneath a landslide of to-do lists and plans in the hope that they'd be squashed so flat that they'd disintegrate without her needing to address them.

'What kind of trouble are you in?' she asked as they made their way through the trees. The residual daylight had pretty much gone now and the woodland had taken on its spindly nighttime shroud.

Robinson half laughed under his breath and shook his head, a hollow, joyless sound. 'Ah, you know. The kind where if I don't get my sorry ass back to Nashville and honour my commitments they're gonna sue me halfway to hell and back.'

Wow. As 'work stuff' went, that *was* pretty stressful.

'Gosh,' she said.

Robinson laughed, softer this time. 'Quite.'

Alice opened the caravan door. 'Coffee?'

She didn't know why she said it. Every last one of her instincts told her that asking him in was a reckless move, and yet she went ahead and did it anyway. Robinson Duff was turning out to be a man who switched her logical brain off and left her vulnerable, and that made him very dangerous indeed.

CHAPTER TWELVE

For his part, Robinson truly considered saying thanks but no thanks. Every last one of his instincts told him that spending time alone with her was unfair on both of them, and yet he went ahead and did it anyway. Alice McBride was turning out to be a woman who pressed the override switch in his head and put his body in charge, and that made her a very dangerous woman indeed.

'Coffee would be good,' he said. 'Bourbon would be even better.'

Alice glanced over her shoulder at him as she led him in to the Airstream.

'One, I don't have any bourbon, and two, it's barely eight o' clock and I haven't eaten. One drink and I'd be legless within the hour.'

'Legless?' he grinned. 'You mean drunk, right?'

She nodded. 'Legless as in I wouldn't be able to stand up.'

'And that's a bad thing because . . .?'

'A very bad thing, because I'd have a headache and probably a gut full of regret in the morning, Robinson,' she said, turning the gas on beneath the kettle like a pro now. 'Sit down.'

He settled on the banquette and watched her busy herself in the small space. She made sandwiches with a practised hand, sliding the filled plate onto the table along with their coffee, and then as an afterthought she pulled a bottle of wine from the fridge and added a couple of glasses.

'It's as good as dessert is going to get around here,' she said, placing the bottle on the table.

'Works for me,' he said. He was a man. Alcohol trumped chocolate in just about every situation he could think of. Alice slid in opposite him and pushed the plate his way.

'Chicken salad. Bit plain, sorry.'

He shook his head, perfectly happy with the fare.

'It's fine. I'm living on pizza and microwave dinners up at the house thanks to that oven from the History Channel. This is a definite step up.'

'No more weird casseroles from Hazel lately, then?' Alice picked up a sandwich as she spoke and pulled her coffee towards her. The conversation batted easily back and forth between them as they ate, mostly about their nearest neighbours in the cottages. Robinson learned that Stewie had turned his spare bedroom into a dedicated wig boudoir and spent a disturbing amount of time and money on eBay buying 'Girl's World' heads to display them all on. He also learned that Hazel claimed to have once cast a love spell that turned the whole village into nymphomaniacs for twenty-four hours, and that one of Niamh's nudes had appeared in the National Gallery.

'And what about you, Alice?' he said, opening the wine as she cleared the table and sat back down. 'What's your unexpected secret?'

She played with the stem of her glass, and he found himself watching her slender, ringless fingers.

'What you see is what you get,' she shrugged. 'I wish I could make me sound more interesting, but this is me.'

'You live in an Airstream in your own backyard, that's pretty interesting,' he said. 'What gives?'

Her pretty blue eyes clouded. 'What do you think?'

'I think you didn't want to live in the house any longer without your husband.'

The look on her face told him that he couldn't be more wrong.

'I love Borne Manor,' she said. 'It's my home, and leaving it broke my heart. I leased it so I could cover the costs of keeping it.'

'You mean you moved out so you didn't have to sell it?'

She sighed, puffing out her cheeks.

'And now my crappy husband and his vile bitch of a girlfriend have decided that they want it.'

Alice looked so delicate, ethereal, and Robinson's only instinct at that time was to protect her from all the crap that life was flinging at her.

'We come from very different worlds, Alice, but in some ways you and I are in very similar situations,' he said, swallowing a mouthful of cold sauvignon and wishing it was warm bourbon. 'We've both found our lives turned upside down by other people and been left trying to find our place in the world again.'

Alice nodded. 'Except you moved thousands of miles to do it and I only moved as far as my own back garden.'

'Maybe that makes you lucky,' he offered. 'You know where you want to be, even if you're not with the person you want to be with.'

'Where as you've ended up in a strange land with bizarre people who have wig boudoirs and cast love spells,' she said, raising her eyebrows at him.

'Exactly, Goldilocks.' He laughed softly. 'You got off pretty darn light.'

Alice topped up their dwindling glasses.

'I'm here, you know,' she said. 'If you ever need to get anything off your chest, you can talk to me.'

At that precise moment, he thought about how much he'd like to get his shirt off his chest and press Alice back against the cushions.

'I mean it,' she spoke again when he didn't reply. 'If anyone is going to understand what you're going through, with your marriage at least, it's me.'

Did he want to talk about Lena? 'You know, Alice, I don't think there's much to say. I found one of my closest friends fucking my wife over our breakfast bar. It all went downhill pretty fast from there to here.'

'Oh my god, Robinson! That's bloody awful.' Alice's mouth twisted in disgust and she shook her head slowly, swirling her wine in her glass. 'It's bad enough with a stranger, but someone you loved and trusted? What's wrong with people? You must have been . . . God, I don't even want to imagine what you must have been.'

'Furious enough to smack his head off that same breakfast bar so hard that Lena called him an ambulance,' he supplied.

Alice didn't flinch. 'I don't blame you.' She swallowed a huge mouthful of wine. 'In fact, in some ways I'm bloody jealous.'

Her reaction surprised him.

'How so?'

'I can't tell you how many times I've fantasised about

taking the bacon scissors to Felicity Shaw's stupid rat-tail hair.' She all but spat the woman's name out. It seemed such an out of character thing to hear her say. Alice was an unlikely badass, but he knew exactly which part of her heart she spoke from.

'I think that's part of the reason I kissed you when your husband came by,' Robinson confessed. 'Somewhere in my head it was Lena standing on that step having to watch me kiss a beautiful woman.'

'I get your need for revenge,' she said, and he knew from her eyes that she absolutely did.

'Is it such a bad thing if he thinks you and me are hitting the sheets?' Robinson's gaze slid unbidden to the bed that filled the other end of the Airstream.

Alice paused, most of the way down her second glass of wine. She upended the bottle between them.

'I just didn't want to play games with him. The moral high ground is just about all I've got left, you know?'

She was wrong, and it suddenly felt important to tell her so.

'You have so much more than just that, Alice,' he said. 'You're gorgeous. You've got this sweet, sexy thing going on, you're blue skies and cotton candy. But then every now and then you're not, and that just makes you all the more goddamn sexy.'

She stared at him, surprised, all tumbled curls and rosy cheeks, and then her lips parted a little to let out a tiny 'oh' that perfectly illustrated his point. He was hard just looking at her.

'I'm willing to bet that right about now that ex of yours is burning up inside at the thought of us together,' he said. 'He doesn't know we're not really fucking.'

Jesus. What was in this wine? His words were tumbling

out of his mouth like he'd just lost a game of truth or dare. Alice looked taken aback.

'I guess he doesn't. Serves him right.' She stood up. 'Want some rum?'

And there she was again, the unexpected bad girl. She went from bad to downright sinful when she moved around the table and stretched up on her tiptoes to reach into a cabinet over his head. Her hips were actually asking his hands to hold them, and he couldn't say no.

She stilled and looked down, her arms still over her head.

His gaze slid up the length of her body to meet her kiss-me eyes.

'Robinson . . .' She breathed his name, and he did the only thing on his mind at that moment. He swayed her body gently towards him, close enough to be able to press his mouth against the slim strip of skin exposed by the hem of her shirt. She stared down at him, and he up at her, and then she seemed to forget all about getting the rum and swung her knee over his thighs instead. He wasn't certain if she sat down or he pulled her down, but seconds later she was straddled over his lap, her breathing so shallow that he could see her breasts rising up and down beneath her fitted shirt and he was desperate to know how she'd look without it.

'Alice,' his voice came out hoarse, and he pushed her hair back and held her face between his hands. 'We both know that this isn't going anywhere, right?' God, he hoped she knew what he meant.

'Neither of us wants complicated,' she said, and he gripped the top of her shirt with both hands and pulled the metal snaps open all in one go.

'Jesus, Mary mother of God,' he muttered, unable to take his eyes off the fullness of her breasts trying to escape from her black lace bra. 'Do you always wear stuff like this underneath your work clothes?'

'Always,' she said, reaching for the bottom of his t-shirt and dragging it over his head.

'You know I love someone else,' he said.

'And you know I don't want a relationship,' she whispered, her eyes all over his body. 'I've never seen a man who looks like this in real life.'

'You're even more incredible than I imagined, Alice,' he murmured, and then pulled her ass right against his crotch with both hands so that her breasts brushed against his chest.

'You've thought about this?' She lifted one eyebrow, stroking her hands all the way down from his shoulders to his stomach, making his muscles jump and pay attention.

'I'm having trouble sleeping, baby,' he offered by way of explanation for his fantasies, and then she stroked his face, her eyes telling him that she understood. He turned his face into her palm and kissed it.

'This is the best I've felt in as long as I can remember,' she said as he skimmed his hands up the length of her spine and lowered his face into the swell of her breasts. Christ, she was smooth, and she smelled amazing, of outdoors and an underlying hint of flowers, just as a beautiful fairy at the bottom of the garden should.

'My sweet, sweet, fucking Goldilocks,' he whispered, on fire for her, filling his hands with fistfuls of her hair and kissing the flushed slopes of her breasts, then her neck when she tipped her head back and offered it to him. Robinson had known from their first kiss in the kitchen that Alice would be hot when she was turned on. He just hadn't counted on her being *this* hot, the kind of hot that could start infernos and stop his heart. She was moving on him, rocking herself against him and he couldn't think straight with needing more.

Reaching behind her, he felt for the clasp of her bra and found only a slim, smooth band of slippery silk. Alice laughed softly when he ran his fingers back and forth along it a second time, feeling more like a horny teenager than a thirty-seven-year-old man who knew what he was doing.

'It's at the front.'

She pulled back a little and reached for the clip between her breasts with both hands, and when she looked up at him through her lashes, all peaches and cream and swells and slopes, she reminded him of those billboards that had guys swerving into trouble on the highways back home. She had a confidence about her that was far more intoxicating than the wine they'd shared or the rum she'd offered him; her eyes said look at me and her body said touch me. He was as drunk on her as a man could be and he was happy to stay that blissful way for as long as she'd let him. It sure beat the hell out of every other emotion he'd felt lately.

And then she opened her bra and he realised that there was still so much more to feel, and for a second it was all he could do to look at her and feel like the luckiest guy ever, because she was more lovely than he had words for. He'd known she would be, his hands had told him so in the kitchen the other night, but to see her bared and bold for him like this took his breath.

'Gonna keep me waiting, cowboy? You haven't even kissed me yet,' she murmured, shooting him a look that almost dared him to make the next move with her ten per cent amused, ninety per cent turned-on eyes.

He shook his head and laughed softly. 'Come here, pretty girl.'

Alice had never in her whole life felt so liberated or powerful. Robinson had a way of looking at her that openly said how much he appreciated what he saw, that he was turned on, that he couldn't take his eyes or his hands off her.

He was so very, ridiculously amazing with his shirt off, skin the colour of warm beach bodies and shoulders that said I've got you, you can cling to me. She'd known he'd be in good shape; his job in the public eye pretty much demanded it of him. But he wasn't gym fit in that too perfect, plastic way; he was raw, and real, the kind of work-outdoors-powerful that said I can protect you from everything. She saw all of that in him and loved the way that he was holding back despite all of that, for not rushing the pace faster than she wanted to go. It was like being given the keys to a Ferrari and free rein to put her foot to the floor. Alice was the kind of girl who'd instinctively go a little slower at first to make sure she could handle the power, and right now she was finding out that yes, she could, and yes, she wanted to go full throttle.

She wanted his mouth so she leaned in and took it, her arms wound around his neck so she could bury her hands deep in his hair. Oh . . . that's how his skin felt against hers, warm as Mediterranean sunshine, and oh . . . that's how his kiss tasted, of wine and longing, and oh *God*, his tongue was so sexy in her mouth and his hands were firm and gentle at the same time all over her breasts. The low growl in his chest thrilled her, and the way he teased her nipples made her moan, and oh Jesus, please do that some more.

They were past words, past any thoughts of stopping, past any thoughts of anyone else.

'Come to bed,' she whispered, reaching for the top button on his jeans.

'Yes,' he murmured into her lips, breathing hard, half

dragging her along the banquette and standing up with her still against him. She gasped when he paused halfway to the bed and pushed her back against the cold mirrored closet door, his entire body pressed against hers as he kissed her deep and hard.

'Alice.' He spoke her name against her ear, then into her mouth when he kissed her again, and she wrapped her legs around him to pull him in. If she could have climbed him she would have, the need to have him closer and over her and inside her was just so damn overwhelming and urgent that she could have cried with it.

'Get me naked, Robinson,' she said, pressing her mouth into the golden warmth at the curve of his neck.

He smiled against her shoulder. 'It's funny. You said pretty much that exact same thing in my head last night,' he said, sliding his mouth down and over her breasts, licking, nipping, and kissing her better again. His hands were on the snap of her jeans and she was barely breathing, and then he dropped down onto his knees, pulled her jeans down and she stopped breathing altogether.

'Filthy buggers!'

Alice's eyes flew wide open and Robinson froze, his thumbs still on her hips hooked under the sides of her silk knickers.

'What the actual fuck?' he muttered as the cry outside rang out again, 'filthy buggers!' this time accompanied by a squawk and a loud clatter on the roof of the Airstream. 'Who ever that is better be a fast runner,' he growled, jumping up and fastening his jeans before throwing her shirt towards her and flinging the door of the caravan open.

Alice dragged her jeans back up her legs and pulled her shirt on, getting a hold on her breathing as she watched

Robinson's back. She knew that the culprit could fly faster than he could run, and at that moment she could have happily wrung Rambo's scrawny, feathery neck.

'It's a goddamn bird,' she heard him say, frustration clear in his voice as he stepped outside and looked up at the roof of the Airstream.

'Yeah, I guessed as much,' Alice said, joining him. 'It's Rambo. He must have escaped again.'

'Hazel's bird?'

'Filthy buggers,' the bird said again, flying awkwardly down onto one of the deckchairs.

'Is he always this rude?' Robinson asked, folding his arms across his still-bare chest. 'I don't like him.'

'Always,' Alice said, then looked closer at Rambo and noticed there was blood on one of his legs. 'Does his leg look injured to you?'

Robinson studied Rambo for a moment and then sighed heavily. 'Grab my t-shirt?'

Alice handed it to him, and rather than slide it over his head he wrapped it around Rambo and picked the bird up carefully. Rambo accepted the help with bad grace, trying to reach any bare skin he could with his sharp beak.

'This is not how this evening was supposed to end,' Robinson grumbled, shooting Alice a look that told her he was in a worse mood than a kid who didn't get his new bike for Christmas.

Inappropriate jokes about him having pulled the wrong bird flickered in and out of her mind as her own lustful haze cleared, and she started to laugh as he shook his head and moved away through the trees with Rambo in his arms.

'We're not done here,' he called out as he disappeared into the darkness. 'Not by a mile, Goldilocks.'

CHAPTER THIRTEEN

'He's a hero. That Bear Grylls has got nothing on him.'

Hazel leaned her back against the Airstream and shaded her eyes from the sun to gaze dreamily in the direction of Borne Manor. 'He'd taken off his t-shirt to wrap it around my Rambo. How many men do you know who'd give up their own shirt to rescue an injured animal, Alice? Found him outside his back door, he said, and he brought him home even though it was almost midnight.' Hazel's glasses all but steamed up as she spoke. 'Between you, me and the gatepost, Alice, I was in my nightdress. I think . . .' she paused to draw air quotes around the word think 'that my love potion might have been a bit on the strong side.'

'Your love potion?' Alice said, already worried where this was heading.

Hazel nodded. 'Slipped some into a casserole I made him a couple of weeks ago.' Leaning forward, she lowered her voice to a hushed whisper. 'If it hadn't been for poor Rambo needing attention, I seriously think he might have ravaged me. He had *that* look in his eye.' Again, Hazel drew air quotes, this time around the word 'that' as she nodded gravely.

Alice knew 'that' look. She'd seen it herself last night too, and just thinking about it now had her nervously plaiting and un-plaiting her ponytail.

'I didn't realise you were looking for love, Hazel,' she said, worrying what people would think if they knew what had happened between her and Robinson. Both Hazel and Niamh seemed to be harbouring crushes on their famous new neighbour.

'Oh, no. I'm not, Alice! What sort of cougar do you think I am?' Hazel put her hands up in front of her with her fingers curled into claws and laughed. 'I was just testing the potion out, and my god, I think it works like gangbusters!' Her eyes were like saucers. 'Not sure I've got the balance right in the batch, might be a bit strong. Robinson looked . . .' Hazel screwed up her face as she cast around for the right word. 'Well, he looked *animal*, if you get where I'm coming from.'

'How's Rambo doing?' Alice changed the subject as she was sure her cheeks had to be flaming.

'Swearing like a trooper, so I'm taking that as a good sign,' Hazel said merrily. 'I better get back to him, actually. He's quite a demanding patient.' She frowned suddenly. 'Do you know what he shouted at me this morning when I went to clear out his feeding bowls?'

Alice braced herself and shook her head as Hazel leaned closer to take her into her confidence.

'He said, and I quote, so excuse the obscenities, *interrupt me like that again and I'll wring your neck like a fucking chicken!*' Hazel's voice shot up an octave at the end of her sentence and she threw her hands out to the sides. 'I mean, Alice, where on earth has he been to hear such foul language? I'm just thankful he ended up back safely at the manor and Robinson found him.'

Shaking her head and biting her tongue, Alice pulled out a basket from beneath the Airstream.

'I found these growing by the boathouse the other day, thought they might be of use to you. Chamomile, I think?' She handed Hazel the flowers she'd gathered.

'They are,' Hazel said, touching the white flower heads. 'Are there more?'

Alice nodded. 'Take as many as you like.'

Hazel tucked the flowers into her bag and pulled out Robinson's t-shirt. 'Can you pass this on for me, Alice? I called by but he's not home.'

Alice took the soft, laundered shirt from Hazel, remembering how she'd peeled it from Robinson's body last night. 'I'll see he gets it.'

Hazel floated away across the grass with a wave of her jangly bangles, and then swung back around. 'Alice, do you like horses?'

Alice had never actually ridden a horse, but she liked them well enough. She nodded. 'Think so. Why?'

'Oh, nothing. I just wondered,' Hazel said airily, blatantly lying and not at all bothered. 'See you soon.'

Alice didn't try to press-gang Hazel for information. She'd had that look of enjoying her secret, the kind of expression that said you can ask all you like, I'm not going to tell you.

Borne really did have more than its fair share of oddness. Robinson must feel as if he'd fallen down a rabbit hole half the time.

*

'Robinson?'

Alice tapped on the open kitchen door of the manor that evening, his t-shirt in her hands.

'Hey you,' he said, coming through from the hallway.

'Hazel came by to drop this off for you earlier.' She placed his shirt on the kitchen table. 'You're officially her hero after last night.'

'And there was me thinking you were going to say I was officially your hero. How's that damn bird doing?' he asked, and a tiny smile tipped one side of his mouth. Alice felt about thirteen, all fingers, thumbs and butterflies.

'Fine, by all accounts. Although he did say something odd to Hazel this morning, along the lines of "interrupt me again and I'll wring your scrawny neck",' she said. 'Can't imagine where he's had that from.'

'He's lucky he's still alive,' Robinson laughed. 'Drink to celebrate the sunshine?'

He made it sound so easy and uncomplicated, but a few glasses of wine had made last night very complicated indeed. Or had it? Was there anything to feel so conflicted about?

He grabbed a couple of beers and led the way outside to the bench by the back door.

'Your weather seems to have finally decided that it's summer,' he said, turning his face up to the low evening sunshine. The skyline had that pretty pink and orange swirl that promises a glowing sunset, turning Robinson's eyes into crystal-green rock pools. Did they contain secrets waiting to be fished out? She was pretty sure they did, and not at all sure she should dip her net.

'We should talk about last night,' he said, straight off the bat. Alice took a drink and swallowed hard.

'That was just so American,' she laughed lightly, taken

aback. 'Straight from talking about the weather to talking about sex. Slow down there, cowboy.'

He grinned and shook his head, looking away with a laugh.

'Right. Noted. More weather chat required, English girl?' He waved his hand in the direction of the tree line. 'Those low hangin' clouds are kind of . . . I dunno . . . pink?'

She nodded, enjoying his attempt to do as she'd asked. 'They are, Robinson. They are.'

He licked his finger and held it up in the breeze.

'The signs all suggest another warm one tomorrow,' he said, then knocked back a good glug of beer. 'How'm I doin' over here?'

'Pretty good,' she smiled.

'Good enough to move on and talk about what happened in the Airstream last night?' he said, angling his body towards hers on the bench. 'Sorry. I'm not a talk about the weather kind of guy, Alice. I like to shoot straight and speak the truth.'

'Okay,' she said, because he was right, and it was kind of refreshing that he wanted to talk about it rather than sweep it under the carpet. 'You go first.'

'I was planning on it,' he said dryly, then finished his beer and put the empty bottle on the ground. 'Here's the thing. I came here because I needed somewhere to be. Somewhere unfamiliar, somewhere private, somewhere where I could be alone. I needed that. Still do.'

Alice nodded and held her tongue.

'I've got a lot of shit going on back home, pressures and hassles from all angles and then some,' he went on, and she waited because he seemed to need to kind of build himself up to talking about what had happened, to set the scene for his own benefit as well as hers. 'So I come here, and it's all so fuckin' ridiculously English, and I find you, Alice McBride, all blonde hair and crazy red boots, and I swear to God you're a breath of pure fresh mountain air. I like you,' he paused and took a breath, his arm across the back of the bench, his fingertips drawing circles on the bare skin of her shoulder where her sweater had slid down. 'I like you so damn much, and being around you makes me feel lighter and easier because you're so un-fuckin'-complicated compared to just about everything back home in Nashville.'

'I like you too,' she said, because she really did like him very much, even though he scared her and she didn't really know him at all.

He looked at her steadily and then blew out a deep breath. 'Alice, I can give you nothing. My head is all over the place. I'm a washed-up country singer, and I can't even do that any more.'

'Don't say that,' she said, rubbing his knee through the softness of his jeans. 'Give it time.'

He shrugged. 'I don't even want to. I'm done with it, Alice. It's a circus, all that pressure and the cameras and never saying the wrong thing. Where did it get me? Sure, I have money, but that doesn't keep me warm at night, does it? I have fans, but they're fickle and will move on to the next guy just as quickly as Lena did.' He rubbed his jaw. 'I'm not saying all of this to make you feel bad for me. I don't need sympathy, I know I have it pretty good compared to most folks. I just need you to see inside my head and know it's screwed up so that I don't screw you up right along with me, okay?'

His fingertips had moved from spiralling to massaging, and when he met her eyes she saw the rawness and honesty there. She went to speak, but he laid his finger against her lips to still the words.

'Let me finish? I need to get this out, okay?' He rubbed his thumb over her bottom lip, and then the back of his fingers over her jawbone. 'Last night was something, wasn't it?'

She didn't know if she was supposed to even answer him, it sounded like a rhetorical question.

'I want you, Alice. I have nothing but my body and my time to give and I want nothing but your body and your time from you in return,' he said. 'Does that make me an ass? Because saying it makes me feel like one. Is it selfish and greedy to say that kissing you makes me feel good, and that all I've been able to think about since last night is how goddamn amazing you looked in my lap?'

Alice appreciated his honesty more than he could know.

'It's not crazy, Robinson. You're not crazy. Or at least, if you are, then I am too,' she said softly. 'I'm lonely. You're lonely. We both know that neither of us is available emotionally, but when you touch me . . . it makes me forget all the bad stuff for a while.'

He wrapped a strand of her hair around his finger, moving closer. 'I don't want you thinking about the bad stuff.'

'So make me forget it,' she said, and surprised them both by putting her bottle down and leaning in to kiss him. He kissed her back, slow and sexy, and then he broke away a little, just enough to speak.

'Alice . . .'

She reached up and put her finger over his lips, her head and her emotions all over the place.

'Ssh. My turn now.'

She leaned into his arm around her shoulders, and smoothed her hand over his thigh.

'If you could look inside my head you'd see it's every bit as screwed up as yours is. I'm scared of a million things all of the time, Robinson. Of losing the house, of never being happy again, of getting divorced from the man I thought I'd be with for ever. The last six months have been one long hell of heartache and press intrusion, of being dragged publicly through the mud because Brad is considered public property. We had the press camped out here for weeks. I had to see him in compromising positions with her on the front of every newspaper every time I went to buy milk. It was awful, and a lot of the time, it still is.'

He listened, watching her eyes, playing with her hair.

'And then there's you. You scare me, Robinson, because you're famous too. Much more so. One whiff of you being here and the press would descend again, that whole circus would start up and I don't think I can face it all a second time.'

'I'll go,' he said, cutting in. 'If me being here makes it harder for you, I'll go.'

'I don't want you to go. For as long as no one knows you're here, I want you to stay.'

'I don't want anyone to know I'm here, either,' he said. 'I feel like I'm on holiday from my own life, and I like it.'

Alice slid her arm around his back and he lowered his head and kissed the crook of her neck. 'We both know that you're going to have to go home,' she said, closing her eyes briefly because the sensation of his mouth on her skin demanded it.

'But I'm here now,' he said, his mouth close to her ear.

'We both are,' she whispered. 'I've been thinking about last night all day.'

'Me too,' he said, bringing her hand to his face and kissing her fingers. 'Be my holiday fling, Goldilocks?'

Alice had never had a holiday romance, or a one night stand, or a relationship where you lay your cards on the table so patently before falling into it head first. In that exact moment his honest, open, hurt no one attitude made complete and utter sense. And then he kissed her again, on her mouth, hot in her mouth, and pulled her so close against the hard heat of his chest that any attempt at thinking sensibly left her head for the summer.

'Making each other feel this good can't be wrong,' he said, still kissing her, stroking her back and moulding her into him.

'I've been the talk of the village before. I don't want that again.'

'And I've been the talk of Nashville for all the wrong reasons, baby,' he said, resting his forehead against hers. 'Let's make this, whatever *this* is, just for us. No one else needs to know. Being lonely together sure beats the hell out of being lonely alone.'

'Secret lovers?' she said, and found the idea turned her on madly.

'The best darn secret I've ever kept,' he said, sliding his hand inside her sweater. 'Come inside?'

She stalled, opening her eyes and looking at the manor.

'Not in there?' he said, perceptive.

'I don't think I can.'

'Then God bless the all-American Airstream.' He smiled that sexy half smile that melted her brain.

'You don't think I'm being stupid?' She looked doubtfully back at the manor with its plethora of bedrooms. God knew she and Brad hadn't used them all.

'I think you're crazy beautiful and I don't care where we go as long as I get to take your clothes off,' he said, holding his hand out.

She got up and he pushed his hand into her hair and kissed her long and hard.

'Wait there,' he gasped when he came up for air, and disappeared for a moment then came back and threw her over his shoulder. Alice dissolved into laughter as he marched across the grass with her, his arm firm across the back of her knees.

'I don't know if you're a cowboy or a caveman,' she said, rucking up his t-shirt and kissing his back. God, his skin was warm and smooth, and he smelled so delicious she wanted to bury her face in him and never come up for air.

CHAPTER FOURTEEN

They reached the Airstream and he opened the door and carried her in, banging the door closed behind him and tumbling her onto the bed.

'What did you go back inside the house for?' Alice asked him, and he dug inside the back pocket of his jeans and produced a gold foil packet without looking the least bit sheepish.

'You're sure of yourself, cowboy,' she said as he slid down onto the bed with her, half covering her body with the welcome weight of his.

'This is a holiday romance, remember? The rules are different.'

'I remember,' she whispered. 'Shouldn't we drink dodgy cocktails or something first?'

'No time. Too horny. We can drink tequila afterwards,' he said, already pulling her sweater over her head and then his own t-shirt.

'This is about the point where Rambo interrupted us last time,' she said, wide eyed and worked up as she revelled in the feel of his chest under her palms. He was firm muscles and soft tawny hair that tapered into his jeans, and she was light headed with the knowledge that this time around she was going to get to see where it went.

'If that bird comes anywhere near this Airstream in the next couple of hours he'll be in the stewpot.' Robinson dipped his head to trail kisses from Alice's shoulder to her collarbone. 'And technically, you're wrong.' He reached behind her and thankfully found the clip of her grey and black silk bra easily this time. 'Lovely as this is, we need to get rid of it before we're at the point where squawk interrupted us.'

And then he peeled her bra from her body and sighed with happiness, and Alice wondered how to make a couple of hours feel like a lifetime because the way he was looking at her made her feel the most beautiful she had in her whole life.

'What would you say if I said let's do it once fast and then again real slow?' he said, his knees either side of her thighs as he held her breasts in his hands and kissed them, his eyes hot on hers.

'I'd say get naked,' she said, smoothing her hands over his hair, raking her nails over his golden shoulders. He groaned, and reached for her jeans snapper at the same moment that she reached for his. Seconds later and they'd pushed their clothes away and lay down again, naked, and the intimacy was so shocking that Alice gasped, almost faltered. Robinson seemed to sense her feelings and despite his own needs he slowed things right down, settling his body weight, his knee between hers.

'Don't think,' he whispered, and then he kissed her, more sweet and gentle than any other time so far, moving her hair away from her face. 'We're on holiday, remember? Listen . . .' He tucked her hair behind her ear. 'You can hear the sea.'

A small smile touched Alice's mouth as she went with him, floating away, closing her eyes.

'Let's be on a beach, pretty girl,' he said, and she heard the crinkle of foil before he moved between her legs then held her hands loosely in his own over her head against the pillows. 'There's no one here but you and me.'

He stopped speaking then and pushed himself into her, his face next to hers when she breathed in sharply. 'It's okay, it's okay, it's okay,' he said against her ear, and even though he'd said he needed to go fast, he didn't, he lifted his head and looked down at her, his kiss barely there on her lips as he held still and let her lead.

She nodded, thinking of no one but him and nowhere but now, overwhelmed by the closeness after months of being alone. Moving under him came as naturally as breathing, and he responded with a gasp of his own as he started to move with her.

'You're so damn beautiful,' he said, his voice ragged against her lips, his hands moving in her hair on the pillows. 'It's like fucking an angel.'

Alice just gave herself up to him, to the feeling of being held as close as a man can hold a woman, to the delicious build and the inevitable high. He touched her everywhere, and then he lost it and she held him through it until he fell against her, heavy and tangled and brilliant.

Holding him, Alice stroked her fingers over his back and looked at his face on her shoulder as he got his breath back. His eyes were closed, his full lips slightly parted, and his whole expression said contented, as if he were sleeping and having the most awesome dream ever.

'Now I get why you moved out here,' he murmured a little while later. 'It's fabulous. Can I stay in the Airstream too?'

'It's only like this because you're here,' she said quietly, and a lazy smile touched his lips.

'Damn, I'm good,' he said, making her laugh and cuff him on the shoulder even though she entirely agreed with him. He was good. He was more than good. He'd turned her on like a moonbeam, as if she were shining from the inside out. She held her hand up in front of her face, half expecting it to glow phosphorous bright in the darkness of the Airstream.

'Can you still hear those waves out there, Goldilocks?' he said, covering her breast with his hand in a thrilling, possessive way.

She tipped her head, listening, and he dipped his head, licking.

'I'm pretty sure I can,' she said, closing her eyes and melting completely into the quilts and into Robinson.

'This is hands down the best holiday I've been on in my life,' he laughed, and then he slid down her body and Alice stopped thinking altogether.

Early Saturday-morning sunshine filtered through the windows into the Airstream, bathing Robinson in a shaft of dappled, golden light. Alice sat up and leaned against the wall in bed, her arms around her knees, watching him. She hadn't realised it up to that precise moment, but this was the first time that she'd seen him truly relaxed. He was on his back, one arm flung above his head on the pillow, the other hand stretched out towards her in his sleep, exuding tranquillity in a way that invited her to lay back down and enjoy the peace of the moment with him. In a while she would, but right now she wanted just to look at him for a little longer. She didn't regret what had happened last night. Not the first time, nor the slower, sexier second time that followed soon afterwards, and definitely not the tender, half awake, half asleep third time in the middle of the night, either. That kind of sex wasn't something any sane person could regret. He'd probably call it smokin'. She'd call it so hot that it was a wonder the Airstream hadn't exploded and burned itself into a hole in the ground.

'Come here, pretty girl,' Robinson said, lifting the quilt and not even opening his eyes. If he had, he'd have seen Alice's gaze slide down his body and appreciate the view. As it was she let out a contented little sigh and snuggled in, enjoying the feeling of his bigger, warm body spooned around hers, his arms holding her close inside the quilt.

'What time is it?' he murmured.

'Just before six.' Alice closed her eyes and listened to his breathing close to her ear. He moved her hair aside and smooched the back of her neck.

'Early.' Alice heard the smile in his voice. 'Feels good.'

'I know,' she said, bringing his palm up to her face and kissing it.

'Let's stay in bed a while,' he said, and from the way he stirred behind her, Alice guessed he didn't have sleep on his mind. That was pretty lucky, because as it happened, neither did she.

'Alice!'

Niamh banged on the door of the Airstream.

'Alice, wake up. I need to talk to you!'

Inside, Alice was instantly wide awake and in a panic.

How do you hide a six-foot sleeping cowboy in a one-room caravan? Answer: you didn't. Niamh couldn't come in, so she'd have to go out. Flinging on her long robe and dragging her hair back in a band, she opened the door just enough to slide out and pushed it shut again behind her.

'Morning,' she said, tying her belt and leaning down to fuss an overeager Pluto. 'Wassamatter?'

Niamh glanced behind her towards the manor. 'Are we still supposed to be keeping it a secret that we have a super-star staying in the village?'

'Absolutely and totally yes,' Alice said, quickly and quietly. Even more so after last night and this morning. 'Why?'

'Well . . . shall we have coffee?' Niamh looked hopefully towards the Airstream.

'I'm all out. Why did you ask about Robinson?'

'Tea, maybe?' Niamh hedged.

'No milk,' Alice lied, getting that sinking feeling. 'Niamh, what's going on?'

Niamh gave up on the idea of a drink and sat down hard on an upturned bucket. Pluto sat beside her with his head on her knee.

'Nothing really,' she said, but her tone suggested otherwise. 'It's just that I was in The Siren last night and a couple of things struck me as odd, that's all.'

'What things?' Alice frowned, perching on the edge of a deckchair and pulling her robe over her knees.

Niamh screwed her face up. 'Dessy, for one. I mean he's always wearing something odd so it could have been nothing, but leather chaps and a Stetson seemed a bit extreme for behind the bar, even for him.'

Alice had seen Dessy pulling pints in many strange outfits, so she didn't panic too much.

'Which would have been fine,' Niamh went on, 'except Jase appeared in an almost identical costume, only without a shirt and a lasso over his shoulder.'

Okay, so that was maybe a little bit more worrying. The landlords of The Siren were divinely handsome men and Alice had no doubt that they'd have carried the look off with aplomb, but Niamh's story was definitely starting to ring warning bells.

'Anything else?' she said, chewing her thumbnail.

'Davina.'

The postmistress's name sent a shiver down Alice's spine. She hadn't forgiven her for the way she'd taken repeated, thankfully failed, shots at Brad during their marriage. There was no way she was going to get her claws into Robinson Duff.

'What did she say?' Alice's heart rattled behind her ribs. If Davina knew he was here, the rest of the world would know he was here before lunchtime. She sighed, already lamenting the end of the sweetest, shortest affair in history.

'She didn't mention Robinson by name, but she tried every which way to get me to tell her who was renting the manor. Seems she's got wind that there's someone in there worthy of gossip and she's desperate to get the low down before everyone else.'

'You didn't tell her though?' Alice knew she didn't really need to ask.

'No, I bloody didn't!' Niamh said. 'But he needs to lay really low if he's serious about keeping his presence here out of the village newsletter.'

'It's more the nationals I'm worried about,' Alice said quietly.

'I know, hon. That's why I came to see you. He might need a disguise if he goes out and about.'

Alice coughed. 'Any suggestions?'

'Borrow one of Stewie's wigs?' Niamh laughed. 'Or get Hazel to cast some sort of invisibility spell?'

Ignoring Niamh's less than impressive suggestions, Alice cupped her chin in her hands.

'Will you help keep his secret, Niamh? I don't want him to leave.'

Niamh tipped her head on one side. 'Something you want to tell me, McBride?'

'Nothing,' Alice said, at the exact same moment as the Airstream door flew back and Robinson stood there buck naked. To his credit he didn't turn a hair, even when Niamh's hand flew to her mouth to hold in her shocked laugh and Alice's hands flew to her face to cover it completely.

'Ladies,' he said, then tipped his invisible Stetson and closed the door again.

'No coffee, huh?' Niamh said.

Alice peeped through her fingers and shook her head. 'Nor milk.'

'But lots of hot sex with a naked cowboy?' Niamh's eyes could not have sparkled brighter if she'd had them surgically removed and replaced with diamonds.

'You can't tell a soul, Niamh,' Alice said. 'Promise me?'

'Alice, relax, you know I won't. I'm just so bloody happy that you're getting some action! And with Robinson bloody Duff!' Niamh somehow managed to squeal, whisper and swoon all in one go. 'In your face, Felicity Shaw!'

'Niamh . . .'

'I know, I know,' Niamh said, rolling her eyes. 'I shouldn't think it or say it, but I'm doing it on your behalf because you're too nice to say it yourself.'

'I'm not. It's just . . . it's complicated.'

'Well don't let it be.' Niamh leaned forward, no longer laughing. 'Alice, this is just what you need, don't make it more complicated than it needs to be. Just take it for what it is and enjoy it, okay?'

Alice nodded. 'I want to.'

Niamh started to laugh and covered her pink cheeks with her palms. 'You know I can't un-see what I just saw, right? It's in there for ever.' She tapped the side of her head and grinned as she stood up.

Alice couldn't help but laugh with her. 'Just make sure it stays in there. If it makes it out onto canvas we are no longer friends, understand?'

She accepted Niamh's outstretched hand to haul her out of the deckchair.

'Only because you're my best friend. But you should know that my fingers are actually hurting from the effort of not painting something so mighty fine.'

'Go. Go back to your ancient farmer willies.' Alice gave Niamh a little nudge.

Niamh nudged her right back and threw a ball from her pocket to get Pluto moving in the right direction. 'Thanks. Go back to your magnificent cowboy willy.'

'Some girls get all the luck,' Alice laughed softly, watching Niamh leave and then sliding back inside the Airstream and locking the door.

CHAPTER FIFTEEN

'Shall I be chair?' Stewie said loudly, leaning towards Alice across the table in the back room of The Siren. It was just after three in the afternoon as Dessy made his way to the table with a tray of drinks, stopping halfway across the room to straighten his sparkly Stetson out of his eyes.

'Crème de menthe,' he said, curling his lip at the smell as he handed Hazel the sherry schooner of emerald green liquid. 'Sure you wouldn't like something in it? Domestos, maybe?'

'You boys just don't know what's good for you,' Hazel said, arching her eyebrows and sipping it with a little mewl of pleasure.

'Whisky for you, Stewpot, no rocks.' Dessy slid the neat scotch over to Stewie.

'And a fruit-based drink for the ladies,' Jasc said, appearing behind Dessy waving a bottle of icy white wine and a clutch of glasses.

'Sorry, kiddo,' Dessy said to Ewan as he slid him a Coke, then leaned over and whispered 'there's a double rum in it,' out of earshot of Hazel and shot the teenager a cheeky wink.

Alice looked around the collective, gathered there by Niamh for an 'invitation only, highly confidential' meeting, if the sign taped to the door of the snug was to be taken at face value. Once they were all inside, Stewie had conducted a completely unnecessary headcount and then shoved a chair under the handle to ensure they wouldn't be interrupted by afternoon drinkers from the bar.

Taking Alice's lack of answer as a yes, Stewie shoved his chair back and stood up, clearing his throat to garner everyone's attention, even Pluto's, who looked up from his bowl of water by the table leg and regarded Stewie sombrely with his good eye.

'Ladies . . . gentlemen . . . and pooches,' he said, embroidering his words with as much drama as he could muster. He attempted to throw in a bow too, but only tipped a fraction forward before his luxurious dark curls, brought in homage to Kevin Keegan in the early eighties, started to slide forwards so he shot back up hastily.

'We seven gathered here today, henceforth to be known as the Borne Seven Society, or the BS Society, have been bestowed with a great responsibility. But as a great man once said, with great responsibility comes great power.'

Dessy frowned and took off his Stetson. 'Shouldn't that be the other way around?'

Stewie ignored him and carried on. 'We,' he gesticulated in a circle around the table, 'have been appointed as the protectors and guardians of the greatest secret ever to be bestowed upon this village.'

A silence settled on the group and they all looked at Stewie, who looked around at them each in turn and nodded gravely, rubbing his silk-shirt-encased gut in circular motions like it was his food baby.

'As we all know, Brad McBride departed Borne Manor in a cloud of flashy suits and light bulbs.' He patted Alice's shoulder. 'Nasty business, my darling, nasty business.'

Alice could only agree.

'And he left behind this poor, defenceless creature to fend for herself,' Stewie said, and Alice looked up at him in alarm and went to stand up.

'Err, I'm not exactly defenceless . . .'she started, then stopped speaking again when Stewie applied enough pressure to plop her back down into her seat and spoke over her.

'And so it came to be that she has fallen on hard times, and has had to move out of the big house into the servants' quarters, and the house has a new master to serve.'

Niamh started to laugh and muttered 'Cinderella', and Alice reached for her wine in resignation. Everyone in the room knew the general truth of what had happened with Brad anyway, thanks to the press coverage at the time, and trying to stop Stewie in full flow was about as pointless as throwing yourself in front of a moving train and expecting to survive.

'Stewie, are you sure this wasn't the plot of one of your movies?' Jase piped up.

Stewie narrowed his eyes as he thought about it for a second. 'Now that you come to mention it, Jason, I did take the part of a rather dashing young lord of the manor in 1973. Similar building, actually. Lined all the servants up and rogered them senseless over the kitchen table,' he said, nodding at the memory with a faraway smile.

Ewan batted his mother off when she tried to cover his ears and Dessy rocked back on the legs of his chair and grinned. 'Hope you're doing your maidly duties, Alice, my darling.' He raised his glass in her direction. Niamh stroked Pluto's silky nose and caught Alice's eye but said nothing. For her part, Alice wondered why she'd ever thought this meeting would be a good idea.

'Some hush so I can continue, if you please, children,' Stewie said, brimming with bonhomie and whisky, flapping his hands until he had everyone's attention again.

'The fact is that we've got ourselves what you might call a delicate situation here, team BS. Robby Duff has chosen Borne as his home for the next few months and he wants to live here in privacy and seclusion. The moment it gets out that there's a superstar in the manor, he'll leave, and I for one want him to stay as long as possible.'

'Didn't he used to be in Take That?' Jase said, knowing full well that he didn't and winking at Niamh, who had dug a pen from her bag and was doodling Alice a caricature of Stewie on a beermat.

'Actually, I don't think anyone calls him Robby,' Alice said, to keep the facts straight. 'Or Robster, or Robin, or Bob, either. It's Robinson.'

Dessy raised his hand. 'Can I say that I think it's extremely unfair that Jase and I are the only members of the Bullshit Society that haven't actually met him.'

'Noted in the minutes,' Niamh said, writing 'never gonna happen' on the edge of the beermat before showing Dessy with an impish grin.

'The man is a bone-fide, walking talking rock star,' Stewie said, full of self-importance. 'If we can keep it under our hats that he's here,' he looked pointedly at Dessy and Jase's matching glittery Stetsons, 'who knows who else might come to visit him over the summer? Think of the private parties at the manor. I'm willing to bet he knows Hugh Hefner.'

Stewie stroked his curls absently. 'Had a wild night in the Playboy Mansion with Heff in 1978. Those bunny girls, I can see them now, all big bare bosoms and waggy little tails.' He sighed, drawing a curvy female outline in the air with his hands and wiggling his backside.

'In all seriousness, it's really important that no one finds out that Robinson is here,' Alice said, shooting Stewie a look that went completely over his curly head as he was still lost somewhere in a Hollywood Jacuzzi in the seventies. 'He's come here because he needs some peace, and I for one understand that. And you know what else? He's a pretty cool, normal sort of guy when you talk to him, just someone who's had his problems and could use our help.'

Alice wasn't speaking out of turn; Robinson's relationship issues had been splashed all over the internet even more than her own had.

'I know you guys haven't met him yet,' she looked towards Jase and Dessy. 'And you have no reason to keep his secrets, but will you do it anyway? Not for him, but for me. I honestly don't think I can handle the press descending on the manor again.'

Everyone around the table nodded. They'd all taken Alice into their hearts as one of their own, and despite their eccentricities and foibles they knew how to close ranks.

'I'd like the chance at least to spend some time turning the gardens of the manor into a glampsite, and I won't be able to do that if all hell breaks loose,' she went on. 'Because if I can't get this business off the ground it's highly likely that the manor will have to be sold, or else Brad will buy me out and I'll have to leave.' Alice found herself becoming emotional and Niamh squeezed her fingers. 'I don't want to leave Borne. I love it so much, and all of you crazy people with it.' She smiled, and a tear slid down her cheek. If Brad had been there, he'd have been crazed with jealousy that he couldn't summon tears with such perfect timing, except that Alice was one hundred per cent authentic and meant every word.

'One for all and all for one,' Jase said, holding his wine glass aloft like a sword. 'Robinson who?'

'Team BS all the way,' Dessy added, taking the Stetson off regretfully and laying it on the table. 'The Siren's lips are officially sealed.'

Hazel drained her crème de menthe and placed the glass delicately back down. 'Robinson can of course rely on our complete discretion,' she said, rolling her 'r's like the queen and laying a hand on Ewan's shoulder to indicate she spoke for them collectively.

Her son looked at her hand for a second, and then slowly around the table as if he'd just noticed they were all there. 'BS stands for bullshit,' he slurred, laughing into his neck and then sliding under the table in a rum stupour.

'That was hilarious,' Niamh said, as they stood by her front gate twenty minutes later. Hazel had screamed in panic when Ewan had hit the deck, and a shamefaced Dessy had confessed that the tiniest splash of rum might have somehow fallen into Ewan's Coke by mistake and then hauled him up and gave him a piggy back home. Niamh and Alice had followed on behind, leaving Stewie in the bar of The Siren where he was retelling his Hugh Hefner story to a startled-looking farmer she half recognised from down the valley.

'I just hope it works,' Alice said, reaching down behind the garden wall into the box of dog treats Niamh stashed there and feeding one to Pluto who'd been leaning against her leg.

'It will,' Niamh said, unlatching the gate. 'I was born in Borne.' She started to laugh at her own joke because she'd drunk too much wine. 'I know the people here. They're bonkers but deep down they're solid gold.' She looked up at her little cottage and sighed. 'There've been a lot of secrets in this village over the years, Alice, we're good at playing our cards close to our chest.' And with that she tottered up the path and opened the front door, ushering Pluto in before blowing a kiss and disappearing inside. Alice looked at the cottages thoughtfully. Although she owned them, technically, they never particularly felt like hers, probably because everybody paid bugger all in rent. She'd never even seen their rental contracts, let alone collected any monies from them. Pausing outside number four, she looked for any signs of life and found nothing. It was strange, really. Her half of the sale proceeds had landed in the bank a few weeks back, much needed funds both to live on and to use to get the glampsite up and running. With the wind behind her and Robinson's rent too, she should be able to hang on to the manor for the summer in time for her to, God willing, get a business mortgage on the manor. The plan had holes in it big enough to keep her awake at night, but it was all she had and she was going to cling to it like a life raft until such a time came as she sank altogether. But it wouldn't. She wouldn't sink. If there was one thing that Alice had learned about herself during the whole debacle with Brad it was that she might look fragile but she was actually a whole lot stronger than people gave her credit for. The meeting in the pub might have seemed quite lighthearted at times, but her friends all knew her well enough to know that when it came down to it, the situation was just about as serious as it got for Alice.

When she opened the Airstream door, she found herself faced with a naked cowboy, aside from his boots, his modesty saved only by a suede tool belt. He threw his hands out to the sides and shot her a sexy grin.

'I got you a gift,' he said. Alice let her eyes slide down his eye-wateringly good chest and looked at his middle.

'You got me a tool belt?'

'I don't want you keeping nails in your pockets any more, Goldilocks.'

She was beyond touched that he'd done something so simple and thoughtful, and then he turned around slowly and treated her to a cheeky view of his perfectly peachy backside before facing her again with a glint in his eye.

'Like it?' he asked, stepping closer.

'A lot,' she laughed, placing her hands on his chest and sighing with pleasure.

'You better try it on then,' he said, then dropped the kitchen blind with one hand and unclipped the belt with the other and let it fall to the floor.

CHAPTER SIXTEEN

'Did you ever take a bath with your husband up at the manor?'

Alice propped herself up on her elbow and studied Robinson's stubble-shadowed jaw.

'No. Why?'

'Because I haven't been able to get the thought of sliding into the water with you out of my head since you took a bath.' He trailed a finger over her collarbone. 'Let's do it tonight.'

Alice faltered. She loved that bathroom, and she couldn't count the number of times that she'd lain in that bath and hoped in vain that Brad would get the urge to come up and join her. It had been one of her favourite fantasies about the manor. Could she adjust the image in her head a little to accommodate a different man?

'Okay,' she said, still unsure. 'I think I'd like that.'

'How about the kitchen table?' he said, kissing her shoulder.

Another unfulfilled wish. She shook her head.

'But you did it on the stairs, right?' he asked, watching her closely. Alice dropped her eyes and sighed, almost ashamed.

'Just the bedroom. And maybe in the lounge.'

'You can't remember for sure?'

Oh, she remembered. She just wasn't certain that particular encounter between herself and Brad even counted, because he'd been so pissed he'd fallen asleep halfway through. It wasn't something she wanted to talk about, now or ever.

'So as long as we avoid those two places, we could maybe spend some time in the house?' he said. 'Because much as I'm fond of this old girl –' he tapped the Airstream wall, '– it seems a shame to have all of those unexplored options, don't you think?'

She did think. It had been one of the thoughts she'd had when they'd bought the manor. It was just going to feel weird being there in that way with anyone else.

'It's only as difficult as you make it, baby,' he said softly, using that trick he seemed to have of looking inside her head.

Alice nodded and curled into his chest, and he stroked her hair until she fell asleep, into mixed-up dreams of her wedding day to Brad, only as she turned she saw Robinson smile at her in the congregation and started to panic. She woke up with a start, her heart racing, tears on her cheeks. The details of the dream left her as she settled back into the circle of his arms, but the unsettled feeling of panic remained.

The tree house was starting to look quite magnificent. It was watertight, and Robinson watched bemused from the kitchen window as Alice's various eBay purchases and vintage-market buys rolled up the drive and headed out there. When the compost toilet installer's van rocked up on the last Friday of May, he finally decided that enough was enough. Alice had held back on telling him why she was making such a thorough job of the tree house, but unless she was planning to actually move into it, then there was something he was missing.

'Alice?' he said, nodding briefly at the guys busily getting to work a little way from the base of the tree. His ubiquitous disguise of baseball cap and sunglasses served him well, they barely looked his way as he made his way up the winding steps.

'Wow.'

He stepped inside and shoved his hands deep into his pockets, whistling in admiration as he did a slow three hundred and sixty degree spin to take in all the changes up there.

Alice stood in the doorway to the balcony. 'You like it?'

The last time Robinson had seen inside the tree house it had been a musty, cobwebbed kind of space. Not any more. Alice's renovations had given it the air of a cosy log cabin complete with a brass bedstead, low tables, a comfy looking sofa and pretty rugs. It was rustic chic and gorgeous, all pretty soft furnishings and cute curtains that made the place magazine worthy. It was quirky, and somehow it was totally, completely Alice.

'The squirrels are gonna live well up here, Goldilocks,' he said.

Alice looked at her boots. 'It's squirrel-tight.'

Robinson nodded, looking up at the ceiling. 'And watertight, and bird-tight. In fact I'd go as far as to say it's the fanciest tree house I've ever been in, Alice.'

She smiled guardedly, and he could see how proud she was of it in her face.

'Feel like telling me what this is all about yet?' Robinson deliberately phrased it casually, because for some reason Alice clammed up whenever he'd asked her about her project in the trees.

'Meet me back here later on?' she said, cryptic as ever. 'About seven?'

'Should I bring anything?'

Alice looked at him for a long minute, and then said something that took the breath from his lungs.

'I'd really like it if you brought your guitar, Robinson.'

He stared at her, and then turned on his heel and left her there.

Alice didn't know why she was nervous. Robinson had been in Borne for over a month now, she'd grown used to having him around and felt easy in both his company and his arms. They'd talked about so many things. He knew stuff about her past, about her father, that she hadn't told anyone else, and she knew that he'd fallen from a horse when he was seven and broken both of his arms. He'd seen her cry, she'd made him laugh, and she especially loved to see the look of intense pleasure on his face when he let go of his control in bed. They were close, physically, and on some level close as friends, even though they'd both acknowledged that they were rebounding like a pair of out-of-control frisbees and agreed upfront that theirs could only ever be a brief but glorious holiday romance.

The balcony of the tree house looked every bit as pretty as she'd hoped, the hundreds of tiny solar-powered white fairy lights she'd wound around the rustic struts of the balcony now glowed softly, having basked all day in energy-giving sunshine. Alice herself had enjoyed the warmth too, and her shoulders had turned a warm shade of pink to match the slick of gloss she'd swiped over her lips. It wasn't the only effort she'd made for the evening; because they'd made this dinner arrangement in advance, it somehow had a more formal, date-like feel than their usual casual meet-ups. She'd dressed accordingly, braiding her hair around her head and digging a lemon sundress out to replace her usual jeans. She ducked inside the tree house and rummaged in the bag she'd brought over from the Airstream, pulling out salt, vinegar and cold prosecco, plus wine glasses to accompany the plates, and cutlery she'd already laid outside on the table. Stepping barefoot back outside onto the deck, she stopped, arrested by the sight of Robinson slowly crossing the lawns, handsome as hell in jeans and an open-necked dark shirt with his guitar slung across his back.

Alice found herself momentarily star struck. Without his guitar, he was just Robinson, the cowboy who'd come to stay. It was easy to disassociate him from his public persona because he didn't speak of it and she didn't really know of it, but seeing him coming towards her with his guitar was a stark reminder of who he really was, and where he really belonged.

She ran her suddenly clammy hands down her dress as he made his way up the tree and had managed to gather herself back together when he appeared inside.

'Something smells good,' he said, sliding the strap of his guitar over his head and propping it against the wall without reference to it.

'Fish and chips.' Alice had nipped down to the village chippy just before he arrived. 'Thought it was time you tried a proper English dinner.'

Robinson smiled. 'Maybe one day I'll return the favour and take you for meat and three,' he said, making her look at him quizzically as she started to unwrap the food from its paper.

'Meat and three what?'

Robinson grinned, nostalgic. 'Ah man, you'd love it. Meat first, so hot chicken or ham, or fried steak maybe, then three of whatever you like piled on the side. I'm a mac'n'cheese, collard greens and heavy on the biscuits kind of guy.'

'You basically just spoke another language,' Alice laughed, laying his food in front of him still on the paper and sitting down opposite him to the same. 'Biscuits with dinner? That's every kind of wrong.'

He shook his head. 'You'd get it if you tried it. Heaven on a plate.'

Alice didn't reply. They both knew that he wouldn't be taking her for meat and three anytime in the future. They had only here, and now, and fish and chips straight from the paper. She watched him eat as she poured the fizz.

'This is good,' he said, squeezing a heavy dose of ketchup onto the paper, warming her insides with his praise even though all she'd done to make dinner was queue up for it.

'Your British fans would probably die on the spot if they could see you right now,' she said, and the shift in his expression from relaxed to guarded happened in an instant, just as it had earlier when she'd asked him to bring his guitar.

'Good job they can't then,' he said, shutting her down.

The problem was that Alice knew from experience that rug-sweeping emotional problems was an approach that didn't work. It might, for a while, but you ended up eventually with a hump beneath the carpet that you'd keep tripping on until you sorted it out, and if you left it there for too long you might just fall and break your neck. She'd allowed herself to use that approach over the last year of her marriage to Brad, and she was still trying to stamp the stubborn kinks out of that particular damn rug.

They ate slowly, making small talk, luxuriating in the simplicity of each other's company, and Alice avoided saying the things that were on her mind until she'd screwed up the discarded food wrappers and Robinson had refilled their glasses. Darkness had blanketed the woods, turning the fairy-lit tree house even more fairytale.

'I like this dress on you,' Robinson said, running his finger beneath the slender strap as they curled up together on the loveseat she'd placed on the balcony for prospective residents to stargaze.

She smiled and kissed his fingers, resting her head back on his outstretched arm.

'Stars are out,' she said, her eyes picking out the great bear and the little bear nestled beside it. She'd spent countless nights as a child studying the skies flat on her back beside her dad, some of the most precious memories she had.

He followed suit and tipped his head back too. 'Same stars, even on the flipside of the world.'

'There are some things you just can't outrun,' she said, turning her head towards him.

Robinson sighed. 'Out with it, Goldilocks. There's something on your mind. Tell me what it is.'

Alice sat up with her feet tucked beneath her, her body angled towards his. She nodded slowly, unsure how even to say the things in her mind, and unwilling to break the easy comfort of the time they shared together.

'It's this place,' she looked around the wood. 'And us,' she added, 'and you.'

'That's three pretty big things,' he said. 'Start at the beginning. This place. You mean the manor?'

Alice nodded. 'I love Borne, Robinson. I love the village, the people, and the manor. When Brad left he left me with very few alternatives to packing up and leaving too. I couldn't keep up payments on a place like this, so I made the choice to rent it out rather than lose it. Everything is only just making it, I cross my fingers before I open bills and hope the bank manager doesn't send for me. I feel like I'm trying to hang on to the stars, running in high heels; I go to sleep scared tomorrow will be the day I realise I'm going to lose it all.'

Robinson rubbed her shoulder absently. 'I know how it feels to lose almost everything you love, Alice. I envy you for still loving the place you call home. It's good that you still have that, even if you're having to share it temporarily with a reclusive cowboy.'

She laughed softly. 'I'm glad you're here. When I advertised for someone to rent the manor, I never imagined that someone like you would come.'

'Someone like me?'

'Don't pretend you don't know how much better you've made things for me,' she said, her fingers rubbing back and forth over the collar of his shirt. 'I'm not lonely any more, and I don't spend my time obsessing over what or who I've lost. You're kind of curing me of loving Brad McBride, and for that I'll be forever grateful to the cowboy who came to stay.'

His green eyes glittered in the reflected lights wound over their heads.

'Backatcha, pretty face. I didn't count on you, either.'

'It's all make-believe, though, isn't it?' she said quietly. 'At the end of the summer you'll go home, and I'll still be here, and I have to find a way to stay here afterwards.'

'I guess I hadn't thought so far ahead for you,' he said. 'Will you rent the manor out again?'

Alice sipped her wine and shook her head. 'Pretty as it is, I can't stay in that caravan for ever, Robinson.'

'I see that.'

'So no, I don't think I'll look for someone else to rent the manor after you . . .' It suddenly felt hard to say 'after you leave', so she let the sentence hang in the air. 'That's why I've renovated the tree house.'

He frowned, not seeing the picture, and Alice haltingly told him about her plans for the glampsite. She gathered confidence as she described how the boathouse looked in her dreams, and the stunning location she'd decided on for the yurt down by the stream, and the sheltered glade at the far end of the woods that she planned to turn into a book nook complete with a gauzy day bed and a little library of books she'd been amassing from charity stores and table sales. Five or six different places people could come and stay in the beauty of Borne woods, more eventually. Hopefully. If the stars aligned and she could string things out financially for long enough to get everything in place by the time he left. She was well aware that her plan had its holes, that it was pulled together from hope and stardust and desperation.

'For a girl with such slender shoulders, you sure have a lot resting on them,' he said, when she finally finished speaking and looked at him for his reaction. She didn't know why she'd kept her plans from him. Or she did, but she didn't know how to put her feelings into words. The thing she had with Robinson was . . . it was other, separate, just for them. Letting reality into it was a risk. They worked because of the strict rules they'd applied to their relationship upfront, namely that it wasn't a relationship, or even a friendship, really. It wasn't set up for them to share worries, or plans, or find pathways into each other's heart. They were each other's holding bay, each other's 'get your breath back' safety net. It wasn't supposed to be touched by reality, and by sharing her hopes, dreams and fears she'd blurred all of those lines. And then he went and said things like that. Simple insights that said I see you, I see who you really are, and in moments like those he stole her breath.

'I'm stronger than I look,' she said, and he just nodded and put his head back again.

'There's something else,' she said, unburdening herself even more than she'd planned on. 'Brad wants the manor back. It's only the fact that it's rented out that's holding him off.'

Slowly, Robinson raised his head again and looked her in the eyes.

'Sounds like it might be easier all round if I just went and shot him,' he said, and Alice loved the way he managed to make light of it whilst also offering his protection should she ever need it. She knew that she had it without question for as long as Robinson was in Borne.

'I think I need to be the one who fires the shots,' she said.

His eyes told her that he understood. 'At least let me load the gun and teach you how to handle it,' he said, his hand warm and reassuring on the curve of her neck. 'By the time I leave here you'll be a sure shot.'

'He won't know what has hit him.'

Robinson smiled, kissing her shoulder. 'Atta girl.' He turned her jaw to his with his fingertips, kissing her lips slow and searching.

'Don't worry about biting off more than you can chew, Alice,' he said, as he pulled her on top of him and held her hair back from her face. 'Your mouth is probably a whole lot bigger than you think.'

She smiled against his lips. 'Cowboy wisdom, eh?' she said, really quite distracted by his hand sliding up her thigh.

'There's a whole lot more where that came from.'

There was a whole lot more that Alice needed to say too, but he blew all of those thoughts from her mind like confetti with his hot kisses and cowboy moves. It'd keep for a while. She really ought to test out that bed anyway.

In the early hours of the morning Alice awoke and looked at Robinson sleeping, all tanned skin against white cotton sheets, so very unexpected in her life. It was as if he'd been sent to her just at the time she needed him most, and she hoped she offered him that same sense of shelter in return.

Moonlight bathed the whole tree house in a pale silvery wash, picking out the outlines of the furniture, the gleam of their used glasses, their hastily discarded clothes on the sofa. His guitar still stood where he'd left it when he came in earlier, untouched and unreferenced over the course of the evening. Beside it on the low side table sat her camera. Not her father's beloved Nikon, but her own top-of-the-range kit that she'd left at the manor, until recently, ignored. Brad had seemed oblivious at the time that he'd chosen her a gift she neither wanted, appreciated, nor used. He'd just given her the camera as it was something she didn't already own and because it made for a substantial, showy gift.

Getting to grips with it in recent weeks had, however, been a guilty pleasure for Alice. She intended on cataloguing the glampsite as it developed in order to commission a website when she was a bit closer to being ready, and already she'd bagged some beautiful images of the various stages of the tree house renovation. It was another integral piece of her gossamer-thin spider-web plan to keep hold of the things she loved. Looking at Robinson's guitar for a few long minutes, she pulled her courage together and touched his shoulder to wake him.

CHAPTER SEVENTEEN

'Play for me?'

Robinson opened one eye and found Alice lying on her side in bed beside him, all naked curves and wild blonde curls, the most heaven-sent woodland nymph ever. The words coming from her mouth, however, were nowhere near as heavenly.

'Go to sleep, Goldilocks,' he whispered, reaching for her, hoping to pull her in and make her forget. She resisted, putting her palm flat against his chest, the resolute look in her eyes clear even in the pale, moonlit cabin.

'Please,' she said. 'Play your guitar for me.'

'I can think of plenty of better ways to help you sleep, baby,' he tried again, smoothing his fingers over the rose tip of her breast. It hardened, and her lips parted slightly, but still she held him back.

'Afterwards,' she murmured, and his body was already awake enough and reacting to hers to find her promise encouraging.

'Anything else, Alice. Ask me for anything but that and it's yours.'

'I don't want anything else,' she said. 'Robinson, I watched you walk over from the house earlier with your guitar on your back and you looked . . . I don't know . . . more complete? I know you as a man, not a musician, but even I could see *that* much. I only know half of you, and I'd love to know the other half too, if you'll let me.'

'Alice, I know you think you're helping me here, but you're really not,' he said. 'I'm not hiding half of myself. I'm changing. It's different.'

'Yet you still went to the trouble of bringing your guitar with you when you came over here,' she said. He had to give it to the girl, she was as stubborn as a goddamn ox when she wanted to be.

'Habit. Pure and simple. I've travelled with my guitar since I was fifteen years old,' he countered, even though the decision to bring his guitar to England hadn't been anywhere near that clean cut in reality. He'd left home without it, driven twenty miles out towards the airport, and then turned back around to fetch it, his heart pounding out of his chest. But just because he had it close by didn't mean he necessarily had to play it. It just meant that he had the choice, and right now he was choosing not to.

Alice stroked his fingers. 'I'd love to hear you. I'm not asking you to sing. Just play for me?'

He knew what she was doing. Little by little. Bit by bit. Piece by piece. Crumb by crumb.

'You remember my dad's camera?'

Robinson nodded. He remembered just fine, the way that she'd huffed and puffed that box out of the cellar and refused his offers of help even though it was obvious she could use it.

'I put that camera away when he died, and it's taken me

eight whole years to find the guts to open the box again. I wanted to follow in his footsteps, to be a photographer, to make him proud, and then he died and I shut a huge part of myself away in that box with his camera, you know?' Alice was sitting up now, the sheet tucked under her arms. 'I let his death change me, and define me, even though I knew it would have killed him all over again if he knew.' Alice swept her hair over one shoulder and held one of his hands in both of her own.

'These last few weeks, since I've been taking pictures again . . . they're better, Robinson. *I'm* better. I don't think I'd realised how much I'd lost, and I regret all of that wasted time, all of those photographs I didn't take.'

Thinking on it, he'd barely seen her without her camera slung around her neck when she was out working in the woods lately, and it seemed such a natural extension of her that he hadn't paid attention.

'What I'm trying to say is that stopping doing something you love as a knee-jerk reaction to being hurt doesn't work, Robinson. It just hurts you more in the long run.'

Outside in the woods a solitary owl hooted, and inside the tree house Alice fell silent and looked at him with those big, honest eyes of hers. She was killing him. Robinson's emotions cycled through the instinctive urge to come out fighting from the corner she'd backed him into and the urge to hug her close for sharing something so personal because it reflected his own feelings so closely. He landed up on the overriding emotion that sat in the driving seat of his life most of the time these days. Fear. Being here in England with Alice quietened the roar, but it was always there, and right now it was like she'd kicked the angry lion in his head. He was frightened of how hard and fast his life had spiralled out of control, and she was right. His knee-jerk reaction had been to turn his back on everything that he loved, shut down, press reset, be someone else because being Robinson Duff got too hard.

He pulled himself up in bed and sat against the bedstead, dragging the pillows behind him. Eight years was a hell of a long time not to do something that came as naturally as breathing.

'Pass me my guitar?'

Alice slid out of bed, hyper aware that she was naked but too scared to grab anything to cover herself in case she slowed things down and broke the spell. His guitar was a solid weight in her hands, black patent wood with a dark, heavy leather strap with his name emblazoned down its length in white swirly script. She'd seen it before in the pictures on the net at Niamh's cottage, back when Robinson first arrived in Borne, and she handled it with the reverence it deserved; there were people out there who would maim and kill for the chance to be near it or the man who owned it.

Holding it in both hands, she crossed back to the bed and held it out to him.

'Hold it right there and hand me your camera, Goldilocks. That's one image I never want to forget.'

Alice shook her head. 'Not a chance.'

'Pity,' he murmured, shooting her a small, intimate wink as he took the guitar from her hands. Alice slid back into bed, sitting cross-legged facing him, the quilt pulled safely up under her armpits again. Robinson leaned forward and slung the strap over his shoulder then settled back against the pillows, illuminated by a moonbeam with the guitar against his bare, tanned chest.

'You look so sexy, cowboy.' She said it because he did, incredibly so, but also because she wanted to make this as easy as she could on him. He might look the epitome of relaxed but she knew him well enough to know different. He looked down at the instrument, moving his hands slowly over it in a way that reminded her of how he touched her; intimate, focused, connected.

And then he lifted his eyes to hers, vulnerable and raw, and she had to force her hands to stay in her lap because every instinct in her wanted to take the guitar from him, to say sorry, to pull him back under the covers and make him forget. Had she done the wrong thing by forcing his hand? Should she have waited? Would she have appreciated someone doing the exact same thing for her, or would she have resented the person who made her do something she didn't feel ready to do? And, oh God, was she hastening his departure from her life? What was she anyway, some kind of evangelical Oprah-style life coach, it worked for me and it'll work for you too? She went to reach out and offer to put the guitar back down, and at that precise same moment Robinson's fingers moved over the strings and he started to play the most hauntingly beautiful melody she'd ever heard in her whole entire life.

She wanted to close her eyes but found she couldn't look away from him. His dipped head hid his expression from her, his gaze lowered to his guitar, and out of nowhere she was almost jealous of the communion. He had her rapt, caught up in the music with him, in awe of how the small movements of his fingers over the strings could create something so effortlessly beautiful. His head came up at last, his eyes closed as he played, and it was difficult to discern if his mouth was set in pain or pleasure. She didn't know what he was playing, but even without words it was a love song. Who was he playing for? Where had he gone in his head? His lips parted on a sigh as he played, fragile music to fall in love to. It said words he would never say to her, and his cheeks were damp with tears, yet still he played on, lost. Alice could only watch him, full of wonder, and behind her ribs invisible needles stitched the holes in her heart and made it whole so she could use it again.

When the song came to an end, he opened his eyes, his dark lashes spiked, and slowly, slowly, he came back.

'That was incredible,' she said, her voice hoarse and barely there in the quiet room.

Robinson lowered his head and lifted the strap over his head then turned away from her and placed the guitar carefully against the wall beside the bed. Was he angry? Was he distressed? Was he hurt? Please, don't let me have hurt him more than he was already hurting, she thought, utterly still as she watched his back.

And then he turned around and moved back beneath the covers. 'Come here,' he said, low and gravel-rich, and Alice could only imagine how good he would sound when he sang as well as played. She could see why women all over the world were halfway in love with Robinson Duff. Right at that moment she was too, and she melted against him, his skin on hers.

'It's afterwards,' he said, filling his hands with her hair, and she rolled over on top him and kissed his still-damp eyelids.

'I know,' she said, and then neither of them said anything else for a while. Afterwards, truly afterwards, as she closed her eyes and they tumbled towards sleep, she heard him whisper thank you.

*

The summer rolled on endlessly, another week of warm days banging in nails and making big plans, until the weekend rolled in redolent and welcoming, beckoning for them to come and laze around on deckchairs and drink Pimm's.

'Robinson.' Alice shook him gently by the shoulder to wake him. 'Robinson, wake up.'

He opened one eye and looked at her blearily, then opened them both and squinted at his watch.

'Alice, it's barely seven in the morning and it's Sunday.' His eyes moved down over her white sun top and denim cut-offs and then back up again to her face. 'I vote you get undressed again and come back to bed.'

Shaking her head, Alice flung open the Airstream door to let the sunshine in. 'No can do.' She picked up a mug of coffee and held it out to him. Robinson scrubbed his hands over his hair and sat up, taking the mug from her, still half asleep.

'No?' he said.

Alice perched on the end of the bed, her own coffee cradled in her hands.

'If this is a holiday romance, there's something vital that's missing,' she said.

Robinson frowned, still too asleep to guess.

'The sea,' she said, grinning. 'I want to take you to the seaside, Robinson.'

The idea had formed in her head after a hushed, late-night pillow conversation as they'd drifted off to sleep the night before. He'd said if she listened hard enough she'd be able to hear the sea, his mouth warm on her ear, and even though she couldn't hear it, it'd sowed a seed. She wanted to hear the sea, really hear it, with him.

'The seaside?' he said. 'In Borne?'

Alice rolled her eyes. 'Of course not in Borne,' she said,

finishing the last of her drink. 'We're just about as central as we can be here, but we can make the coast in a couple of hours on a good run.' She glanced at the cool box by the door. 'I packed us a picnic.'

Robinson swallowed a mouthful of coffee. 'Sounds like you've got it all worked out, Goldilocks,' he said. Neither his words nor his expression gave away what he thought of her plan.

'I know you don't want people knowing you're here, but if you put on a cap and sunglasses no one will look twice,' she said, bobbing with suppressed excitement. 'I think we could both do with a break from the manor for a day, don't you? You even more than me. You've barely left the grounds since you arrived.'

'I've never been to the English seaside,' he said, making it sound quaint.

'Strictly speaking, you won't today, either. We're heading for Barmouth, which is Welsh.'

'Welsh, huh? Remind me to grab my passport from the manor,' he said, winking as he leant over to take her empty cup and put both mugs down on the floor. As he lay back he reached out and pulled her down onto the bed on top of him.

'Fancy skinny dipping in the ocean with me, Goldilocks?' he said, sliding his hands up the back of her thighs and inside the edge of her shorts to cup her backside.

Laughter bubbled up in Alice's throat.

'It's the Irish Sea, Robinson, not the Pacific.'

He looked up at her with serious eyes. 'No nakedness at all?'

Alice shook her head, and then giggled as Robinson whipped her top up and off.

'In that case Wales can wait half an hour,' he said, reaching for her bikini ties behind her neck, and Alice decided he was absolutely right.

'Mr. Whippy?' Robinson said doubtfully when Alice handed him an ice-cream cone on the beach a few hours later. 'What is he, an ice-cream seller or a male escort?'

Alice tried to picture the bald pensioner who'd just served her ice cream as a male escort and started to laugh as she flopped down beside him on the towels.

All around them, the beach buzzed with activity; children playing cricket and building sandcastles, teenagers sunbathing and posing, and harassed parents erecting wind breakers to stake out their territory even though there was barely a breeze in the air. The shore line was as busy as a city pavement at Christmas, and the whole beach rang with the happy chatter and shouts of people out to play in the sunshine.

'I came here often as a child,' Alice said, licking her ice cream.

'With your dad?'

She nodded, remembering days spent messing around in rock pools with sandy toes and eating candy floss from the bag on the sleepy car ride home.

'He loved to people watch, always had his camera at the ready just in case the perfect shot appeared.'

'Like father, like daughter,' Robinson said softly, rubbing ice-cream cone crumbs from his fingers before tapping the camera that hung around her neck.

Alice finished her own cone and unsnapped the camera from its case. Holding it to her face, she swept it slowly around the beach, clicking off shots, and then finally turned it towards Robinson, now lying back with his eyes closed and the peak of his cap resting on his nose. He tilted his head when he heard the camera and opened one eye.

'Put it down and relax, pretty face. You're on holiday, remember?'

Alice took a couple more shots and then did as he'd suggested, stretching out and basking in the sunshine. Robinson's fingers played idly with hers between them in the sand.

'Feels good,' he murmured.

'Mmm,' she said, thoroughly relaxed.

She felt him wriggling, and when she looked at him he'd removed his t-shirt and lay back again with the cap once more in place over his eyes. Glancing around, Alice noticed that his beach-beautiful body hadn't gone unnoticed by pretty much any woman in the vicinity, and an undeniable thrill of pride rippled down her spine. He drew attention not because he was famous, but because he was hot as hell, even with his face covered.

'You should probably put your t-shirt back on again, you're attracting attention,' she said, rolling onto her side to face him.

'Too hot. You should probably take yours off,' he said, feeling for her hand again. 'You look sexy in that bikini. They'll all be too busy looking at you to notice me.'

'Just keep your face covered, for God's sake,' she whispered, feeling as if she'd just brought Magic Mike to Barmouth beach. He had a point about her t-shirt though. She was baking, it needed to come off. Besides, bikinis seemed to be the order of the day on the beach anyway, so contrary to what he'd said she felt pretty sure she'd blend in just fine.

Robinson slid his sunglasses back over his eyes and jammed

his cap into place on his head, sitting up to mess in the beach bag for a second then rolling on his side to face her.

'Sun cream,' he said, flipping the lid on the bottle. Alice went to take it from him but he held it out of her grasp. 'Let me.'

A small part of her thought of saying no, you really shouldn't, but the rest of her screamed oh my god, yes, you really should, so she lay still and let him drizzle a blob of white sun cream onto her navel, and then another dot onto each of her shoulders.

'Imagine we're on a deserted island in the Indian Ocean,' he said quietly as he began to massage the cream into her stomach in slow, circular motions. He lingered across the waist band of her shorts, and then flicked the top button open and made her gasp.

'Robinson, don't,' she said, breathing faster.

'I won't,' he said, letting his hand slide up her body again to rub the cream into her shoulders and down the length of her arms. 'But not because I don't want to. If we were on that beach on the Indian Ocean, I'd have you naked in seconds.'

Fond as Alice was of Barmouth beach, she wished with all of her heart that she was thousands of miles away at that moment.

'You're a bad, bad cowboy,' she said under her breath, opening her eyes behind her dark glasses to look up at him. 'Want me to do you now?'

He shook his head. 'Not unless you want me to make good on my promise to have you naked in seconds,' he said.

Alice laughed softly, enjoying the effect she had on him.

'You sure? I'd do a real good job. Why don't you lie back and let me show you?'

Robinson coughed. 'I'd probably get arrested if I lie back in this state on a public beach.'

'Want me to tell you what I'd do if we were on that deserted beach in the Indian Ocean?' she asked, biting her bottom lip. His eyes watched her mouth.

'Behave, Goldilocks,' he muttered eventually, his voice gravel-low as he rolled onto his stomach until he was safe to be out in public again.

Alice laughed again, more carefree than she could remember being for a long, long time.

Between them in the sand she drew their initials inside a love heart, like a teenage girl doodling in the back of her exercise book.

Robinson watched her, his eyes on her handiwork. After a pause he wrote 'I want you,' beneath the heart.

Alice kissed his shoulder. 'I want you too,' she said, loving the sun-baked heat of his skin and the smell of sun cream on their bodies.

'Just you wait until I get you home,' he said.

Alice rested her chin on his shoulder and looked out to sea, trying not to concentrate on the way her heart contracted when he said home.

Back in the Airstream a little after midnight, Alice closed her eyes and listened to Robinson breathing steady against her ear as he spooned himself around her. It really had been the most spectacular day in every way, from the unbroken blue skies to the sand in their toes and how he'd made good on his promise to get her naked in seconds as soon as they were alone. An owl hooted somewhere in the trees outside in Borne woods, but as Alice drifted towards sleep she heard seagulls, and the Airstream wasn't

her makeshift home, it was their romantic holiday hide-
away.

Alice watched with quiet satisfaction a couple of weeks later
as the yurt took shape before her eyes beside the stream.
Purchased second-hand from a Welsh campsite on eBay,
she'd been lucky enough to drop on sellers who'd been
happy to come and show her how to erect it properly in
exchange for lunch and the petrol money to bring it over.
She'd warmed to the ever-so-slightly bonkers pair of brothers
the moment they'd tumbled out of their transit and hauled
the yurt down towards the site.

'He's Barry Jones,' one said, jerking his thumb.

'And he's Brynn Jones,' the other said, nodding towards
his brother.

'He likes cheese with his onion,' Barry said.

'And he likes onion with his cheese,' Brynn said, with a
grin. They were remarkably similar, both thickset with a mop
of dark hair and merry eyes.

'Cheese and onion for lunch, then?' Alice said, leading
the way to the stream, excited to see the yurt in place.

If they'd seemed comical when they arrived, the way they
worked was anything but haphazard. They had the yurt up
and looking brilliant with breathtaking speed, as if there
were ten rather than two of them. Alice tramped down to
the site around midday with a plate heaving with sandwiches
and found them three-parts done already.

'Wow!' she laughed, putting the plate down on a tree
stump and clapping her hands with delight. 'This looks
amazing!'

Brynn gave her the thumbs up as Barry helped himself to
a sandwich. He looked at it and then passed it to his brother.

'This one's yours. There's onion on it.'

Brynn nodded and handed Barry a different one from the plate without a flicker of amusement.

Alice liked them so much she wondered if they'd stay for ever.

Brynn lay back and basked in the sunshine after he'd eaten, his hands behind his head.

'Best summer I can remember in my lifetime,' he said, smiling broadly.

'Probably the best in mine too,' Barry said, striking an identical pose beside his brother.

Alice considered stretching out beside them because it was probably the best in hers as well, then turned as someone called her name out sharply across the garden. Hazel half stumbled half ran across the grass, a jumble of long skirts and clanking bangles as she reached them. She stood with her hands on her hips, gasping heavily to get her breath back.

'Alice, have you seen him?'

Alice shifted the plate of sandwiches hastily from the tree stump and guided Hazel down to sit on it.

'Seen who, Hazel? Is Ewan missing?'

Brynn and Barry sat up and leaned back on their elbows, interested, as Hazel shook her head, her hands twisting in her lap.

'Rambo. I haven't seen him since last night. One minute he was on the windowsill shouting at the people queuing for the bus, the next he'd gone.' She sighed, her hand flat against her still-heaving chest. 'I didn't panic at first, you know what he's like. He does this sometimes, but he doesn't like the dark, Alice. He's been out all night!' Hazel's voice skittered up an octave at the end of her sentence and Alice put a comforting arm around her shoulders.

'Oh Hazel, I'm sure he'll come home soon,' she soothed, although privately she wasn't so certain. The village was alive with foxes and wildlife at night. Rambo was a domesticated old boy, he wouldn't stand a chance against the wily ways of the natural creatures of the countryside.

'Have you checked up at the manor?' she asked.

Hazel nodded miserably. 'First place I thought of. Hoped he'd gone back there like last time.'

Brynn and Barry polished off the plate of sandwiches and watched the exchange in fascinated silence. It had been a while since they'd come across folk odder than themselves.

A mile or so away at the village post office, Davina stared wide eyed at the big glossy black bird that had swooped in through the open door and landed on her counter. She wasn't a fan of birds in most cases, and especially not of this one in particular. Rambo shouted at her every time she walked past the cottages down by the manor, preening himself like a peacock on the open windowsill. 'Put yer clothes on, hussy!' seemed to be his favourite insult for her, and she hadn't failed to notice the way people queuing at the bus stop opposite nodded in agreement when he yelled it. Just because she favoured skirts that skimmed her knickers, it wasn't for this bird or anyone else in the village to judge her. She knew enough to know that Rambo was only repeating what he'd heard. She reached for the broom to shoo him out, and he fixed her with his black bead eyes and squawked.

'Don't you start on me in my own shop, bully bird,' she said, lifting the brush and waving the bristles gamely towards him.

'Everyone can see her bosoms!' Rambo cackled, and

Davina glanced down her low-cut blouse at her favourite red bra.

'And lucky buggers they are too,' she shot back, not pausing to question the fact that she was having an argument with a bird. 'Be off with you!'

Rambo didn't budge an inch, utterly indifferent to Davina's threats.

'Don't tell a soul that he's here, Ewan Spencer!' Rambo mimicked Hazel's voice perfectly, then picked up a book of first-class stamps and hurled it across the room.

Davina paused, conflicted. She wanted the bird off her counter and out of her post office, but then . . .

'Mum fancies Robinson Duff! Mum fancies Robinson Duff!'

Davina narrowed her eyes at Rambo, who'd switched from impersonating Hazel to her weirdo goth kid who came in every now and then to try to buy booze.

'Robinson Duff?' Davina breathed. Hazel wasn't the only one with a crush on the country music star. Half the women in the world loved Robinson Duff, Davina included. That was why Rambo's next sentence, a perfect impression of Alice McBride, made her head spin and her red fingernails dig into her palms with excitement.

'Get me naked, Robinson.'

CHAPTER EIGHTEEN

Stewie leaned on the bar in The Siren, resplendent in a billowing Indian kaftan chosen to combat the July heat wave.

'Not wearing a jot underneath it, chaps,' he said, winking archly at Jase. 'Swinging low and free as a whistle under here. Quite liberating, actually.'

'Behave, Stewie, I've just been a bit sick in my mouth,' Dessy said, fake heaving. 'Wet wipe that stool when he leaves, Jase.'

Stewie ran his hand down the thick black ponytail that he hoped lent him the air of an exotic tribal chief.

'Wanted to talk to you two. I think our Robster needs a night out.'

Jase glanced quickly around the bar and shot Stewie daggers.

'I didn't say his actual name, did I?' Stewie said, unabashed. 'He's barely left the manor since he arrived here. It's been weeks, and a man has . . . needs.' He looked down at his apparently unfettered nether regions tellingly and then up at Dessy and Jase again.

'Are you suggesting that we take he who must not be named out to get laid, Stew-pot?' Dessy said, pouring himself a large gin and tonic stacked with ice.

'I'm fairly sure that the clubs we go to aren't really his scene, and your Thursday bridge club ain't gonna cut it either, Stewie darling,' Jase laughed, wiping wine glasses dry with the cloth draped over his muscular shoulder and hanging them up.

'You say bridge, I say . . .' Stewie started, and Jase held his hand up.

'Des, pass me that sick bucket. It's my turn. I'll never look at Agnes Turner and her American-tan support tights the same way again.'

'That woman certainly knows a few unexpected moves,' Stewie acknowledged, miles away, leaving both Jase and Dessy fervently hoping he was referring to Aggie's card skills. The village stalwart only ever came in to the pub to attend church committee meetings and even then had just one schooner of sherry at the vicar's insistence and left two thirds of it untouched.

'I bet Davina would be more than willing to visit him on a mercy mission,' Dessy suggested cattily.

'I don't think so, Desmond,' Stewie sniffed. 'That woman has had more men than I've had wigs.'

'You're a fine one to talk,' Jase said, stating the obvious.

'Well, if not a night out then a boys' night in,' Stewie said, changing tack as Dessy replenished his scotch. He laid a hand over the glass and scowled when offered ice.

'Boys?' Jase said. 'One, two,' he counted, pointing at himself and then Dessy. 'And you, three?' he added, looking at Stewie with an expression that conveyed he was anything but a boy. 'So four, including the guest of honour? It's hardly a party, is it?'

Dessy, however, laid a hand on Jase's solid forearm. 'Sshh. Let's not be so hasty, lover,' he murmured, because the chance to get inside the manor for an evening with their secret superstar wasn't to be dismissed lightly. 'I'm sure we could schedule something in.'

'Top banana,' Stewie said, drinking the whisky in one shot and sliding down onto his flip-flop-clad feet. 'I'll bring curry. Make it myself from goat testicles. Out of this world.'

'We'll bring the beer,' Jase said doubtfully, reaching for the wet wipes as Dessy shot towards the loos, not even needing to fake his heaves this time.

Alice, Niamh and Hazel stood inside the yurt and admired their handiwork at length. They'd spent the last few days giving the roomy interior a fantasy makeover, aiming for the feel of a spicy Moroccan bazaar and knocking it right out of the ballpark. The space flowed centrally from the huge, ornately carved bed in a celebration of jewel-coloured soft furnishings and sumptuous sheepskin rugs, with huge floor cushions that invited you to loll on them and read a book, and a low red velvet couch perfect for snoozing. When night fell the clear central dome over the bed was strategically positioned to stargaze.

'I'm glad you suggested siting the yurt here,' Alice said, and Hazel preened with pride.

'It's a honeymooners' delight,' she said in a faraway voice. 'Many new spirits will be made here, Alice.'

Niamh raised her eyebrows at Hazel. 'You mean babies, right? Because that bed has baby maker written all over it and I'm not sure it's anything to do with the spirits, unless you mean gin and tonic.'

Hazel looked at the grand wooden bed fondly and shook

her dark curls. 'Mother nature is a powerful woman, Niamh. She's here in this space. You mark my words.'

Alice caught Niamh's eye over Hazel's bowed head. 'Drink?' she mouthed.

Niamh nodded.

'Time for a glass of wine, Hazel?' Alice asked, having waited politely for her neighbour to open her eyes and cease communing with the spirits. Hazel shook her head.

'Better not. Need to get back and keep an eye on that ruddy bird. Bloody Scarlet Pimpernel he is at the moment. Turned up at the post office of all places last week.'

'At least he came home in the end,' Alice said, smoothing Hazel's feathers as they left the yurt and headed through the woods towards the Airstream.

'He didn't. Davina locked him in the post office and came down the high street shrieking at me to fetch him.' Hazel rolled her eyes. 'By the time I got to him he was alarmed and had pecked a hole in Davina's poster of George Clooney in the buff.' She leaned in and spoke behind her hand for effect. 'I won't tell you which bit of George was missing, but let's just say that Davina was furious.'

Parting shot delivered, Hazel wandered away towards the manor, an ethereal vision of strappy tie-dye and long, knotted strings of jangling beads. The women of Borne had each tailored their individual looks to accommodate the continuing heat wave; Niamh rocked a white denim mini and scarlet Minnie Mouse t-shirt, while Alice stuck with her beloved denim, this time in the form of dungaree shorts layered over a white vest.

Alice dipped inside the caravan, deposited her ever present camera and opened a bottle of white, knowing it wasn't anywhere near enough reward for Niamh for all of her help with the glampsite, and knowing also that Niamh was a true enough friend not to want any reward at all. Between the yurt, the tree house and the Airstream they'd amassed three super pretty places for people to stay, and now that the compost loos and a matching rustic shower block had been installed she was getting close to the point where she could think about renting out at least some of the accommodation. There was more to come too; she cherished the hope of a romantic renovation of the boathouse, and she had one eye constantly on the net looking out for other quirky abodes to add to her collection. She couldn't quite believe it was all actually happening, but it was, thanks largely to the support and love of her weird and wonderful crew of neighbours and friends.

'So how are things going with the naked cowboy?'

Alice settled into the deckchair beside Niamh, kicking off her Converse and stretching out her bare legs to catch the glorious warmth of the summer sunshine. As English summers went, this one was shaping up to be a record breaker; the weather forecaster had practically swooned over the high pressure charts on breakfast TV that morning and the shops were stockpiling factor 50 sun cream. The newspapers were happily forecasting hosepipe bans and offering water-saving tips, and people old enough to remember the summer of '76 were reminiscing wildly about bouts of sunstroke caused by drunken space-hopper races.

'He's...' Alice closed her eyes, the smallest of smiles on her face as she considered how to answer Niamh's question. She and Robinson had the strangest of arrangements, really, doing their own thing sometimes, dropping in and out of each other's lives and beds, although never in the room she'd shared with Brad.

'We're just enjoying each other's company,' she said in the end, even though it was a poor summary. 'No pressures, just . . .'

'Pleasures?' Niamh supplied, arching her brows and then slumping back in her chair with a dramatic sigh. 'Some girls get all the luck.'

'It's only a holiday romance, Niamh. He's got a life to go home to, and I've got a home to claim back.' Alice looked over towards the manor wistfully.

'Even better, I say. Great sex with no strings attached.' Niamh slugged her wine. 'They played one of his songs on the radio this morning. If the man shags as sexily as he sings you must be having the time of your bloody life, Alice.'

Alice laughed into her wine glass, not willing or ready to share the juicy details of quite how eye-wateringly good Robinson Duff was in bed.

'Shut up and enjoy the sunshine,' she said instead, laughing as she put her glass down on the grass to braid her hair around her head.

Movement over by the manor caught her eye, and Niamh's too judging by the way she sat up and lifted her sunglasses to squint in the direction of the house.

'What's going on over there?'

Alice shielded her eyes from the sun and leaned forward in her chair.

'I have absolutely no idea,' she said slowly. 'Is that Stewie?'

It was always difficult to know for certain from a distance with Stewie, because one day he might be Elvis and the next he was more Boris Johnson.

'Think so. Well, it's either Stewie or Donald Trump,' Niamh giggled, wine-silly. 'Maybe he's helicoptered in to persuade Robinson to join his election campaign.'

186

'And is that Dessy and Jase with him?'

Niamh nodded. 'Who else would risk hot pants like that in Borne?'

Alice slouched back in her chair, perplexed. 'How very odd.'

'He's not expecting them?'

'Don't think so.' Alice picked up her wine. 'Was Dessy carrying pizza boxes?'

'And beer,' Niamh confirmed, sliding her glasses into her hair and turning her face up to the sunshine.

Alice reached for the wine bottle and topped up their glasses. Funny, Robinson hadn't mentioned anything about expecting visitors. She shrugged the thought away, along with the tingle of disappointment that glittered down her spine at the realisation that her plans to give him the grand tour of the yurt might need to go on ice for the evening.

'Robster!'

Robinson looked up in surprise at the voice outside the kitchen door, his knife poised over some nameless ready meal he planned to bang in the microwave for his dinner. He knew before he even opened the door that Stewie would be on the other side of it. No one else in his life had ever called him Robster, and no one else would get away with it in the future. Would it be wrong to hide underneath the kitchen table until Stewie gave up and went away?

'Come on, Robbie, don't keep an old man waiting on the doorstep!'

Robinson sighed as his southern manners won out, sending him across the room to open the door for his unexpected visitor. Except when he opened the door he found not just one visitor but three, two of whom he didn't recognise. Instantly on his guard, Robinson gripped the handle of the knife he hadn't thought to put down.

'Steady on there, Robster,' Stewie said, alarmed, his eyes on the blade. 'We come in peace!'

'With dinner,' one of the guys behind Stewie piped up with a disarming grin. What was going on? Robinson placed the knife down on the countertop and frowned lightly.

'What is this?' he asked, looking between the three guys at the pizza and beer, not to mention the glass dish covered in foil in Stewie's hands.

'Boys' night in,' Stewie supplied. 'Stand aside, lad, this dish is taking the skin off my hands.'

All three men trooped into the kitchen and placed their spoils down on the table as Robinson closed the door.

'Robster, meet Dessy and Jase, my dear, queer friends, fine landlords of The Siren on the Rocks and proud members of the BS.'

Robinson was pretty sure that was a completely politically incorrect thing to say, but the two guys obviously took no offence as they shouldered each other out of the way to be first to shake hands with him.

'Dessy,' the guy closest to him said, winning the battle and pumping Robinson's hand enthusiastically. He looked as if he was going to say more and then closed his mouth again and just kept on silently shaking hands.

'Jase,' his friend cut in, clearing his throat and rolling his eyes towards Dessy. 'You'll have to excuse Des. He's been playing your music all day and worked himself up into a state this afternoon in case he barfs all over you when he sees you in person.'

'I so have not,' Dessy hissed. 'I brought you pizza,' he said, turning back to Robinson. 'There's Hawaiian if you like it fruity, margarita in case you're more of a plain Jane lover, and of course a good old meat feast in case you prefer it, err, nice and meaty,' he said, almost squeaking by the end of his sentence in a way that had Jase laughing into his muscled shoulder.

'You'll have to excuse my husband's fan-girling. He really doesn't mean to ask you for sex by pizza toppings, he's just nervous.'

'And anyway, who needs pizza!' Stewie said, peeling back the foil on the glass dish he'd been carrying to reveal a gloopy brown curry.

Jase cracked the slab of beer and handed Robinson a can. 'Trust me. You're going to need this,' he said, 'for that.' He gestured towards Stewie's dish.

'Nut curry,' Dessy said.

Robinson baulked. 'You know, I'm really not so much of a vegetarian kind of guy.' The garlic waft from the curry hit the back of his throat and took his breath.

'Course you're not, Robster,' Stewie thundered, slapping him hard on the shoulder. 'I wouldn't insult a cowboy with vegetables. This here curry isn't squirrel nuts. It's goat. Goat balls. Testicles. Melts in your mouth. Tender as scrambled eggs and rammed full of testosterone and protein, guaranteed to put hairs on your chest.'

Dessy looked physically pained as he peeped down the front of his neon green vest. 'I paid a fortune last week to have this baby waxed, I'm smooth as a peach all over. Keep that bowl of balls to yourself, thank you very much, Stewart, I'll stick to the salami.' He patted the pizza box affectionately.

'You boys today don't know what's good for you,' Stewie said. 'Grab some plates would you, Rob?'

Jase caught Robinson's eye, a moment of understanding

and humour, and Robinson relaxed and gave up. The beer was cold, the sun was out and Dessy and Jase seemed decent enough guys. He hadn't realised it until now, but he missed the simple act of having a beer with the boys. He didn't let himself dwell on the fact that most of his beers back home had been shared with the guy he'd found banging his wife in his kitchen. Some lessons were just harder learned than others.

Over at the Airstream, Alice and Niamh shared a huge prawn and avocado salad and the rest of the bottle of wine, lazing in the balmy evening sun and speculating over what was happening in the manor.

'Pizza and beer. Man stuff going down,' Niamh said, eyes closed and deckchair cranked back almost horizontal.

'You reckon?' Alice lay alongside her, stuffed full of dinner and sleepily relaxed by the pinot grigio.

'Wig trying on sesh?' Niamh said, giggling and then hiccupping. 'Imagine Jase might look pretty good in that Rod Stewart thing Stewie had on the other day.'

'You think?' Alice said, wondering if Robinson could carry off the ginger eighties mullet Stewie sometimes sported around the village. 'Should we go over there and see if Robinson needs rescuing?'

'He's a big boy, Alice. Leave him to look after himself. Just make sure you remember all of the juicy gossip afterwards, I'm dying to hear all about it in the morning.'

Robinson squinted at his watch. It was just after ten, the sun had gone down, and he was as drunk as he could remember being in years. They'd ploughed through the beer and pizza then moved on to a now almost empty bottle of bourbon produced from nowhere by Jase an hour or two back. Robinson had tactfully suggested they keep the curry back for a late-night snack, and then covered it over with the fervent hope that he'd never have to see it again.

They were crashed out on the sofas in the lounge, and one of Stewie's Hawaiian shirt buttons had pinged off to let his furry, orange-tanned belly spill out. Dessy gesticulated in his general direction with his whisky glass.

'Did any actual hamsters die in the production of that wig, Stewie?'

Stewie groped for his head, missed it the first time and then swiped the wig off and peered at it.

'I can't be one hundred per cent certain, Desmond, but I seem to recall that this one is Himalayan yak.'

Dessy, Jase and Robinson all stared at Stewie.

'Do you know, Stewie, I think that's the first time I've ever seen you without a wig on, and you have the most delightful head,' Jase slurred, blinking. 'It's like a freshly boiled egg.'

'Can I touch it?' Dessy said, leaning over and giving Stewie's head an approving buff. 'You should dare to go bare more often, it looks good on you.'

'Alice looks so damn good bare,' Robinson said to no one in particular from the recesses of the armchair.

All eyes swung from Stewie to Robinson.

'O.M.G.!' Dessy said, clapping his hands in delight. 'Have you been getting down and dirty with the lady of the house?'

Robinson realised too late the words hadn't just stayed in his head as he'd thought.

Stewie clutched his wig in both hands, misty eyed. 'Marvellous news, marvellous news, mon cherries! Just between us boys, our Alice is a dead ringer for one of my favourite co-stars from back in the day. Went like a bloody racehorse, she did, all hair and teeth and sexy rump. Fine filly. Wasn't averse to a good flogging, either, if I remember rightly.'

Jase took Stewie's wig and tried it on for size. 'So, just so we're clear as crystal chandeliers . . . you and Alice are . . .' He screwed up his nose in distaste and made a lewd poking gesture with his hands.

Robinson frowned. 'I don't think I actually said that, did I?'

Dessy sidled up to Jase and stroked his hair. 'God, that suits you, sexy boy, you look like Marilyn Monroe,' he purred. 'Give us a go.' He moved the wig from Jase's head to his own and blew Robinson a kiss. 'Err, sailor? You so did say that you were boffing our chatelaine.'

Robinson scratched his head, confused. 'All I said was that she looked good bare.'

'That's right, good boy,' Jase laughed. 'And unless you've taken to perving through caravan windows, that means you've taken her clothes off.'

Robinson closed his eyes, wishing Alice was there right now so he could take her clothes off.

Dessy stood up, unsteady on his feet, and picked up Robinson's guitar.

'I'm gonna play you a song,' he said, his feet planted wide apart.

Jase jumped up and took the guitar from Dessy's uncertain fingers. 'You know how much this thing must be worth?' he said, passing it carefully to Robinson.

'Firewood,' Robinson croaked, holding his old familiar friend more like gold than kindling nonetheless.

'Know any Elvis, Robster?' Stewie said. 'I'm sure I met him once.'

'Where, down the chip shop?' Dessy said, smirking.

Robinson had lost the thread of the conversation, because he had his guitar in his hands and his defences were down and someone had mentioned Elvis.

His fingers moved unaided by his brain, striking up the opening notes of 'Jailhouse Rock', and he didn't even think about whether or not to sing, the words just fell out of his mouth unbidden. He was singing, and everyone was clapping and drunk singing with him, and then he was on his feet, and somehow he was wearing Stewie's wig, and that was precisely, exactly how he looked when he stumbled, laughing, to answer the front door when Alice who looked good naked knocked five minutes later.

Except it wasn't Alice.

CHAPTER NINETEEN

'Marsh?'

Robinson squinted through his bourbon-soaked haze at the familiar outline of his manager in the doorway of the manor.

Donald Marshall dropped his fat cigar in shock and ground it into the front step of the manor underneath his boot. 'Sweet baby Jesus and his beautiful virgin mother Mary, this situation is even worse than I thought.'

Behind him, Robinson could feel Dessy, Jase and Stewie gathering, horribly like he'd assembled the worst backing singers ever.

'Marsh,' Robinson said again, rendered stupid by booze and shock, trying to work out how his tiny but mighty manager who never left Nashville had landed here slap bang in the middle of his English fairytale.

Dessy leaned forward. 'I think he's another cowboy,' he whispered in Robinson's ear. Given that Marsh wore double denim beneath his blazer, a huge Stetson and three-inch Cuban-heeled cowboy boots, it wasn't much of a stretch.

Throw in the fact that he had skin the colour and consistency of a walnut and a belt buckle that could be seen from Mars and it was fairly safe to assume this man would be able to lasso a stray horse with his eyes closed.

Stewie, reading the mood more accurately, reached up from behind and slowly slid his wig from Robinson's head and placed it back on his own.

'Are you going to invite me in, or just stand there in the doorway until someone takes your picture and the whole wide world knows you've checked into crazyville with a capital C, son?'

Jase looked at Dessy, deeply offended. 'Capital C? He took that too far,' he muttered.

Dessy nodded. 'Fucking liberty.'

Robinson scrubbed his hands through his flattened hair and knew he needed to try to get a hold of himself and the situation. Marsh was here. That changed things. He stepped backwards, forcing the three men behind him to move flat against the wall so that Marsh could come inside. The smaller man stalked in, his heels banging on the flagstones floor.

Stewie recovered himself as Robinson closed the door, stepping forward and extending his hand.

'Good evening,' he said formally, with the smallest of bows. 'Stewie Heaven, film star.'

Marsh shook the offered hand briefly and then withdrew anti-bacterial spray from his inside pocket and spritzed his palm.

'Rude,' Jase said under his breath, catching hold of Dessy's hand when he went to extend it and pulling it back down again.

'What in the name of all that is good and holy is this

place? A low-rent remake of *One Flew Over the Fuckin' Cuckoo's Nest*?' Marsh said, glaring around at all four men. 'Who's in charge around here?'

'Here's Stewie!' Stewie tried jazz hands and a wide grin.

Jase lifted the side of Stewie's wig and hissed, 'Wrong movie,' in his ear.

'Fuckin' cuckoo. He made a rhyme,' Dessy tittered, then looked across at Marsh and attempted to sound sober and hospitable. 'Goat-testicle curry?'

Robinson opened the front door again.

'I think we better call this party done for the evening, guys,' he said, looking warmly at his three new best friends.

No one moved.

'You heard the man,' Marsh clapped his hands like he was refereeing a classroom of rowdy teenagers. 'Go back to your hen houses, out houses and shit houses, strange people. This man has a plane to pack for.'

'Are you leaving on a jet plane?' Dessy sang mournfully to Robinson, wide eyed and out of tune.

'The hell I am,' Robinson said, more forcefully than he expected.

'God. Say that again, I think I just orgasmed,' Jase said, stroking Robinson's cheek slowly as he passed.

Stewie turned back around on the doorstep and looked at Marsh.

'Don't suppose you happened to know John Wayne, old boy?' he said thoughtfully. 'Met him once, hung like an absolute . . .'

His next words were mercifully carried away on the breeze as Dessy and Jase lunged forward and lifted him clean off the floor by the elbows, then ambled off down the gravel driveway with Stewie floating between them, regaling them with ribald stories about Dallas and Debbie and a rather unfortunate donkey.

Marsh clicked his fingers loudly right by Robinson's ear, making him flinch and his eyes flicker open.

'Coffee, or as near as I could muster in that antique museum that passes for a kitchen.'

Robinson lifted his head from the kitchen table at the strong smell underneath his nose. He didn't want coffee. He wanted Alice, and he wanted to go to bed, preferably in that order. He'd been asleep no more than fifteen minutes yet he'd already managed to wipe all recollection of Marsh's arrival at the manor from his brain, so it came as a fresh shock to find his manager slap bang in the middle of his holiday from reality, and an unwelcome shock at that.

Blah blah 'tickets'. Blah blah 'concert'. Blah blah 'quit belly achin''. Blah blah 'home'. Blah blah 'plane'. Blah blah 'tomorrow'. Even given the fact that he wasn't really registering Marsh's conversation, enough words filtered through into Robinson's consciousness to provoke a reaction neither of them expected.

Hot coffee sprayed across the kitchen as he flung out his arm and smacked the mug clean off the work surface.

'I don't need coffee,' he said, getting to his feet. 'There will be no concerts, or planes, or . . .' Robinson paused and made yap yap hand gestures in the air, 'or any more of that talk in my kitchen. Am I making myself perfectly clear, Marsh?'

'Frankly, no. You're making absolutely zilch in the way of sense and haven't been for two months or longer, Robinson,' Marsh shot back, sweeping his silvery grey hair back over his head. 'Why do you think Mohammed has been forced to come to the mountain? Let me clue you in here, sunshine; it sure ain't to eat testicles and play nurse-maid! You are a man with responsibilities, and you're just gonna have to cowboy up. First thing tomorrow you're on a bird back to Nashville, an' that's that.'

Robinson watched his manager make his speech and wondered if he was going to have a seizure. He was certainly mad enough.

'Marsh, you know I respect you more than pretty much anyone else in this world, and the fact that you've come here means something to me,' he said, enunciating as clearly as he could. 'Now, as you may or may not have noticed, I'm kind of soaked, and I'm real tired, and hell will freeze over before I get on a plane tomorrow. So here's what's gonna happen. I'm going to bed. You can stay here. Pick a room, any room, there's hundreds of the things, and I'll see you later when my brain doesn't hurt.' He yanked the kitchen door open. 'G'night, Marsh. Sleep tight.'

Marsh followed him to the door and watched him weave his way across the grass.

'Robinson,' he called sharply. 'Where in God's name are you going?'

'See my girl,' Robinson called back through the darkness, still walking, thoughts of Alice making him happy.

'What is she, a goddamn sheep?' Marsh yelled. 'You better make some serious sense come daylight, Robinson Duff, or I'll be ripping up your contracts and wiping my bony white ass on them!'

Robinson laughed as Marsh's insults rattled through the air, and seconds later he heard the door bang closed as his manager gave up on him for the night.

*

Alice woke up as the door of the Airstream opened and Robinson filled the doorway.

'You okay?' she said, because he didn't look it. He looked three sheets to the wind and mildly manic as he veered inside and banged the door shut again behind him hard enough to rock the caravan.

'S'not good, Goldilocks,' he murmured, shucking out of his clothes and leaving them in a heap in the middle of the floor.

'What's not?' she said softly, smiling as he lifted the bottom of the quilt and crawled underneath it. He surfaced near her pillow, close enough for her to taste the whisky on his breath when he spoke again.

'He thinks I'm leaving on a jet plane,' Robinson said, all of his words running into one as he rested his head on her shoulder.

'Who does?' Alice stroked his cheek as he snaked his arm across her waist and pulled her against him.

'You're not wearing any clothes,' he said, groggy, already half asleep.

'No,' she said, pressing her lips to his forehead. 'I'm not. Go to sleep, Robinson.'

Alice couldn't be certain, but as she wrapped her arms around him and closed her eyes, it sounded very much as if Robinson muttered something along the lines of 'Stayin' right here with my sheep.'

Alice rose a little after six the next morning and put the kettle on, finding Robinson a far less enjoyable bedfellow than usual. If the state he'd been in last night and the way he was fidgeting and grumbling in his sleep was anything to go on, he was going to need more than a cup of coffee and a smile to get him going when he finally surfaced.

Jeez, it was warm already. Gorgeous as these endless summer days were, the Airstream had a tendency to become sauna-like in the sunshine. Cranking open the skylight and a couple of windows to get some air circulating, Alice curled up on the banquette at the opposite end of the Airstream and slid the SD card from her camera into the slot of her laptop. She sipped her coffee, soaking up the peace as she enjoyed the anticipation of seeing the latest batch of photographs she'd taken in the last day or two around the site.

Bright, jewelled images of the yurt popped up one by one, flashes of turquoise, hot pink and gold as they downloaded. Pictures of Niamh screwing the bed together, and of Hazel positioning the batik wall hanging, plus lots and lots of images of Robinson. Shots of him cooking bacon at the Aga, and of him sunbathing with his shirt off outside the Airstream, of him sleeping in front of a romantic movie she'd chosen because she'd won the toss, and of him taking a bath with his Stetson on because she'd insisted she wanted to see him like that. Looking at the shot, she was glad she had, and her brain raced with editing options to make the image even more eye popping, if that was possible. Robinson really was a photographer's dream, all sweeping dark lashes and glittering green eyes, not to mention that sinful, 'oh my god it hurts my eyes to look at you' body. If this was to be a holiday romance, then Alice was going to take enough pictures of him to last the lifetime after they'd said their tearful goodbyes at the airport, never to see each other again.

She closed her laptop with a sigh and reached for her mug again, curling her hands around it as she leaned back and looked at Robinson, still deeply asleep. Life was odd, really. When Brad left, she'd never have imagined that she could ever feel whole or happy again, yet distilling her life down to this twenty-one-foot space had actually expanded it in so many other ways so that in an abstract way she now had more space than ever. And it wasn't just Robinson, although of course he'd played a major part in it. It was Alice herself. She felt older, and wiser, as if she'd grown so much on the inside that it was a wonder she hadn't gone up a dress size on the outside. Since moving to Borne she'd got to know so many new and brilliant people, but the person she'd learned more about than anyone else was herself. She was becoming her own close friend and trusted confidante, which was a strange but kind of brilliant and comforting thought.

As moments went, this quiet, warm one with just the birdsong and her reflective thoughts felt altogether lovely, which made it all the more shocking when ear-splittingly loud music suddenly blasted out across the still morning from the direction of the mansion.

She bolted to the Airstream door and threw it open.

If Robinson was here in bed, who the heck was in her house?

CHAPTER TWENTY

'Hello? Dessy?' Alice called out, banging on the back kitchen door and then turning the handle and letting herself in. Robinson must have left his own party early last night; she fully expected to find Dessy, Jase and Stewie still going strong in the lounge. Please don't let them have trashed the place, she thought, and found herself alone in the kitchen, a congealed bowl of something dark brown and revolting half covered in silver foil left uneaten on the table.

If she'd thought the music sounded loud from the Airstream, it was nothing to the decibel level in the mansion. If it had been anything other than Robinson's voice blaring around the house Alice would have found it unbearable, but as it was she found it plain unsettling. Hearing his voice – so accomplished and confident and vibrant – was a window into the world he really belonged in, the world he'd ultimately go home to. It irritated her that Dessy would be so insensitive as to play Robinson's music so loudly when the whole point to him being here was to have space to breathe and re-evaluate.

Alice screwed up her nose as she lifted the foil on the

suspicious-looking bowl of brownness, then looked up as movement in the hallway caught her attention.

It wasn't Dessy, or Jase, or Stewie. To give him his dues, the small man in the doorway looked as scandalised to find a blonde woman in her dressing gown in the kitchen as Alice looked to find a compact little man with skin tanned the colour of tree bark, naked aside from a pair of glowing white budgie smugglers that left little to the imagination, in front of her.

'Who are you?' he bristled, shouting over the music.

Alice did a mental double take, both at the audacity of his question and the fact that in those three short words she'd learned that he probably wasn't a stranger to Robinson. That accent was pure country, a perfect match for the music still rattling the windows. 'I was just about to ask you the same question,' she said loudly, wrapping her dressing gown around her body and belting it securely. 'Do you think you could turn the music down?'

He looked as if he might say no, and then swung around and strutted off, the cheeks of his backside jumping aggressively in his tight pants. He managed to look indignant, even from the back. Alice pulled out a chair and sat down then breathed out a sigh of relief when the music stopped abruptly, and then another one when the guy returned to the kitchen fully clothed.

'I'm Alice McBride,' she said, when he looked at her in speculative silence. 'I own this house. Robinson rents it from me.'

He absorbed the information, eyeing her shrewdly. 'I'm Donald Marshall. Marsh. Robinson's manager.'

They regarded each other across the table, weighing up each other's status to see who'd come out on top.

'Would it be rude to ask you what you're doing in my house?' she said, going for the direct approach because she sensed that this wasn't a man who cared to beat around the bush. He looked her up and down, making her wish she had something more suitable on than her nightclothes because he was clearly drawing his own unsettling conclusions.

'Oh crap,' Marsh said, looking in physical pain. 'Do not, I repeat, do NOT tell me that you and he are hitting the sheets.' He smacked his palm hard against his lined forehead. 'Oh, now that has *really* soured my milk.'

Definitely not a man to beat around the bush, then. Alice wasn't certain how to respond, or what Robinson would prefer his manager not to know. Besides, he was just plain rude.

'There's coffee in the cupboard above the machine,' she said shortly, standing up. 'I'm sure Robinson will be over in a while.'

'You do know he has a wife, don't you?'

Right. Gloves off, then. Alice picked up the Pyrex dish of disgustingness from the table and crossed to the bin.

'I know he's separated, yes. If you expect me to feel guilt or sympathy for the woman who cheated on him then you're fresh out of luck.' She flipped the bin open and dropped the bowl and its contents in.

'Is it money?' Marsh looked at her with his cold, seen it all before grey eyes. 'How much will it take?'

Alice looked at him, incredulous. 'You think I'm after Robinson's money?'

'I should have known he'd get himself into trouble,' Marsh said, almost to himself. 'Where's he hidin' his sorry excuse for an ass, missy?'

'He isn't hiding. He's sleeping,' Alice said mildly. There wasn't a cat in hell's chance that she was going to tell this man where Robinson was.

'He's awake now,' a familiar, if a little gruffer than usual voice said from behind her, and when she turned she found the man in question himself standing in the doorway. He looked rough; tired eyed, wearing last night's clothes he'd obviously dragged on in a hurry and his hair said he hadn't looked in the mirror on the way out of the Airstream.

'You owe Alice an apology, Marsh. That was out of fucking order.'

Marsh looked thoroughly unrepentant. 'I'll reserve judgment on that,' he said.

Alice headed over to the door, moving past Robinson. 'Headache pills in the cupboard in the corner,' she said softly, not touching him because she didn't know how to be around him in front of Marsh.

He solved her dilemma by sliding his hand into her hair and kissing her brief and hard. He tasted of last night's whisky and of desperation and uncertainty, and her stomach performed a slow somersault because even like this he took her breath away.

'See you later,' she murmured.

'Count on it,' he said, stroking her arm tenderly as she walked away. He closed the door behind her, and she walked away with a growing sense of foreboding that no amount of coffee was going to wash away. Halfway across the lawns she turned around and changed her mind about going back to the Airstream.

'Another cowboy in just his pants? They're not fond of clothes, this lot, are they?' Niamh laughed twenty minutes later, having heard the whole sorry story as they sat out on the rickety iron bistro chairs on her tiny back patio. The old blue cobbles made the chairs even more unstable, and Pluto wasn't helping by nudging Alice's leg, asking her to play with the damp, dirty ball he'd dropped at her feet.

'Yeah, but this one wasn't sexy without his clothes on,' Alice said, miserable.

'Or pleasant with them on, either, by the sound of it,' Niamh said, offended on Alice's behalf as she distracted Pluto with scraps of toast crust from her plate.

Alice shook her head and tore her toast in half without eating any. 'Not a bit.'

Niamh watched her friend over the rim of her mug. 'So what's really on your mind?'

Sighing heavily, Alice let the words fall out. 'I'm not ready for him to leave me yet.'

Niamh nodded, and after a while said, 'He might not.'

'He will. He was always going to, Niamh. Just not so soon.'

'And you're all right with that, the idea that he's going to have to go at some point?'

Alice nodded, then shrugged and half shook her head. 'I'll miss him, of course I will. He was . . . unexpected in my life, and he's turned my worst times into some of my best. We both knew it was only ever going to be temporary.' She put the toast down uneaten, butter glistening on her fingertips.

'Right,' Niamh said softly, standing up to adjust the umbrella so that the sun wasn't in Alice's eyes. 'Only I think you might love him.'

Alice looked up, startled. 'You're seeing romance that isn't there, Niamh. I enjoy his company, and he makes me laugh.

We stop each other being lonely. I've probably let myself like him too much, but it's not love.'

'And you know this because you loved Brad,' Niamh reasoned, watching her friend closely.

Alice nodded, frowning, because she knew she'd loved Brad but somehow comparing her feelings for Robinson against her feelings for her soon to be ex-husband was confusing and not as clean cut as it should have been. Robinson filled parts of her life she hadn't even realised were empty, and he built her up where Brad had been so needy himself that he hadn't had enough left over to support Alice too. Robinson just felt like a broader, safer foundation to rest on.

'He has an easy way about him, Niamh. He makes me feel beautiful when he looks at me.'

'I see that when he looks at you too,' Niamh said.

'You're not helping. You know that, right?'

Niamh smiled, but her eyes were serious. 'Be careful, Alice.'

'I will. I am. I knew this wasn't going to last for ever, that was kind of the point. If he goes home tomorrow, or the next day, I'll be okay. I'll be sad for a while, but I'll be okay in the end. Honestly, I will.'

Alice stood up and scooped up her keys. 'I better get back. Hazel mentioned she needed to drop something around this morning.'

'Probably Rambo.'

'It better not be. That bird's been given fair warning about coming anywhere near the Airstream,' Alice laughed as they made their way through the cottage and out onto the front path.

'Hey, Alice,' Niamh called out as Alice walked away down the lane. 'I meant be careful not to give up too easy.'

Alice backtracked to Niamh's gate and hugged her friend, then set off back home ready to face whatever came her way.

'I've packed your bags for you. Get your ass in the shower, Duff, we leave in three hours.'

Robinson opened the cupboard in search of those head-ache tablets. 'I'm sorry, Marsh,' he laughed, sarcasm rolling off him. 'I don't remember signing anything that put you in charge of my whole goddamn life. I'll go home when I'm good and ready, and when I do I'll pack my own suitcases.'

He shook a couple of pills from the pack and then a third for good measure. Two for the headache, one for the additional ball ache of having to deal with Marsh. The fact that his manager was here was wrong on every level. Marsh didn't travel easy; he was pathologically terrified of flying. It would have cost him dearly to get on that plane, so Robinson could only assume that it was going to cost *him* dearly too. More than that. Marsh's arrival had stuck a needle into the bubble he'd been living in in Borne. He was part of his other life, and having him here overlapping with this life muddied all the waters. Going home wasn't part of his plan yet. The problem was he didn't actually *have* a plan, something to produce with a flourish and present to Marsh as a fait accompli, and it left him vulnerable, like a petulant teenager whose dad had turned up to fetch him home from a party early.

'Need I remind you about the concert? The tickets that thousands of fans have paid for?'

'It's not for weeks,' Robinson said.

'They put you where you are, son, and they'll turn on you just as fast if you don't show up for your own goddamn party.'

It was true and Robinson knew it, and somewhere in the back of his brain he knew he wasn't a guy who could sleep easy at night if he let his fans down. Maybe he did have a plan of sorts, after all.

'I'll do the concert, Marsh.'

The other man puffed up his chest like a turkey. 'Too dang right you will! What the hell are you doing here, spinning your wheels and makin' out with blondie when you've got a wife keepin' the bed warm at home and a job to do? Goddamn you, Duff. You're too young for a midlife crisis, and I'm too old to nursemaid you.' Marsh thumped his fist down hard on the table. 'We leave. Today.'

'Whoa, back on up there one second, Marsh.' Robinson really wanted to keep a lid on his temper, but his manager sure was testing his limits. He could feel the hot, sickly burn of injustice in his gut.

'I am not, as you so kindly put it, "spinning my wheels", and I think we both know that my soon to be ex-wife is keeping someone else's bed good 'n' warm these days – a fact you knew long before I did and decided to keep to yourself, I might add.'

Marsh wasn't a man who cared what people thought of him. He'd earned his tough-as-nails reputation in the business by having very few ethics and a lot of ruthless ambition, and he made his decisions based on how to get the best out of his artists rather than how to do the best for them. He'd known Lena was cheating for months before the shit hit the fan, and he'd kept his mouth shut and hoped she'd tire of it before Robinson found out. His only regret on the matter was not turning up with his cheque-book and paying off the dufus who'd been banging Robinson's wife, because it didn't look as if the woman

Robinson had tangled himself up with here was going to take the bait.

'Cab's booked for midday.'

Robinson scrubbed his hands over his face. 'I'm not leaving here yet. I haven't done what I came here to do.'

'Which is?'

'None of your damn business, Marsh.'

'It looks a lot like you're hidin' out to me. I didn't have you down as yellow, Duff.'

Robinson sighed. 'I know what you're doing and it's not gonna work. I'm not twelve years old. You can't goad me into getting on that plane.'

'Your sister misses you like crazy. Why do you think she told me where you are? She wants me to bring you home. Your poor momma, too. Have mercy, Duff. I saw her just last week and the woman was in tears on the street.'

Robinson laughed at the idea of his wise-cracking mother in tears in public. It was a standing joke in their family that Janna Duff's tear ducts had long since gone rusty from lack of use. She was the toughest woman he knew and he loved her all the more for it. 'I highly doubt that,' he said, drily. 'So. You've tried threats, and you've tried emotional black-mail. What's your next trick gonna be, Marsh?'

The smaller man shot out of his chair, too fired up to sit still. He'd always been that way, a firework forever on the edge of going off.

'This is no game, Duff! Do you know how many pills I had to take to get on that plane? I'm rattling louder than an angry rattler, here!' He stopped stomping around the room to make a violent rattlesnake motion in the air with his arm, the loose wrinkled skin of his forearm juddering. 'Damn it, Duff, I did it for you, because your career matters to me. You go down the pan and you take me with you, son, and there ain't a universe out there where that's gonna happen.'

The fact was that, even if he was a fully paid-up member of the self-preservation society, Marsh had something of a point. Sentimentality aside, Robinson owed his manager for his career and all of the good, life-changing things that had gone along with it, and he was a guy who always honoured his debts.

'Look, Marsh,' he said. 'I hear you, okay? I know how much it must have taken out of you coming over here. I appreciate it.' He reached for the coffee from the cupboard and filled the machine. 'Now I'm gonna make us some coffee and take a shower, then we can sit down and talk this through, man to man.'

Marsh looked at his watch and started pacing again. 'Two and a half hours, Duff. Say your goodbyes if you need to, because by hook or by crook, you're going home.'

CHAPTER TWENTY-ONE

'The cab's outside,' Marsh yelled out of the back door at the top of his lungs and could only hope it reached Robinson's ears. 'I'm getting your bags loaded, Duff. Time's up. Get your ass over here.'

In the Airstream, Alice and Robinson lay on the bed and heard every word.

'He means it, Robinson. I don't think he's taking no for an answer.'

'It's not in his vocabulary. He's gonna find this real hard,' Robinson said, smoothing her hair behind her ear. They lay facing each other, forehead to forehead, fingers tangled, their hearts heavy with foreboding.

'He's loading your luggage.'

Robinson shrugged. 'I'll buy new shirts.'

Alice kissed him, lingering, achingly sweet. 'You're going to have to go back sometime. Maybe now's as good a time as any,' she whispered, even though every selfish bone in her body wanted to hold on to him for a while longer.

'My holiday ain't over 'til I say it is, pretty face. The sun's still hot and I can still hear those waves.'

They fell silent. The long summer days had all added to the illusion of their holiday romance, and if she concentrated really hard she was certain she could hear the sea too. Or was it the rumble of jet engines? Was this to be their tearful airport farewell?

'Yoohoo! Aliiiiiiccce!'

Alice groaned. She'd forgotten all about the fact that Hazel was coming over.

'That woman and her damn bird have the world's worst timing,' Robinson growled.

'Alice! Get out here!'

'I'll get rid of her,' Alice said, sliding reluctantly out of Robinson's arms. 'Stay right there.' She opened the door and then leaned forward to get a better look at the commotion happening over by the house. 'Scrap that. You need to see this.'

She pushed her feet into her flip-flops and smoothed her sundress out, grabbing her sunglasses and jamming them on her head at the same time. 'Seriously, Robinson, come look.'

Alice stepped down from the Airstream and raised her hand.

'Be right there,' she called, waving at Ewan, now loping across the grass at Hazel's behest to fetch Alice. He waved nonchalantly back as she approached him.

'What's going on?' she said, looking past him towards the drive of the manor.

'You better ask my mother,' Ewan mumbled, shrugging his bony shoulders.

Robinson caught up with them, pulling on his t-shirt as he walked. Alice swallowed hard, wondering wretchedly if that was the last time she'd get to behold the beauty of him.

'Alice!' Hazel shouted. 'Come and see what I've got for you!'

Robinson's hand stole around her waist as she walked, warm and reassuring.

'This could be about to get interesting,' he said as Marsh popped out of the manor in a burst of denim and Cuban heels, and Alice could hear laughter behind his tone.

'Get that thing out of the way!' Marsh shouted, waving his hands at Hazel.

Hazel glanced at him and then seemed to decide not to acknowledge him. She practically bounced towards Alice instead and grabbed her hands and clutched them excitedly.

'Isn't it fabulous,' she gushed, glancing over her shoulder. 'Do you love it?'

Alice looked at the beautiful, ornate bottle-green gypsy caravan currently blocking the exit from Borne Manor and fell instantly in love. Rambling flowers covered the intricately painted panels, their colours prettily weathered by the years and country living. Its big wooden cartwheels were a faded cherry red and the stable door was half open revealing a gauzy lace net fluttering in the warm breeze.

'Where's it come from, Hazel?' she breathed. There's no way someone would give something this beautiful away. It was going to be way out of her budget and she was missing it already.

'Now there's a story,' Hazel said, taking Alice by the hand and leading her towards the caravan. 'My mother's sister's husband's uncle was Romany, see? Well, he had a son, and that son had a daughter who I grew up with as close as sisters, even though she was a cousin. Starling, her name is. She's never liked it, goes as Stephanie, but I always thought it was romantic.'

Alice frowned, trying heroically to follow Hazel's complicated family history.

Over by the house, Marsh stood on the top step and
clapped his hands loudly to get everyone's attention.

'Lovely as this is, folks, you're blocking the exit and I
need out of Toy Town! Robinson, get over here and get in
the cab or we're gonna miss that bird.' He shot his arm into
the air to mimic the take-off of the plane he fully intended
them to be on.

Robinson shrugged his shoulders helplessly and laughed,
sitting down on a sawn-off tree trunk. 'Things around here
never go quite to plan, Marsh.'

'Anyway,' Hazel said loudly, shooting daggers at Marsh for
interrupting her flow. 'Starling married a man called Defiance
Loveridge, right smarmy rick he was, all jet black Brylcreem
quiff and dirty fingernails to match. I never liked being left
alone with him and his clammy, wandering hands.' Hazel
shuddered and curled her lip. 'So of course he's gone and
took up with some flighty piece in Ireland with her own static
caravan, leaving Starling with this on the drive of her council
house,' she gestured at the caravan, 'and Banjo to deal with.'

'He played the banjo?' Alice said, completely lost.

'No, darling!' Stewie's voice carried suddenly around from
behind the caravan. 'This beauty here is Banjo.'

Alice crunched across the gravel and found Stewie in
ill-advised leather trousers, a silky black wig and no shirt,
clearly channelling his inner gypsy as he held on to the bit
of the largest and most magnificent black and white shire
horse Alice had ever encountered.

'Give him a sugar lump,' Stewie said, managing by some
miracle to pull one out of his skintight trouser pocket. 'He
loves them.'

'I didn't know you were a horseman, Stewie.'

Stewie nodded and looked off into the middle distance as he adjusted his red bandana. 'One of my earliest movies was a remake of the classic Dick Turnip.'

'Turpin,' Alice corrected him automatically.

'Oh, no. This was a turnip all right,' Stewie said, puffing his chest out. 'Along with a ruddy great bunch of carrots and an eye-wateringly large cucumber, if my memory serves me correctly.'

Alice could feel her shoulders starting to shake. Marsh was still yelling in the background and windmilling his arms around, apoplectic at being out of control, and two of Ewan's equally goth mates from the village appeared, attracted by the noise. They sat on the low wall around the front lawn like the three stooges, watching proceedings keenly with their dark ringed eyes and gangly limbs.

The taxi driver got out of the car and looked at Marsh.

'This is all on the clock, JR,' he said, sparking up a cigarette and leaning against the bonnet of his car.

'You can squeeze past it!' Marsh shouted, as if just saying it would make the non-existent space between the caravan and the gateposts wider.

'How did it get here?' Alice asked in wonder.

'Banjo pulled it,' Stewie said.

'Get that horse up front and this caravan shifted this cotton pickin' minute!' Marsh yelled.

'No can do,' Stewie said amiably, stroking Banjo's nose. 'He lost a shoe down the drain just back there. He's officially on the box.'

Marsh turned puce. 'On the box? On the box? I don't know what that even means! Speak English, man.'

'Said the American,' Ewan said, and all the goths'

shoulders moved up and down together in silent humour, vampire-like in their black t-shirts and three-quarter shorts, their only concession to the heat.

'Then drag it. You three, get over there and haul that thing aside,' Marsh said, gesticulating at Ewan and his friends.

Ewan looked at Robinson, who shook his head out of Marsh's eyeline, by now enjoying the whole thing immensely.

Rubbing his shoulder, Ewan looked regretful. 'Shoulder sprain, man.'

Beside him his friend cottoned on and stretched his leg out and pulled a face. 'Bone in my leg. Sorry.'

On Ewan's other side, his other friend massaged the back of his neck. 'Mosh-pit whiplash.'

'If you'll take Banjo you can have the caravan for free,' Hazel said, joining Alice beside Stewie.

Alice wanted to say yes really badly. 'I don't know anything about horses,' she said, tentatively feeding Banjo the sugar lump from the flat of her hand. For such a huge horse, his velvety mouth felt as gentle as butterflies dancing on her palm.

'I can teach you,' Robinson said, coming down the drive to meet Banjo. 'Hey, old timer,' he whispered softly, fussing the horse's nose and scratching his ears. 'You like that, huh?'

Alice turned to Hazel and hugged her. 'This is the best gift anyone's ever given me,' she said. 'I don't know how to thank you.'

'You don't need to, silly girl,' Hazel said, quite overcome.

At that moment, Niamh appeared from the lane in a paint-splattered apron with an equally paint-splattered Rambo under her arm.

'Hazel, you're going to have to shut him inside. He's flying round my living room and I'm trying to paint,' she said, exasperated, and then looked slowly around the unusual gathering outside the manor. 'Did I miss something?'

Marsh all but howled and hurled himself inside the manor in a temper and slammed the door.

Niamh handed Rambo over to Hazel, but he broke free of her grasp and fluttered up to sit on top of the caravan, a streak of bright yellow paint along one glossy black wing.

'Get me naked, Robinson!' he called out in Alice's voice, still his favourite phrase.

'I've never liked that bird until now,' Robinson murmured as Alice blushed, mortified.

The taxi driver straightened up off his bonnet, clearly delighted at an entertaining hour spent sunbathing rather than tackling the horror of the airport run on what was shaping up to be the hottest day of the summer so far. Mopping his balding head with his handkerchief, he smiled broadly.

'Take the cases out again then, shall I?'

While the rest of the residents of the cottages were up at the manor, someone unlocked the door of number four and pushed it open, giving it a good shove to move the accumulated junk mail and newspapers behind it. Closing the door and dropping their holdall on the hall floor, Borne's newest resident sat down on the bottom step of the creaky stairs and looked bleakly around at the old, threadbare furniture left there since the death of Albert Rollinson almost a year ago. It wasn't much. In fact it was pretty hideous, but from here on in, it was home.

*

'I was never leaving today,' Robinson said later that evening, lounging back naked amongst the many cushions and throws on the huge bed in the centre of the yurt.

'I know.' Alice looked up at the night sky through the yurt's clear dome. 'The stars tell me so.'

'You're making that up, right?'

She laughed. 'Maybe.'

They fell silent, lying on their backs side by side, and then a thought occurred to Alice.

'Hazel said that mother nature is especially present in here. She thinks I should market it as the honeymoon suite.'

Robinson rolled onto his side and drew gossamer fine patterns on Alice's stomach with his fingertip. 'Do you think she's right?'

Alice wasn't sure why his question felt more ominous than it ought to.

'It is pretty romantic,' she said, eventually.

'It is,' he said softly, moving over her and parting her legs with his knee. 'It's romantic, and you're incredibly beautiful, Alice, and when the time comes that I do have to leave you and go home, I want to close my eyes and be able to see you here, just like this.'

He was inside her body and her mind, and in that moment, he was inside her heart too. And then she knew why tonight felt so serious. Robinson had come close to leaving today; he'd been forced to think about it at least. Tonight was the start of their long goodbye. It might be tomorrow, it might be a few days, or if they were lucky it might be weeks, but something inside him had shifted, and this tender, melting sex was his way of putting them on notice.

CHAPTER TWENTY-TWO

The gypsy caravan looked spectacular down at the far end of the meadow behind the woods. It had been home to an ecstatic Banjo for the last couple of weeks, too. The first time Alice had opened the door and glimpsed inside the caravan was a moment she'd never forget. She'd expected to find it dated, a bit of a renovation project, but what she got was something so unexpectedly perfect that she'd actually welled up. The double bed sat raised over polished cherry-wood cupboards across the far end, and its heavy velvet side curtains turned it into a stage for those inclined to put on an all-star performance between the crisp white sheets topped with a colourful patchwork quilt. Gilt and deep green leather ran amok all around the interior, every bit original and obviously cherished by Starling Loveridge when it had been her marital home. Mother-of-pearl flowers had been intricately inlaid into all of the gleaming wood-work, and the graceful curve of the roof had been painted all over with the most marvellous fresco of cherubs and angels. It was utterly, unashamedly kitsch, and Alice felt more like its fortunate caretaker and custodian that its owner.

'Morning, Alice,' Dessy called out across the meadow, resplendent in neon jogging attire.

Alice stepped out of the caravan, clean sheets over her arm. 'You do know you're jogging on private property,' she grinned.

'And here's me doing you a favour.' He popped his earbuds out and handed her a bundle of mail. 'Saw the postman by the gate and offered to bring this up for him.'

'I don't suppose you were hoping to bump into a certain easy on the eyes cowboy while you were up here,' she teased, on to him.

'He's a damn sight more charming than that evil little sour puss we've got the pleasure of at The Siren,' Dessy grumbled. Marsh had been left with no choice but to check in at the only B&B in the village after missing his flight home and Robinson's refusal to book new tickets.

'I leave when you do,' Marsh had said, digging his heels and fully expecting luxury full bed and board at the manor in the meantime. He'd been disappointed. The last thing Robinson needed was his manager around as a perpetual and extremely loud reminder that the clock was ticking for him to return home.

'He's allergic to so many things that it's a wonder the man isn't living inside an oxygen tent,' Dessy went on. 'Honestly, Alice, he's a nightmare.'

Alice flicked through the mail. Ominous-looking brown ones, and official-looking white ones. They all made her nerves jangle.

'Can you sing, Alice?'

She looked up, confused by Dessy's sudden change of tack. 'Umm, a bit, I suppose? Why?'

'Karaoke at The Siren next Friday night. Bring Niamh.' He glanced slyly over his shoulder in the direction of the manor. 'And anyone else you might know who can sing.'

Alice started to laugh. 'You don't have a hope in hell of Robinson coming, if that's what you're angling after.'

Dessy sighed. 'Worth a try.'

Alice lifted her camera and shot off a volley of images of Dessy as he jogged away towards the woods, a bright flash of pink as he disappeared, leaving her alone with her thoughts, her shire horse, and a handful of unwelcome mail.

'I've got an appointment with the bank in three weeks' time,' Alice said, full of nerves. 'It came this morning.'

Robinson gathered small, early apples that had fallen from the trees for Banjo. 'That's a good thing, right?'

Alice rolled her shoulders. 'I suppose so. It just means I need to try to write a convincing business plan. I don't know what I'll do if they say no.'

'My offer still stands, Goldilocks.'

She shook her head as they walked across the meadow, just as he'd known she would. He'd offered more than once over the last couple of months to act as her unofficial banker for the project and she'd refused him every time. He didn't push it. He knew her well enough by now to know that her independence mattered a great deal to her, more and more so, and it was one of her many qualities he'd grown to admire. To look at Alice it would be easy to make lazy assumptions that she might be fragile and need taking care of, but to believe appearances would be to woefully under-estimate the girl. She was fragile, but she was also iron willed, and much as sheltering her under his protection fed his caveman soul, she soared highest and happiest unfettered.

Banjo ambled across the meadow as they approached him and pushed his nose into the bag Robinson held.

'Easy there, big fella,' Robinson laughed, feeding him his haul and giving Banjo's ears a good scratch. 'He's looking well, isn't he?'

Alice nodded. 'In rude health.'

She hadn't the first clue about horses, and Robinson had delighted in taking complete charge of Banjo when he arrived in Borne. She'd watched as he washed the horse's legs down and brushed his heavy mane, and listened as he'd ordered supplies of food and kit to settle him in. A brand new stable had been erected at the side of the meadow within days, a cute building fashioned by Robinson from reclaimed wood to sit happily in its surroundings, the perfect shelter for the village's new gentle giant.

'I'll teach you to ride him, if you want,' Robinson said. 'It's easy enough. Kinda like dancin', you just need to feel the rhythm and go with it. You couldn't ask for a better first ride than this old boy.'

'I'd like that,' she said. Horse riding wasn't something that she'd ever tried, but watching Robinson with Banjo over the last week made it look appealing. Caring for Banjo as a method of payment for something as glorious as the caravan seemed almost like robbery, because he was a gentle joy to be around and added rather than detracted from the glampsite. Looking at him, Alice had fanciful notions of wedding parties coming to stay, and of the bride riding Banjo to church with flowers twined in his mane. She could even rent out rooms in the house as well as in the gardens for bigger parties.

Robinson dropped down on the uncut grass of the meadow and lay flat on his back.

'I don't believe a word they say about British weather

being awful,' he said, peeling off his t-shirt and tucking it beneath his head as a makeshift pillow. He squinted up at her and patted the ground for her to lie down beside him.

Alice flopped down and propped herself up on one elbow to study his profile. His eyes were closed as if he were sleeping, and a smile hovered around the corners of his lips as if he were having the most delicious of dreams.

'You sure brought your cowboy sunshine with you,' she said softly, plucking a long blade of grass and using it to tickle Robinson's bare chest.

'I'll leave it behind for you when I go,' he said, a promise they both knew he couldn't keep. He opened his eyes and looked at her when she brushed the frond of grass slowly across the skin above the waistband of his jeans.

'I can always take them off if they're in your way.'

She laughed lightly and shook her head.

'Don't want to startle Banjo.'

She looked towards the huge horse happily grazing at the far end of the meadow.

'I think he's happy here,' she said, dropping back flat onto the grass.

Robinson rolled onto his side and took the slender blade of grass from her fingers.

'Of course he is. He's with you.'

Alice let his compliment settle over her, warmer than the sun's rays. She jumped a little when he drew the grass along her arm from fingertip to shoulder.

'Sunshine suits you,' he said. 'You look as if someone dipped you in gold dust.'

No one had ever made Alice feel the way Robinson could with a few uncensored words. He wore his unavailable heart on his sleeve and was always generous with his compliments.

As confidence boosters went, he was right up there with losing a stone and pillar-box-red Chanel lipstick.

She laughed as he traced an intricate pattern from shoulder to shoulder across her body with the strand of grass.

'What did you draw?'

Robinson flicked the grass out of his fingers and slid his hand up her thigh until he reached her cut-off shorts.

'I didn't draw. I wrote,' he said.

Alice turned her head to look at him, shading her eyes from the sun.

'What did you write?'

He leaned in and kissed the corner of her mouth.

'My name,' he said.

She wistfully wished he'd tattooed it in ink instead of invisible, blow-away-on-the-breeze letters.

'I should probably pay you for your autograph then,' she said, making light of it.

'Only if you let me write it again in indelible ink,' he murmured, his words too close to her own thoughts for comfort.

'I think it probably breaks the rules of holiday romances to leave a permanent mark.'

'Bit late for that,' he said, sliding his hand up inside her vest, warm and sure on her skin. 'You've already left your mark on me, Goldilocks.'

And then he kissed her for a good, long time under the heat of the afternoon sun, a slow, lazy smooch, a holding card for later.

'I'll do it, you know,' she said, looking towards the gypsy caravan as she laid her head down on his chest. 'I'm going to make this glampsite happen, and it's going to be brilliant.'

Robinson tightened his arm around her shoulders. 'Darlin', I don't doubt you for one minute. If you told me that you were gonna fly to the moon and back I'd believe you. You're just that kind of girl.'

Alice glowed with pleasure and pride under Robinson's praise. They said that it took a village to raise a child. In Alice's case, it took a village and a hot cowboy to turn that child into a woman to be reckoned with.

Every seat in The Siren was taken the following Friday night, and the fire doors thrown open to combat the ongoing summer airlessness and the heat of having pretty much the whole village in one confined space. Alice and Niamh had bagged an early table, and Hazel, Ewan and Stewie had straggled in and dragged chairs around it too.

'Are you sure you can't persuade Robinson to come?' Niamh said, flaking cobalt blue oil paint off her thumbnail. 'Imagine this lot if he just strolled in here and knocked a few tracks out.'

Alice glanced around the village collective; farmers, WI members, with a smattering of goth teenagers sprinkled through. 'I'm not sure they'd even know who he was,' she said.

'I can think of one person who definitely would,' Niamh said, glancing over towards Davina standing at the bar, her hair backcombed into a 1980s crow's nest. 'She'd eat him alive.' Given the fact that the postmistress was also wearing a basque with white lace elbow-length gloves and had numerous strands of knotted pearls draped around her neck, it was a fair bet she was planning to perform a few Madonna classics.

On the small, makeshift stage Dessy tapped the mike

experimentally, making everyone cringe and cover their ears. He waited until their shoulders moved back down from around their ears and then did it again just to wind them all up, earning himself dirty looks and a peanut in the eye from one especially irate member of the audience.

'Welcome ladies, gentle-farmers, Death Eaters,' he said, throwing a wink over at goth corner, whose inhabitants glared back at him impressively, 'and a special welcome to Queen Madge. We're honoured.' He dipped a curtsey at Davina, who accepted his deference by raising her pina colada in his direction and wiggling her lace clad fingers in a dodgy royal wave.

'I've got a book to pass round,' Dessy said, holding up a red folder. 'If your song isn't in here you can't sing it, simple as.' He flicked through it, frowned, and then tossed it aside as he glanced up at Davina again. 'There's only "Like a Virgin", sorry, Davs. Not really up your alley.'

Niamh rolled her eyes at Alice as Dessy ran through his pantomime introductions.

'What will you sing?' she said to Alice, reaching over for the red folder off the table where Dessy had flung it.

Alice laughed. 'Err, nothing, of course,' she said. She'd never sung a note in public and had no intention of changing that this evening.

'You will,' Niamh said, flicking through the pages, unruffled. 'It's addictive. You'll have a couple of glasses of wine and suddenly realise that you're Lady Gaga.'

'I highly doubt that.'

She watched as Stewie patted himself down absently looking for his reading glasses before Hazel reached up and fished them out of his Mick Hucknell-esque curls. He'd teamed the wig with a Bob Marley t-shirt and flowing harem pants, quite out there even by Stewie's standards.

'I'm hoping to do "Wuthering Heights" if it's in there,' Hazel said, adjusting the velvet bodice of her strapless purple dress. The chiffon skirt fell in various layers around her knees, and she'd pinned her hair back with a large rose clip. The overall effect was somewhere between a country singer and a pagan witch, and it suited her well.

'"Do You Think I'm Sexy", Stewie?' Hazel suggested, taking the file from Niamh and sliding her fingertip down the list.

'Yes, Hazel. As a matter of fact, I do,' he said. 'Bewitching, actually.' He picked up his whisky and knocked it back in one go, then pushed out his chair and headed off for a refill, leaving Hazel staring after his printed, multi-coloured back-side in a daze.

Alice smiled into her wine glass as Hazel's cheeks turned pink. She hadn't seen that one coming, but then she'd been so preoccupied of late with everything going on at home that she'd barely had time to notice what was going on outside the walls of Borne Manor.

On the stage, Jase kicked off proceedings with a rousing twist on Beyonce's 'All the Single Ladies', complete with a low-cut tight black sequin t-shirt and dance moves he'd clearly gone to some effort to perfect, watched and egged-on by a shiny-eyed, entranced Dessy.

'Stewie, will you do "Islands in the Stream" with Hazel? It always reminds me of happy childhood memories,' Niamh said mistily when he came back from the bar. She managed to say it without a flicker of acknowledgment that she'd heard the earlier exchange between Stewie and Hazel and decided to meddle shamelessly. She had no special memories of the song, but hoped to after tonight now. Scribbling their names against it before they had time to even consider her

228

question, she got up and treated the pub to a flirty version of 'At Last' by Etta James.

Alice noticed a dour-faced Marsh sidle in and take a stool at the end of the bar, his feet not touching the floor from his perch. He caught her eye and looked away without greeting, which didn't bother or surprise her in the slightest. He was a small man with an ego as big as his oversized hat, a fish out of water amongst the villagers that he made no attempt to talk to.

Dessy killed 'Wake Me Up Before You GoGo', thrusting his hips and swinging the mike in a way that had a couple of tweed-clad farmers in their sixties slacking off their ties as Alice drank the last of her glass of wine and wondered what Robinson was up to back at the manor. Niamh topped them both up as Dessy consulted his list and beckoned Stewie and Hazel up to the microphone, plugging a second one in for the duet. Across the pub, Ewan slid down almost under the table muttering that he wanted to die as his friends elbowed him in the ribs.

'Put your hands together for Borne's answer to Dolly and Kenny,' Dessy said, presenting them with his jazz hands as Hazel looked down at her chest doubtfully. 'This one's for you, sir,' Dessy added, and threw a theatrical wink across the room at Marsh, who looked over his own shoulder at the wall for someone behind him in sarcastic response.

Hazel cleared her throat as the music struck up, Stewie swaying beside her with his mike ready by his lips. He started to sing, not especially to the tune, merry eyes only for Hazel. She almost whispered her way through her first line, and then Stewie reached for her fingers and gave them a squeeze until she piped up louder. They sang to each other rather than the room, sweet, romantic words that neither of them would have otherwise dreamt of uttering to each other. When Stewie ensured her she could rely on him whatever, the whole room sang ah ah, and when Hazel agreed to sail away with him, they oo oo'd. And then came the line that mentioned riding away together to make love, and Stewie abandoned all attempts at singing and bent Hazel backwards over his arm for a massive snog.

'Stewie, you old sea dog! Get a room!' Jase called from behind the bar as Dessy heroically took up the lyrics and stood in front of Stewie and Hazel to preserve their modesty. They emerged when the track finished, Hazel holding Stewie's red wig in one hand and Stewie wearing more of Hazel's plum lipstick than she was.

'Gin, dear,' Hazel said, sliding unsteadily into the chair between Alice and Niamh.

Dessy reached down and half pulled Alice out of her seat. 'Save me, Alice,' he murmured, lining up the next track. 'Sing. I'm desperate for a pee.'

It seemed that Dessy had decided to stick with the country vibe, because the song he'd left her to grapple with was 'Crazy', the Patsy Cline classic. Alice looked pleadingly in Niamh's direction but found her head to head with Stewie, laughing as she wiped the lipstick off his face with a paper napkin. Other than leave the karaoke to fall on its face, Alice had little choice but to just get the job over with. It wasn't that she didn't love to sing, she did. She just wasn't a performer. But then hadn't the last few months taught her that she was stronger than she thought and braver than she knew? Taking a deep breath, she gave herself a lightning-fast pep talk. She'd got this. Rolling her shoulders a little, she opened her mouth and just started to sing as if she were alone in the Airstream, or maybe in the bathtub at the manor looking out over the gardens. She closed her eyes and laid her palm flat on her chest, feeling the words vibrate huskily from her body. When she opened them she found that practically every eye in the room was on her, and the buzz of chat had faded away as they all listened to her sing. Dessy was back, standing in the doorway rather than coming to take over, and when she looked to him for help he just laughed and shrugged for her to carry on. Niamh sat shiny eyed, her hands pressed together beneath her chin, and Stewie sat still wigless beside a distinctly squiffy Hazel.

In all of the hubbub, no one noticed the door open and someone slip into the bar. He wrote a false name beside his chosen song as Dessy reached for the folder to scan for any final acts before handing Davina the stage for the finale, and stepped up on the stage just as Dessy pressed play.

'Brace yourself, girls, it says Brad Pitt here,' Dessy grinned as he squinted at the folder, and then the smile fell from his face as Brad took off his hoody and dropped it on the table. Taking the mike, he smiled round at his old neighbours, aiming for bashful, shy even.

'Umm, wrong Brad,' he joked badly, with a half laugh that he no doubt expected to be reciprocated. It wasn't.

'The prodigal son returns,' Jase said from behind the bar as the opening beats of the intro ended and Brad started to sing the beautiful opening lines of 'When a Man Loves a Woman' from Percy Sledge.

Alice sat rooted to the spot. Was she still breathing? She wasn't even sure. Brad had a decent enough voice, and it cracked with emotion as he sang without taking his eyes off her. He was here, the man she'd hoped to love for ever, and it looked for all the world as if he was making the most public of apologies. Looking at him, she saw the face that had turned to watch her walk down the aisle, and the arms she'd hoped would hold her children. She saw the glisten of tears on his cheeks, heard the tremor in his voice as she stood up and slowly edged closer to the stage, every eye in the place on her once more. Brad reached the crescendo of the song and reached out a hand towards her, never one to miss the chance to pile on the drama. It had all of the elements of the final scenes of a romantic movie, boy makes impressive apology and wins his girl back, which only made it all the more spectacular when Alice threw the contents of her freshly refilled wine glass straight into Brad's symmetrically handsome, shocked face.

Niamh stood up and cheered, thumping the air while Brad picked up his jacket and wiped it across his face, and Dessy hastily yanked the plug on the wine-soaked karaoke machine in case the whole place went up in smoke. Alice shook her head in disgust at Brad and then bolted out of the fire doors into the darkness, knocking a finally interested Marsh's hat on the floor as she went by.

CHAPTER TWENTY-THREE

'I woke up and you weren't there, Goldilocks,' Robinson said, tapping on the open Airstream door the following morning. 'Thought I better come and make sure you didn't run into any bears in the woods last night.'

Alice buttered the toast she knew she didn't have the stomach to eat and put the plate down on the table.

'Hungry?' she said, sitting down and nodding for him to come in and do the same. He sat opposite her at the table, studying her closely. She knew there was no way he could miss the pale grey tint to her complexion nor the bags underneath her eyes from lack of sleep.

'Hangover?' His clear green eyes danced with amusement. 'Hair of the dog is your best friend right now. Whisky in your coffee should get you there in five.'

Alice's stomach flipped unpleasantly and she pushed the plate towards him.

'Brad's back.'

Robinson blinked, wrong footed, and then nodded slowly

and took a bite of toast. 'You don't look cock-a-hoop, pretty face.'

'Should I?' She'd lain awake for most of the night, and when she had fallen asleep it had been to dream of being in bed in the Airstream with Robinson, only to look twice and find it was Brad's face over hers, his body pressing hers into the mattress. The dreams made her cry and left her troubled heart trying to work out how it was supposed to feel and who for.

She regaled the whole sorry story of last night to Robinson, leaving nothing out to spare his feelings because they'd never lied to each other once and it was a blessed relief not to have to consider how to present the truth.

He laughed approvingly about Stewie and Hazel's un-anticipated lust, and said how much he wished he'd been there to hear Alice sing, and he reached out and held her hand across the table when it came to the part about Brad turning up. His thumb moved reassuring and warm across her knuckles, and for a minute or two they just sat like that in silence, each of them considering how this changed things.

'You should speak to him,' Robinson said, after a while.

'I don't know what to say. So much has changed.'

Robinson moved around and scooched her along so he could slide in beside her, his arm along the back of the bench as she leaned gratefully against him.

'I guess you need to take some time to think about things,' he said. 'Work on your own timescale, not his or anyone else's. You don't have to make your decisions today, or tomorrow, next week or next month. Just hear what he has to say and then come home again and think.'

The way he said come home again brought a lump to her

throat. Come home to the Airstream, to the manor, or to him? They all seemed to be one and the same at the moment. It should have been odd to have this conversation with Robinson; he was probably the last person she ought to be having it with, yet at the same time he was the only person in the world she wanted to talk to. He knew how she felt without her needing to spell it out, because he'd been through the same emotional wringer then tumbled into these last strange and fabulous few months where their worlds had collided at the exact moment they each hit the bottom. Without him, she might have drowned. Without her, he'd probably have not bothered getting up again. And now reality was knocking on the door, and sooner or later they were each going to have to answer it. Marsh was here. Brad was here. Robinson had a concert he needed to be at and a career to hold on to in the States, and Alice had a meeting with the bank manager and hopefully a brand new career of her own. Rural England might still be baking under its unseasonably hot summer, but for them the season was drawing to its inevitable close.

'He's staying at The Siren,' Niamh said without preamble when she came by the Airstream a couple of hours later. 'I've just been down there and spoken to Dessy. He's taken a room and hasn't said when he's leaving.'

Alice poured Niamh a glass of chilled water and they settled outside on the deckchairs.

'You were my hero last night,' Niamh said, raising her glass to her friend as if it were champagne rather than water.

'It was childish,' Alice sighed. Good as it had felt at the time, throwing wine over Brad hadn't made her feel any better in the morning.

'No, it was well deserved. In fact he deserved you to hit him over the head with the actual bottle. He got off lightly.'

'What did you make of it all, Niamh?'

Niamh swirled her water as she considered the question. 'I think Brad fully expected you to melt. It was quite a stunt.'

Alice waited to hear what came next, resting her head on the side of her chair to look at her friend.

'And I think his timing was off. If this had happened three months ago you'd have fallen into his arms. He's left it too late.'

'You think so?'

'I know so. And I'm bloody glad he waited, as well. I bet she's ditched his sorry ass so he's come crawling back here.' Naimh shot Alice a guilty look. 'Sorry. That sounded as if I was saying you're second best and you're not. But then you know that.'

'Don't be sorry, you're probably right.' Alice fiddled with the pendant around her neck. 'You didn't see him today?'

Niamh's laugh echoed with sarcasm. 'He's lucky I didn't. He'd have more than a drink in his face to worry about if I had. The nerve of him.' She looked at Alice with a sudden frown. 'You're not regretting chucking your drink, are you?'

'No.' Alice shook her head, struggling to explain her feelings because she didn't fully understand them herself. 'It came naturally. He just seemed more concerned about his performance than he did about me, which just about sums up our entire relationship. But he's my still my husband, Niamh, on paper at least. I have to hear him out.'

Niamh scowled. 'I'm worried that he'll switch on the charm and you'll cave in. I know how much he meant to you, and I saw how much he hurt you. I don't want you to go back there again when you've come this far.'

'I won't,' Alice said, her feelings crystallising as she voiced them. 'You're right. If he'd have come back a few months ago I'd have taken him back. But he didn't, and now I'm not the same girl any more. This happened,' she turned and gestured at the Airstream. 'And the glampsite happened. And this happened, too.' Alice touched the camera around her neck, then lifted it and took a shot of Niamh raising her glass. 'I can't believe I let myself go so long without taking pictures. So much of the world I've missed.'

'And Robinson happened,' Niamh added to Alice's list.

'I was just coming to him,' Alice sighed wistfully. 'He's going home in a few weeks, but I'll never be sorry that he came, and I'll never be sorry that we got to spend this long, hot summer together.'

'Won't you be sorry that he's gone?'

Alice closed her eyes and did the same thing she did every time the subject came up. 'I don't want to think about it until it happens.'

'Any chance he could kill Brad before he leaves?'

'Niamh,' Alice chastised her friend softly.

Niamh shrugged. 'Not sorry.'

'Come on. I'll walk you home on my way to The Siren.'

Alice sat in the middle of the otherwise empty bar at The Siren nursing an orange juice while Jase let Brad know that she was downstairs. He'd hi-fived her silently when she'd walked in to the pub, and murmured that he'd be there in a heartbeat if she shouted for him, as he put her drink down and went to find her errant husband.

She glanced over at the door as it opened a few minutes later and Brad sheepishly poked his head inside.

'Is it safe to come in?'

His attempt at humour felt wide of the mark. Alice looked at him steadily, taking in his freshly shaven face, his still-shower-damp dark hair, the shirt she'd given him for Christmas. He looked like the man she'd shared her life with for years, and at the same time like a stranger. He glanced at her juice warily.

'You're not likely to throw that one as well, are you?'

'Quit with the lame jokes and just sit down, will you?' she said, suddenly weary. She'd had so many imaginary conversations with Brad since he left, and none of them had gone quite like this, nor had they taken place in The Siren for safety. Times really had changed.

Brad scraped the chair opposite Alice's back on the flagstones and dropped into it, his hands cupping his slightly tilted chin. It was a pose that said look at me I'm gorgeous, rather than I'm looking at you and you're gorgeous, and the staged element of it set Alice's teeth instantly on edge.

'I would have come to you,' he said, magnanimous.

Alice sipped her juice and knotted her fingers in her lap.

'Why did you do that last night, Brad?'

He sighed and looked forlorn. 'I honestly thought you'd like it, Ali.'

Brad was the only person in the world who called her Ali, and the tiniest piece of her heart thawed at the sound of it on his lips. She looked away, out of the window at the deep blue sky and the road stretching away towards the manor. Towards home. Her home, not Brad's.

'Did you really think that after everything you put me through one public display of not even very good singing was going to impress me?'

He looked offended, and she knew him well enough to know that the slur on his singing ability had cut deeper than the rest of her question.

'I hoped it would help you see that I mean it,' he said, petulance edging into his tone at her lack of appreciation.

'You mean what, Brad? What is it that you've come here to say?'

He looked at her as if she'd asked a stupid question. 'Isn't it obvious? I'm coming home, baby.' He smiled, and his eyes said you love me and you know it.

'Am I supposed to tie a yellow ribbon round the old oak tree?'

He looked nonplussed. 'Being sarcastic isn't going to help anyone, is it?' He glanced around. 'Look. Let me take you for dinner tonight. Anywhere you fancy. You pick.'

'You really think it's going to be easier to talk in a crowded restaurant than an empty bar?' He always did like an audience to play off.

'Ali, I want to come home. I made a huge fucking mistake and I regret it more than you know,' he said, suddenly reaching out across the table and gripping her hand as she went for her drink. 'Felicity was a nightmare. Total and utter crazy shrew, all she cares about is how she looks in the newspaper, her reviews, and her next career move. She's cold and so damn needy, she couldn't care less about my career as long as hers is all right.'

Alice couldn't help but see the irony. He'd managed to find someone more narcissistic than himself.

'So it's over between you two?'

He huffed. 'She's gone to the States for a job that by rights should have been mine. Couldn't have us both on the show, they said, too much personal conflict. Load of bollocks, of course. She was obviously more obliging on the casting couch than I was.'

Listening to him reminded Alice all too starkly of many mornings spent poring over the morning papers for reviews, full of bile and bitterness for anyone who'd fared well with the critics. Pulling her hand out from under his, she played with the stem of her glass.

'So because she's left you and gone to America, you've decided to come back to me?'

He looked aghast. 'That wasn't what I said at all. It was over between us before that. I should never have left you for her.'

He stopped short of saying sorry. In fact he'd never said sorry at all.

'I'm not saying we can just pick up where we left off, I know it's not going to be as easy as all that, but we're still married, Ali. Let's move back into the manor and get our lives back on track.'

His mention of the manor had her heart beating harder.

'What's the big deal about the manor, Brad? You were never really fussed when you lived in it, but now you suddenly love it?'

Brad tried the puppy-dog eyes. 'I miss it. I miss living there with my favourite girl.'

They were words clearly designed to soften her heart, yet strangely they had the opposite effect.

'The manor's rented out. You couldn't move back in there even if you wanted to.'

Brad laughed. 'I can get us out of that agreement early. I've already spoken to the leasing agency to get on it.'

'You've asked them to speak to Robinson about leaving sooner than planned?' The red mists were descending.

Brad nodded, staring at her through narrowed eyes. 'Is that a problem?'

He was testing her, playing games she didn't want to play. 'Yes,' she said, quiet and clear. 'Yes, it's a problem. That's what this is really about, isn't it? You were fine when I was heart-broken, but now that you can see me moving on you can't stand it. You've come back here to throw your weight around, to prove to yourself that you can have me anytime you choose. Well, here's the thing, Brad. You waited too long. You gave me enough time to see that there is actually such a thing as life without you, and what's more it's bloody good, too. I've got friends, and I've got plans, and I've got . . .'

Her voice grew slowly louder as she spoke, and Brad's eyes grew slowly colder as he realised that his charms weren't going to be enough to get his own way this time.

'What? You've got what, Alice, or should I say you've got who? Because let's face it, we both know you're shagging our tenant. It's a bit desperate, isn't it? You love that fucking house so much that you're prepared to sleep with any random yank who turns up, blows smoke up your ass and pays the rent?' He half laughed and then put his hands up to stop her from interrupting him. 'But you know what, it's okay. I deserved you to do that to me. I deserved you to sleep with someone else. In a funny way it sort of makes us even, doesn't it?'

It was difficult for Alice to know which bit of his speech pissed her off more. On reflection it was the fact that he'd called Robinson names, so she started there.

'Some random yank? You really don't know who he is?' she raised her eyebrows. 'You surprise me, what with him being a fellow celebrity and all. Only far more famous, of course.'

A slow red flush crept up from Brad's neck, as if he were actually on fire on the inside. 'Who is he?' he ground out.

Alice shrugged. 'It doesn't matter who he is. He's not blowing smoke up my ass, but you're dead right about the sex, Brad. We are having amazing, brilliant sex, the sort of sex that I didn't even know people really actually had, and he's not going home until he's good and ready, no matter what you or the stupid letting agent says.'

In the long run she probably wouldn't be proud of the things she'd just said, but in the heat of the moment she meant every word and enjoyed the fact that Brad looked as if he was going to spontaneously combust with fury.

'Who. Is. He?' Brad forced the three words between his gritted teeth.

Alice shook her head. 'That's what's really got under your skin here, isn't it? It's not that I'm sleeping with someone else, it's that I'm sleeping with someone more famous than you, isn't it?' She rammed her chair back and stood up. 'Well, let me tell you something, Brad McBride. He's not just more famous than you, he's kinder, and sexier and all round better in just about every way. Go back to London, Brad. Go back and find yourself another Felicity to massage your ego, because I'm officially done with you.'

'Fine!' he yelled at her back as she walked towards the door. 'Fine. Go back to your love nest, Alice. Go back and make the most of it while you still can, because that house is bloody well mine and I'm having it back whether you like it or not!'

Alice turned back to him at the door, willing her voice to sound stronger than she felt inside.

'Go ahead, Brad, do your worst. When you left I felt as if I'd lost everything in my life that mattered to me, but I was wrong. I still had my home. Borne Manor is the one thing I'm not prepared to lose in all of this.'

'Then I'll see you and lover boy in court,' he said, with what she could only describe as a flounce.

She shook her head and sighed. 'One day you might realise that real life isn't some corny soap opera.'

'Says the woman addicted to sleeping with the stars,' he snapped.

'As always, you overestimate yourself.' She walked out of the pub and left him there to stew in his own jealous juices.

Alice was too worked up to notice The Siren's other resident lurking outside in the hallway. Marsh turned smoothly away from her as she stormed from the pub, and then sidled into the bar when she was safely out of the way.

He looked at Brad and feigned concern. 'You look like a man who could use a whisky,' he said, then knocked on the bar for service.

'Bottle of bourbon and two glasses,' he ordered when Jase appeared, then took the seat that Alice had recently vacated and bared his teeth in what he hoped might look like a sympathetic smile.

CHAPTER TWENTY-FOUR

Alice stomped back to the manor, turning the air bluer than even Rambo could as she passed the cottages, muttering under her breath. She crunched up the driveway and straight up the side of the manor, and kept on going over the lawns and past the Airstream. She slowed as she walked beneath the cool shade of the trees, letting the quiet calm of the woods soak up some of her rage. Who did he think he was? He'd pushed all of her buttons and she'd found herself angrier than she'd ever been before. Short of turning green and clubbing him, she needed to think how to handle things, because she'd just hurled a hand grenade into the remains of her marriage and pulled out the pin.

She found who she was looking for contentedly eating grass on the edge of the meadow. Banjo dipped his head towards her, letting her lay her forehead against his warm nose and wrap her arms around his wide neck.

'Why can't everyone be like you, Banjo?' she whispered, scratching behind his ears just the way he liked it. 'People are so bloody complicated.'

The gentle old horse nuzzled into her, giving her his warm, solid comfort and simple, unconditional affection.

'I won't let anyone take this place away. I belong here, and so do you now.'

Crossing to the gypsy caravan, she sat down on its green wooden steps, tracing her finger over the painted flowers as she replayed the ugly scene from the pub in her head. She hadn't intended to say any of those things, but Brad had taken her breath away with his audacity and thinly veiled selfishness. He'd never been a person who fared well on his own. He needed to be the centre of someone's world, to be revolved around and adored, taken care of and feted over. It must have been a bitter blow to hear that she wasn't going to happily reprise her role of chief ego massager, and the bitterest blow of all to hear that she'd moved on to someone higher on the celebrity scale than he was. She closed her eyes and leaned her head back against the caravan door, letting the sun warm her cheeks and the peaceful meadow calm her nerves.

'Hey there, gypsy girl.'

Alice opened her eyes and watched Robinson as he drew near, his green eyes filled with gold glitter by the sunlight.

'Hey there yourself,' she said, moving across on the step to let him sit too. He chose instead to step up behind her and sit on the top step, his legs a welcome and protective frame around her body.

'So, how did it go?'

As he spoke he lowered the straps of her vest down her arms and began to massage her shoulders, warm firm circles that made her sigh and drop her chin down onto her chest.

'Just about as badly as it could have,' she said, sweeping her hair over one shoulder and plaiting it.

Robinson rolled his thumbs down the bumps of her spine between her shoulder blades and then back up again. 'That good, huh?'

Alice slipped her arms out of her vest and turned it into a boob tube. 'You'll be hearing from the letting agency soon to ask you to leave before the end of your tenancy.'

'Already did. Told 'em no can do.'

He seemed so utterly unfazed by it that Alice could feel the tension draining from her body too. Maybe it was his relaxed company, or maybe it was the skillful way he massaged her shoulders, but as she lapsed into silence and let herself just feel pleasure, her eyes closed and her breathing slowed. He was speaking, but she couldn't hear his words because sleep had caught hold of her. His words were a lullaby, and there on the caravan steps leaning on Robinson's knees, she fell asleep.

It came as easy as breathing to him. Alice had seemed so in need of soothing, her muscles wound tight even though her skin was so soft and smooth under his fingers. He'd felt her slowly beginning to relax, listened to her breathing, and then he'd found himself singing to her. Maybe it was because he knew she wouldn't hear him, or maybe it was because a small place in his heart wanted her to, but he sang his old country love songs and stroked her hair until she was deeply, blissfully asleep and those knots in her shoulders had melted away. Whatever it was, holding this sleeping girl felt like the kind of therapy money couldn't buy, the kind that removed every obstacle and freed every blocked pathway in his head and in his heart. This wasn't his ranch and Banjo was a long way from a stallion, but in every way that mattered, Robinson Duff felt like he was home. He closed his eyes too.

The sun had slipped down behind the tree line when he opened his eyes again, the peach and pink layers sliced across the horizon letting him know that they'd been there for quite a while.

'Alice,' he whispered, shaking her shoulder lightly. She responded, tipping her head back and smiling, her eyes still closed.

'Don't ask me to move. I'm too comfortable.'

He kissed her full, soft mouth and then scooped her up with ease, carrying her across the meadow like a child in his arms.

'Where are we going?'

'Wherever you like,' he said, kissing her again, more deeply. 'The Airstream?'

Alice moved her arms around his neck more securely, and then said, 'Take me to the manor.'

Robinson didn't ask why, just kept on walking, his fingers moving lightly over the side of her breast, her mouth warm against his neck.

He opened the back door of the manor and stepped inside.

'Where to now?'

'Upstairs,' she whispered, unbuttoning the top buttons of his shirt.

He paused on the landing.

'Bath?' he said. 'I could light the candles . . .'

Alice shook her head. They could have just gone inside the gypsy caravan, or over to the Airstream, and a bath sounded divine, but she'd asked him to bring her to the manor for a very specific reason. Sliding down out of his arms, she opened her old bedroom door, the room she'd shared with her husband. There was one last ghost she needed to lay to rest.

'In here.'

Robinson didn't move for a few seconds, just studied her face. 'You sure?'

Alice held out her hand and led him inside slowly. 'It's your bedroom now, not mine, and certainly not his.' She didn't even want to say Brad's name. He had no place here between them. 'I want you to make love to me in your bed, Robinson.'

She let her words sink in and then lifted her vest over her head and let it fall to the floor and stepped out of her shorts, watching his eyes. He was turned on, the dark gleam in his eyes told her so, but still he held back, letting her lead because no matter what she said, this was different.

'Help me?' she said, turning her back for him to unclip her bra. She closed her eyes when he stepped near and lifted the weight of her hair over one shoulder, pressing his warm lips against the back of her neck as his fingers moved over the clasp and opened it.

Alice slipped her bra down her arms and dropped it, then turned around to face him, vulnerable.

Robinson looked at her, his breathing a little shallow, and traced his hand down from her throat to the silk edge of her knickers.

'These too?' He asked permission, even though they both knew he didn't need to.

Alice nodded, closing her eyes when he eased her under-wear down her legs for her to step out of. Robinson lingered to place a kiss against the curve of her stomach before straightening up again, a tender gesture, the slow build she needed.

His Adam's apple moved in his throat as he swallowed, his eyes dark and hungry as they moved over her body. His fingers were already at his wrists unbuttoning his cuffs, and then moving down his body to get his shirt open.

'Every day you surprise me, Alice,' he said, putting his hand behind her head as he kissed her slowly, intimately. His other hand worked the rest of his clothes off, and then he was naked too and lifted her back into his arms. Being held against his chest had seemed caring and sexy when they were dressed. Now that they were naked it was different; intimate and protective, a sensual prelude.

'You're a warrior, and then a wood nymph. The softest girl I know, and then the toughest.'

He crossed to the bed and lowered her carefully onto the covers, following her down and blanketing her body lightly with his own. It was familiar and alien all at the same time for Alice, overwhelming and gorgeous and sad and beautiful.

'Okay?' he whispered, stroking her hair back from her face and fanning it out on the pillow with his fingers.

Alice felt her lips tremble when she tried to smile and tell him that yes, she was more than okay, and yes, she wanted this with him here, and that yes, there was no one else in the world she could imagine lying here with.

She nodded, stroking the back of his head as he settled himself between her legs.

'I might cry,' she said, her voice small. 'It's not because I'm sad, okay?'

Robinson kissed her forehead, her eyes, and then her mouth.

'You're so darn lovely, Alice,' he said, holding her hand beside her head, his thumb stroking her pulse point.

'Don't think,' he whispered, rocking his hips down. 'Just feel.'

He was gentle and she treasured him for it, kissing the tears from her cheeks as he moved slowly inside her, holding her close and murmuring her name.

If Alice had been asked who she cried for, she wouldn't have known what to say. She cried for herself; sadness for the finality of losing her marriage today even though in reality it had been dead in the water for a while, and she cried tears of pride for how far she'd come since she'd found herself unexpectedly alone. She cried tears of regret for how much of herself she'd kept buried over the years, and for the time she'd wasted not being the person she really wanted to be. But most of all, she cried tears of pain for the inescapable truth that she was going to have to give Robinson back to his real life soon. Beautiful, generous Robinson Duff, the drop dead gorgeous cowboy who'd come to Borne to save his own sanity and somehow saved hers too. She missed him already.

'Remind me again why I'm doing this,' Robinson muttered a couple of mornings later, running his hand around the inside of his shirt collar in the back of the car flying along the empty motorway in the early hours.

'Because I am making hay while the British sun shines, Robinson. Because I haven't travelled to this tiny rock just to wipe your ass. Do you know how many strings I had to pull to get you a slot on this show? A lot, that's how many, so suck it up and be grateful. Tell them you love their little country and smile for the camera. Tell them you're coming over here on tour soon.'

'You're advising me to lie on breakfast TV?'

'Doesn't necessarily need to be a lie, son,' Marsh said smoothly, snapping his black silk eye mask over his eyes to indicate that that the conversation was over.

Robinson leaned his head back and watched the lights whizzing past his window in a blur. Trust Marsh to get his money's worth out of being in England. The man was always looking for the next opportunity to make money, and to give him his dues he was the best in the business at his job. Robinson knew that on a professional level he ought to be grateful for the exposure, but coming to England had never been about that. It had been about the opposite, in fact. It was an unwelcome intrusion, his real life seeping further and further in around the edges, like ink bleeding on blotting paper.

Alice switched on the TV in the lounge at the manor and curled up in the armchair to watch Robinson appear on Lorraine's famous morning sofa. She'd grown accustomed to watching Brad being interviewed when they were together, but the idea of Robinson on TV seemed so much more bizarre. She didn't know him in his professional capacity at all, in fact while he'd been here she'd made a point of not looking him up or listening to his music. It felt important, almost like it would be disloyal to know more about him than he knew of her courtesy of Google and skewed information from people with vested interests.

'And coming up after the break we've our weekly round-up of the soaps,' chirped Lorraine, 'and I'll be talking to Brad McBride about the explosive scenes coming up for his character this autumn in Doctors On Call, plus country music superstar Robinson Duff will be here to tell us all about his latest album. More in five.'

Alice gasped out loud in pure shock and horror. This had to be a mistake. It was just too co-incidental that Brad could end up on the same show as Robinson. Breathing fast, she slid her tea onto the table and covered her face with her hands.

'Oh God, oh God, oh God,' she whispered. 'What did you do, Marsh?'

'So, Robinson, it's an absolute treat to have you here! I know your legions of fans here in the UK will want me to ask if you've any plans to tour here soon?' Lorraine smiled broadly and crossed her fingers at the camera on the viewers' behalf as she twinkled at Robinson seated opposite her on the couch.

Alice sat dry mouthed on the edge of her seat, her hands gripping the undersides of her thighs with clammy hands. The camera loved Robinson, picking up the tawny lights in his hair and sprinkling green glitter in his beautiful eyes. He came over exactly as he was in real life, honest and open, and Lorraine looked so smitten that she might crawl across the floor in her fabulous shoes and mount him at any moment. Alice couldn't blame her. Seeing him doing his job was an incredible aphrodisiac; he was confident and sexy, and when Lorraine cut to a clip of him in concert Alice wanted to lick the screen because he was so shatteringly sexy. In that moment, she saw what the world saw and fell for him afresh as a spellbound fan. For a few seconds she forgot all about the fact that Brad was coming on and just appreciated the man in front of her.

'You spend a fair chunk of your time globetrotting, life must be pretty stressful,' Lorraine said, leaning towards him a little. 'What do you do to relax in your down time?'

A loud off-screen clatter made Lorraine jump violently in her seat, and as Robinson looked over his shoulder Brad stumbled into view, shaking his foot free of a trailing camera cable that he'd clearly tripped on as he barged onto the set.

'I'll tell you what he's doing with his down time, Lorraine,' he shouted, jabbing his finger wildly in Robinson's direction. 'He's boning my wife!'

Lorraine looked as if she might be about to have a heart attack on the spot, and Robinson got to his feet.

'I'm real sorry about this, darlin',' he said to Lorraine, and then to a purple-faced Brad, he said 'this is neither the time nor the place.'

'Oh, I think it is,' Brad said. 'And you can tell my slut of a wife from me that . . .'

He didn't get to finish his sentence because Robinson's fist connected squarely with his jaw.

'Never miss a good chance to shut up,' Robinson said, shaking the blood from his knuckles as Brad stumbled backwards out of view again and could be heard screaming loudly at Lorraine's crew to get off him as they hauled him off set.

Robinson sat back down again as if nothing untoward had happened, and after a moment Lorraine followed suit and smoothed a hand over her perfectly coiffed hair.

'Where I come from, it's not polite to speak like that about a lady.'

Lorraine looked as if she might commando roll across the floor and kiss Robinson's feet. She coughed to clear her throat and then smiled into the camera.

'Quite. Coming up after the break, all the inside gossip from the cobbles of *Coronation Street*. We'll be right back.'

They cut to adverts, and Alice switched the TV off and curled up on the sofa in silence. As far as she was concerned, real life wasn't just ink seeping in around the edges, it was crashing in over them like a tidal wave, and she was drowning in it.

He came home and found her at the kitchen table.

'I guess you saw what happened.'

'Did Marsh set it up?'

Robinson sat down beside her. 'He says not. But yeah, I reckon he did.'

She put her hand on his thigh, wincing when she noticed Brad's blood on Robinson's shirt. 'You shouldn't have hit him.'

'I should have hit him harder.'

'Will it damage your reputation?'

He shrugged. 'Marsh thinks not. No publicity is bad publicity, that old chestnut.'

'I shouldn't think Brad's manager is looking at it that way right now,' Alice said, a small smile hovering despite everything. She kissed his cheek.

'Thank you for protecting my honour, even if he was technically correct.'

'What was that phrase he used? Boning?' Robinson said, frowning.

'As in having sex with,' Alice said, grimacing.

Robinson looked sideways at her and then started to laugh under his breath, and then pulled her into his lap.

'As in "let's take our clothes off and bone"?' he asked, sliding his hands inside her t-shirt.

'Not sure that makes literal sense,' she said, settling into him. 'At least he didn't say fucking. Lorraine really wouldn't have liked that.'

'I like how you sound when you say it,' he said, pulling

her t-shirt off and lifting her up onto the kitchen table in front of him as he stood up.

'I like how it feels when we do it,' she breathed, gasping as he pushed her backwards, dragged her hips to the edge of the table and settled himself between her thighs. And then, as had become their way, they blocked out everyone and everything else and lost themselves in each other.

She made them omelettes at midnight and he opened the beers. They sat close at the kitchen table and spoke quietly, then went back to bed and slept tumbled together, wrapped up in the sheets and each other until someone unceremoniously woke them the next morning by banging on the door knocker and shouting through the letterbox.

'Open the damn door, Robinson Duff. I know you're in there and I'm not going anywhere until you open this door!'

Robinson dragged the pillow over his head and groaned, and Alice pulled it back off again and looked at him, still half asleep.

'Who is it?'

Robinson sat up and rubbed his hands over his face.

'I hate to say it, Goldilocks, but it sounds very much like my ex-wife.'

Robinson threw his clothes on and jogged downstairs pulling his t-shirt down his chest, craning his neck to look through the small, bevelled hall window to get the full picture before he opened the door.

'Fuck,' he said, banging the back of his head lightly against the wall as he cursed. 'Fuck, fuck, fuck.'

Opening the door had just become even more of an issue, because it wasn't just Lena out there on the driveway. From what he could tell, the entire British press had set up camp on his doorstep as well.

Grabbing his mobile from the hall table, he called Marsh on speed dial. His manager answered after a couple of rings.

'What the fuck did you do?' Robinson said, dispensing with any greeting.

'Good morning to you too,' Marsh said, sounding pithy and bored.

'I'm not in the mood for your games, Marsh. Did you do this?'

His manager sighed heavily down the phone. 'I've done what needed to be done, Robinson, because you weren't going to man up and do anything yourself any time soon.'

'So what, you called every newspaper in the whole of goddamn England to tell them where I am, and then threw my estranged wife in to the mix for good measure?'

Behind him he heard Alice's footsteps on the stairs and turned to glance at her. She looked stricken, and he wasn't a bit surprised. The only thing she'd asked of him was that he didn't bring the press to her door again, and here they were surrounded by long lens cameras. He mouthed sorry as she fastened her robe around her waist and sat on the bottom step of the stairs to wait for him to finish on the phone.

'What the hell are you saying, Duff?' Marsh barked. 'The press are over there?'

'Don't even bother playing the innocent, Marsh.'

His manager fell silent for a minute and then, typically, started yelling at the top of his lungs. 'Under no circumstances do you open that door until I get there, do you understand me? One sniff of there being truth to that infidelity story and your fans will throw you under the nearest goddamn bus!'

Marsh hung up, and from the way Robinson heard him cursing as he stabbed the end call button of his mobile he felt fairly confident that although Marsh had contacted Lena, he wasn't the one responsible for the press invasion. But if not Marsh, then who?

'Robinson! Let me in, for God's sake,' Lena hissed loudly through the waist-high letterbox. 'If you don't let me inside this house in the next thirty seconds I swear to God I'll give them something to point their lenses at.'

Robinson crossed the hall and dropped down on his haunches in front of Alice. Reaching out, he cupped her cheek in his hand.

'Alice, I'm so sorry. I'll make this all go away, I promise you. By the end of today you'll have your privacy back, okay?'

Her eyes were blue in every sense of the word; cornflower in colour, melancholy in mood. They both knew that the only way to get the press off the driveway of Borne Manor would be for Robinson to leave too.

'You're going to have to let her in,' Alice said. 'They'll eat her alive.'

Robinson laughed sourly. 'You haven't met Lena.'

Alice stood up. 'No. And I'm not planning on meeting her in my robe.' She squinted through the bevelled window and saw the sea of press part to allow the tiny but mighty Marsh to march through the middle of them. 'Marsh is here. I'm going to take a shower while you guys talk.'

'Alice . . .' Robinson caught hold of her hand as she turned to go upstairs and Marsh thumped heavily on the door. She stepped back down and kissed his cheek, lingering to breathe in the scent of him for a precious second.

'It isn't your fault, Robinson,' she sighed, bringing his

fingers to her mouth and kissing them. 'This day has been coming from the moment you arrived. That's the thing with holiday romances. They have to end.'

Across the village, Davina flicked the open sign over to closed as she locked the door and jumped into the waiting taxi. There'd be no catching the bus for her today, nor for the foreseeable future thanks to the tidy sum she'd received in exchange for revealing the whereabouts of Robinson Duff. After his performance on live breakfast TV he was the hottest story in the country; opportunity had come knocking and Davina hadn't needed to think twice before answering. She was taking the morning off, and she might even buy Hazel's stupid bird some fancy seeds as a thank-you for his insider info. She probably wouldn't have trusted the intel from a human; she'd yet to meet one who didn't lie for his own convenience. She wasn't one bit sorry.

CHAPTER TWENTY-FIVE

Alice bolted the bathroom door and after a moment's thought turned on the bath taps instead of jumping in the shower. Whatever was going to happen downstairs was going to happen anyway, and she wasn't in any hurry to meet Robinson's wife or get caught up in the crossfire with Marsh. Sliding into the bubbles, she closed her eyes and tried to work out what on earth was going to happen next, how she could play it and come out with both her heart and her home intact. For a few weeks back there life really had been quite magical, long luxurious days of sunshine and exciting plans, and even longer, hotter nights in the Airstream with Robinson. It had only ever been an interlude, a decadent escape from reality for both of them. Looking back, Marsh's arrival had marked the beginning of the end, and Brad turning up out of nowhere had further hastened the end of their idyll. And now there was Lena to contend with, not to mention the entire British press involved in the spectacle again too. She'd recognised a few of them when she'd peeped quickly out of an upstairs window just now, guys who had spent so much time on her driveway last year for her to know them by first name, faces she'd hoped never to need to see again. Every now and then she heard raised voices from the kitchen, snippets and tones that made her want to stay in the bathroom forever.

Marsh paced the kitchen floor, his jacket discarded and his steel grey hair all over the place from pushing his hands through it. He was in an absolute rage about the press involvement; he ruled the PR side of his client's business with an iron rod and this situation had potential disaster written all over it. He needed a cast-iron damage-limitation strategy, one that definitely didn't include Robinson and Lena having an all out slanging match within ear shot of England's most influential hacks.

'Will you two pipe the hell down?' he shouted over them, waving his arms in the manner of a man landing a plane. Lena shook her glossy dark waves and flashed her eyes at him.

'I'll pipe down when I've said what I hauled my ass halfway across the world to say, Marshall,' she shot back. 'Or what *you* hauled my ass halfway across the world to say.'

'I am *not* listening to her, Marsh,' Robinson said. 'I want her out of the house, out of this village and out of this country before nightfall, do you understand me? She has no place here.' He sighed, infuriated and exasperated. 'What did you think was going to happen?'

Marsh glowered at him. 'I'm gonna ask you a question here, Robinson, and I suggest you think damn carefully before you open your mouth to answer it.'

Robinson stared back hotly. This shouldn't be happening here. It shouldn't be happening at all, but it certainly shouldn't be happening in Alice's house. Marsh pulled out a chair and attempted to look calm.

'Robinson. Am I, or am I not, your business manager?'

Robinson sighed hard and looked out of the window. 'Make your point.'

'My point? My point? You pay me to manage your career, and I'm sure you don't need me to point out the goddamn obvious about how this is gonna look in the press if the truth comes out, which it cata-fuckin'-gorically is not gonna, regardless of that pack of hounds out there.' He jerked his thumb violently towards the front of the house.

'Tell me this, son. Are you, or are you not, planning on turning up in Nashville for your sold-out home-coming concert in three weeks' time?'

Robinson sat down at the table. 'You know damn well I'll be there.'

'And you expect to still have a career after it?'

Robinson swallowed hard. Truth was that he'd deliberately pushed away all thoughts of beyond the commitment he'd made to the concert. He plain old didn't know which direction he wanted his life to go in, but Marsh would have a meltdown at that kind of indecision.

'Here's the deal, Robinson. You want us to stay in business together, then this is how we're gonna play it.' He paused, then said, 'You're a sex addict.'

'The hell I am!' Robinson said, genuinely startled, and even Lena let out a strangulated laugh from her stance over by the Aga.

'Yes, you arc. You're a sex addict, and you came here to check in to therapy in London but ended up being seduced on the way there by some star-fucking blonde in Toy Town and everything spiralled out of your control.' Marsh drummed his fingers quickly on the table. 'I can make this stick. Have you *seen* your damn neighbours? A washed-up porn star and some pagan nutso, not to mention Alice in fuckin' Wonderland herself. It's one step away from a cult and you've been sucked right in. Enter Lena, your beautiful, caring and well-known wife who has selflessly flown over here to step in and rescue you.' Marsh stopped to breathe and slapped his hand down. 'This thing right here is a good old American intervention.' He gestured between Lena and himself, hitting his stride and shouting like an evangelical preacher. 'What you're looking at is your bona-fide rescue party, and if you're wise, son, you'll shut the hell up and let yourself be goddamn rescued!'

Marsh stopped talking and stared at him, wide eyed.

Robinson stared back, incredulous. 'Have you lost your mind?'

Marsh's eyes bulged. 'I'm trying to help you here, son. Work with me.' He made son sound more like a curse than a term of affection.

Robinson turned to look at his estranged wife. 'Why are you really here, Lena? Last I heard we were filin' for divorce.'

Lena shrugged one slender shoulder prettily and crossed to sit beside him. 'I still care 'bout you, baby. I thought we could . . . talk.'

'Which I'm guessing roughly translates as you've realised that good old Buck doesn't have enough money to bankroll your expensive tastes.' Lena had always been the one who revelled in his income, her closet stuffed full of the latest designer clothes and her calendar stuffed full of dinner dates at the most exclusive restaurants. She was high maintenance in every sense, a big spender with a hot temper. It had made for a tempestuous married life, and Robinson hadn't missed the drama one bit.

Lena laid a hand on his arm and twirled her hair around

her finger. 'Sex addiction's a serious thing, Robinson,' she said with wide-eyed fake sincerity. 'I just wanna help you.' She leaned forward to give him a bird's-eye view down her low-cut white dress and whispered close against his ear. 'You know I can help you with that addiction of yours. Remember how hot it was between us?' She slid her red nails up his thigh. 'Buck just didn't measure up, honey.'

Robinson closed his eyes and summoned up the image of Buck and Lena over his kitchen work surface to combat the lies being poured like warm wax into his ears. Had it really only been little more than a year since he and Lena had been together? It seemed like a lifetime. Her perfume was new and stuck in his throat, and her over-long dark lashes were as fake as the new boobs she'd insisted on two Christmases ago. She was a beautiful fraud, both in body and in her heart. Pushing back his chair, he got to his feet.

'Marsh, if I ever hear the words sex addict come out of your mouth about me again, you are no longer my manager. If I hear you say another bad word about Alice or anyone else in Borne, you are no longer my manager. Am I making myself entirely clear?'

Marsh watched him in silence.

'Now, take Lena to The Siren and wait for me,' he said, looking at Marsh. 'Give me until morning. You say nothing to the press, understand? Give me tonight, and you can book the flights.' He looked up as Alice appeared in the doorway. 'Give me one more night, and then I'll go home.'

Lena looked Alice up and down, her hands on her hips. 'Really?' She looked across at Robinson skeptically. 'Oh, please. She's practically a Girl Guide.'

*

Even after her bath, Alice felt woefully under armed in the face of Lena's perfectly groomed glamour. Converse shoes, yesterday's cut-off shorts and her pink vest proved no match for the other woman's white linen dress and heels, and the no make-up look didn't help the situation.

'What are you, nineteen?' Lena looked her over again.

Alice met her eyes head on, uncowed. You don't scare me, lady. Not these days. 'I think Robinson asked you to leave.'

Attractive as Lena undoubtedly was, the sneer that twisted her lips at the sound of Alice's soft English accent was ugly by any definition.

'And I don't think that's any of your business, darlin'.'

Alice didn't flinch. 'It is while you're in my house.'

Robinson crossed to the back door and looked at Marsh. 'Go this way and round the side. You can walk across the woods at the back and follow the path, or go down the drive through that lot. You choose, but Marsh, I swear to God, if you say even one word about sex addiction or cults I will not be on that plane.'

Tension radiated from every bone of Robinson's body as he stared at his manager.

Marsh looked at Lena, and then down at her shoes pointedly.

'You're gonna have to take those things off. We're goin' hikin'.'

Lena looked at him as if she was Jerry Hall and he'd had a frontal lobotomy. 'I don't hike.'

Marsh sighed and rolled his eyes as he stalked past Robinson. 'Then you better put your prettiest smile on for the cameras and keep that big mouth of yours well and truly shut, sweetheart.'

Lena glanced at Alice one last time and then followed Marsh across the kitchen. She paused beside Robinson.

'I'll see you tomorrow, baby,' she murmured, low and sultry. 'I'll make sure he books first-class tickets. They have beds.'

Robinson closed the kitchen door and turned his back against it, and Alice, in the way that only a true Brit can, put the kettle on for tea that she didn't especially want.

They sat down at the kitchen table, both of them subdued and wary in a way that they'd never been with each other up to now.

'Reality bites,' she said after a while as she slid a mug of tea in front of him.

He nodded, sipping it even though it wasn't a drink he could ever imagine being fond of unless it was Long Island Iced.

'We always knew it would,' she added, when he didn't speak.

'Not like this,' he said, raising his eyes to hers. Up until Marsh's arrival those striking green-gold eyes had looked untroubled; right now they were dangerous tropical storms. 'Not with a pack of hyenas on your driveway and your husband and my wife bunked up half a mile up the road. It wasn't supposed to be this way.'

Alice couldn't disagree. They were kind of under house arrest.

'There's something I need to show you,' he said suddenly, standing up. He crossed to the fridge and threw things in a bag and then opened the back door. 'Come on. Bring your camera.'

*

Alice followed Robinson out across the back lawns, wishing she couldn't hear the press out the front still having a frenzy over Marsh and Lena's departure. They jogged quickly over into the cover of the tree line, and he led her beyond the Airstream and through the woods.

'Where are we going?'

Marsh slung his arm over her shoulders.

'On a date.'

They paused to give Banjo a handful of carrots, and then skirted around the meadow towards the lake. The back of the boathouse loomed into sight, the same as always but subtly different, and Robinson tugged her down the side of it and around onto the deck.

'Oh,' she said, drawing the tiny word out on a long whisper. 'Oh, Robinson.' She pressed her hands to her cheeks. She hadn't been down to the boathouse for weeks, not since the day she'd pulled her dad's camera from the cellar of the manor and sat out there to look at it. She'd noticed at the time that some of the deck boards were rotten. Not any more. The deck had been repaired and yacht varnished, and the whole frontage of the boathouse had been restored. New panes of glass where there had been broken ones in the wide doors, fresh antique green paint on the clapboards, even a window box spilling with wild, trailing flowers. She looked around in wonder.

'When did you do all of this?'

He smiled his bashful, crooked smile. 'Here and there. I needed to fill my time.'

It was such an understatement it left her reeling.

'Can I see inside?'

In answer Robinson pulled a key from his jean pocket and unlocked the door.

'It's not completely finished inside,' he cautioned. 'I thought I had more time.'

The boards on the floor were all sound now, as were the shuttered windows and the pitched roof, and in one corner a tiny kitchenette had been hand fashioned from reclaimed wood.

'Did you make this?' she said, running her hand over the mellow wood surface.

Robinson reached over and clicked on the radio he'd had in there over the last few weeks and looked at his hands, rueful. 'Once a carpenter, always a carpenter.'

'I love it,' Alice said straight away, admiring his craftsmanship, but feeling so much more than that too. It would have taken him hours and hours, days to do all of the renovation work he'd done here, trained carpenter or not. It was eighty per cent done, and already she could envisage it furnished and decorated, another perfect romantic retreat for her expanding collection.

'I don't know what to say,' she said, turning to him in the middle of the room. 'Thank you.'

'You're incredibly welcome, Alice,' he said, drawing her hips into his. 'You're so very, incredibly welcome.'

Her hands slid up around his neck as he dipped his head to kiss her, and they stood locked together in the centre of the boathouse, wrapped around each other like wartime lovers on a train platform. Something sentimental played low on the radio, a love song.

'Dance with me, pretty girl?' Robinson linked his hand through hers and lifted it against his shoulder, holding her close with his other hand on the small of her back, old-fashioned chivalry that brought a lump to her throat. This was their first official date, and already their last ever dance. She laid her cheek against his solid, warm chest and moved with him to the music, his chin resting on the top of her head. Alice had been on a fair few dates and even to her own wedding, but this was by far the most profoundly romantic moment of her life.

CHAPTER TWENTY-SIX

They sat out on the deck and dangled their bare toes over the water, skimming stones and murmuring about the accidentally amazing summer they'd shared.

Alice dipped her toes into the water and watched the ripples. 'What will you do when you go home?'

Robinson sighed, his arms braced straight at his sides, his palms flat on the deck. 'Concert's in three weeks. There's rehearsals, and Marsh will already have a schedule of PR junkets and radio interviews lined up. It'll be a crazy time.'

She hadn't really been asking him about work. 'And Lena?'

Robinson thought for a while, his eyes on the water. 'You know, Alice, when I arrived here I brought so much more baggage than just my suitcase and my guitar. I brought my bitterness, and my anger, and what was left of my love for Lena. I couldn't work, couldn't think straight. Spending the summer here in Borne with you changed all of that.' He shook his head, looking pained as he found the words. 'Before Lena . . . before she did what she did, I thought I had life all pretty much all worked out. Right career, right woman, right life.' He shrugged. 'I was wrong about at least one of those things.'

Much as Alice wanted to ask him which one, she didn't. 'It's turned out to be a more life-changing summer than I'd bargained on, too.'

'Then I guess you could say we're even,' he said softly. 'You fixed me, and I fixed you.' He hi-fived her. 'Good job, partner.'

'Who knew sex therapy could be so successful,' she laughed, tearful.

'Especially with me being a sex addict, an' all,' he said, rolling his eyes and muttering an obscenity about Marsh.

'Our holiday romance would never survive out there in the real world, would it?' she said after a while, missing him already.

He shook his head, wistfully. 'You belong here, and I belong back in Nashville. You have this screwball, wonderful life here that suits you perfectly. You're part of the fabric of this place. You need to be in Borne.'

Alice loved that he understood her so innately, and she also knew that what he was going to say next was going to be harder to hear.

'My life isn't here, Alice. Back home it's high octane, full throttle a lot of the time, endless rounds of publicity and all the stuff you'd hate. I can't change that. As people, we fit, but we still don't belong together. Our lives are just too different.'

She leaned against him and put her head on his shoulder.

'It was pretty magical while it lasted, though, wasn't it?'

'Best ever.' He wrapped his arm around her and kissed the top of her head. 'And we still have tonight.'

'I want to remember it for ever,' she said, finding it hard to see the lake through her tears.

'No pressure, then.'

She shook her head. 'None. I'll remember it as the best night of my life even if we just sit in silence and stare at each other.'

He slanted a sidelong glance at her, breaking her heart with his lopsided grin. 'Can we be naked while we do it?'

Alice bumped her shoulder into his. 'Manor or Airstream?'

'Absolutely the Airstream.' He stood up and held his hand out to help her up. 'Come on. Let's end this thing in style, Goldilocks.'

At The Siren, Brad sat at the bar nursing a swollen nose and his third tequila when an outlandishly glamorous woman stormed in and hurled herself onto the only other barstool. She glanced briefly across at Brad and looked away, and then looked at him again, only longer.

'You're him,' she drawled. It was one of his absolute favourite things, to be recognised in public, but even with just two words Brad knew she must be connected to the other two Americans in Borne, one of whom had set him up and the other one had smacked him live on breakfast television that morning. Despite her lithe body and attractive face, he didn't warm to his new drinking buddy at all.

'And you're who?' He didn't even attempt to sound interested.

She flicked her long glossy hair over one shoulder. 'Lena Duff. I do believe that my husband is sleeping with your wife.' Her accent and delivery made the line sound straight out of an episode of *Dallas*. Even Brad was impressed, and he signalled to Dessy for a second shot glass. Dessy slid it down the bar along with the bottle and then left them to it with an inhospitable growl of 'I'll put it on your bill.'

'He always did have a good left hook,' she said, eyeing his nose.

'Lucky punch,' Brad tried to feign nonchalance. It hurt like buggery. 'Brad McBride.'

She downed her first shot of tequila in one and he refilled her glass, sensing a fellow pro drinker.

'Good news is we're going home tomorrow morning. You can have Pollyanna back.'

Brad processed the information as she downed her second drink as if it were water. The tequila had hit his system already and he could feel the effects numbing the pain in his face and loosening ill-advised words from his mouth.

'She's not all sugar and spice, our Alice,' he said, pitching the conversation poorly, as if Lena were one of the lads rather than an attractive and pissed-off woman. 'She can be quite the little wild cat, on the quiet.' He made a claws motion in the air and threw in a halfhearted 'raarrgh' for good measure.

Lena looked at him speculatively. 'Then she sure will have had a good time with Robinson.' She draped her hand over Brad's forearm and leaned in. 'That man is *such* a tiger in the bedroom.' She nodded knowingly and tipped him a subtle wink as she spoke. 'More roar than raargh, if you catch my drift.'

Perturbed and suitably goaded, Brad swallowed another measure of tequila and poured them both another round.

Caught up in their bizarre game of my ex is better than yours, he said, 'Alice likes to take control.'

'Maybe,' Lena shrugged one shoulder. 'Or maybe she just hadn't been with a guy who knew how to control her.' She drew her shot glass towards her. 'Until now. I wonder if he brought his handcuffs with him . . .'

The idea of Alice in handcuffs had him reaching for his shot glass again.

'She has her own,' he said, even though she didn't, not as far as he knew anyway. 'Among other things. I bet he was surprised to see her toy collection.' In reality, the only toy Alice actually owned was a threadbare teddy she'd kept since she was five years old. 'And sometimes she doesn't wear any knickers on a Sunday.'

'Go Pollyanna,' Lena scoffed openly. 'They call Robinson captain commando for a reason, honey.' She downed her latest shot of tequila and waved the empty glass at him. 'Anyhow. They don't do jockey shorts in his size.'

Brad was having trouble bringing Lena's face into focus. 'Yet you shagged his best mate,' he slurred. He'd googled. He knew the gist of it.

'And you still screwed your leading lady,' she said, cattily. She'd googled too, as soon as Marsh had called her to fill her in and tell her he'd booked her on the next flight. Funny how he'd ignored all of her emails trying to get to Robinson until he deemed her useful.

'And right now they're probably boffing each other's brains out in my house,' he said, wondering if he could stand up.

'While we drink tequila in an empty hellhole of a . . . pub?' she said the word as if it were another language, and one she had no interest in learning.

A thought occurred to Brad.

'I have a room upstairs. I don't suppose you fancy . . .' He attempted a seductive look that actually looked more like someone in the advanced stages of a stroke.

Lena squinted at him, and then laughed so hard that tears streaked her mascara. 'You're joking, right?'

Brad scowled, and she laughed even harder and refilled their glasses.

'Honey, there ain't enough tequila in this whole wide world to convince me to go upstairs with you. For one, I can't feel my legs, for three, you and your big split nose are definitely not my type, and for...' she paused, confused. 'For two, and this is the important one so listen the hell up,' she said, jabbing him hard in the chest with her finger. 'For two, I'm taking my husband back home tomorrow and I'm gonna make life so sweet for him that he forgets all about this damn place and every last person in it, Pollyanna included.'

She lost her moral high ground when she attempted to slither haughtily off her stool and crumpled into a heap on the floor at his feet.

Offended, Brad rubbed his chest where her nail had gouged into him. Bloody ungrateful woman couldn't even count. Did she not know who he was?

'Is it too late to run away?'

Alice curled into Robinson's chest in the sanctuary of the Airstream, or as she would forever more refer to the caravan in the soon-to-be-put-together glampsite brochure, the love bubble. They were in bed, as they had so often been, and she was somewhere between euphoric and catastrophic because she'd just had the best sex ever with a man who was soon going to leave her forever.

'I've tried running,' he said, pressing his lips against her forehead. 'Life has a way of following you and setting up camp on your doorstep until you go home again.'

She nodded and sighed. Knowing he was right didn't make it any easier to stomach.

'How will you get out of the manor without being seen?'

He shrugged his shoulder beneath her head.

'I could borrow one of Stewie's wigs?'

Alice considered the various options and couldn't see Robinson as a convincing Elvis, Rod Stewart or one of the Bay City Rollers.

'Be serious,' she chided, stroking his chest, committing him to memory.

'Not today. I'll be serious tomorrow, but right now I'm still on holiday and I'm going to make the most of every last precious second. Listen . . .' He smoothed her hair behind her ear. 'I can still hear the sea.'

The unfamiliar sound of rain on the Airstream roof heralded the arrival of morning, heavy grey clouds ushering in the end of their summer idyll. They dressed quietly, pausing sometimes to hug hard or kiss slow, not saying very much because there wasn't much left unsaid. It was a little after seven when Robinson closed the Airstream door for the last time, laying his hand flat against it for a few seconds before turning away.

Alice walked beside him in her red wellingtons, not bothering with an umbrella because she wanted her hands free to hold his, to hold him. They made their way slowly through the woods, the leaves all glossy with the much needed rain. England had sweltered for weeks under the heat of the summer, unexpected bliss for the humans, not so much for the parched plants and trees. The rain gilded the scorched meadow grass where they went to bid farewell to Banjo. Alice needed to look away when the horse dipped his huge head against Robinson's shoulder, still and sombre as Robinson whispered words she couldn't hear and stroked Banjo's velvet soft nose.

'You should ride him,' he said as they walked back across the meadow. 'I think he'd like it.'

Alice nodded. 'I will. Promise.'

Her fingers tangled with his as they walked the gardens, pausing at the tree house, and again at the yurt.

'You should be proud of everything you've done here,' he said. 'It's going to be brilliant. You're going to be brilliant.'

'Thank you,' she said, trying to smile and struggling because her mouth was trembling with the effort of swallowing her tears. She didn't want their last moments to be sad, even though they were the saddest of times.

His cases were packed and ready in the manor, his guitar leaning against the wall.

A glance at the clock told her his taxi would be here in five minutes, and she wanted each of those minutes to matter.

'This is it, then,' he said, holding both of her hands.

'Time to go,' she whispered, watching a rivulet of rain run slowly down the side of his face. His damp lashes spiked around his beautiful green eyes, and his full mouth had never tasted sweeter than when she stood on tiptoe to press her lips against his.

'It's been more than I ever expected it to be,' he said, holding her against him. Their clothes were damp and clung to them as they clung to each other.

'A life-changing summer,' she said, with the smallest, saddest smile. 'I'm so very glad you came, Robinson.'

'I'll never forget it,' he said, crushing her against him as the sound of tyres and increased activity out on the drive alerted them to the arrival of his cab.

Alice fought the desperate urge to throw the bolts across the door and keep him for ever. 'I'll always remember it,' she said, instead.

A horn tooted and he stepped reluctantly back.

'Ready?' she said, standing behind the door.

'Stay out of sight,' he reminded her. 'And remember the golden rule of holiday romances.'

She nodded. 'Don't call.'

'I won't, either,' he said. 'But know this, Alice. Every time I don't, it'll be because I've had to stop myself, not because I didn't want to.'

And with that, he touched his fingers to his forehead in silent salute, and then opened the door to a deluge of flash-bulbs.

Robinson moved his cases outside and closed the door, his game face well and truly in place as he faced the waiting press.

'Robinson, over here!'

'Robinson, is it true that you're having an affair with Brad McBride's wife?'

'Robinson, are you planning a permanent move to the UK?'

The shouts came at him from all angles, and he held up his hands to silence them. Once the hubbub had calmed down and he had their attention, he spoke.

'I'd like to thank everyone in England for their hospitality and kindness. I've spent the time here writing, and I hope to come back real soon.' Even as he said it he knew he'd never return to Borne.

'Tell us about Alice, Robinson!'

He looked at the guy who'd shouted from the back of

the pack. What could he possibly say about Alice that was fit for public ears? He knew many things about her, all of them too intimate to share with the world. She looks like a beautiful mermaid in the bath? She looks like an angel when she sleeps? He thought both of those things and many more besides, but he couldn't say them. Digging in his jacket pocket, he pulled out a pen and an old receipt and scrawled something on it.

The press hounds watched him with baited breath, waiting to see if he'd hold it up for them to see, but he just turned and pushed it through the letterbox.

'Just an IOU, folks. Forgot to settle the bill.'

He dipped his head and jumped into the cab, shutting the impromptu press conference down abruptly without any further comment.

The slip of paper fell through the letterbox and fluttered onto the slate tiled hallway. Alice waited until the taxi had disappeared through the jostle of photographers before she picked it up, taking it through to the kitchen to read his bold, masculine script.

'Keep listening for the sea, Goldilocks.'

She closed her eyes as she pressed the slip of paper against her heart and listened really hard, but all she could hear was the rain drumming on the kitchen window.

CHAPTER TWENTY-SEVEN

Back home, back to earth with a bump. Marsh had Robinson working around the clock and Lena was making what little down time he had as difficult as she knew how. She was clearly going with the idea that she'd crack his resolve if she just kept chipping away at him, and after two relentless weeks he still hadn't worked out how best to handle her without bringing a storm down around his shoulders. He wasn't sure he had it in him to cope with her drama; all he could think about was getting through until the concert. He had one week of final rehearsals and publicity to make it past and then afterwards he'd take stock, decide how best to deal with Lena once and for all. Maybe he'd also be able to work out why the hell he felt as if he'd been blindsided by a freight train.

He didn't think of England. Or else he *did*, but he shut down all thoughts as soon as they arose because it was the only way he could function.

He didn't miss England. Or else he did, but he shut down all of his emotions outside of his professional ones because he needed to keep going, to give his fans what they'd paid good money for almost a year previously.

He was a showman. He could, and would, do this.

Marsh, on the other hand, wasn't so sure. He'd been at every rehearsal and frankly, he was concerned. It wasn't enough to have the star up there on the stage. Thousands of people were coming to see Robinson Duff perform, to bask in his star quality, not to watch him just turn up and go through the motions. The way Marsh saw it, he could either wait it out and pray that things clicked into place on the night, that the lights and the adrenalin and the crowds were enough to kick-start some star quality in Nashville's favourite son, or he could do something risky to force Robinson's hand. Marsh wasn't a wait and see kind of guy. He hadn't got where he was today by leaving things to chance. He dealt in certainties, and right now he wasn't at all certain that Robinson was going to pull this one off without intervention. Lena had turned out to be precious little help, either. He'd been on the phone to the woman most days and from what he could gather she was making no inroads with Robinson, much to her own shock. The inescapable truth was that there was something huge missing from Robinson's performance, and Marsh knew exactly what it was. However tough and uncompromising he might appear to be to the outside world, Marsh had an innate sense of how to get the best out of his stars and he'd made a handsome living on the back of it. Sitting in the stands watching Robinson rehearsing up there on the stage, he shook his head and cursed under his breath, sourly acknowledging the fact he'd been trying to avoid. He knew precisely what was missing from Robinson's paint-by-numbers performance. His heart. Heading out of the stadium, he hurled his breakfast roll in the nearest trashcan and yanked his cell phone from his pocket, stabbing his fingers at it viciously, as pissed off as a cat served curdled milk.

Back in Borne it was a little after three in the afternoon as Alice paced the floor of her bedroom, running through her words for the hundredth time as she adjusted the uncomfortable waistband of the only remotely official-looking skirt suit she owned. Robinson's rental period covered the manor for a few weeks longer and then it was going to be open warfare with Brad. He was still holed up at The Siren and badgering her endlessly to take him back. His moods swung wildly; some days he was contrite, almost begging her forgiveness and for a second chance in her heart and her bed. Other days he was furious, screaming at her down the phone or through the letterbox that he was going to take the manor and change the locks so that she was homeless and destitute the very minute the rental agreement expired. A lot depended on today. Everything, in actual fact, because if the bank manager didn't see enough potential in 'To The Manor Borne Glamping', as the site had been unanimously christened by the villagers, then Brad would get his way and she'd have to hand over the keys in defeat. Giving herself one last glance over in the mirror, she nodded assertively at herself and headed downstairs, picking up her business plan from the hall table as she strode out to the car, brimming with determination. At the bottom of her handbag, her mobile went straight to voicemail as instructed that morning. There was no way that Brad was going to harass her today of all days.

*

Half an hour later, Alice stalled momentarily as she walked in to the small branch of Bibbs & Downey, the only bank within thirty miles of the manor. Straight out of the fifties, it still had the same original fitments and by the looks of it, most of the same staff too, aside from a couple of fresh out of school trainees. But it wasn't the out-of-step surroundings or the blue-rinse staff that had Alice pausing in the doorway, it was the row of occupied chairs along the far wall.

She spotted Niamh first, waving madly at her in her best flowery dress with paint in her tied-up hair.

Beside her, Hazel, dressed in shoulder to ankle emerald velvet, looked like she might burst with excitement, and Ewan lounged in the next chair along, wearing black as always and looking at the floor as if he'd rather be anywhere but there. Between them on the floor in a golden cage sat Rambo, silent for now, no doubt deciding what he could say for maximum impact.

Stewie rose from the last chair and executed a deep bow, majestic in some kind of tribal robe and a huge feathered head dress.

Alice's heart sank into the pit of her stomach. Much as she loved them all, the last thing she needed was an audience today.

Crossing the floor and ignoring the curious glances from other customers, she dropped into the last empty chair next to Niamh and smiled warily at her friend.

'Niamh. What's going on?'

'Umm, I'm sorry,' she said, pulling a face that said she understood, and that she was very, very sorry. 'I just wanted to be here to support you and thought I'd, umm, you know . . . surprise you.'

Hazel leaned forward across Niamh's lap.

'We were just going to get the bus back to Borne when we spotted Niamh coming in here. Two minutes later and we'd never have seen her. How lucky is that?'

Alice flicked her eyes back to Niamh's still desperately apologetic ones.

Stewie stood up and did a sort of twirl, hopping from foot to foot as if the floor were covered in hot coals.

'What do you think, Alice, darling? The fancy dress shop next door to the vets were having a bit of a sale, couldn't resist it. Actual eagle feathers, you know,' he said, running his hand proudly over his headdress. 'Possibly a bit much for the bank, but hey ho. Put the frighteners on that lot,' he laughed, nodding towards the disapproving staff watching him from behind the safety of their glass screens.

'They'd taken Rambo to the vets,' Niamh added, as Alice looked doubtfully from Stewie to the birdcage.

'Infection in one of his claws. Pus everywhere this morning.' Hazel shuddered, and Alice wondered if it would completely scupper her chances with the bank manager if she threw up in the nearest plant pot. Between her nerves and Hazel's talk of pus, she was beginning to feel distinctly green.

On that note, a door beside Stewie opened and a tall, bald man stepped out and looked down his long nose at the unlikely gathering.

'Alice McBride?' he said, and Alice crossed her fingers in desperation as she got to her feet, her business plan clutched to her chest.

'That's me,' she said, with a tiny, brave smile and an even tinier wave of acknowledgement. She walked past the world's most unlikely police suspect line-up, nodding at each of them as she passed, praying none of them said a word.

They did her proud down to the last man; it was just a shame that the same could not be said of Rambo, who timed his moment to mimic Hazel to perfection as always.

'Come here, handsome, let me rub your big, bald head!'

The bank fell completely silent, and no one moved aside from Stewie who slowly removed his feather headdress and stroked a proud hand over his shiny pink head. Hazel had made it clear on several occasions that she found it a wild turn on and had set a special duster aside to buff him up in what some might consider a bizarre form of foreplay. It had clearly made quite an impact on Rambo, and now on the staff and customers of Bibbs & Downey too.

Ewan's shoulders shook as he tried to hold his laughter in, Hazel went scarlet and threw herself bodily over the cage to prevent the bird from revealing any more of her secrets, and Niamh mouthed sorry over and over as Alice walked slowly towards the glowering bank manager. She felt about thirteen years old, dragging her feet after being sent to the headmaster's office. Stewie, completely unfazed, buffed his head with his handkerchief and then offered it to the equally bald man standing stiffly beside him.

Alice grabbed it and thrust it back at Stewie, then smiled broadly at the clearly outraged bank manager, who eyed Stewie through narrowed eyes, and then stepped inside his office and indicated for Alice to follow him and close the door.

'I'm so sorry about my neighbours,' she said quietly, 'they didn't mean to offend you. They're really very nice when you get to . . .' she trailed off, remembering back to the words Robinson had said right after he hit Brad live on *Lorraine*. Never miss a good chance to shut up. Never had a phrase been more apt, so Alice sat down at the desk opposite the bank manager and swallowed hard. This was it.

'He couldn't even *pronounce* the word glamping,' Alice said to Niamh an hour or so later, turning dejectedly back into the drive of Borne Manor. 'He thought I'd made a spelling mistake.'

'Surely he loved all of your photos though, and the brochure?'

Alice huffed and shook her head. She and Niamh had spent days poring over the hundreds of shots Alice had taken as the glampsite had taken shape, choosing only the very best ones to go in to the business plan as photographic evidence of the hard work involved and the viability of the project. They'd produced a glossy specimen brochure selling the romantic, fairytale aspect of the site; it was a great shame then that the man in charge of deciding whether or not to fund them seemed to be a strong candidate for the world's least romantic man. He'd looked at her as if she were speaking a foreign language when she'd talked of honeymoon love nests and romantic tree house holidays, and he'd actually shuddered at the sight of Banjo and the gypsy caravan. As the meeting progressed it had become more and more clear to Alice that the only way this man was going to green-light funding was if he had a complete personality transplant while he mulled on his decision over the weekend.

'Maybe we could slip some of Hazel's love potion into his tea,' Niamh suggested, her eyes full of sympathy as they climbed out of the car.

Alice searched her bag for her house keys to unlock the front door. 'I should think she's used it all up on Stewie.'

'You should have seen them when you were in with the

manager,' Niamh laughed. 'He lifted her off Rambo's cage when you'd gone into the meeting and handed her his hankie to buff his head to calm her down.'

'Did it work?'

Niamh shuddered. 'In a way. She wasn't embarrassed any more. More, err . . . excited.'

Alice paused, startled. 'Excited?'

'Like, she was going to strip off and shout "do me now, my big bald lover" at any moment. It's a good job their bus was due or they'd have got themselves thrown out, along with any hopes of funding for you, probably.'

'Oh, I think I've managed to blow that all on my own,' Alice sighed, pulling the keys from her bag at last along with her flashing mobile. Unlocking the door and pushing it open, she led the way inside her beloved manor and hoped for a miracle to help her keep it.

'Wine? I think we've earned it.'

They didn't bother with the wine, as it turned out. The first thing Alice saw when she walked into the kitchen was the mess all over the window, bright red sprayed letters that could be clearly read, even backwards. She gasped and fumbled to unlock the door, running outside to look at what had happened. BITCH. Someone had sprayed the kitchen window, and the glass doors leading into the lounge too in the same huge, abusive scarlet letters.

'Who . . .?'

'What the . . .?'

Both Alice and Niamh stood and stared at the mess, horrified.

'Brad?' Niamh suggested.

Alice sat down on the bench at the back of the house,

mortified. 'I don't know. God, I just don't know.' Despite Brad's many faults, it just didn't seem his style of trouble. As she stared ahead, a flash of red on the trees caught her eye.

'Oh God, Niamh, there's more . . .'

She was up and running for the tree line as she spoke, stumbling in her stupid high heels so much that she flung them off. More red paint on the trees in the woods, haphazard flashes leading her deeper in.

'Oh no,' she said, her heart pounding as the Airstream came into sight.

WHORE.

'Shit.' Niamh caught her up and put an arm around Alice's shoulders as they looked in horror at the caravan, now daubed on all sides with huge, ugly blood red insults.

'We need to check the rest,' Alice whispered, half running through the trees towards the tree house. More graffiti, more crude insults.

Standing looking up at it with her hand over her mouth, Alice felt tears spring into her eyes. All of her hopes and dreams were tied up here along with all of her happy memories of her romance with Robinson.

'A jealous fan, maybe?' Niamh offered, obviously meaning someone connected to Robinson.

'I guess it could be,' Alice said, looking at the deck and remembering the fish and chip supper she'd shared there with Robinson. It seemed a lifetime ago now.

'Come on,' she said. 'I need to get down to the yurt. If that's been sprayed, there's no way I'll get it out.'

It was worse than she could have imagined. It hadn't just been sprayed. The fabric sides had been slashed through completely.

'No, no, no!' Alice ran to it, tears running down her face as she ran a hand down one of the gashes as tenderly as if it were a wound. 'Why, Niamh? Why?'

Niamh pulled her in to a hug, crying herself too at the shock and the unfairness, at the vandalism of something so precious to her friend.

An awful thought had Alice running again, no thought for the fact that she was barefoot as she hurled herself through the woods towards the far meadow.

Banjo. Big, beautiful Banjo.

CHAPTER TWENTY-EIGHT

Indescribable relief washed through Alice's body at the sight of the horse grazing unharmed near to the stable Robinson had built for him. She gasped for air, her hands on her knees as she bent double to try to get her breath back. Niamh was right behind her, her hand resting on Alice's back as she breathed heavily.

'He's fine, he's fine, he's fine,' she soothed, repeating it over and over to reassure both Alice and herself. And then she gasped and took off across the grass towards the gypsy caravan at full pelt as Alice straightened to see what had Niamh running again.

There was someone there.

A figure dressed in dark jeans and a hoody ran away from the caravan towards the cover of the woods, back towards Alice because there was no way out from the other end of the meadow.

Acting purely on instinct, Alice gave chase too as the figure spotted her too late and tried to veer away. Her fingers were within inches of the intruder's hood when her bare

foot caught in a branch and she went down hard, still grabbing out for an ankle, a shoe, anything to stop whoever it
was that hated her so much that they'd do this.

'No!' she yelled, the sound wrenching from her body as
the dark figure put more space between them. Niamh faltered
beside her, caught in the agony of indecision between helping
her friend or catching the intruder.

'Go!' Alice yelled, half dragging herself up despite the
pain that shot through her ribs. Niamh glanced down once
and then hurled herself off again, determined. Whoever it
was was almost at the house now; if they made it round to
the front and into the street there was every chance they'd
melt away into the spider's web of old alleys and gardens
that made up the village. Niamh knew she had two minutes
at best and gave it her all, her chest on fire, and then
someone else came striding up the driveway directly into a
collision path with the intruder, way too late for them to
do anything else but smash straight into each other and both
hit the ground hard.

'Catch them!' Niamh yelled at Brad, who looked up in
dazed confusion as the intruder scrabbled away from him
across the gravel. He reached out and managed to grab hold
of a leg, and a second later in a show of surprising strength
he dragged the person on their back and managed to sit
himself astride their middle.

Alice stumbled across the gravel, bleeding from a gash
near her hairline, her feet cut to ribbons and clutching her
ribs, and Niamh dropped down beside Brad and his wriggling
catch. All three of them stared down in horror as the hood
on the intruder's jumper fell back to reveal who had felt
such a level of hatred for Alice as to wreak such destruction
and horror.

Brad blanched.

'Felicity?' he said, staring in shock at the woman bucking furiously beneath him.

'Oooh, this is just too much!' Niamh said, and launched herself at the woman on the floor.

Brad managed to pull her off, at the same time as dragging his ex-lover to her feet and staring at her accusingly.

'You're supposed to be in America,' he spat out. 'Doing my job, remember?'

Even the prettiest of faces could be ugly in anger, and in that moment Felicity Shaw was hideous.

'I got fired,' she hissed. 'Because of you!' She jabbed him in the chest, catching the spot that was still tender from Lena doing the same thing.

'Me?' he said, rubbing his chest and scowling.

Felicity had the dangerous glint in her eye of someone with nothing left to lose. 'I took too much time off, they said. Wasn't sparkly enough for them, and it was all your fault. You reduced me to this because you never loved me enough, it was always Alice this, Alice that, Alice the fucking other.'

Felicity shot daggers at Alice, who would later see the irony of the woman who'd wrecked her life accusing her of doing the very same thing.

'And where are you when I come back to England? Exactly where I knew you'd be, sniffing around her again like a diseased bastard dog.'

Brad's eyes flickered wildly between his ex-wife and his ex-lover, wary and clearly trying to work out what the hell was going on.

'She's ruined everything,' Niamh said hotly to Brad. 'You should see the damage she's caused to all of Alice's hard work. She's a goddamn crazy cow!' Niamh went for Felicity again, and this time Felicity was more than ready to fight back. Once more Brad stepped into the breach, casting himself as the hero in the latest edition of the soap opera that was his life.

'Ladies, please,' he said, pushing them apart and holding them at arm's length.

Alice wanted to do something. She wanted to tear a strip off Felicity, to hold Niamh safely back, to give her ex-husband the dressing down he deserved for bringing all of this down on their heads in the first place. She wanted to do all of those things but she did none of them, because the pain in her ribs was so excruciating that she passed out.

'Don't you ever do that again, Alice McBride, you scared me bloody stupid!'

Alice squinted up at Niamh and then smiled weakly. She was lying down on the huge, comfortable sofa in the manor lounge, her favourite blanket pulled up to her shoulders and her best friend hovering close by looking as if she'd aged ten years.

'The doctor gave you something to help you sleep,' Niamh explained, kneeling beside the sofa and smoothing Alice's hair back from her face. 'How do you feel now?'

The honest answer was that she didn't know. She pushed herself awkwardly up on her elbows and pulled herself up into a sitting position, wincing a little. The pain was still there, but thankfully nowhere near as amplified as it had been earlier on.

'Did the doctor give me pain killers, too?'

Niamh nodded. 'Pokey ones. He left you a supply in the kitchen, said he thinks you've bruised a rib rather than broken it and it should ease over the next few days, as long as you take it easy.'

Memories of the destruction outside flooded back in and Alice slumped against the cushions and closed her eyes again.

'That's that then,' she said, resigned. 'It's over.'

Niamh rubbed her hand. 'Don't say that. I know it looks bad today, but I'll help you put it right. We all will. Me, Stewie, Hazel, Ewan, Dessy, Jase . . . I bet even Davina will lend a hand if we ask. You're not on your own.'

Alice smiled, sad and tearfully grateful, her eyes still closed. She was so incredibly tired, and despite being bolstered by the love and friendship of her neighbours, she was ultimately a girl who knew when to walk away.

Enough was enough. It was time to let Borne Manor go.

At The Siren, Dessy and Jase packed up Brad's things and flung them out on the car park in a heap.

'And don't come back!' Jase shouted, as they stood shoulder to shoulder in the doorway and watched Brad load up his car in the gathering dusk.

'God, I almost feel sorry for him,' Dessy whispered. It was true that the mighty had indeed fallen, his dejected shoulders slumped, his trademark glossy hair flattened beneath a base-ball cap. 'He has had a shocker of a day.'

'What comes around goes around. Karma at its best,' Jase said, unmoved, his arms crossed over his broad chest.

'That Felicity turned out to be a proper fruitcake, didn't she?' Dessy stage whispered, always one for a good gossip even if it did involve Alice. 'You'd never have guessed it from the look of her.'

Jase shook his head and huffed regretfully. 'I just wish we'd sussed her out beforehand. She must have been living in number four for a good couple of months and none of us even noticed.'

It had come as a shock to everyone to hear that Felicity had been the mystery buyer of the end cottage. It seemed that she'd always half expected Brad to do the dirty on her and move back to Borne, so seeing the cottage come up for sale had been a gift dropped in her lap. She'd bought it with the intention of making his life as difficult as possible if the need arose, and she'd spent the last few weeks observing the comings and goings in the village with increasing frustration. Bloody Alice McBride was like a flower filled with nectar, the rest of the village worker bees gathered constantly around her and protecting her. All of this had spilled out of her like hot, furious venom as she'd been bundled into the back of the police car on the drive of Borne Manor and repeated verbatim from person to person ever since.

Brad shot them a long, baleful look as he slammed the boot and they both pushed their chests out in a firm 'no room at the inn' message.

'I hope they throw the book at her, silly little cow,' Dessy said. The screaming police sirens had ensured that word had spread like wild fire of what had happened up at the manor. 'Poor old Alice, she doesn't seem to have had a minute's peace since she bought that place, does she?'

The exact same thought weighed heavily on Alice's mind as she walked slowly along the upstairs corridor to sink into the bath that Niamh had filled for her. She trailed her fingers lovingly over the door handles as she passed them, and she knew each creak in the old oak floorboards as she stepped. Much as she truly adored the house and would have done anything to keep it, she couldn't think of a day since she'd owned it that she'd known true peace. She'd known from the moment she and Brad moved in that his heart wasn't in it and she'd spent all of her days trying to over compensate and force him to love it as much as she did. And then he left, and all she could think of was how to cling on to it by her fingernails, carried along by desperation and longing and emotion. No more. Tomorrow she'd call the estate agent who they'd bought the house from and get the wheels in motion to put it back on the market. No doubt Brad wouldn't be interested in buying it once he knew that she'd conceded defeat anyway. Stepping out of her clothes, she sank gratefully into the warm, scented bubbles. She was tired. Really, really tired, and it was almost a relief to just let it all go.

As Alice wallowed in the bath, below her in the kitchen Niamh answered the home phone and listened to the long-distance clicks as the call connected across the Atlantic. Seconds later, Marsh's voice blasted out across the kitchen, every bit as loud as if the tiny American whirlwind was in the same room rather than four thousand miles away.

'Now you look here, blondie! There's nothing to be gained from ignoring my calls to your cell, you hear me? Because I can and I will keep on calling, every minute of every dang day until I get an answer. Duff's going to hell in a handcart here and you're just about the only thing that stands between him and total annihil-fuckin'-ation when he gets on that stage next week. Are you even listening to me? Unless you want to see it all over the internet that Robinson Duff is a washed-up has been good for the scrap heap nobody you'll get your bony ass on the next plane out here and put right what you made wrong, you hear me? I'll pay for the goddamn ticket. Hell, I'll pay for the entire population of freakin' Toy Town to come over here, if that's what it's gonna take. Speak, for God's sake, woman! Speak!'

By the time he reached the end of his speech he was yelling so loud that Niamh had the phone held at arm's length as her brain scrambled to keep up with Marsh's rant. Throwing caution to the wind, she cleared her throat.

'Okay, okay,' she said calmly, knowing full well that Marsh wouldn't have a clue he wasn't speaking to Alice. 'Okay, Marsh. I'll come. We all will. I'll send you a list of names for the tickets, we can come just as soon as you can make the arrangements.'

Marsh fell silent, clearly expecting Alice to put up more of a battle.

'Dandy,' he barked after a pause, rattling off his email address to send the information to.

'Umm, what's the weather like over there at the moment?' Niamh asked, wondering what she should pack.

'What do you think I am, the goddamn weather channel? Ask Siri!'

And with that, the line went dead, leaving Niamh standing alone in Alice's kitchen. Fetching Alice's flashing mobile from the table in the hall, she listened to Marsh's messages and then pressed delete, hoping like hell that she hadn't just made the biggest mistake of her life.

CHAPTER TWENTY-NINE

In Nashville, things went from bad to worse for Robinson. Going through the motions wasn't turning out to be as easy as he'd hoped; every time his cell phone buzzed he hoped against hope to see Alice's name pop up on the screen, and then the ensuing disappointment each time it wasn't her was like a hangover that kept on coming back.

It blindsided him; he just hadn't expected to feel so damn bereft without her. His eyes were drawn to every blonde head, and his unreasonable heart sank every time it wasn't Alice, even though he knew full well that it wasn't going to be. It shouldn't have surprised him that she was harder to get over than he'd bargained on; their summer of temporary love had been so incredibly sweet that he missed it terribly now he was back on the bitter diet of Lena and sheer hard work. Even the sunshine here felt different; harsher, more relentless, unleisurely.

'Robinson?'

Lena's voice rang out down the hallway like fingernails down a blackboard, making him bang his head on his pillow and vow to take her front door key back. This wasn't her house any more. She'd forgone the right to let herself in unannounced when she'd allowed another man to bend her over the breakfast bar.

God, he wished he'd stuck with his plan to rise early and hit the gym. He was no great fan of pumping iron, but he'd take it over an unexpected audience with his ex any day. Maybe if he'd spent less time last night drinking bourbon with the band he'd have stood a better chance of honouring his good intentions. Sitting up, he scrubbed his hands through his hair and wished he was anywhere else but there. Actually, he wished he was somewhere very specific; back in England, wrapped up in bed with Alice in the Airstream.

He threw the quilt back to get up at the precise same moment that Lena flung his bedroom door wide, and for a moment they both froze.

She recovered first, placing her hand on her hip and raising her eyebrows as her eyes travelled slowly down to his naked crotch.

'Not pleased to see me, honey?' she drawled.

Robinson yanked the quilt back across and glowered at her.

'Why are you here?'

She smiled. 'I thought I'd make you pancakes.'

Wow. The woman was unbelievable.

'Dressed like that?'

She glanced down at her skin-tight black mini dress and killer high heels.

She shrugged. 'You always liked me in this dress.'

'I still like the dress,' he said, matter-of-fact. 'It's you I have the problem with.'

Funnily enough, he found he didn't even like the dress

much any more. It was so Lena's style, and not at all Alice's. He tried to picture her in it and found that even in his imagination she'd teamed it with her red rain boots.

Lena's expression flickered, registering his comment.

'I'll be in the kitchen when you're ready,' she said, then turned on her spiked heel and closed the door on the room they used to share.

'You're still here,' he observed, deadpan, as he walked into the huge kitchen half an hour later. He'd taken his time in the shower in the vain hope that she'd get the message and leave, but even as he'd let the water course over his body he'd known it was futile. Lena would still be waiting out there if he'd stayed under the jets all day.

She didn't reply, just slid a plate of pancakes out of the oven and onto the breakfast bar.

'I'm not hungry,' he said, pulling out a chair at the dining table and dropping down a safe distance away from her.

Lena looked at the pancakes for a long second, and then picked the plate up with a cloth and carried it over to the dining table.

'I made them for you, so you could be polite enough to eat them. I'm trying, okay?'

Robinson looked at the plate.

'You're trying to what, exactly?'

Lena stood behind the breakfast bar and gazed at him.

'Concert's in a couple days, honey. I know how you get before a show.' She softened her voice. 'I only want to help.'

He almost laughed at her sheer audacity.

'Did you take a recent blow to the skull, Lena?' He shook his head, incredulous. 'Because amnesia is the only reasonable explanation I can come up with for why you'd think

299

it acceptable to turn up here this morning and attempt to play the good fucking wife.'

Lena leaned her elbows on the breakfast bar, her face a study of distress, her brown eyes brimming with tears. In all the years they'd been together, this was one in the handful of times he'd ever raised his voice at her.

'I was a good wife to you, Robinson,' she said, her voice trembling. 'I made a mistake. People do that. We can't all be Pollyanna.'

Robinson silently absorbed the way her acerbic reference to Alice almost choked her.

'What do you want me to say?' she said when he didn't respond, throwing her hands up in the air. 'I'm sorry? Is that it? You want me to grovel and beg you to take me back?'

He shook his head.

'I don't want your apologies, Lena. I don't want your apologies, and I don't want your pancakes. The only thing I want from you is the key to my house, because you're no longer welcome here.'

Lena straightened her shoulders and wiped her eyes. He watched her draw herself up to her full height and set her jaw high in the air, like a cobra preparing to strike.

'I'm a strong, proud, southern woman, Robinson Duff. Since when did it become okay for you to be rude to me?'

He shoved his chair back and crossed the room, suddenly more angry with her than he'd ever been before.

'You come in here, and you dare to preach at me to be polite, whilst you lean over the exact same breakfast bar I found you having sex with my best friend over?' He slammed his hands down hard on the counter, making her jump.

'I'll tell you something, shall I? This,' he banged his hands down flat against the surface to make his point, 'this, is the first time I've laid so much as a hand on this fucking break-fast bar since that day. I couldn't even stand to look at it.'

His face was inches away from hers now and he could see the shock in her wide eyes.

'Now, let me make myself real clear here, Lena, because I don't want to have to say this again. I don't want your food, I don't want your apologies, and I don't want your cold, hard body in my bed ever again. I don't want you.'

The words ground out of him, released after too long trapped inside, cathartic for him, catastrophic for her.

Lena's mouth opened and then closed again, and the look in her eye hardened from hurt to furious.

'This is about her, isn't it? Polly-fuckin'-anna.'

He knew what she was trying to do and he wasn't prepared to play her games.

'Much as it must be convenient for you to blame someone else, Lena, no, it's not about Alice. It's about me realising I don't love you any more.'

She shook her head, bitter fury turning her face un-attractive.

'She'll never make you happier than I can.'

Robinson looked at her levelly.

'She already did.'

They stared at each other in angry silence, and then Lena banged her fist down on the breakfast bar and stormed for the door. He said her name as she put her fingers on the handle and she turned back, triumph in her dark eyes because he hadn't been able to let her walk away after all.

'Your key,' he said, picking up the pancakes and dumping them in the bin. 'Leave your key on the hall table on your way out.'

*

Two mornings later in Borne, Alice pulled her suitcase out of the front door of the manor and locked it behind her, still unable to believe what she was about to do. Or what they were about to do, to be more precise. Her eyes settled for a long moment on the 'For Sale' sign that had been unceremoniously banged against the driveway wall by the eager estate agent yesterday afternoon. The bank manager from Bibbs & Downey had wasted no time in sending her a brief and to the point 'no way on God's green earth am I loaning you any money' letter in the mail that morning, he must have written it as soon she left his office and raced to the post office to make sure he made the evening collection. She wasn't at all surprised, and it had been the final push she'd needed to make contact with the estate agents. It had taken them precisely ninety-two minutes from taking her instructions over the phone to put the house on the market to arriving at the manor in a screech of Porsche tyres on gravel to get the ball rolling. Seeing the sign there broke another piece of Alice's already battered heart, but she was doggedly determined. There was no other way.

Dragging her case awkwardly over the uneven drive, Alice glanced back once at the manor slumbering quietly under the steel grey skies and then resolutely headed along the lane.

She paused at Niamh's gate, and a couple of seconds later her friend emerged pulling an equally cumbersome case behind her and slamming her front door with a grin.

'I am so bloody excited!' she laughed, yanking her case down the path to Alice. 'Isn't this mad?'

'That's one way to put it,' Alice said mildly. 'I'm still not sure we're doing the right thing.'

Niamh opened her gate. 'Do you think this is all right?'

She gestured down at her bright red skinnies and Converse boots. 'I've tried to go for the "American girl about town" look.'

'Niamh, you're neither American nor a girl about town. You're an English village rose through and through.'

'So what, I should be wearing a vintage tea dress and have my hair in a neat bun?' Niamh's hair was never tidy. Messily pulled back with paint splatters was the usual order of the day, although today it was glossy and hung in loose curls around her pretty face.

'Niamh. You look gorgeous, okay? God, will you calm down? You're making me more nervous than I already am.'

'Why are you nervous? You don't need to be,' Niamh said quickly. 'I think it's brilliant that Marsh invited us all to go over. Maybe he's not as cuckoo as he seemed.'

Alice nodded. 'It's a bit strange though, don't you think? He couldn't get Robinson away from Borne fast enough, and now he's suddenly inviting half of the village to be VIP guests at the concert and flying us all around the world?'

It just seemed such a turnaround. Alice hadn't heard a word from Robinson himself, and neither had she expected to. She hadn't tried to make any contact either; they'd agreed and she wasn't going to go back on her word. It didn't mean she hadn't thought of him and their magical summer every damn morning as she woke alone in the manor, at noon as she ate lunch and each night as she closed her eyes to sleep; it just meant that she understood the rules of the game.

She'd railed vociferously against Niamh when she'd turned up yesterday and declared that they were flying out to Nashville en masse in twenty-four hours' time. It was thoroughly outlandish, and so ridiculously out of the blue and short notice that it caught her unawares. Why? Why on earth would Marsh, who had so very clearly disliked them all, decide that a visit from the Borne Seven would in any way be a welcome surprise for Robinson? Niamh had of course told everyone else before letting Alice in on the secret, taking away any chance she might have had of vetoing the trip.

They were all in a state of near hysteria, and it was clear that the Borne Six would be hitting Nashville even if their seventh member decided to stay at home. It made no sense, and Alice had a feeling in her gut that it couldn't possibly end well, but none the less they were all meeting the minibus on the car park of The Siren in ten minutes to head out to the airport. It was just what she needed, Niamh had insisted, a total change of scene. Her injuries had thankfully turned out to be minor, easily controlled with the pain killers, and the last thing she needed was to show gawkers around the manor until she'd at least had chance to get her head around the fact that it was even for sale. Let's be spontaneous, she'd said. Let's throw caution to the wind and have a mini adventure seeing as it's landed in our laps. In the face of extreme pressure and beseeching smiles, she'd finally agreed to set aside her own misgivings and go with the flow. How bad could it be? And somewhere in Alice's heart of hearts, buried too deep to be acknowledged, was a tiny flare of hope.

'Darlings! There you are,' Stewie boomed as they rolled their cases onto the smooth tarmac of The Siren's car park a few minutes later. 'You're the last, we're all here and raring to go!'

Alice sighed inwardly at the sight of Stewie. What else would he be wearing besides his Elvis tribute costume? His jet-black wig stood a good six inches on top of his head and his belt buckle was so huge that had it been a solar panel it would have powered the entire village. Rummaging in his bag, he produced a wavy ginger wig followed by his favourite Rod Stewart mullet. Turning to Dessy and Jase, he held them out.

'Do me the greatest favour, chaps? I need to get these to the US of A and I don't think they'll be allowed on the plane in my bag. Bloody rules and regulations gone mad, if you ask me.'

He handed the ginger one to Dessy.

'Goes with your eyes,' he said, winking devilishly. Dessy held it at arm's length between his thumb and finger as if he'd been handed a live hamster.

'You are joking?'

He stared at Stewie, who ignored him and placed the ash blond shag wig on top of Jase's buzz cut.

'God, you look beautiful! If only you were a woman and I was twenty years younger. Reminds me of a film I made in nineteen seventy seven . . .'

Dessy shouldered Stewie aside, the ginger curls now firmly in place. 'Out of the way, old man, this cutie pie is mine, all mine.'

Jase didn't miss a beat. 'Hello, handsome. Haven't seen you around these parts before.' He manhandled Dessy's leather-trouser-clad ass. 'Fancy a holiday romance?'

Alice turned away from the scene, jolted by Jase's choice of phrase. It couldn't have been less similar in circumstance to her own holiday romance, but nonetheless the words stung. She'd come so close to getting in touch with Robinson over the last day or two, because she was not at all sure that they, or more specifically she, would be a welcome intrusion into his real life. If it hadn't been for Marsh's insistence that it had to be a surprise, she would have. Or maybe it was closer to the truth that she hadn't got in touch in case he stopped her from coming. God, she was confused.

She looked up when the others started jostling and clapping with excitement as the mini bus pulled onto the car park. Pushing all of her worries and misgivings to the back of her mind, she smiled at Niamh and rolled her case across to join the others.

'Right then,' Dessy said, as they neared the front of the queue to go through customs. 'As soon as we get through this bit I need to buy a litre of gin from duty free.'

Jase slung his arm around Dessy's shoulders. 'Chill out, babe.'

He looked over Dessy's shoulder at Niamh and Alice and mouthed 'nervous flyer', tipping his head towards his husband.

'Our turn,' Hazel said brightly, ushering Ewan forward.

'Earphones and iPod in the tray,' the security guy said, and Ewan looked mortally wounded, as if he'd been asked to amputate his own head and pass it through the scanner.

Stewie stepped up next. 'Belt buckle, please, sir,' the guard said, and then glanced over the conveyor belt at Stewie's feet. 'And the boots,' he sighed. Stewie's two-inch stacked cowboy boots came off, and as he stood there in his socks holding up his trousers, the security guard tapped his head to indicate that Stewie's wig needed to come off too.

Beside him, Hazel smiled and patted his arm.

'Let me do that for you, dear.'

Stewie bowed his head for Hazel to do the honours, and as she removed the huge black wig Alice noticed the way she ran her hands quickly over Stewie's freshly revealed head and shuddered, closing her eyes for a second.

'Christ, Stewie, hurry up and get it back on will you. I think Hazel's about to orgasm,' Dessy muttered, earning himself a slap on the arm from a pink-cheeked Hazel.

As Stewie passed through customs in his socks, the guard looked pointedly at Jase and Dessy's wigs, and they sighed in unison and removed them slowly, laying them side by side in the plastic tray like guinea pigs cuddled in a hutch.

Dessy gave them a quick stroke as they started moving away from him and looked at the guard as if he were the child catcher from *Chitty Chitty Bang Bang*.

'I just feel so naked,' Jase sighed, running his hand over his own perfectly usual hair.

'And cold,' Dessy said, shivering for effect as they all gathered successfully on the other side of customs and retrieved their trays.

'Hang on . . .' Jase said, reaching for the Rod Stewart wig and placing it on Dessy's head instead of his own.

'Sexy,' he growled, as Dessy lifted the ginger wig and pressed it into place on Jase.

'You look so hot as a ginge,' he said, running his hand down his husband's cheek. 'Stewie, can we come and play with your wig collection when we get home, please?'

'You can have them all,' Hazel said. 'Stewie's thinking of giving them up, aren't you, my love?'

Stewie looked conflicted. He'd fallen hard for Hazel, but that wig collection had taken years to build up and he was extremely fond of it.

Jase grinned. 'We don't want the doll's heads though. That's just creepy, man.'

Alice and Niamh walked a little way behind the others arm in arm.

'How are you feeling about seeing him again?' Niamh asked, feeling safe enough to talk about Robinson now that they were almost on the plane. She'd avoided the conversation up to now in case Alice lost her cool and called the whole trip off.

Alice sighed, sickly with nerves. 'Terrified. What if he hates us turning up like this?'

Niamh had had the benefit of listening to Marsh's messages she'd erased from Alice's mobile and felt pretty sure that Robinson would be glad to see Alice at least, but she couldn't say that without revealing what she'd done.

'It'll be fine,' she soothed. 'We can just hang out, see the concert and say hi. No biggie. You guys should totally have dinner while we're there though, and you know . . . catch up.'

Niamh made it all sound so doable and light hearted. No biggie, she'd said. Except it felt like a biggie. It felt massive. Huge, like either the biggest mistake of her life or the best thing she'd ever done.

'Bloody hell! I know how the three wise men must have felt after they trekked across the desert on camels to get to the baby Jesus now,' Dessy grouched as their plane touched down. They'd been travelling for over fifteen hours, changing planes in New York to finally reach Nashville around four in the afternoon local time, which would make it just turned midnight and coming on for bedtime back in Borne.

They all filed out of the plane and through customs again, this time taking their wigs off without even being asked to, desperate to get outside and find the driver Marsh had sent to ferry them to the hotel he'd arranged for them to stay in. He'd taken care of everything, or else his people had, and looking at the hotel they arrived at half an hour or so later, they hadn't cut any corners. Nashville had sped past the windows of the luxurious cab, a bright blur of sky-scrapers, neon lights and party people, infectious and awe inspiring, whipping them all out of their sleepy states with its glittering buildings that had them craning their necks to see the tops and the wide roads and intersections.

'It's like being in a real-life movie,' Ewan breathed, awed out of his gothness by the overwhelming otherness of Nashville compared to Borne.

'Only hotter,' Hazel said faintly, wilting as she leaned against Stewie, who fanned her with the Stetson he'd bought at the airport.

The hotel had a similar, dazzling effect. Everything was bigger and brighter, from the luxurious fittings to the perfect white smiles of the staff behind reception. By the time Alice and Niamh finally made it into their accomodation a little after six in the evening they were fit to drop, but even that didn't stop them from gawping in amazement at the glamorous suite Marsh had reserved for them. Two huge, sumptuous beds sat in the generous air-conditioned space, and floor-to-ceiling windows offered them an uninterrupted view across the sparkling city skyline. There were fresh flowers and plump cushions everywhere, and the dark polished wood cabinets gleamed under the subdued lamp-lights. It was a complete oasis, just what both women needed after travelling around the world and the clock to be here.

'God, I don't even want to imagine how the others are reacting to their rooms,' Niamh said, falling like a starfish onto the nearest bed. They were all on the same corridor, and Ewan had been ecstatic at the prospect of a suite all to himself.

'I predict that whatever Jase and Dessy are doing, it will involve keeping those wigs on,' Alice mirrored Niamh on the other bed and sighed with relief.

'Your rib?' Niamh asked, concerned. She'd checked up on Alice's health at least once an hour over the journey, making sure that she took her painkillers when they were cramped up for hours in the aeroplane.

'I'm okay,' Alice said, because in all honesty it wasn't her rib that was troubling her. It was something a little to the left. Her heart.

CHAPTER THIRTY

Someone was banging on the door. Alice jolted awake, disorientated, needing to think for a second while she got her bearings. Oh God! Had Marsh told Robinson already and he was here right now? She wasn't prepared, and if it was him on the other side of that door then he didn't sound in a particularly good mood. Niamh stirred on the other bed as the door knocked again, more insistent.

'Come on, blondie, open up!'

'Marsh,' Niamh whispered, pulling a face as she looked at her watch, freshly reset to local time when the captain informed them they were thirty thousand feet over Tennessee. 'At midnight.'

Alice opened the door, barefoot on the deep pile carpet and bleary eyed.

'I knew it,' Marsh said, dispensing with pleasantries as usual as he strutted in. 'You're on my payroll and on my turf now, ladies, which means being bright eyed, bushy tailed and ready for action. When I say jump, you say how high!' Marsh executed a tight, angry little jump to demonstrate his point. 'Are we clear here? You're not in Kansas any more.'

Alice and Niamh looked at each other, and then at Marsh.

'You don't expect us to go out right now, surely?' Niamh said, her mind firmly on the deep marble bath and fluffy white robe she'd spied when she'd been to the loo. 'We've been travelling for almost an entire day and Alice is injured.'

His eyes raked Alice up and down, completely unsympathetic. 'You better not be, girly.'

'I'm all right,' Alice sighed, privately adding a sarcastic 'thanks very much for asking' in her head. 'It does seem kind of late to get everyone up to surprise Robinson now though?'

He rolled his eyes. 'Are you crazy? The car will collect you, and ONLY you, at nine sharp in the morning. Do not, I repeat do NOT, bring your bunch of Toy Town nutso crazies with you.' He glared accusingly at Niamh for a second and then swung back to Alice. 'It's bad enough that they're all here at all, let alone coming to shock the living fucking daylights out of Duff this close to show time. You at nine a.m., and then a car will collect everyone else at six for the concert.' He glared over at Niamh. 'Try and act sane.'

And with that, he spun on his heeled boot and left the room as abruptly as he'd entered it, leaving both Alice and Niamh staring at the open doorway in shock.

Alice closed it carefully, thinking about what he'd just said.

'What did he mean, Niamh? I thought he'd invited everyone here by choice?'

Niamh avoided Alice's gaze and blustered it out. 'Jeez, you know what he's like, Alice! He's . . . he's an oddball. He says one thing and then does another.'

Alice pulled her case over to the bed and flipped the lid

wide to find her PJs, still turning the conversation over in her head as she dug around.

'That's just the thing,' she said, perplexed. 'Marsh doesn't blow hot and cold, actually. He *is* an oddball, and God knows he rants, but he's possibly the most terrifyingly efficient man I've ever met.' Alice sat down on the edge of the bed, her PJs in her hands as she looked at her friend.

'Niamh, is there anything you need to tell me? Because if there is, right now is the time to do it.'

Robinson pushed away the plate of hot pancakes and grabbed the coffee that had been freshly delivered to his dressing room. He couldn't face food this morning. He wasn't one for eating much on concert days anyway, and he had the makings of a hangover from a couple of too-heavy-handed bourbons he'd knocked back late last night to help him sleep. Marsh frogmarching him over to the arena at what felt like the crack of dawn hadn't helped much, either.

He knew his lines, he knew the running order; he was as ready as he was going to be for tonight. The one thing Marsh couldn't control and Robinson couldn't manufacture was charisma. He had it in his bones, but so far it was staying locked inside and privately Robinson was terrified. He'd never felt this way about being up on stage before, stage fright had never troubled him. He knew his rehearsals had been lacklustre, and he could feel the silent panic settling over the crew with every passing hour. It wasn't a conscious choice he was making; Jesus Christ, if he could bring the good stuff up there on stage he would. He was a professional and thousands of people were paying their hard-earned money to come out tonight and see him. The last thing he ever wanted to do was disappoint them, the thought of it drenched him in sweat. He just kept on telling himself that he'd feel better tomorrow, and then the next day, but they were hours away from curtain up now and he'd run out of tomorrows. It was so nearly show time. Tipping his coffee into the nearest pot plant, he kicked the table leg and got to his feet. His name was being called over the PA system for him to hit the stage for yet another run through. He still felt wretched.

In the car racing towards the arena, Alice felt pretty much the same way. She'd spent so many days and nights with Robinson Duff, but the man she was going to see today felt like a stranger. She looked up at the huge poster boards as the car came to a stop outside the venue, at the huge digital posters of the man she'd shared her love-drenched summer with in the Airstream, his name emblazoned in sky-high, scrolling letters with a countdown clock to show time.

This was a world away from Borne. If she'd needed any reminder that their lives were just too different ever to be compatible, then this was it. The man she'd spent the summer with wasn't the real Robinson Duff. This was. If she wasn't entirely certain that Marsh would hunt her down and drag her back kicking and screaming, she'd have asked the cab driver to turn around and take her to the airport without even stopping by the hotel first. She was well and truly terrified.

Marsh met her in the foyer as soon as she walked through the huge glass doors, practically wrestling her off down a side corridor and out into the vast, empty auditorium. Jesus, it was *massive*. How could he do this? How could he stand up there in front of all these people?

'So here's what you're gonna do,' Marsh barked. 'Sit down

314

just here in the stands and watch.' Marsh gave her no choice on where to sit, half pushing her into a central seat where she'd have a decent view of the whole stage.

'Now listen up, blondie. He's gonna break your goddamn heart.'

He left her alone there, feeling tiny and invisible among the sea of empty seats. Staff milled around, and Alice caught snippets of that same gorgeous soft country accent that had punctuated her summertime conversations and whispered in her ear in bed in the Airstream, and the tree house, and the yurt. She let all of those memories wash over her, drawing in a sharp breath as the huge screens around the stage flickered into life and various images of Robinson appeared. Scenes of him up on stage playing to other packed-out arenas, and shots of him backstage chatting to crewmembers. She watched him laugh with someone bringing him a beer, and then saw him hug a teenager whose eyes shone with tears because she'd met her idol and he was every bit as gorgeous as she'd hoped he'd be. Snapshots of Robinson's life, making him real again because behind all of the artificial glamour and razzamatazz she could see glimpses of the man she knew. Down on the stage musicians from Robinson's band warmed up and joked around easily with each other, and then she caught her breath because Robinson himself strolled out onto the stage, deep in conversation with another guy. Alice recognised the guitar around his neck as the one he'd played for her back in the tree house, another silken thread of connection weaving between their two lives.

The energy on the stage changed instantly with his arrival, in fact the energy in the whole arena sparked. The staff couldn't keep their eyes off him, and the crew seemed to spring into action, moving with renewed purpose. In short, there was a buzz, and Alice couldn't fail to feel it too. In that moment she saw Robinson through different eyes; she saw the star.

Her heart beat a little faster just from seeing him again, and her throat dried out with the anticipation of watching him perform. She wanted to stand up and wave her arms over her head until he noticed her there in the stands, but in another way she didn't want him to see her at all because this was his world and who knew what would happen when he knew she was here in it. Would it piss him off, threaten his performance? Or was she overstating her own importance to him because she'd come to realise his true importance to her? She still couldn't work out why Marsh had wanted her here so urgently, even since Niamh had explained what had happened back at the manor when she'd answered Marsh's call. Would she have done the same if she'd have picked up the call herself?

The truth was that she probably would have, because if Robinson really needed her then she'd have come, although probably without the rest of Borne in tow behind her. It was reassuring to have Niamh along for the trip though, and she couldn't really blame her friend for making a snap decision to twist Alice's arm. She'd been certain Alice would say no and decided not to leave it to chance, she'd said, and Alice knew her well enough to know that she'd made her decisions with a good heart and only Alice's best interests in mind.

When the band started to play, loud and powerful modern country, an undeniable thrill rippled down her spine. They sounded incredible, full and melodic, the kind of music that made her instantly want to get up and dance. Alice stopped thinking about anything at all other than Robinson Duff, because down there doing his stuff he was simply mesmerising. Electric. He had an effortlessly cool way about him, he looked entirely comfortable on stage, very definitely the boss. And that was all before he started to sing.

The moment he opened his mouth, Alice lost any tiny pieces of her heart she'd held on to. His voice filled every single bit of space in the arena with the upbeat song, clearly designed to kick off the concert with a bang. Jesus, if this was rehearsal, he was going to take the roof off this place when he did it for real tonight. The hairs on the back of Alice's neck stood up when he turned to the guy on the drums and said something that caused the band to laugh. He laughed along with them, and the sound off his voice and his beautiful, easy laughter made her laugh too, her fingertips pressed against her trembling lips as tears slipped unchecked down her cheeks as she sat alone in the stands. His laugh had been the soundtrack to her summer, she hadn't even realised how much she missed it until she heard it again. He bent and took a slug from a water bottle tucked behind a speaker and then picked out the opening notes of the next song on his guitar, something slower, bitter-sweet. Robinson's whole demeanour changed too, rolling his shoulders tensely and glancing at the floor as he started to sing the opening verse of the love song. It was so achingly hard to listen to him sing about the woman he loved, his heart on his sleeve, pure and crystal clear.

Had he written the song for Lena? The screens around the stage zoomed in close on his face, and as she studied him from the safety of her seat, she finally saw what it was that had Marsh rattled enough to ship the crazy people of Borne across the world in time for the concert. Robinson had lonely eyes, and the melancholy words really had him on the ropes up there. It was one thing to put emotion into his performance. This was a long way beyond that. He looked as if he didn't want to sing the words, as if they actually hurt him as they wrenched themselves from his throat. Without conscious thought, Alice was on her feet and moving down the aisle towards the stage, towards him.

He didn't notice her as the words fell from his lips, and then he glanced over as she drew closer, probably a reflex reaction to spotting her movement out of the corner of his eye. He looked her way fleetingly and then back down at the floor, and then slowly, slowly he lifted his head again for a longer, more searching look. Either side of the stage she could see his face up on those digital screens, and she saw the exact moment he recognised who she was, that she was there in Nashville watching him. He was only part way through the song but the words faded away in his throat, and wary glints of incredulous hope lit his face as he narrowed his eyes to make sure they weren't playing tricks on him.

And then it happened, that sexy, slow trademark smile that women the world over adored and Alice had missed every day since he'd left Borne. He shrugged his guitar off quickly and left it behind him on the stage as the band looked at each other in confusion, unsure whether to go on or not. They took it down a notch as they waited to see what happened next, curious spectators along with the crew and the staff of the arena who'd also stopped whatever they were doing to see what had caught Robinson's attention.

It didn't matter to Alice who else was in the arena. The only person in the building she could see was Robinson Duff, and from the way he clambered down from the stage and broke into a run to get to her, he was just as glad to see her as she was to see him. He slowed down when he was an arm's length away, and suddenly anxious, Alice stopped too.

'You're really here, Goldilocks.' His voice cracked, and his eyes raked searchingly over her face as if he couldn't believe it even though she was barely three feet away. 'You're really here.'

She half laughed and half cried as she nodded, and he laughed too and closed the space between them in two quick strides. Alice closed her eyes as his hands moved around her, pulling her into the closest, sexiest hug of her life.

'How?' he said, tipping her chin up to look in her eyes, stroking her jaw.

Alice shrugged softly.

'I was in town. Thought I'd come by and see the show,' she said, as if it were the most casual coincidence in the world.

'Sorry, pretty face. I think we're sold out.' He smiled, his hungry eyes still moving over her like a man looking at the winning lottery ticket in his hands.

'Shame,' she whispered, loving the familiarity of him under her hands again. 'I came a long way to see you.'

'You're trembling,' he said, and then at last, he lowered his mouth over hers and kissed her, long and emotional and so full of sweeping, bone-melting romance that it almost made the lonely weeks they'd spent apart worth all of the heartache. Alice swooned into him, her arms around his neck, her fingers buried in the back of his hair.

Up on stage the band finished the track and broke into a spontaneous round of cheers and applause, along with the crew and just about everyone else in the arena too.

Robinson cupped the back of her head in both hands and kissed her forehead, laughing.

'You'll stay?' he said, and she didn't know if he meant for the concert, for a holiday or for ever, but it didn't matter because whichever he meant the answer was the same.

'Yes.'

Behind them they heard a clatter of swing doors, and then Marsh came strutting towards them waving his Stetson in the air.

'Thank you, Marsh!' he yelled down at them. 'Why, you're welcome, Duff!'

Robinson pushed his hand through his hair and grinned, shaking his head at his manager.

'You did this.'

'Who needs Nicholas Cage to save the fuckin' day when you've got me,' Marsh shouted. 'Now, moved as I am by . . . this,' he rolled his eyes sarcastically and gestured between them with a wave of his hand, 'by this thing, you need to hustle your ass out of here quick as a whip, little lady.'

Robinson held on to her hand. 'No way. She stays with me.'

'To distract you all day? No way on God's green earth, son. Ain't never gonna happen.'

Robinson opened his mouth to argue, but Alice reached up and kissed him to still the words on his lips.

'It's okay,' she said. 'Marsh is right. I'll be back in time for the show.' She glanced back at Marsh. 'I hear there happens to be a spare seat after all.'

Marsh tapped his pocket, and Robinson nodded reluctantly.

'Just don't disappear on me afterwards,' he said, running his thumb softly across her bottom lip.

'No chance,' she whispered, turning her face into his palm and pressing her lips there before stepping slowly away from him. 'I'll see you tonight.'

'Count on it,' Robinson said, unable to take his eyes off her as she moved away.

Marsh cleared his throat pointedly, and Alice started to

laugh. She paused when she reached him and leaned in and quickly pecked him on the cheek.

'Thank you, Marsh.'

He made a show of huffing, taking her by the elbow and frogmarching her out into the foyer where huge stands were being stocked full of show merchandise.

'Don't thank me, blondie. I've got a swimming pool riding on the back of tonight's merch sales.'

CHAPTER THIRTY-ONE

At seven that evening, a thoroughly overexcited Borne Seven sat in a row close to the front, right on the floor of the arena where they had a bird's eye view.

'I can't wait to hear him sing,' Hazel said, already dreamy eyed before Robinson had even come out on stage. She looked more Dolly Parton than even Dolly Parton could tonight, except for the obvious physical differences. She and Stewie had hit the stores downtown that afternoon, and Hazel was now the proud owner of a snowy white leather jean jacket encrusted in rhinestones and matching cowboy boots. Stewie sat beside her decked out in an identical outfit, except he'd opted for jet black to match the Elvis wig he still sported. Along the row from them, Jase and Dessy looked as if they'd cleaned out the merchandise stands in the foyer. They both wore Robinson Duff t-shirts, his face emblazoned across their broad chests, and had Robinson's signature across the front of the baseball caps on their thankfully wig-free heads.

Even Ewan had accessorised his usual black goth attire

with a Robinson Duff beanie as he slouched in his seat on the far end of the row and took videos of the arena on his mobile.

'It's going to be so weird seeing him how his fans see him,' Niamh said, twisting round in her seat beside Alice to look at the rapidly filling arena behind them. A tangible buzz of excitement fizzed around the whole place, and the huge screens around the stage scrolled through the images and films of Robinson that Alice had watched earlier that day during rehearsals. Glancing around, she saw countless fans watching the screens with dreamy, faraway expressions, no doubt having wildly inappropriate thoughts about their favourite drop dead sexy country star. Alice couldn't blame them, she was doing the exact same thing. But she was the luckiest girl in the arena, because when the lights went up at the end of the night and they all went wistfully home, she was going to get to go backstage and meet the superstar. She didn't really know what would happen after that; it was enough for now just to know that she was going to see him again. To hold him, talk to him, to kiss him.

'I wish I'd had my mobile with me that day he popped out of the Airstream door naked,' Niamh whispered, grinning. 'I could have been a millionaire five times over if I had that image on me right now.'

Alice touched the camera hanging around her neck, thinking of the hundreds of images she'd taken of Robinson over the summer, all of them memories captured to look at when they were no longer together. She'd never imagined this, being here as a visitor in his world as he'd been a visitor in hers. All through the long plane journey she'd agonised over whether things would be different between them in Nashville, and then the moment his eyes lit up when he spotted her in the arena she'd known that it didn't matter where in the world they were, things would always be the same way between them.

The warm-up act did their job brilliantly; by the time they were done they had the packed-out arena rocking and the anticipation levels for the main man himself off the scale. The excitement was a palpable, beating heart, and the sound of thousands of stamping feet shook the foundations of the building as they chanted his name over and over. Duff. Duff. Duff. Alice was so glad she'd never seen this aspect of Robinson's life before he came to Borne, because there was no way she'd have been able to treat him as just a regular guy if she'd had any concept of the level of his fame. Her ignorance had been a blissful gift to them both.

Niamh's hand slid into hers and squeezed it tightly as out of nowhere Robinson suddenly strolled onto the stage, his guitar slung casually around his neck as always. All of the screens around the stage centred in on his face for the benefit of the crowds at the back, and the stadium rose to their feet as one and went into absolute meltdown as he lifted a hand in greeting and laughed with pure joy at the rapturous reception from his fans. Alice didn't think the cheers could get any louder, and then he thanked them all for coming and told them how good it was to be back home in Music City, and she found herself proved wrong. These were his people, and this was his beloved town. She'd devoured every word of the double-page interview in the centre of the concert programme, and she'd studied the tour photographs where he'd played to sold-out audiences from Australia to Moscow to New York. He'd obviously experienced so many thrills in his career, but performing right here in Nashville had to be the best feeling in the world for him; every man, woman and child in the arena adored him and celebrated him as one of their own.

Glancing along the line at the Borne Seven, Alice found herself tearful once more. At the far end Ewan looked like a little boy, all pretence of goth coolness dropped as he cheered and whooped along with the crowds. Jase and Dessy had their arms in the air and the hugest, gooniest grins on their faces, and Stewie punched the air and yelled 'Go Robster' while Hazel dabbed her eyes with Stewie's hankie, overcome with the emotion of it all. She wasn't the only one; a quick glance around the arena told Alice that seeing Robinson in the flesh was overwhelming for quite a large proportion of his female fans.

The band kicked off with the track Alice had heard in rehearsal that morning, and as she'd predicted it absolutely blew the roof off the place. The beat, the volume, and most of all the awe inspiring, sexy as hell man up there centre stage. No one could take their eyes off him; in that moment he was easily the coolest man on the planet. He sang with a sexy, laidback confidence, those big screens filled with his wide, melt your ovaries smile and laughing green eyes. Alice saw what every other woman in the arena saw, and she couldn't believe her own good fortune at having had him to herself for so long over the summer in Borne. Even if today turned out to be the last day she had with him, she'd never forget him or regret him.

Just like earlier, the band dialled the pace right down after the opening number, filling the place with a beautiful, haunting melody, and the accompanying cheers told Alice that it must be one of his big hits. She wasn't surprised; it was stunning, stripped back and emotional to showcase his vocals, and the arena seemed to swoon as one as his raw voice blanketed them like warm velvet. She watched him, really watched him, and what she saw filled her heart with so much tender love for him that had it burst and flooded her veins, she'd have drowned happily in Robinson Duff. His performance was so entirely different to that morning's rehearsal. He was still emotional, more so even, but his eyes weren't lonely or fixed on the floor tonight, they were smouldering and sweeping the rows at the front of the stage. He was searching for her, and when he finally found her, his slow, sexy smile amplified on the huge screens was hers alone, even though she shared it with thousands.

Niamh squeezed Alice's fingers so hard she almost broke the bones.

'He's spotted you,' she shouted, loud and excited, her dark eyes shining with triumph.

Alice nodded, loving every second but wishing the concert away because all she wanted to do was get him to herself. The two-hour set seemed to go by in moments, an absolute celebration of the coolest country music Alice had ever heard in her life. Sometimes loud, fun and infectious, at other times heartbreakingly sweet and romantic, all punctuated with anecdotes and lines from Robinson that had the crowd hanging from his every word. He had them eating out of his hand, and when he finally took his guitar from around his neck and left the stage at the end, the thunder of the crowd chanting for more went from a rumble to a roar until he strolled back on again, laughing with an expression of pure, raw elation. For a couple of minutes he could do nothing but let the roar happen and soak it in, and then he picked up his guitar and slid the strap over his shoulder and held his hand up, waiting for the roar to quieten again before he spoke.

'Wanna hear something brand new?' he asked them, grinning as they erupted again, laughing as he waited for them to calm down.

'Okay, so I wasn't planning on doing this tonight, but it suddenly just feels kind of right.' He cleared his throat. 'I wrote this recently, it's called "One Hot Summer". See what y'all think.' As he settled his guitar into position and picked out the opening notes, a hush fell around the crowd, and when he started to sing, everyone else in the place ceased to exist for Alice. There was just Robinson Duff, singing to her, just as he had in the tree house back at Borne Manor. He looked her way as he told the story of their romance through his lyrics, managing to capture perfectly the essence of their time together and distill it into three perfect minutes.

'There's an angel in my bed,' he crooned, low and intimate. 'She runs through my dreams, all red boots and sunshine, her blonde hair flyin' in the wind.' Robinson sang for the crowds, but he made love to Alice with his words. He opened his heart about wishing summer had never had to end, and he closed his eyes as if saying his prayers when he sang about the beautiful girl who seemed to carry magic in the back pocket of her jeans.

It was a song that made every woman in the whole place sigh, all wistful to be the girl Robinson Duff saw when he closed his eyes.

It was a song that made the Borne Seven lean forward in unison to look down the line at Alice knowingly, fat tears coursing unchecked down Dessy's cheeks as he gestured between Alice and Robinson and mouthed 'it's about you', in case she hadn't realised.

She had. Of course she had. It was a song that made Alice

decide that nothing else mattered in her life except for being with Robinson Duff.

'Robster!'

Robinson knew straight away who was shouting his name, because no one else on the planet had ever called him Robster. Turning to scan the backstage crowd, he made his excuses to the girl whose arm he'd just signed and pushed his way over to Stewie, delighted. After a two and a half hour set his brain was fried, and sudden affection for this weird and wonderful bunch of people came out of nowhere and choked him up.

'You guys! You're all here.'

Stewie hugged him robustly, and then handed him down the line to Hazel, who shimmied her rhinestone shoulders at him with a dreamy, tearfully proud smile.

Ewan went for a manly handshake, and then got shoved aside by Jase and Dessy who manhandled Robinson into a three-way hug punctuated by hearty backslaps and congratulations.

He soaked them all in like a family reunion, and then moved along to Niamh.

'I didn't recognise you with your clothes on,' she joked, making him laugh at the memory of that day back in the Airstream doorway. When he leaned down and kissed her cheek, she took the opportunity to whisper in his ear.

'Break her and I swear I'll kill you in your sleep.'

Robinson wasn't offended. He just wished he had the kind of best friend who had his back like that rather than an eye on his girl. His eyes slid to the empty space at her side, looking for Alice.

'Where is she?' The damaged edges of Robinson's heart

banged painfully against his ribs. *Please don't let her have left without saying goodbye.* Niamh must have read his fear in his eyes, because she laid a hand on his bicep and smiled.

'It's okay. Marsh took her to your dressing room, I think. We're heading out for dinner but she's not coming with us, so I assume she's eating with you. Or...' Niamh shrugged and grinned, 'whatever she's doing, she's doing it with you.'

Relief washed through his body like cool water on a hot day. She was here somewhere; he just needed to find her. Excusing himself with a promise of getting together over the next few days, he slipped out of a side door and away from the signature-hungry crowds.

CHAPTER THIRTY-TWO

Alice didn't know what to do with herself. She'd tried sitting down on the battered leather couch, and comfortable as it was, she couldn't settle. She sat instead at the spot-lit bank of mirrors along the back wall, fiddling with empty coffee cups and guitar picks for a few minutes before getting up again and pacing the patterned rug as she looked at the framed pictures of previous stars who'd performed at the arena. It was a comfortable, lamp-lit space designed to soothe the nerves of anxious artists, but even the understated southern luxury couldn't settle the butterfly farm in her stomach.

God, what if he didn't want her here? What if he'd had time to think about things since this morning and decided on balance that she should have let their romance rest where they'd left it in Borne? That was the way it was always supposed to be, after all. The butterflies stilled as if they were playing a game of statues and someone had turned the music off.

But then . . . that song. He wouldn't have written it, and

surely he wouldn't have performed it tonight knowing she was there if he wasn't glad she'd come to Nashville? The butterflies slowly started to flap their wings again, gathering for flight and swooping as she let herself remember how he'd looked and how he'd sounded in that encore.

She heard a door close down the hallway outside, and the footsteps coming nearer threw her into panic mode. She didn't want to be standing in the middle of the room when he came in, it looked weird. She tried out the sofa again, and then at the last moment wriggled up and perched on the arm with her ankles crossed. And then the handle turned and the door swung open, and it didn't matter at all whether she was sitting on the sofa or standing on her head, because Robinson burst into the room and pulled her right into his arms and kissed her until she was breathless and euphoric, and the butterflies all lay punch drunk and delirious.

'I was scared I'd dreamt you,' he said, holding her face in his hands. 'God, I've missed you so much.'

'You didn't dream me,' she whispered fiercely. 'I'm here for you for as long as you want me to be.'

His slow, sexy smile tipped his mouth at one edge.

'What if I say I want you to stay with me for ever, Goldilocks?'

Alice didn't hesitate for a second. 'I'd say yes.'

Robinson studied her, intent.

'What about your life back home in Borne? The manor . . . the Airstream . . . you have so much to go home to.'

Alice shook her head, and found that thinking about giving up all of those precious things he'd mentioned didn't hurt anywhere near as much as she'd thought it might. It was as if being with Robinson had given her padding on the inside so that none of the bad stuff could hurt her any more.

'It's for sale.'

'Then I'll buy it for you.'

She laughed softly. 'I don't want you to.'

'I'm serious, Alice.' He stroked her hair behind her ear. 'Let me buy it. It's your home. I know how much you love it.'

Alice didn't doubt for one minute that he could and would buy the manor in a heartbeat if she asked.

'Home's a funny word, Robinson. I learned this summer that it's not a place.' She'd already moved out of the manor in her head and into him, into the equally protective walls of his arms.

'I do love the manor,' she said. 'But I love you so much more.'

If she could have pressed record on just one scene in her entire life, it would have been that one, the way Robinson Duff looked at her when she told him that she loved him for the very first time.

He made a sound in his throat, low and intimate, somewhere between a relieved moan, a sexy sigh and a territorial growl, and to Alice's ears it was even more special than their love song because it was for her ears only.

'My beautiful Alice,' he said, his mouth moving over her face, her tear-damp eyelashes, and then down to her trembling mouth. 'I love you too, so much more than I have the words or the love songs to tell you. I think I've loved you from the moment you opened the front door in Borne.' He kissed her then, a kiss that said welcome home, I'm going to love you for a lifetime.

'If you hadn't come tonight, I'd have come for you,' he said. 'I still will, if you want me to. We can live in the manor and make babies, tiny little fairy girls in red boots with flying blonde hair and summer skies blue eyes.'

Alice closed her eyes and saw them running wild in the woods at Borne Manor, the ragtaggle bunch of blonde girls and sun-kissed little boys with dirty faces and autumn green-gold eyes. She could almost smell them, a seductive mix of Borne woods at dawn and vanilla cookies, almost hear their loud, infectious laughter. It was the most wonderful of fantasies, and letting it go hurt even more than letting the manor itself go. She shook her head reluctantly and opened her eyes.

'Can I stay here with you instead?'

'For ever,' he said in a heartbeat. 'Stay with me for ever.' He kissed her, exploring her mouth slowly with his tongue, from sexy and delicious to scandalously hot in seconds.

'If I didn't need a shower so badly, I'd have you naked now,' he said, palming her breast with his hand, moaning when she pushed into him.

'Don't do that,' he said, half laughing and half panting. 'Not unless you want the dirtiest five-second sex you've ever had.'

Alice peeled her t-shirt over her head and smiled.

'Where's your shower?'

'I'm the luckiest man alive,' he said, his eyes suddenly hot and serious.

'Just take your clothes off, cowboy.' Alice breathed in sharply when he flicked the front catch of her bra open and winked in lazy, sexy triumph.

'I'd rather take yours off.'

He tugged her towards the bathroom by the hand, yanking his belt out of its loops.

She paused suddenly and he looked over his shoulder, his eyebrows raised.

'What's wrong?'

She bit her lip.

'What about the golden rules of holiday romances?'

He rolled his eyes and pushed the bathroom door open. 'I've never been a fan of stickin' to the rules, Goldilocks.'

Leaning in to switch the oversized shower on as they discarded the rest of their clothes, he glanced up at her through his lashes and smiled, heart-achingly sexy.

'I'm so glad you came, Alice. My life is all round better with you in it.'

She couldn't speak because his words had brought a lump to her throat, so she stepped into the cubicle with him and just laid her head over his beating heart and thanked her lucky stars.

'There is just one thing though,' she said as he turned her face up into the water and then slicked her hair back under the spray with both hands. His wet mouth slid over hers as he backed her against the glass.

'I'm gonna hold you to those babies.'

EPILOGUE

Robinson did, of course, buy Borne Manor for Alice. He gave her the keys in bed on their first Christmas morning together, and when she protested, he just shrugged it off and reasoned that they were going to need an English base and he couldn't imagine a better place than Borne.

It was just as well really, because it made the perfect backdrop for Hazel and Stewie's wedding on midsummer's day of the following year.

'How do I look?'

Hazel twirled slowly for Alice and Niamh in the lounge at Borne Manor, making the crystals on the short train of her pale lavender dress bounce rainbows around the room.

'Like the most fabulous fairy godmother in the land,' Niamh said, spritzing more of Hazel's homemade glimmer dust in the air for good luck.

'Stunning,' Alice agreed, coughing on the dust cloud as she slid Hazel's handmade tiara into place. It was her gift to Hazel for something new, an intricate tangle of tiny sparkling stars that looked fabulous against her dark, upswept hair.

Stewie had provided her with her something old in the form of an exquisite antique silver wand, perfect, he'd said, for the most enchanting woman he'd ever known. Niamh had decorated it with wild flowers gathered that morning from Borne woods, turning it into a special and unique bridal bouquet befitting of the village's most mystical resident.

'Not long now, Mum,' Ewan said, popping his head around the lounge door and doing a double take when he caught sight of his mother. 'Wow.'

Niamh whistled.

'Not looking too shabby yourself, Ewan.'

This was probably the first and last time that any of them would see Ewan in a suit, and he'd tied his hair back with a skinny leather band because he knew his mum preferred it that way. His shirt toned perfectly with Hazel's dress, and he'd even forgone his beloved black eye liner in honour of the occasion. Hazel hadn't told anyone except for Alice and Niamh, but she'd tucked Ewan's baby bracelet from the hospital inside her dress for good luck.

'What about your something blue?' Alice asked, her mind already racing through her jewellery box to see if she could come up with anything.

Hazel laughed merrily. 'I'm marrying Stewie, my love! I think I've got blue covered.'

'Five minutes,' Niamh said, and Alice automatically glanced towards the clock on the mantle. It was one of the few pieces they'd shipped across from Nashville, first steps in making the manor theirs instead of hers. The huge painting over the fireplace was a new addition too, a handmade house warming gift courtesy of Niamh. Lavish in both size and style, it featured a bold baroque representation of Alice and Robinson in a broad gilt frame. In the scene, Alice sat side-saddle on Banjo's back, grand and quite naked aside from her red wellingtons, her modesty protected only by her cascading pre-Raphaelite blonde waves. Robinson stood beside Banjo's head holding on to his bit, Stetson on, shirt off, his muscles remembered with almost disturbing accuracy by Niamh. His low-slung jeans were held in place by a gilt belt buckle and, of course, he had his beloved guitar slung over his tanned torso. The manor stood behind them in the distance; the whole vibrant painting was alive with jewel colours, humour and love. Niamh had hung it as a surprise for them on their first trip home to the manor, and Alice had laughed until she'd cried, overcome with emotion and relief. She was head over heels in love with Robinson, with Borne, with her friends, and with her newest treasured possession.

A huge, brand new yellow and white candy stripe bell tent had replaced the damaged yurt, and Alice and Niamh had spent the previous day transforming it into the quirkiest of pretty wedding venues for Hazel and Stewie's special day.

Robinson and handsome Huck, his chief roadie, had kindly dismantled the bed, doing most of the heavy lifting to bring all of the dining chairs from the manor and most of the cottages down into the bell tent for the congregation. It didn't matter at all that they were mismatched; it all just added to the vintage charm. Lavender bunting wound around the guy ropes and fluttered in the warm breeze, while jugs of wild flowers filled the tent with the scents and colours of an English cottage garden. It was like a scene from a fairytale, made complete by the little wedding carriage Hazel's cousin Starling had managed to borrow for the day on a 'no questions asked' basis.

'Your carriage awaits, Cinderella,' Ewan called from out

on the driveway, and all three women made their way outside into the sunshine.

Banjo looked magnificent harnessed to the navy-lacquered open top carriage, a jaunty plume of lavender feathers on top of his head, as handsome Huck appeared and opened the carriage door. Ewan offered his mother a hand as she stepped inside and then hopped in beside her.

'Come on up, Goldilocks,' Robinson said, nodding at Alice to join him up front on the padded driver's bench. Alice grinned, and then turned to hug Niamh quickly. Loosely allocated the role of bridesmaids, they were both dressed in Hazel's choice of identical pink mini dresses with white cowboy boots and wild flower circlets in their plaited hair, blending seamlessly with the bohemian and mildly eccentric tone of the day.

Alice skipped up to the carriage and then paused, unsure how to clamber up without showing her knickers.

Handsome Huck hovered, on hand to give her a boost if needed.

'I'm watching where you put your hands,' Robinson warned, winking at his buddy.

'So am I!' Niamh said. She smacked Huck on the ass smartly, and he twisted around as he boosted Alice and kissed Niamh hard on the mouth. From the moment Niamh and Huck had met backstage at Robinson's concert, they'd fallen irrevocably in lust with each other, and it would come as no surprise to anyone if the next wedding at Borne had a distinctly Anglo-Southern twist.

As the carriage made its way sedately off across the lawns, Niamh clapped her hands happily and then climbed up aboard Huck's back, arms around his neck, her cowboy boots crossed over his crotch. He growled, sliding his hand behind him and up her bare thigh until she slapped him away.

'Later, my big handsome Huck,' she whispered, biting his ear. 'I'm gonna wrap myself naked in the American flag and pledge allegiance to your huge, mercifully un-fig-like todger.'

Huck laughed and jiggled his belt. 'Darlin', I don't even know what half of that means, but I sure as hell am lookin' forward to findin' out.'

'Yee haa!' Niamh shouted, kicking his hips and lassoing the air as they set off after the carriage, keeping a safe distance until Huck was once more respectable enough to be seen in public.

It really was the most marvellous of weddings. Stewie was every inch the Prince Charming in his white suit and lavender frilled dress shirt, his head gloriously bare and buffed at his bride's request. Dessy and Jase assisted him ably as his best men, both in powder blue shirts that hugged their muscled biceps as they directed people randomly to any spare seat they could see.

Most of the village had turned out, a curious collection of farmers, WI members and the obligatory smattering of goth teenagers keeping Ewan company at the back.

The only person in the village who hadn't been invited to the wedding was Davina. Hazel and Stewie had boycotted the post office as soon as it became clear that Davina had been the one responsible for tipping the press off about Robinson's presence in Borne. They weren't the only ones to take umbrige with the post mistress; most of the village had wised up to her ways now and she'd had to turn to internet dating for the attention she craved.

Finally the ceremony got under way, and there was barely a dry eye in the tent when the happy couple made their personalised wedding vows. A ripple of laughter moved around the tent when Hazel vowed to let Stewie wear his Elvis wig once a year on the King's birthday and in turn Stewie agreed to become foster father to both Ewan and Rambo. On cue, Rambo, who had of course attended the wedding as guest of honour in his huge gold cage, preened his feathers and shouted his now legendary phrase.

'Come here, handsome, and let me rub your big bald head!'

Stewie ran his hand over his smooth head and then bent Hazel back over his arm, Rhett Butler to her Scarlett O'Hara.

'I rather think that's a job for my new wife, don't you, darling?'

Everyone clapped and wolf whistled as Stewie whipped his hankie from his top pocket for Hazel to do the honours, and Ewan slunk lower into his chair and covered his eyes when a few moments later she flung the hankie aside and pulled Stewie down into an X-rated snog.

As dusk fell, hundreds of fairy lights glittered in the trees and tea-lights shone in the hand-painted jam jars Alice had hung from the branches. Inside the tent Stewie and Hazel danced slowly to live music provided by Hazel's cousin Starling on violin and handsome Huck on his antique mouth organ, and outside in the grass Robinson pulled Alice in to his arms too.

'You did good today, Goldilocks,' he said, sliding the hairbands from the bottom of Alice's plaits and unpicking them with his fingers.

'We all did,' she said, sliding her arms around his waist and leaning her head on his shoulder. 'I think we can safely call our first wedding at "To The Manor Borne Glamping" a roaring success.'

'I was never in any doubt,' he said, kissing her neck, sending a shiver down her spine when he ran his hands down her bare arms. 'I like this dress.'

All traces of Felicity's destruction had been professionally removed from both the manor and the glampsite, with the exception of the yurt, which had sadly been damaged beyond repair. They'd also purchased the last of the cottages back and were in the process of finding a couple to tenant it and manage the day-to-day running of the site. Alice and Robinson planned to come home as much as their schedule allowed, happy to wander, safe in the knowledge that Borne Manor slumbered quietly in the English countryside waiting for them to come home.

'Let's sleep in the Airstream tonight, for old times' sake,' Robinson said, leading Alice away beneath the canopy of stars and fairy lights.

'We should make the most of it being just the two of us,' she said softly.

Robinson paused to press her against a tree trunk, one hand on her neck, the other tender and protective over her abdomen as he kissed her lingeringly.

'You know we're not stopping at this one, right? I'm thinking six or seven.'

They made their way through the trees, laughing softly, his arm slung over her shoulders. If anyone watching them had cared to look hard enough, they might have just been able to make out the magical midsummer shadows dancing around them in the woods, tiny little fairy girls in red boots with flying blonde hair, and sun-kissed little boys with dirty faces and autumn green-gold eyes.

As fairytale endings went, Alice and Robinson's would take some beating.

What happens when Mr Wrong turns out to be Mr Right?

'*Laugh-out-loud fun with a real romantic heart*'

MIRANDA DICKINSON

Funny, romantic and dangerously sexy, *Undertaking Love* is a delightful read, perfect for fans of **Miranda Dickinson** and **Jane Costello**.

Finding love isn't always black and white…

'Citrus-sharp humour, a glorious cast of characters, a hero you'll want to run off with and a heroine you just want fate to smile on. Can't think of a more perfect summer read'

CLAUDIA CARROLL

A hilarious, feel-good, sexy romantic comedy and an ideal summer read for fans of **Lucy Diamond**, **Mhairi McFarlane** and **Giovanna Fletcher**.